CW00835672

MY MAN AND ME

Nick Dahlgreen

Published by New Generation Publishing in 2021

Copyright © Nick Dahlgreen 2021

First Edition

The author asserts the moral right under the Copyright, Designs and Patents Act 1988 to be identified as the author of this work.

All Rights reserved. No part of this publication may be reproduced, stored in a retrieval system or transmitted, in any form or by any means without the prior consent of the author, nor be otherwise circulated in any form of binding or cover other than that which it is published and without a similar condition being imposed on the subsequent purchaser.

ISBN
	Paperback	978-1-80031-189-3
	Hardback	978-1-80031-188-6
	Ebook	978-1-80031-187-9

www.newgeneration-publishing.com

 New Generation Publishing

AUTUMN 2017

Saturday 4 November

Before

Chapter 1

She took another sip of red wine, and stared again at the face of her watch. Strange that she looked at her watch when there was an enormous clock on the wall opposite, behind the bar. The bar where she'd just spent the last six hours dutifully smiling at customers and serving drinks. Sitting now near the terrace area, it was as though looking at your watch might deliver a different result. Baume and Mercier, Maison d'Horlogerie Geneve 1830. But there was no change in the result.

Rupert had bought it for her. It had cost one thousand pounds. At least that's what it said on the website. Not the Baume and Mercier website. That would have been too common. Swissluxury.com. That was it. Right now, a thousand of anything would have come in very useful indeed. Pounds, euros, dollars. Although it wasn't the lack of funds that was preoccupying her. She'd actually been paid this week. The German motor manufacturers' conference Granada 2017 must have filled the coffers, even at the Sala Aliatar bar. Despite it being off the beaten track, over half a mile from the Plaza de la Trinidad.

It was nearly midnight. The clock and the watch agreed. Where was he? Nowhere to be seen, even though he absolutely knew her shift finished at eleven thirty.

She looked back at her watch. Rupert had bought it for her twenty-fifth birthday, just over three years ago. A present from Rupert. Not Mum and Rupert. Not Elaine and Rupert. Just Rupert de Villiers. Her stepfather with a Norman name. Amazing really. All that land he owned just because William the Conqueror gave it to one of his mates a thousand years ago. Not a bad man, Rupert that is, better than most really. Certainly better than that bastard Rodolfo who was supposed to be picking her up. Half an hour ago.

3

She took another sip. It was the cheapest red they served. No need to wince now, she was settling in to the taste and the wonderful anaesthetic effect. It must have been looking at the watch that got her thinking about him. That, and the one-in-a-million encounter last week, of course. Rupert. How could anyone be called that name, without, you know, thinking of, a bear? With a red jumper and yellow check trousers. Surely his parents would have worked that one out. That you'd get mercilessly taunted at school, even the incredibly posh one he'd been to. That it would probably preclude half the women in the world having anything to do with you. Not her mother obviously. She must have learned to live with it. But what was wrong with a normal, down-to-earth name – like George, or Paul?

She stared at the packet of cigarettes on the table. Just wait one minute longer. But if you smoked the cigarette, in the end it would do the same damage to you. It was only if you managed to smoke nineteen a day rather than twenty, that you were making progress. Humans were the only species capable of deferring gratification. Don't smoke because you'll get cancer when you're sixty-five. Don't drink too much because your liver will be knackered. Even when you really want another drink. Don't go out to a party because you've got English Literature A level tomorrow. Well, none of that had worked for her. She really had gone to that party. That must have accounted for the grade D.

Maybe she was closer to a dog than a human – eat every scrap of food in front of you, even if it makes you sick. Don't save any for later. Instant gratification. She was good at that. She had the legs to go with it. Beautiful long legs, well-tanned in the Andalusian sun, and slim hips. Men spent a lot of time looking at those legs. The old guy in the corner was looking at them now. She still wore her short summer dress even though it was November. He was pretending to look out the window, but squinting in her direction at the same time. Anyway, if she was a dog, she was a stylish well-

groomed Afghan hound, owned by a French fashion model living on a wide tree-lined Parisian boulevard.

Sod it. She lit the cigarette. She was in the terrace area or as near as damn it, and Juan didn't seem to mind too much after midnight. She finished off the glass of wine in two more mouthfuls. No need to savour the subtle flavours of blueberry, black olive and coffee in this one. Not at one euro a bottle wholesale, seven euros at the bar. She'd perfected the technique of drinking red wine, smoking, and talking at the same time. Or that's what Rodolfo said. She'd get another glass in a minute if he didn't turn up. That bastard Rodolfo. It was certainly all about instant gratification with him. No long-term plan there. Just like she'd had no long-term plan when she moved out here.

It was Katrina who'd told her about the commune. Nestling in the foothills of the Sierra Nevada mountains. It was fine when they'd arrived in May when it was thirty-five degrees at midnight. It didn't matter that you were sleeping in a half-converted barn. The solar panels had worked at first. The water for the shower wasn't boiling, but it was warm enough. And Rodolfo was very handsome, with long flowing dark hair and eyes to match, great abs and biceps. And he wrote poetry and played the guitar. Good technique.

There was some water from the spring, but nobody had planted any crops. Nobody knew anything about farming. No leaders, no patriarchy. But no decisions, no actions, and no food. Lots of drinking and drugs, and romance, yes. But none of that stopped you feeling hungry. So, in the end there were trips to the local store in the battered truck. The food was to be shared. But if you'd paid for it, you wanted to eat it. It was just human nature.

Then she'd got the job in the bar. Rodolfo gave her a lift into town five nights a week on his old motorbike. He said he'd go busking, but no money ever appeared. It was her wages to be shared. From each according to his abilities. To each according to his needs. Except it was always her abilities, if only working in a bar, and his needs.

So, when Roberto came along, with his short hair and clean fingernails, and his good manners and job at the bank, compromise didn't seem so bad. He'd started calling in at the bar with his books to study for exams. They'd got talking. His flat was clean. The fridge was full. Less sexual electricity, but more real electricity. The sort that makes light bulbs work. And he was a good man. Loved his mother.

And he loved her. Rachel, from Hackney, East London, the gentrified bit. Daughter of a lawyer. Stepdaughter of an architect who owned a lot of land. In possession of a good education, apart from English Literature, grade D. With a wayward side that nobody could explain.

But the real problem was, their names were so similar – Rodolfo and Roberto. Both beginning with R, both three syllables, and both ending in O. Not great planning that. You had to be very careful, especially in the morning. She'd got it wrong once, but got away with it. Roberto hadn't noticed. Or was it Rodolfo?

Where the hell was Rodolfo?

He'd been late a week ago as well. The night when so many things changed. It hadn't been Rodolfo, or Roberto, or Rupert, that she'd been thinking about for the past week. She'd done nothing about it for too long, but now she was determined.

She stubbed out the half-smoked cigarette, took out her phone, and sent the text message to Danni.

PART ONE

Tuesday 7 November

Chapter 2

With the ice-sharp needles of rain pricking his rapidly-numbing face, he stood outside his house and wondered how an estate agent might describe it. It was detached, by way of two narrow passages flanking it on either side, but it was squashed into a tiny plot and there were only three bedrooms. It was an anomaly. Something to do with the angle of the plot when it was built. The description might well include 'well-presented', 'deceptively spacious', 'private rear gardens', and 'benefits from recent conservatory extension', and might even squeeze in 'select development'.

But what did any of that mean? 'Well-presented' could mean that you'd rushed around and tidied up ten minutes before somebody came to look at it. 'Deceptively spacious' usually meant that it wasn't quite as small as it looks, inside. It didn't just mean small – that was 'compact'. And 'private rear gardens' just meant back garden. There was no need to use the plural. That was for stately homes or Gardener's World – the African Garden, the White Garden. As for the structurally unsound conservatory, it was difficult to see how anybody benefitted from it. There was a draught at the far end all year round, and a fridge-like quality for at least six months. He couldn't remember why they'd had it built. They didn't need the extra space. Paul had already gone to university by then. Maybe they were trying to add a bit of value, compensate for the lack of the fourth bedroom. Or maybe it was to try to take their minds off all the other troubles.

What about 'select development'. They used to be called housing estates. Now they were developments. How did you win promotion from a 'development' to a 'select development'? Jesus Christ, did any of this matter?

Well, somehow it did matter to him. And it mattered whether you'd refer to it as an 'executive home' or not. Prosser and Butcher estate agents might do, at a push. When Andrew Prosser had come to value their house, he'd clearly referred to it as an executive residence. He'd exclaimed, with what seemed like sincerity at the time, 'oh what a beautiful property', and almost offered to market it within their Platinum Collection. Almost but not quite. Another bedroom might have done the trick. The conservatory hadn't quite pushed it over the line.

The reality was that it was virtually the same as the other properties on the Sycamore Meadows development on the outskirts of Leeds, West Yorkshire. The three-bedroom ones that is. But, nowhere near as nice as the distinguished detached five-bedroom house at the far edge, backing on to open fields. Word had it there was a view of the sunset on a summer's evening, whilst sipping your chilled Chablis. This had been the show home when the properties were built seven years ago, and was definitely a cut above, luxuriating in a slightly elevated position. Not exactly the top of a hill. More of a mound. But definitely looking down on the rest of them. Not so much with ancient paternalistic tolerance, more a new money sneer.

He remembered reading somewhere that whether you felt good about yourself depended on whether you were a bit better off than your neighbours. He felt about the same as the other twelve families with the three-bedroom houses, two of whom had also added a conservatory. But not as good as the Pearson family with five bedrooms. Five bedrooms, a Georgian portico, two en-suite bathrooms as well as a family one, and a double garage to house Derek Pearson's midnight blue five series BMW, replaced every three years as part of the company car scheme. You'd move to a different chapter in the estate agent's lexicon for Derek's house.

But on the other hand, he felt better off than the residents on the Grimes Pride council estate on the other side of the main road. They only had two bedrooms. Not really a council estate any more. Most of the houses had been sold off as part of the eighties' drive to create a property-owning democracy. But you could always tell. Grimes Pride was almost out of sight from his own front garden, but not quite. Light years from Derek Pearson's property though.

So, there it was. The class system in microcosm on the outskirts of a northern city. And he George Stephenson, the same name as the inventor of one of the world's first steam locomotives, just about in the middle. Depending on your view of the conservatory.

*

George looked at his watch. It wasn't always easy to read the time with it. The top half was permanently steamed up after he'd dropped it in the washing-up bowl last year. But the bottom half was OK. You could make out the numbers between three and nine. So he could see that it was twenty to five in the afternoon. There were a few slivers of daylight left in the sky, but basically it would be dark until he got up at just after seven tomorrow morning. Whatever sun there had been that day, had long disappeared. This was an English autumn in the north of England, about to turn into an English winter, with the sort of cold rain that gets right into your bones. Not much to lift the spirits, and the long stretch of dark nights and dark mornings until spring lay ahead.

He'd been standing there for about three minutes now. In the rain, in November, outside his own house, having got back from work earlier than usual. That was long enough.

Out of the corner of his eye, he sensed some movement, then saw old Bernard with his dog.

"You alright George, forgotten your key?"

He hesitated before coming up with a reasonable half-lie.

"No, I've got my key Bernard, and I think Dawn is in anyway. I was just looking at the roof. I thought one of the tiles might want replacing."

Bernard looked up and surveyed it for thirty seconds in what was left of the light, and then came up with a diplomatic reply.

"I can't see a loose tile George. But your eyesight is better than mine. That guttering needs clearing out though. There's something growing in the corner. Anyway, we'll be on our way. C'mon Lucy, let's finish your walk."

Bernard shuffled off with the dog, leaving traces of that familiar smell hanging in the air. George watched them go, reflecting on the relationship between man and dog. No complications, just unqualified loyalty and love. George had never had a dog. Bernard had a dog – but Bernard was also a convicted murderer. He really was. It was all a long time ago, in a far-off village in East Yorkshire. Bernard had killed his wife with a kukri – a Gurkha knife. They'd had an argument about what to watch on TV. Obviously there must have been some underlying problems. But he'd snapped. When the rumours started on Sycamore Meadows, somebody tracked down the old newspaper headlines. He'd served nine years in Armley prison. But he'd done his time, paid his debt to society, and was now a free man. Walking the streets with Lucy the faithful cocker spaniel. No longer a danger to anybody. The incident was never mentioned. But every now and again, George thought he might just have seen a certain look in Bernard's eye. The look of a man who had killed.

*

There were some lights on in the house, all of them downstairs apart from on the landing. He stared at the sitting room window of number two Sycamore Meadows. His house. The house he shared with his wife of nearly twenty-five years, Dawn. There was no activity that he could see.

Nothing in the kitchen either. But through the hall window, he could see somebody scurrying around. He'd give it another thirty seconds to be safe. A few minutes earlier he'd parked his car in the garage which was set back from the house. The garage with just enough space to park one medium-size car. His car, a seven-year-old Toyota Yaris. He'd revved the engine as he pressed the remote control to open the garage door. To make a bit more noise. He'd sat in the car for a minute after he'd switched the engine off. Now he was standing in the bloody rain, making himself visible, to give them even more time. God, he was being helpful.

Now it was time for George to go into his own house to see his own wife. He wasn't sure what was going on between Dawn and Derek, but he feared the worst. Not romantic liaison, some awful fumbling in the spare bedroom. Dawn wasn't that stupid. She wasn't stupid at all. She was intelligent. She was lovely. She was a lot better than George deserved. He knew that, but he just didn't have it in him to turn things around. So, he carried on making things worse. He didn't mean to, it just seemed to happen. He was weak. That was it. But so were most people. What was it about his brand of weakness that singled him out for special disappointment?

What he did think was going on between Dawn and Derek was worse than passion. He suspected real conversation, proper communication and connection. Perhaps even some smiles and laughter. It had been a long time since he'd made Dawn smile. Derek could connect with people, he made eye contact, he shook your hand firmly, he seemed interested in what you were saying. He'd probably been on a course to learn how to do all of this, but it still worked. George had decided that Derek was less handsome than himself. But it was those communication skills, and the badges of success, that elevated Derek up the attraction ladder. The house, the car, Cassandra the ridiculously beautiful wife, Begonia the talented daughter. Carefully thought out life plan. Work and leisure in perfect harmony. The Chinese bank that employed him, and the expensive road bike. The well-cut work suit, the tight-fitting lycra gear. Flexible working and international business travel. Cycling challenges with the high-achieving chums. The alpha male from Surrey. Compared to the distinctly average beta male from West Yorkshire, with the over-riding feeling of a life that could have been more fulfilled.

'I could have been someone,' Sean McGowan had said.

'Well so could anyone,' Kirsty McColl had said.

Fairytale of New York. A classic. Wasn't actually the Christmas number one though.

*

Dawn would know that he wouldn't like it if Derek had been at their house. That afternoon, and other afternoons. That's why he'd waited outside, to give Derek time to get out the back. It avoided confrontation. Avoided having to deal with the hundred and one issues that he should tackle with Dawn. He knew that wasn't a long-term strategy, but it was all he could manage at the moment.

But, more and more, the pictures of Dawn and Derek floated into his consciousness. Still sepia pictures, and sometimes moving pictures in slow motion for more effect. Not a lurid porno film with them locked in mortal sexual combat. Worse than that. Face to face, looking into each other's eyes, holding both hands. Laughing together, at ease in each other's company. Derek pointing at something. Dawn looking surprised, then smiling. All in subdued colours, slightly hazy, always a hot summer's afternoon. Dawn wearing that flimsy cotton dress with the shoulder straps. Running through a corn field. He usually managed to press the off button at that point. If there was a tap anywhere near, he would splash cold water on his face. If there was a mirror, he would stare at himself, examine the lines and imperfections, the ravages of time. The sad, sad eyes. The decades of disappointment reflecting back at him.

In the darkest hour, he saw Derek standing behind him looking into the mirror, illuminated by a single bare light bulb. A cruel smile creeping across his face, devil horns peeping through his hair. What would a psychiatrist make of that? But psycho-analysis wasn't a good idea. All the other stuff could come out. The stuff that was better buried away, deep underground, in a bunker.

He blinked back to reality. There was no water from a tap to splash on his face, but the rain was falling more heavily now, seeping down the back of his neck. If he'd had his winter coat on, he would've pulled up the collar at the back, buttoned it up at the front, and hunched his shoulders. But he wouldn't get that coat out until December.

About to open the front door, he hesitated one second more. There was a malevolent hissing sound, and a flash of black. In the near darkness he could still distinguish the outline of the black cat belonging to Dorothy from the flats round the corner. Dorothy was not a witch. She was a retired primary school teacher. But this was definitely a witch's feline familiar, an evil spirit that crapped in George's back garden. She'd been duped into thinking it was a simple domestic cat, which she'd called Timothy. And why did it choose their garden when there were at least ten others more conveniently placed? He couldn't remember whether a black cat crossing your path was supposed to be a sign of good or bad luck. He hoped it wasn't a harbinger of doom for him and Dawn.

With a sense of dread and resignation, George finally pushed open the front door and stepped into the hall.

*

"Hi. You alright? Had a good day?"

Dawn was sitting on the settee, pretending to read the paper. She looked up, and he could see the redness around her eyes, and the tiniest quivering of the lips.

15

"You're back early," she said, looking at him with a definite sadness in those dark brown eyes, knowing that he suspected she'd been crying.

"Yes, the last meeting was cancelled. Things aren't going too well, and I couldn't face sticking around. Are you OK?"

How was she supposed to answer? I've had a crap life with you and I've spent the afternoon with that tosser Derek Pearson. Or maybe she was supposed to say – yes, I'm fine.

"Yes, I'm fine," she said, with the full certainty of meaning the opposite. "I never think I make the best use of my half day on Tuesdays. I end up just sorting things out, doing jobs. There's definitely a leak in the conservatory, George. You keep saying you'll get it fixed. And I did a bit of reading. I'm going to the book club tonight."

He took a longing look at his wife. Honestly, Dawn had kept herself in pretty good shape. She was a good-looking woman. Not just for her age, which was forty-seven, two years younger than him, but generally. She was still slim and classy, with silky chestnut brown hair. He liked it when she wore her pink vest to go to the gym, and the hair rolled down onto her soft bare shoulders. So many women dye their hair blonde as they get older, daub lots of make-up on like war-paint. Dawn wore just a touch of make-up. Stylishly understated. She looked natural, a few lines on her face, but her skin was clear and fresh. She had big round brown eyes, thick dark eyelashes, high cheekbones, full lips, and a sort-of knowing smile. He remembered that smile from the first time they'd met, and the eyes, and the hair. He reckoned other men didn't notice hair, but he did. He wanted to touch it now, to softly stroke it. But it was all a bit late for that. She'd stare at him with a bemused look and ask him what on earth he was doing.

Dawn worked for a debt advisory charity, and she was good at her job. Her colleagues liked her, the clients liked her. She helped people. She helped the community. She was his wife, the mother of his son. When you added it all up, why couldn't he bring himself to enjoy their life together, to make the most of it? There must be something missing from him, some genetic flaw or something in his upbringing. Flawed from both a nature and nurture point of a view. But no, it was just because he was George Stephenson, and he let everybody down, and messed everything up. That's why.

Walking into the kitchen to make a cup of tea, he wondered why he was pondering on his life in general these days – in summary form, big picture stuff. Fleeting reflections were coming thick and fast. But it was the cumulative effect. It crept up from behind, and pounced. He couldn't fight it off. It held him in a wrestler's grip. Perhaps it was because his half-century was approaching. He wasn't special. Everybody thought – where have all those years gone? Henry VIII had thought it. But where had they gone? Being fifty was what happened to your Auntie Brenda, it didn't happen to you. It couldn't be fifty years since his birth, twenty-five years since he married Dawn, twenty-two years since the birth of Paul, their only son. Not so much a life of shattered dreams or inexplicable disasters. More a life of consistent under-achievement. But there was no need for everybody to be a high-flyer, to pursue the glittering prizes. He'd learnt to cherish mediocrity. A Lower Second from Hull had served him reasonably well. He felt a slight burst of pride. Like the pilot light in a central heating boiler. Sparking to life for a second, before going out again. A fault with the boiler.

His thoughts were interrupted by the familiar call.

"Watchya Brian."

He turned his head to look at Polonius through the open door into the utility room. The African grey cocked his head, before letting out the second catchphrase.

"At the other end."

It was a shock when he'd been left something in Uncle Walter's will. More of a shock to learn it was a fifty-year-old African grey parrot. Uncle Walter wasn't their real uncle. He was their next-door neighbour when George was growing up. And although young George was entertained by the parrot, he didn't expect it to turn up again years later. Dawn had refused to have the bird, but they ran out of options. There was no parrot rescue centre in the area. So in the end Polonius had been allowed into Sycamore Meadows as an interim measure, while they found him a suitable home, but in the end had stayed the last six years. Living in the cramped utility room in a cage hanging from the ceiling just above the washing machine, with a view out on to the wheelie bins. They'd tried to decipher the two phrases, but there was no clue who Brian was, and at the other end of what?

George thought Dawn tolerated Polonius in the same way that she tolerated him. Both in the house, but not necessarily in the relationship. So he found the bird to be a kindred spirit, a muse. It listened to him, without judging him. He'd describe his inability to communicate properly with Dawn. Polonius would listen intently, consider the issues, cock his head, then deliver his response – 'Watchya Brian' or 'at the other end'. Those were the two options.

'How can I show Dawn that I still love her, and I'm really sorry for what I've done. Not that she knows the full story, or I don't think she does, although she might suspect something. And I am worried about Paul. We're both not sure whether Danni's right for him. And there's something else that's wrong. Something that he's not telling us about.'

Response one or response two. Both unfathomable.

He switched the kettle on, and put two teabags in the teapot. There was a small crack in the spout, so that it always dribbled. Dawn had instructed him to get a new one. But he'd failed, he hadn't completed the task. He didn't see the need. Most teapots dribbled. He'd fight off Dawn's demands. Ride it out, avoid emotional engagement.

Except that was exactly what Dawn wanted. Not the new teapot bit, although she did want one. No, the emotional engagement. Intimacy. Not necessarily physical intimacy unfortunately, but closeness and connection. He knew that because she'd told him when they saw the relationship counsellor. And he'd failed her on that score as well. It sounded so easy. Talk more, share thoughts, the ups and downs of the day. But it was always easier to read the paper, or watch the telly. You could always talk tomorrow. But in his heart, he knew Dawn was right. She was always right. So perceptive. So wise. So strong. He just hoped she was prepared to live with both imperfections. The teapot, and her husband.

*

She was already looking at him as he walked into the room and handed her the cup. Was she expecting a miraculous transformation on a Tuesday afternoon? He hadn't been a bad husband. He hadn't been a bad father. He just hadn't been very good at either. He'd fallen short. But that's what most people did. He was slap bang at the centre of the normal distribution curve. Except he knew Dawn thought there had to be more. He just couldn't work out what the 'more' was. So he fell back on trusty inanities.

"It's not going well at work. I've got my annual performance review tomorrow, but there's not a lot of performance to review. The project's dead in the water, and I haven't got a clue how to get things moving. Still, I've been there over two years so if they boot me out, I'll get a pay-off."

There, how about that for communication! Showing plenty of vulnerability. No macho posturing. Possibly a life-changing event around the corner. Over to you, Dawn.

"I'm sorry about that George. But you always find something. You'll get sorted out."

God, not much empathy there. Just overwhelming neutrality. You could have put your arms around me. Kissed me on the cheek. Said something about 'at least we've got each other'. But no, 'you'll get sorted out'. Is that it?

"George, there's something I want to talk to you about."

Oh Jesus Christ, here it comes. It really is going to happen this time. This is 'The Big Communication'. She's going to leave me. She's going to tell me now. I'll be on my own. We'll have to sell the house. We'll have to fix the conservatory first. It probably needs knocking down and rebuilding. She's leaving me for Derek. They're going to set up home together. In a trendy riverside apartment in the city centre. Everybody'll feel sorry for me, but at the end of the day they'll be on Dawn's side.

He felt a tidal wave of nausea. He was going to throw up, there and then, on the sitting room carpet. He could try begging. Maybe that would work. Abject grovelling. Please don't say it, not today. Wait until tomorrow. Wait until next week. He could change. Just one last chance. Please. Please.

Maybe she did see the terror in his eyes, the dread, the pleading look. Maybe she did think of the twenty-five years, the son, the house, the conservatory, the sporadic good times. He would never know.

"I'm going away for a long weekend with Sandra. We're going on Friday morning and coming back on Monday. We'll be away three nights. I've booked two days off work. It's a spa weekend. She won it at a charity auction – well, paid for it actually, but you know what I mean. She was going to take her sister, but she couldn't make it. She's having a bunion removed. It's quite a big operation. You have your foot in a cast for weeks. The consultant had a last minute cancellation. So Sandra asked me. It's only in Harrogate. You don't need me."

Yes, I do need you. I absolutely do need you Dawn.

He felt like a condemned man who'd just won a reprieve from the Home Secretary, or the State Governor, or the President. The nausea passed, to be replaced with something close to euphoria, or at least relief. He would make the most of this second chance, he absolutely would. He'd said it before, but this time would be different. He'd learnt his lesson.

"That's great news. You'll have a wonderful time. I've always liked Sandra. Apart from when she left John, and he had to move into that awful bedsit before they sold the house. It'll be relaxing. Take your mind off things. I didn't realise anybody got bunions these days. I think my mother had one, but I don't remember her having an operation."

Maybe he sounded a bit gushing, and there was definitely too much focus on bunions. He wasn't saying it's great news that you're going to Harrogate. He was saying it's great news you're not leaving me. Thank you for not leaving me. He should have left it there, but he had a few more lines.

"But will Sandra be alright with a spa weekend? I thought she'd converted to Islam."

"You can still go to a spa if you're a Muslim, George. Even in Harrogate. Anyway, she didn't go through with it. Decided she liked Sauvignon Blanc too much. And Argentinian Malbec."

"Hadn't she been drinking Argentinian Malbec when she nearly killed that waiter?"

"She didn't nearly kill the waiter George. She tried to put her arms round him. Gave him a kiss on the cheek. But he stepped back, fell over, hit his head on the corner of a table."

"But he ended up in hospital. Had to have an operation to relieve pressure on the brain. It was touch and go for a while."

Still, he could have left it there. A semi-humorous reflection. But no, why not dish a bit more dirt on one of Dawn's best friends.

"So she's been through Christianity, Islam, and didn't she go to Stonehenge for the summer solstice with a bunch of druids last year? There won't be many more religions left for her. And remember when she became a vegetarian but carried on eating roast chicken."

Dawn stared back at him. Incredulity etched on all of her features. He knew straight away. He looked down at his shoes. It was months since he'd polished them.

"For Christ's sake George! What have you got against Sandra? You've never liked me seeing her. I don't understand you. Why do you turn everything into a big argument?"

She looked at him not with anger, but perhaps something closer to despair, or even pity. Why oh why did he say those things? Snatched defeat from the jaws of victory. He looked back with his best pleading eyes, and stumbled on.

"I didn't mean it like that. I just meant that she keeps changing her mind. I like her, honestly I do."

She said nothing. Silence was an effective weapon.

"Maybe you and I could go away Dawn, for my fiftieth birthday in January. Or we could have a big party."

She used the effective weapon again.

Chapter 3

It was the first Tuesday of the month, so that meant Dawn went to the book club in the evening, and George stayed in. He didn't have to stay in. There was no young child to look after. There hadn't been for a long time now. The fact was, he didn't have anything else to do. Maybe he should have started that foreign language course, or gone to the pub quiz with a bunch of good mates that he didn't have, or the oil painting course at the college in town. But no, usually he just stayed in, watched television, and thought about what went on at the book club. Was it a policy decision to exclude men? Dawn had only ever read half the book, but it didn't seem to matter. The pushy professionals that she knew would have read all of it. It was a mystery where they found the time. Clever old Amelia had even written a book. She was a solicitor with five children. A good Catholic. How could you do all of that, and read the book every month for the sodding book club? Maybe it was all a cover. Orgies, devil worship, recreational drugs. But he couldn't imagine Amelia being keen on conjuring up the devil. You'd have a job explaining that one to the priest on a Sunday morning. No, probably they just discussed books.

He switched the TV off. Five hundred channels and nothing on. He looked down at the book on the coffee table. The travel book that Dawn bought him last Christmas. Progress was slow. About two pages a day, in bed, before falling asleep. Eleven months and less than half way through. It was meant to kindle a spirit of adventure. Get him excited about the two of them trekking through the Alps. A last-ditch attempt to breathe some life into their marriage. But what would they talk about? When they'd gone out for a meal on Dawn's birthday, he'd actually written a list – five things on a scrap of paper, hidden in his jacket pocket. He'd tried to remember them, but got stuck on number four just as the main course arrived. When he tried to sneak a look, Dawn spotted him, and gave him a kindly smile. Like you'd give to a child. At least she didn't pat his head.

He didn't bother picking the book up. He'd put some music on. A vinyl record. The digital world couldn't compete. Looking at the album cover, the pictures of the band, reading the lyrics. Removing the record from the sleeve, holding it in both hands at the edges, placing it on the turntable, slowly moving the stylus over and lowering it. The wait of a few seconds before the music kicked in. It was a tactile sensual experience. Like when he held the back of her waist that night, and gently pressed against her. That one night all those decades ago. He could still feel the electricity now.

He should have put on a soul classic, something to lift the spirits. The Temptations with My Girl. Maybe not such a great idea. Aretha Franklin R-E-S-P-E-C-T. Maybe that would hit the spot. But he selected Joy Division's second and last album, Closer. Ian Curtis' anguished tones as he spiralled towards oblivion. A strange choice. With the music still playing, he switched the TV back on. Put it on mute. He didn't think he could get through the night without it. There was a match on one of the free channels from the lower German league. Two teams he'd never heard of, playing out a nil-nil draw. Perhaps that was the sum of his life. A goalless draw.

He'd poured himself a second glass of wine. He'd only put the bottle in the fridge as Dawn left the house. The first glass was warm, but the second was nearly cool enough. It was only Tuesday night, but what the hell. He'd spilt some wine on the carpet as he walked back in the room. Strange how he looked around while circling his foot on the faint stain on the carpet, rubbing round and round. Almost like the presence of Dawn could see what he was doing. Any minute she'd say, 'Just go and get a damp cloth from the kitchen'. That would be another one to ask the psychiatrist about. The general feeling of being watched. Maybe it was just when he was alone in the house. Maybe everybody got that feeling sometimes. It had been stronger over the last few days though. There's no hope for you George.

Another gulp of wine gave him a temporary boost. The record had finished, so he switched the sound up on the TV. Just in time for the after-match analysis. Hearing humans talking made him feel less alone. God, he needed to feel less alone. He was staring at the screen but not really seeing anything. He took another gulp of wine, only thirty seconds after the previous one. This time he sank a few notches. He shook his head to try to get the thought out of his mind. But no, it was stuck there. She was stuck there. The L word. Linda.

Boy, he'd tried to banish the unhappy saga of Linda. His betrayal. He'd like to have it removed by intricate laser surgery from the part of his brain that dealt with it. But neurosurgery hadn't come that far. It would fester, eat away at his self-worth, for eternity. Or for this life at least. He hadn't meant to get that piece of furry green decomposing cheese out the fridge tonight. But here it was again, an unwelcome racist uncle come to say hello. Like toothache. You couldn't help pressing the painful gum, to make it hurt a bit more. Or the 'Don't touch, wet paint' sign. You couldn't resist touching it, then looking at the smudge of white on the end of your finger.

Sometimes he managed to convince himself that he and Dawn had just generally run out of steam. Just the normal course of events. It happened to everybody. He'd read somewhere that for the first eighteen months in a relationship, the body pumps a whole load of chemicals around your system. That's the feeling in love bit. And it keeps going long enough so that you have your first child. Then you're bound together by parenthood. Then eighteen years later the child leaves home, and the trouble starts. It couldn't be as simple as that, but that's the model they'd followed. Or that he'd followed. So it wasn't his fault. It was a chemical reaction.

Except there was the small matter of his affair with Linda from work. If you could call one night in a Premier Inn in Rochdale an affair. Even if you took into account the second night in the Premier Inn in Sheffield, he still doubted whether his relationship with Linda constituted an affair. More a minor indiscretion. Yes, that was right. A minor indiscretion. The idea of an affair conjured up thoughts of something French, with electrifying passion, uncontrollable urges, tortured regret, enduring pain. Not something conducted in budget hotels in Greater Manchester and South Yorkshire. Dull, overcast, with light rain, on both occasions. He wondered whether the staff on the reception desks were trained to be discreet with couples checking in for a night of passion, not with their spouse. Probably not part of the Premier Inn training programme. In Rochdale you didn't even have to trouble yourself with human contact. You just stuck your credit card into a machine and out popped a key card. The machine wasn't working in Sheffield. No, for discretion, you'd be talking about the front desk of Le Bristol Paris. Parisian life at its most elegant. They'd know how to handle these things. Discretion guaranteed. All part of the service. Five hundred euros a night for crisp white bed linen and a Michelin-rated gastronomic experience. Derek had stayed there once, on a business trip. He'd dropped that one into conversation.

The relationship with Dawn had hit rock bottom at that time. The time of Linda. He'd convinced himself that Linda was effect not cause. He would do, wouldn't he. Such a gentleman. He'd managed to disconnect from Linda, but there were still excruciating encounters at work, embarrassing glances and nods, deviations at the bottom of the stairs, sudden U-turns in the corridor. He'd left it as a 'grey area', but he sensed Linda regarded it as unfinished business, so there was an ever-present peril at work each day. It wasn't clear to him whether Dawn knew about it. Or whether she knew, but chose to keep it in reserve. The secret weapon. But in the end, with or without the Linda factor, they'd decided not to split up. Not to sell the house. He'd phoned Andrew Prosser to tell him, but only got to speak to Janey in the general office. Prosser must have been out dealing with the Platinum Collection. 'Give us a ring if you change your minds,' said Janey in a cheery voice. She didn't sound too devastated that they'd missed out on the commission.

So here they still were. Him and Dawn, and a parrot. In the same house. He'd like to think it wasn't the subsiding conservatory that had kept them together. But maybe it had played its part. Probably a bigger factor than the sessions with the relationship counsellor, Sarah. And, with his distorted logic, Dawn's relationship with Derek seemed fair to balance things out. Perhaps not complete equilibrium. His relationship with Linda had been physical if not romantic. Whereas he hoped and prayed that Dawn's relationship with Derek was just low-level emotional support, even if Derek had baser motives. In the end he thought he'd made the right call not to start the fling with Linda until after the sessions with Sarah, otherwise he'd have had to confess all in front of both Sarah and Dawn. Humiliation and blame in front of two women. No, better to get the relationship counselling out of the way. Then have the affair. Then end it, just about. Then turn a blind eye to your wife's relationship with Derek Pearson, your neighbour from the five-bedroom executive residence backing on to open countryside. That was all a lot more straightforward. In keeping with his general approach to life. Far better to let everybody down. Lie and cheat. Mess things up some more. Stick together because of a conservatory. Then wait outside your own house until Derek had slipped out the back. Yes, that was the George Stephenson way.

*

Dawn should be back by now. It was nearly eleven o'clock, and he'd finished off two large glasses of wine. He was desperate for a third, but somehow managed to dredge up the self-control to resist.

He drew the curtain back to look outside. He wasn't quite sure why, because he'd hear Dawn's car turning off the road. He recognised the engine noise. When she changed her car last year, she'd invested in a slightly sportier Polo. That worried him at the time, and still did. Particularly the alloy wheel trim. A statement of intent perhaps.

The rain had stopped, and in the dark sky there was a glowing moon edged with subtle misty clouds. An eerie moon casting a cold light onto the modest drive in front of their house. The black cat was sitting there looking directly back at him. Piercing shining diamond eyes drilling its evil into his soul. Staring him out. Forcing him to blink first. The night, the moon, the mist, all definitely belonged to the black cat.

George walked into the hall, then opened the front door. Fortified with white wine, he took a few paces outside to scare off the cat, stamping on the paving stones. The cat held its ground for a few seconds longer. George heard Polonius give out a solitary shriek. He didn't usually do that. As if on cue, Dawn drove up, ending the stand-off. The cat slowly walked away.

"What are you doing standing in the drive George?"

He could hardly say he was trying to frighten the cat.

The numbness enveloped her like a giant black cloak flung round her whole body from the neck down, leaving just her head exposed to deal with the details. Rupert had buried his head in a cocoon formed by his gripping hands and hairy forearms, exposed by untidily rolled-up shirt sleeves. The cuffs were dirty, he hadn't shaved, and he needed a haircut. She hadn't seen him for nearly a month, except briefly through the side window of his Bentley when he'd dropped the boys off last Sunday. No, a week last Sunday. He'd blocked the road with that monstrosity as there were no car parking spaces. He'd had to speed off as soon as they'd stepped onto the pavement. Realistically you needed two spaces to fit it in, and even then it jutted out into the road at the side. It was a complete liability in London, and he usually kept it for the country lanes of Kent, which although narrow at times, could be a bit more forgiving in their openness. He was putting on weight as well. With his upper body bent forward, his blue striped shirt tightened against two rolls of fat spreading across his middle. The shirt buttons were straining, but holding for the moment. And why on earth had he kept his tie on for the last twelve hours? He'd had it on since she'd met him at the airport. It was dangling down now, hanging between his knees parted at a near right angle. Perhaps it was an attempt at English decorum. The last vestige of standards, hanging there like a hangman's noose.

She spoke to him through dried lips that she couldn't even moisten with her tongue, handing him the last two euro coins from her purse.

"Can you get me a bottle of water from the drinks machine."

As he turned his face up out of his hands, she glimpsed his red eyes which had deepened between puffy cheeks and drooping eyebrows. He'd aged since the airport.

"Do you want a chocolate bar as well?" he offered.

"No, just the water Rupert."

Wednesday 8 November

Chapter 4

He had dreamt the strangest of dreams last night. He was a young deckhand on a sailing ship in the South China Sea. An early nineteenth-century vessel, with three square-rigged masts. Pitching up and down through towering walls of water battering it on all sides. Surges of wind trying to lift it out the sea. Dark brooding skies, lightning flashes, thunder claps, torrential rain. The full works. Like in a film. They were being dragged towards jagged rocks, certain to be wrecked and sink deep into the ocean. But then a moment of calm. Clear skies, a shaft of sunlight, clear air. Melodic distant voices carried towards him on the breeze. Then the view of the mermaids on the rocks illuminated by sunlight now. Beautiful faces, long flowing hair, bare breasts, glistening fish tails. Lilting music and orchestrated singing. Peace had descended from heaven.

About to set off for work, that's pretty much what he felt about life. Disaster and calm as bedfellows. Unable to fathom mermaids. No dramatic resolution. At least the black cat was nowhere to be seen. It was daylight now, even if only an emotionless grey-painted sky. A time for humans not evil cats. Humans and dogs. He nodded to Bernard and Lucy. Bernard nodded back. No need for words from the dour Yorkshire men. George's spirits lifted at the sight of man and dog bonded in trust and companionship. The past could all be forgotten and buried. Redemption was possible.

The breath of optimism was fleeting. The half second of delay in pulling out allowed another car to come round the corner. Not just any old car. The gleaming five series BMW of Derek Pearson. His nemesis Derek Pearson. The car looked newly cleaned and valeted. So did Derek, as he sped off to meet the challenges ahead for a thrusting executive.

George followed dutifully behind, stalled, and held up a Tesco delivery van. The driver mouthed 'fucking idiot'. Hope had dissipated before eight in the morning, and now it was time for anxiety about work. The seamless switch from mild optimism to dark pessimism. It was one small step for man.

Work. Over ten years ago when Paul had asked him what he did for a job, he'd felt incapable of providing a meaningful answer. Train driver, policeman, farmer, were all something that an eleven-year-old could picture. But project manager, what did he do? George struggled to explain it to his son just starting secondary school, and if he was being brutally honest, struggled to understand it himself. He'd stumbled into it in a similar way to marriage, and remained confused by both. He'd told Paul that he worked in an office. That was the best he could do.

So, in an office, he managed projects – for companies, for Government departments, anybody who would pay him. He produced action lists and traffic lights to show progress, but he didn't actually have to do anything himself. That should have been the beauty of it. Other people did the real work, and the project manager monitored progress, gave direction.

It was a choice of career to which he was perfectly ill-suited. A general meandering, unstructured, let's be honest – lazy and puzzled, approach to life, was hardly the set of skills that would ruthlessly drive forward a strategically important project. He was out of his depth at all times. Not just paddling in a country stream with water gently lapping over his feet; but up to his waist in a tidal estuary, ankles locked in mud and silt, with the torrent about to power over him and end it all. The only saving grace was that while he fully understood the awful inevitability, that one day he would indeed drown in the Humber, it took other people a while to fully detect and comprehend his deficiencies. But even the uninitiated and uninformed did in the end, and then drastic action was needed.

That was now a matter of weeks or even days away.

*

It was just over two years since he'd marched confidently into Horizon Global, watched with indifference by Geoff Thompson on reception. Geoff allowed him to walk ten paces before shouting to come back and get an access card. It was a trusted routine for Geoff with new starters, establishing his authority as guardian of the gates. Reinforced by a navy blue uniform with epaulettes and brass buttons, a peaked cap, and excellent voice projection. After three months, you could start calling him Tommo. They were now confidants, chewing the cud on matters of life, love, and disappointment. And Tommo was more forthcoming as a muse than Polonius.

Two years was the average life cycle of one of George's job campaigns. A cheerful march to war, fortified by pipers and kisses from sweethearts. Followed by protracted and unproductive skirmishes, ultimately leading to an ignominious retreat and a vindictive peace settlement.

There had been one exception. The implementation of a sales-order processing system fourteen years ago for a budget ladies' fashion chain in the West Midlands. The incumbent had retired hurt for unpleasant abdominal surgery. George had been wheeled in, put up in the Wolverhampton Hilton, and managed to see it through without undoing all the good work that had gone before. He took the credit, without shame. It meant that when asked at an interview to give an example of a project that you feel proud of, he could give a half-honest reply. As he'd done at the Horizon Global interview.

Horizon Global, HG, occupying three floors of an office building about ten minutes' walk from the city centre. The building was an architect's mess of smoked glass, galvanised steel, and purple-coloured cladding, but lacked a workable air-conditioning system. The time of thick jumpers and fan-heaters was approaching. But despite that, a decorative plaque in reception happily informed all who entered that it was a workplace promoting creativity and wellbeing.

HG. 'Global solutions, local accountability'. That's what it said on the mouse mat. George had tried to fathom it, he really had. It had been explained to them at the annual European conference at the Harrogate Exhibition Centre. Chuck McNorton, Global CEO and President, had flown in from the corporate HQ in Columbus Ohio to explain the new global strategy. Chuck had replaced the previous guy, Ed somebody, and was bringing new vigour and purpose. He'd stood on the stage in front of nearly a thousand people to explain his vision. Combining the experience of the last fifty years with the opportunities of globalisation. Harnessing the power of technology with human creativity. Wow.

At the end of his speech to the multitude, Chuck shouted 'If you're with me, follow me now. If you're against me, get out of my way.' Everybody rose, applauded, and pledged their allegiance. They were with him. They would follow him. Even the French contingent. Even George. It would have been churlish not to.

The Americans on the stage did a lot of whooping. Somebody shouted 'who's number one?', and somebody shouted back 'the customer'. That brought the house down. They linked arms and soaked up the adoration. Balloons were released from the ceiling. The music came on. Carmina Burana. Stirring and rousing, guaranteed to get the heart pumping. There was a hint of the Nuremburg rallies, but George chose not to mention that.

But what did a global strategy mean? What were you supposed to do about it sitting at your desk on a Wednesday morning? He was haunted by the thought that everybody else had worked it out. You were supposed to align your actions twenty-four seven with the strategy. That's what Chuck expected. You had to live and breathe it. Gosh.

George hadn't worked out how to align his actions twenty-four seven. Or nine to five. Or nine to ten for that matter. He was more focused on covering up his own deficiencies for a bit longer. He'd been selected to lead the European pillar of the Global Change Programme – the 'GCP', that's what they called it. There were five strands to it. He could remember three of them, struggled with the other two, although one began with a 'D'. But the whole thing was now a runaway train heading over a cliff, plunging into a canyon below. The driver with his eyes closed, fingers crossed, hoping for the best.

And today, the glazed cherry, on the icing, on the cake, was the supreme horror of his annual performance review. It would be like standing naked in the middle of Wembley stadium on a cold day, a flaccid member on display, with the capacity crowd pointing and laughing. He'd read about imposter syndrome. 'A psychological pattern in which one doubts one's accomplishments and has a persistent internalised fear of being exposed as a fraud'. That hit the nail on the head. Except that he really was an imposter. It wasn't a syndrome.

Chapter 5

He followed his usual route into the city that he'd lived in all his life. Apart from the three years at Hull university, the month in Wolverhampton, and an unproductive three weeks in Skelmersdale at the beginning of his career. This was the city that he felt comfortable in, and where he would stay. A twenty-five-minute drive. On average. Depending on the traffic, the road-works, school holidays. An uninteresting mix of dual carriageway, single carriageway, and a couple of short-cuts now discovered by everybody, stripping away the advantage. Some people liked to use this time to plan the day ahead. George preferred to delay things twenty-five minutes longer.

His routine was carefully worked out. News and sport for fifteen minutes, music for the last ten, ending with a rousing rock anthem. Less to fire him up for the day, more to drown out the fear and self-loathing.

On the short stretch of dual carriageway, which only showed any colour with a short burst of daffodil yellow in the central reservation each spring, he made his switch from words to music. At the same time, he switched from the inside to the outside lane to position for the roundabout ahead, a manoeuvre that he'd practised diligently over the last couple of years. Doubly pleasing today, as it carved up a scarlet Audi R8, which he knew would have a retail price approaching one hundred thousand pounds. If only he could apply the same focus to work. He caught a glimpse of the driver, noticing only a dark moustache and a tweed jacket. Serve you right mate, for having an expensive car, a dark moustache, and a tweed jacket. The other driver flashed his lights, sounded his horn, and no doubt shouted a few obscenities in his cockpit. But George was in front of him, smiling in the rear-view mirror. The joy of a small victory.

The final stage of the sequencing didn't go to plan. Entering the car park, he fumbled to get the right song on. The iPod classic had seen better days. He didn't think Apple sold them anymore. You were supposed to buy an iPhone for a thousand pounds. On came a country and western ballad that may have been called Misery and Whiskey. A cowboy bidding a bitter-sweet farewell to his love who he'd just strangled, and was now ascending to heaven accompanied by a choir of angels. The piece of music to start the working day.

As he grabbed his bag and ran across the car park, the portent of the song was reinforced by a darkening sky, a deep rumble of thunder, and marbles of raindrops starting to bounce off the paving. A bit like the storm of last night's dream, but without the mermaids. The gods must be angry with you George.

*

"She was in early today, George. Not the red dress though. Think you'd call it emerald green. Looked ready for trouble, I'd say. But she went straight up to the third floor, so you might be safe for a while."

Tommo liked to get bad news in early, in his undiluted cockney accent, and added a sly wink and an angled nod for dramatic effect.

"Thanks Tommo, I'll be on the lookout."

He'd confessed to Geoff Thompson a few weeks after the demise of his relationship with Linda, during one of their late Friday afternoon heart-to-heart sessions. Geoff had told him about his earlier dalliance with a lady butcher from Sheffield. George had felt an obligation to reciprocate, whilst reflecting that it was a strange profession for a lady.

Having escaped further interrogation, George walked into the main office, and strode twenty paces to his desk. He knew it was twenty paces, he had counted them, and it was always twenty. His desk was next to the window. It was very dark outside, and he caught sight of his reflection. It wasn't like looking at yourself in the mirror, not that clear, and the office lights reflected back, but he could see his face, his body. He observed himself full frontal, then slightly to one side, then slightly to the other. He was five foot eleven and a half inches. He usually said he was about six foot. No sign of middle-age spread. He had a very good physique. It was unjust. He never went to the gym, never went running, never played any sport. But there you go, suckers.

He stood more upright, pushed his shoulders back, half remembered the things he'd been taught at the Pilates classes Dawn bought him for his fortieth birthday. Engaged his core. Strengthened his pelvic floor. That was it. God, he thought he was old at forty, but that was nearly ten years ago. What he'd give to be only forty now.

He stared at the reflection of his face. There was no vision of Derek behind him, and he ignored the sad eyes. Not bad bone structure, a prominent lower jaw. A strong chin, as his mother put it. Linda had called it rugged. Dawn hadn't called it anything for a long time. He had a full head of hair, with just a few grey streaks. He thought that made him look more dignified. And a decent haircut. Even if it did cost him twenty-five pounds every six weeks. His mother had told him that – invest in a good haircut. She'd told him he was classically handsome. But that was his mother saying it. She'd say he was better looking than Derek as well. And he did get five Valentine's cards when he was fifteen. He had a slightly crooked nose. Not broken playing sport or in a punch-up, it had just always been that way. Just like his father's in that one very old photo. Paul had the same nose. But this was only a slight imperfection. The nose, the sad eyes, with a few lines growing. Otherwise, a pretty good specimen. If it weren't for the fatal character defects, he'd be a decent catch.

It was an open-plan office, and this desk was nearly always his. But not absolutely always, because they had a hot-desking policy. So if he was in late, or had gone off-site, then somebody else might grab it. He hated that. It was like seeing a stranger in your own bed. That was the main reason for getting into the office early. To stake your claim. Even if it did mean watching people eating cereal at their desks. When did that start?

He switched on his desk-top. It took a while to start up, but the dread started immediately. He'd given up reading e-mails after work. That made for a more relaxing evening, but it meant the horror e-mails had built up overnight. That was the problem working for an American company with global reach. There were the extra hours of US time, and then the Far East lot opened up. Not that anybody seemed to stop sending e-mails to go to sleep. They had to adopt a twenty-four-hour business culture to survive globally – that's what Chuck had said. But it didn't matter what part of the globe the e-mails were coming from, or what time they'd been sent. They were all asking the same question – why was there no progress on the project?

As the emails appeared on the screen, he felt a deep well of nausea building. Twenty-three new ones since he switched off at nearly four o'clock yesterday afternoon. He could recognise a few killers straight away. The deadly assassin one was from Bud Ellis, the corporate liaison director, or spy. George hardly dared open it, but there was enough in the heading to make him shiver. 'Progress on Project Argonaut'. Why did they need a code name? It was hardly a state secret. The e-mail had been sent at 21.42 the previous evening UK time, just when George would have been pouring his second glass of wine.

'George, I thought it best to contact you directly to say how very disappointed I am with progress on Argonaut. I cannot see that we have driven forward any of the key work-streams over the last six months. Armando himself has contacted me to express concern. He will be flying in from Asia next week. Please send me the updated action plan immediately, with timeline to completion. We all need to pull together and deliver on this one George. Please be assured of my support. Hope Deonne and the family are fine. Bud.'

Well, that's that then. It's all over.

*

The e-mail had been copied to Samantha Pena, George's boss. A Spanish surname because she'd married a Cuban American living in the UK. How did that work? But Samantha was from Halifax. The accent was well-hidden but kept peeping out especially when she got angry – which she did a lot these days. If Bud hadn't quite got there, Samantha definitely had. She'd worked George out, and done that sooner than most. She was in her mid-thirties, she was bright, and she was closing in on him.

His performance review with Samantha was at eleven. So that left him a few hours to fill in the form the best way he could, and work out whether to try to salvage anything out of it, or just say it's a fair cop and I'll come quietly. He'd better get on with it then. But first a quick trawl of the news websites, a cup of coffee, and maybe order a CD on Amazon. Oh, and work out what that was all about with mermaids. The answer was only a few clicks away.

'Mermaids foretell and provoke disaster. Cause shipwrecks. Stir up terrible storms.'

Oh dear. But hang on.

'In other folk traditions, they can be benevolent, predicting a return to calm waters, and can fall in love with humans.'

That was as clear as mud then.

What about sirens? Are they the same as mermaids?

'In Greek mythology sirens were dangerous creatures who lured sailors with their enchanting singing voices to shipwreck on the rocky coast.'

No ambiguity there. Sirens were out to get you. But there was a picture of them and they had legs not a fish tail. So, he had been dreaming about mermaids not sirens. There was hope.

What about black cats? That was all over the place. Could be good luck or bad luck, depending on which way they were walking, and which country you were in. Apparently in Japan they were hugely lucky for single ladies, bringing lots of good suitors. George didn't bother looking which way it worked for males, nearly fifty, in West Yorkshire.

The in-depth research, reading an article about a massive snake swallowing an alligator, two cups of coffee, and nearly ordering a CD, took longer than planned. He'd also looked up werewolves, even though he hadn't dreamt about them. So, it was about ten o'clock before he got down to any work. Then Tommo phoned him to say Linda had left to get a train to London, so he'd be safe for the rest of the day, and carried on talking for another ten minutes.

All of that meant that he walked into the meeting room at four minutes past eleven, armed only with a crumpled draft, marked with hand-written notes in blue and red – he'd lost the blue pen half way through. He could tell Samantha had been sitting there since ten fifty-nine. She was what his mother would call a hefty woman, which was unusual for somebody called Samantha. But she'd lost a lot of weight recently, acquired a new wardrobe, and the mischievous smile was back in town. And this morning she looked a lot taller. He shook his head, blinked, and looked again, transfixed by the conical shape slightly pointing backwards. It was indeed a 1960's beehive hairdo, newly unveiled, perched on top of Samantha Pena's head. She'd always had very long hair, down to her waist nearly, so it could be physically possible. But was there some form of structure in there to wrap it round before starting on the hairspray?

"Hello George. How are you?" she said, almost with warmth, "sit down, get yourself a glass of water if you want one." No mention of the far-reaching changes to her hairstyle.

Disarmed by the calmness, having being used to glares and raised voices over the last few weeks, and feeling a few beads of sweat building on his forehead, he pulled out a chair and sat down as instructed. And with super-human effort, managed to look at her face, and trot out a lame response, feeling that it would be inappropriate, in the circumstances, to refer to her hair, riveting as it was.

"I'm fine Samantha, thank you," he said hesitantly, putting the sorry document on the table. "I've made a few notes on the review form. I haven't finished it yet though. Thought I'd get your feedback, then complete it properly."

She didn't look at the form, but turned her head with poise to maintain eye contact. The manoeuvre reminded him of the Tanzanian lady carrying a large water bucket on her head, that he'd seen in a documentary.

"That's fine George. Actually, we're going to handle the meeting differently. Anna from HR is going to join us. She was meant to be here by now. I'm sure she won't be long…"

As if on cue, the door opened, and in walked Anna, the angel of death. A tall, slim shadowy figure, about the same age as Samantha. Too tall and slim. She reminded him of a long-necked wading bird – a stork or a crane, her head moving with a pecking motion. Jet black hair slicked back, perfectly groomed. Dark piercing eyes etched around by green eye shadow, thin lips glistening with purple lipstick, and a cruel smile. A smart black suit and shiny stilettos, perfect for walking over you. Vampire corporate, but revealing a small rose tattoo on her left ankle as she sat down and crossed one very long leg over the other very long leg. He felt a momentary arousal. She fixed his gaze, and began the exquisite torture.

The agony was short-lived in the end. More of a one-sided boxing match over in the first round, rather than two hours on the rack in the Tower. Perhaps it was out of pity, or perhaps she had more important things to do, but Anna from HR put him out of his misery within two and a half minutes, including the softening up, the body punches, and the final knock-out.

"Need to right-size the cost base. Match skill-sets with business needs. Armando flying in from South East Asia. Hand over duties to Angel Wei. Just got her MBA. New blood. Arriving from Hong Kong. Bring her up to speed. Talk detail about contractual arrangements tomorrow."

*

Back at his desk, gathering his thoughts, he stared idly out of the hermetically sealed window.

There was no beauty to behold in the view. Just a few spindly trees shorn of their leaves, half-heartedly interrupting the view of the diesel lorries thundering past.

He didn't feel like sharing his news of the morning. Everybody around looked busy. Chuck would be heartened to see them beavering away bringing his dream to reality. There'd be a briefing note from HR in the morning.

'George Stephenson decided to pursue his career outside of HG… made a significant contribution over the last two years… handing over to Angel Wei… flying in from Hong Kong… wish him well for the future.'

It was a relief, an act of kindness. It had been coming, and now here it was. He rewound some of Anna's corporate speak. There was a reference to four month's pay. That would do. And he had the impression that he could walk out unscathed, no public black marks. Well sod it. It was time to move on from HG. Move on from Samantha and Anna, the beehive and the tattoo, Bud and Armando. Bud who he'd only glimpsed in the far corner of a video conference call, and the unseen mysterious Armando. And who the hell was Angel Wei? His mother used to give him Angel Delight for pudding. Escape the temptations of luscious Linda and the red dress. This could be the turning point for him and Dawn. The spark that lit the tinder box. Darkest hour always comes before dawn. No pun intended. Sunlit uplands and all that. Definitely, maybe.

Briefly filled with modest hope, the man of action bought himself a sandwich from the canteen. Cheese salad on a brown baguette – it was Wednesday after all. But on the first bite, his peace was disturbed. His phone vibrated and he saw Dawn's name appear. He'd switched it to silent for his meeting with Samantha. It was rare for Dawn to ring him at work. The phone carried on vibrating. He stared at it. She only rang when it was bad news. Eventually he answered.

"Hi."

Funny how they never used each other's first name on the phone. Usually you just said 'It's me.'

Dawn dived in with no preamble.

"It's me. I've just had a call from Paul. He was at work, but he seemed strange. Seemed like he wanted to tell me something. But he didn't tell me anything. Just small talk about a take-away pizza last night. They sent the wrong one, but he ate it anyway. He wouldn't ring me just to talk about a pizza. I could tell he was holding back. There's something wrong, but I can't put my finger on it. Something to do with that awful woman. I can't understand why he's still with her. I want you to talk to him."

Dawn still worried about Paul. Worried even more about the influence of his girlfriend Danni. Two years older than Paul, and named after the younger less successful Minogue sister apparently. Dawn called her dreadful Danni. Thought she was rude and disrespectful, and rough. A bag of mystery. They'd only met her a few times, and Paul knew that his mother didn't like her. She'd worn a black leather mini-skirt to Paul's graduation ceremony. It was way too short. Fishnet stockings with a big hole in one knee, and silver Doctor Marten boots. Hadn't even combed her hair. Looked like she'd just crawled out of bed. Dawn had spotted two tattoos and suspected more.

George liked the small silver ring in her nose though, the piercing green eyes, and the chaotic peroxide-blonde hair. Her roots needed doing, but there was an unusual boyish beauty about her. Audrey Hepburn in *Breakfast at Tiffany's*. Small but perfectly formed. Something mystic as well, and an attractive irreverence. He'd felt it the very first time they'd met, but it was a lot stronger at the graduation ceremony. Some sort of connection. It wasn't sexual, he told himself. He couldn't explain it. It was deeper. More primitive. Something in the way she moved, the way she looked at him. God, he'd better put that out of his mind. Certainly never mention it to Dawn. Life was complicated enough. Anyway, Paul was only twenty-two. Plenty of time to find a nice girl. Or go back to the original nice girl.

"I'm sure he's fine Dawn," he said with a breezy air, which he knew as soon as he'd said it would be annoying her, "probably nothing to worry about," he continued weakly, "he's still getting used to the new job."

There was an uncompromising tone in her response which he recognised immediately.

"George, I'm telling you, there is something wrong. I can sense it. He wouldn't spend ten minutes talking about a fucking pizza. That's why I'm ringing you. I want you to get in touch with him. I'm going to be busy for the next few hours. Take some responsibility George. Don't leave it all up to me."

It took him one second to back down, and he didn't ask what type of pizza it was.

"OK, I'll ring him, see you later." He didn't feel like telling her about this morning's events. He'd tell her tonight.

On the face of it, Paul had his life sorted out. A decent degree from Hull university in economics. One notch better than his father, so there's progress down the generations. Strange why he'd gone to the same university, when you were supposed to rebel against your parents. The lure of Hull must have been too great. Then he'd got an accountancy training contract with a food company on an industrial estate on the edge of Hull, and was doing professional exams. That was all mainstream stuff, a proper job, a salary, prospects, and a one-bedroom flat near the centre of the city. George could remember the area from his student days, a bit run down, but Paul was just starting out. Plenty of time to move up the property ladder.

Then there was Danni. You had to admit, there was a bit of a juxtaposition there – Paul having a degree in economics, training as an accountant; but living with the wild and mysterious Danni. Belladonna. Deadly nightshade. Or the mermaid. A picture of Danni's naked human top half, with the strange tattoo on her bare shoulder, exposed breasts and slim waist merging into silky fishtail bottom half, flashed unwelcomely into his mind. He quickly pressed the erase button.

Dawn's female intuition was probably spot on. Danni would be at the root of the problem somehow. He ought to speak to Paul. Dawn had given him very clear orders with no room for ambiguity or delay. On the other hand, he didn't want to engage with any more trouble. If there was a problem to sort out, he couldn't face doing it now. He'd rather put it off a bit longer, ring Paul tonight, or tomorrow. But the fear of Dawn was greater, and she could smell his lies from a great distance. He had his instructions. He pressed Paul's number on his phone. It rang, nobody answered, and it went to voice mail.

"Hi Paul, it's Dad, just ringing to see if you're OK. I think you talked to Mum earlier. Wondered if we could come over and see you. Give me a ring, or I'll ring you again tonight or tomorrow. See you."

Not a bad result. He'd done what Dawn had commanded, without having to deal with any difficulties just yet. It was a message that didn't say anything. The fact was, the forty-nine-year-old father had lost touch with the twenty-two-year-old son. He hadn't meant it to happen. No father meant it to happen. Well not many. There were exceptions, obviously. One notable one. But generally, it was just the unstoppable force of nature. The six-year-old hanging on your every word, listening to the story in bed, a goodnight kiss as you switch the bedside lamp off. Then the blink of an eye, and the metamorphosis to the teenager who is simply embarrassed by your very presence, not worthy of a hello or goodbye. Quickly followed by the departure to university, the awkward hug, the difficult look. That's it. All over. Apparently when an adolescent lion leaves its mother, it just wanders off and never comes back. At least with humans, you get to see the offspring for the odd weekend here and there, even if it's only to use the washing machine.

Maybe when he worked out the communication secret with Dawn, he could use it on Paul. The three of them reunited. That would be good. It really would.

Chapter 6

"Sorry to hear the news George. Leaving a week on Friday I hear. Hope you're having a do. We could all do with a knees up. You're bound to find something else – a man with your brain."

You had to hand it to Geoff Thomson, thought George as he was about to walk through the main exit doors at four thirty that afternoon. His communication network was top notch. He knew George's leaving date before he did. But you wouldn't have compassion on the list of attributes for the hardened East End bruiser.

"Thanks Tommo. I was thinking of a cross-dressing karaoke night. What do you reckon?"

"Ha, not with my legs mate. Look terrible in anything above the knee. Look on the bright side though. It gets you away from her. She's not in tomorrow by the way, staying the night in London."

"Every cloud has a silver lining Tommo."

"Spot on. By the way, have you seen that facking monstrosity on top of old Samantha's head? She's left her husband you know. That Latin-type. Moved in with a joiner bloke from Glasgow. Scottish, so I hear. He was doing some joinery work on that kitchen extension they were having, and one thing led to another. Doing a lot more dove-tailing now I reckon, old jock-face. That's why she's got that new hairdo. I sent a picture to my missus. She thought she looked like Dusty Springfield. You wouldn't remember her."

George wondered if Tommo would simply ramble on forever, giving his mildly offensive views on life, love, and the universe. He only needed an audience of one, and didn't require much in the way of interaction. George tried to picture the tryst of Tommo and the lady butcher from Sheffield, the lovers' romantic rendezvous on a summer's evening in a secluded glade, the last splashes of sunlight filtering through the leaves.

"I'll give it three months, then she'll be back with Mario. He's got money you know."

With a superhuman effort George managed to extricate himself, walking at pace through the doors, and leaving Geoff speculating on the reconciliation of Samantha and Mario, who'd only just been wrenched asunder.

Dawn was at work until eight this evening. There was a late-night counselling session each Wednesday, so she wouldn't be home until about half eight. He'd driven home in good spirits, and found an unopened tube of wine gums on the passenger seat under a fleece that he kept in the car during the winter. When he opened it, there was a red one on top, his favourite. Things were looking up.

Turning into Sycamore Meadows, he spotted Mr McManus pulling away from number five in the hearse. He was the only undertaker that George had ever met, except at a funeral. It was unusual to see the hearse. Normally it was parked up at the business premises – that's what he'd told George. You wouldn't want to see it parked on the drive every evening. Too big and too depressing. There'd be complaints. Perhaps he'd popped back for a snack before some early evening embalming. Strange that they had a murderer and a funeral director living so close. Maybe the two of them hooked up every now and again to discuss, what? – bodies?

Approaching their drive, George waved to Mr McManus, and then focused on his old adversary the black cat. It was sitting there unperturbed by him aiming the car directly at it. It was a tricky manoeuvre, but he managed a short final acceleration before braking hard to avoid hitting the garage. The cat scattered and ran for the hedge. Another small victory.

Inside, he greeted the bird. "Good evening Polonius. How's it going. Had a good day?"

He went through this routine most evenings after work. The fact is, Polonius must have had a pretty dull day, stuck in that cage, standing on that perch. George emptied some food pellets into the feeding tray and topped up the water. You were supposed to provide stimulation to avoid behavioural problems in African greys. They were high maintenance pets. They usually bonded to one family member. That was George. Polonius was indifferent to Dawn, and didn't like strangers. Sometimes George closed the utility room door, opened the birdcage, and let the bird flap around. Not enough room for serious flying, but it was a brief taste of freedom. Not tonight though, he had other things on his mind, but there was time for a quick catch-up on the day's events.

"They booted me out at work today Polonius. It was on the cards. It's a relief really. I'll probably be at home during the day for a while. We can spend more time together. Go for walks. Oh, and Samantha's run off with a Glaswegian joiner. Got herself a fancy new haircut – it'll take a lot of maintenance, add twenty minutes in the mornings. We're still not sure what's wrong with Paul. I pictured Danni as a mermaid. It suited her."

The bird looked back at him with that intelligent stare, and made his choice from the two options.

"Watcha Brian."

Such profound thoughts from a bird.

*

When Dawn had the evening session, he usually made some tea for both of them, ate his, then she had hers when she got back. He made some pasta, mixed in a sauce, but the only vegetables he could find were three blackened carrots. He put them in the compost bin. Today, he'd probably only had two of out the required five a day. He'd have to bring the average up tomorrow.

He ate his meal, then a Cornetto. There was only one Cornetto left in the freezer, but Dawn didn't like them as much as he did, so it was fine to take the last one. There were some nuts in that. Perhaps he was up to two and a half.

He looked at his watch. It was a minute past six, and pitch black outside. It might have been the sugar rush of the branded frozen dessert cone, but he was suddenly spurred into action. He could get another job if he tried. He'd done it before. Whispering a few snippets of clichéd self-motivation to himself – 'be decisive', 'positive thinking George' – he delayed the washing up, and plonked his laptop down on the kitchen table. He found the version of his CV when he'd got the job at HG. So, he just had to update it, embellish it, avoid the awful truth. Mission accomplished at HG. Success factors ticked off. Time to move on to the next challenge. After about an hour he sat back and admired his work. You could almost believe it.

Now it was time to update his LinkedIn account. This would be more challenging. He hadn't touched it for a couple of years, but he somehow remembered his password. There was an old picture of him with the bright pink tie. That must be seven years old. No need to change it. Lots of messages from Richard Branson, Jack Welch, and Bill Gates offering nuggets of wisdom. Directed at everybody presumably, not just him. A few people wanting to connect. There was that idiot in HG Finance beaming out, smartly dressed, looking all professional –Brian Van Halen. Same as the rock band. From Holland. 'Do you know Brian Van Halen?' 'Yes, connect' 'No, I don't'. Well, he did know him, but George certainly didn't want to connect. He clicked 'No, I don't'. Then he clicked on his own picture. Apparently, his profile strength was intermediate. He was surprised it was that strong. He could build his network, subscribe to newsletters, and get notified about new jobs. The last one seemed a good idea in the circumstances. He did a bit more work on it, updated his contact details, and managed to upload his CV. Then ran out of steam. He'd had enough of being thrusting and dynamic. It was eight o'clock now, and Dawn should be back in half an hour for a bit of uneasy communication.

He made himself a cup of tea, using the last tea bag. Dawn wouldn't be pleased about that. He printed out his CV, using the last two sheets of paper. She wouldn't be pleased about that either. He was reading the document with some modest pride, when the phone rang. The landline. Nobody ever phoned on that. Just the annoying lady from BT trying to persuade you to upgrade the broadband for an extra £4.99 per month. Or Auntie Maureen from Basingstoke to ask Dawn how her mother was. He eventually tracked down the phone, stared at it trying to remember which button to press, then hesitated. Somebody had died. It was the police about a car accident. It was Dawn. It was Paul. He pressed the green button and said 'hello' in a worried tone. Nothing. No police constable from West Yorkshire or Humberside. No lady from BT. No Auntie Maureen. He said 'hello' three times. You could usually tell when it was a marketing call in a queuing system – there'd be a click or something. But there was only silence. A strange sort of silence. The silence when you know there's somebody there. He pressed the red button.

Then another strange thing. A knock at the door. The bell didn't work anymore. He was supposed to get it fixed. Who the hell was knocking at the door at this time? Too early for carol singers. The ex-convicts selling oven gloves usually came on Saturday mornings. A bit late for a delivery. A bit late for somebody collecting for charity. He strolled through to the hall, peered out of the small window, but couldn't see properly. Just have to open it then. So he did, and saw Derek Pearson looking back at him.

"Hi George. I was hoping to speak to Dawn about something. She's been kind of, advising me, you could say. If she's in, I'd really like to speak to her, if that's convenient."

"Sorry Derek, she's out. She does a late session on Wednesday."

He was pleased with his self-restraint. Keep it factual. No need for confrontation at this stage. Don't strangle him just yet, and he probably wasn't strong enough to overpower Derek, drag him in and chain him up in the cellar overnight, ready to torture him in the morning, or perhaps at the weekend. Anyway, they didn't have a cellar.

"I'll tell her you called, Derek. I think she'll be tired by the time she gets back. She'll just want a quiet night in. Just the two of us. You know how it is Derek."

"Of course George. I'm sorry to trouble you. Yes, tell her that I called round. Nothing too urgent. It can wait a few more days."

"Did you just ring our landline Derek?"

"No, it wasn't me George. It could be one of those annoying marketing calls."

There were no signs of lying on Derek's face, but he did look different. The self-confidence had faded, he was hunched up, his hair dishevelled. He looked at George with heavy eyes. Then it happened. At first George couldn't work it out. Then it happened again. Derek moved his jaw and bottom lip to one side. Closed one eye, and opened the other one wide. There was a bit of shoulder movement as well. George stared at him transfixed. Oh joy. Oh joy of joys. A nervous twitch. There was a pause. Maybe he'd regained his self-control. But then another one. It was definitely a pattern. With a bit of a body twist this time. Similar to a boy at school who they'd taunted mercilessly, said he was trying to catch flies in his mouth.

"OK George I'll head off. Cassandra will be back soon from tennis lessons. I don't like to leave Begonia on her own too long. Although she is fourteen now."

George considered an acerbic one-liner, but was too stunned to summon up anything original.

"Bye Derek. Take care."

That's all he said. But he couldn't keep the grin off his face. And as Derek trudged away, he couldn't resist a tiny wave goodbye. Like at a football match when a player from the other team gets sent off. Well, those are the twists and turns of life. One minute you're up, the next you're down. One minute you're standing astride the corporate world. The next minute you're twitching on the doorstep. Shame about that Derek. Couldn't happen to a nicer guy.

But what had caused it? There must be a reason. It didn't just happen. Some trauma perhaps. But whatever it was, it was to be welcomed. He'd ask Dawn. Very diplomatically of course. He'd look serious. Concerned. No sense of, what do you call it? Schadenfreude. He looked it up quickly on his phone. 'Pleasure derived by someone from another person's misfortune. A complex negative emotion.' That was it. Schadenfreude. But nothing complex or negative here. Just pure unadulterated pleasure. Poor old Derek.

*

George's spirits lifted, his belief in life renewed, and with a gust of second wind blowing from behind, he got back to job searching. He took his notebook out, and flicked through the disorderly lists of recruitment consultants, websites, and previous employers. By half eight, he'd fired-off e-mails, uploaded his CV, scattered his contact details in every direction, and generally done what was needed to find a job. Or phase one at least. Two and a half hours, even allowing for the Derek interlude, and he'd got the wheels in motion. No wallowing in self-pity for George Stephenson, miraculously transformed into a man of action. He even managed to tidy up the kitchen and put Dawn's tea on the table, with a bottle of chilled white wine.

He heard Dawn come in and kick off her shoes in the hall as she usually did. He stood up as she came into the kitchen, as if the teacher had walked into the room. She was wearing a cream blouse tucked into black trousers. He took a few seconds to admire the slimness of her waist and the elegance of her neck, then blurted out a scatter gun of greetings and explanations.

"Hi Dawn, had a good day? I tried to ring Paul but I couldn't get through, I left him a message. I got booted out at work, but I've sent my CV around. I'll sort it out."

She looked around at the tidy kitchen, the tea on the table, the bottle of wine. She could tell that it was chilled. She gave him a suspicious, searching look, but decided to let him have the benefit of the doubt.

"I'm fine George," she said, still half-heartedly looking for the catch. "What was that about losing your job? You said it might be on the cards, but it's happened has it?"

He told her the whole story. Not that there was a lot to tell. She knew his failings better than anybody. He focused on the cash to cushion the blow, tide them over for a few months, and that in the last couple of hours he'd got on with the job search. He thought that was worthy of praise. They'd only told him that morning.

"I'm sorry that's happened George. I suppose you've had time to prepare for it. And it's good that you've got on with things. You seem pretty positive. You've got a lot of experience, you've always worked. I think you'll get sorted out, won't you?"

Not bad. A squeeze of the hand would've been nice.

"Did you say you'd tried to get in touch with Paul? I do think there's something wrong George. I can feel it."

She'd calmed down a bit about Paul. He told her that he'd left a message, and that he'd ring him in the morning. He told her that he had a week and a bit left at work, according to Tommo. She ate her pasta, and didn't notice that he'd eaten the last Cornetto.

"George, I bumped into Bernard this morning. He definitely smells of cannabis. He did the last time I spoke to him as well."

"I think he's got a new supplier. The last one didn't do home delivery. You can probably get it on Amazon these days."

"He must start in the morning."

"No, I think his clothes smell of it. He told me he doesn't start until after four in the afternoon."

"What, you mean he's talked to you about it. He's admitted it?"

"The great thing is, it's not even medicinal. He just likes to get high. He's a child of the sixties. Free love and all that."

"He grew up in Goole. I don't think the Summer of Love got that far."

He smiled. Good comic timing. You see, there was still a spark there.

"It probably takes his mind off, you know, what happened."

"When he butchered his wife, you mean."

"He's haunted by it Dawn. You can see it in his eyes."

"So he should be. All that rubbish at the trial about dark forces. He was responsible. It's as simple as that."

"It is, you're right."

They didn't talk anymore about Bernard, or about anything else. They tried watching the ten o'clock news, but gave up after eleven minutes of relentless misery, and trudged upstairs to bed. Each of them followed their own routine of pre-bed actions. Switching lights off, locking doors, brushing teeth, swilling mouthwash. Urinating. Putting on nightwear. Climbing into bed. George switched his bedside light off first. Dawn kept hers on five minutes longer while she read a few pages of her book. He'd ask her about Derek tomorrow. Now didn't seem a good time.

She looked at him as he slept. There was some moonlight falling on his face. He was such a handsome young man. A beautiful face and thick dark wavy hair, cut short at the sides, but tussled on top. She hadn't tired of running her fingers through it, stroking it with the back of her hand. He looked like something out of a Renaissance painting. A fine torso. And he must be about six foot two, a good eight inches taller than her, but gentle. He looked peaceful. Almost childlike. There was peace in the first few hours of his sleep. Before the nightmares kicked in. He nearly always went to sleep before she did. Even with all of his troubles. All of their troubles. She only ever needed four or five hours' sleep. So, when she wasn't partying, she could either pace around the flat like a caged animal, or go to bed to do her thinking. She touched his cheek softly with her fingers in the hope that it would delay the bad dreams a bit longer. Then she got on with her thinking.

They were not original thoughts. She'd been thinking them for the last week and a half. What were the odds of what happened? It must be a million to one. No, a lot longer odds than that. Perhaps there was a formula that could calculate it. She'd been good at maths at school until she was about thirteen or fourteen. It wasn't hard for her. She wasn't bad at English either. She could make sense of a bunch of poems when the other girls just stared out the window, or looked at their phones, or chatted mindlessly. It was the roughest school around, but she stood out.

It had all gone wrong since then. She had enough self-knowledge to know that. But she'd kept her brain, and she'd kept her looks, and one day she was going to turn it all around. Just not today. She could be polite, charming, warm, funny, endearing, flirtatious, when she wanted to be. It's just that she didn't always want to be. The white wine topped with vodka in a half pint glass didn't help. That's what had happened on his graduation day. She'd meant to look normal, with a pretty dress. Enough dress to cover up the tattoos. Normal make-up. Do her hair. Be nice to his parents. But it hadn't worked out. She was nervous. She'd got horribly drunk the night before. Woke up in the wrong place, with the wrong clothes. No shower, no doing her hair. Steaming hangover. And rude to his mother. She hadn't meant to be, it just happened, the wrong words had flowed out of her mouth and she couldn't stop them.

Despite that, he stuck with her. And despite the other troubles he stuck with her, even though she was partly responsible.

And now she had this knowledge. This insight. And he didn't. They'd decided not to share it with him.

She could change that now. She could wake him up, and tell him right here and now. She'd promised not to. But that was a promise to a stranger in a bar. You could break the promise. Tell the truth to the man that you were sharing a bed with. Or tell his father.

But there was some force compelling her not to. And that strange magnetic force had grown stronger over the last few days. She could feel these forces, when others couldn't. Auntie Lelia had told her that.

Thursday 9 November

Chapter 7

This was the room with no windows, no natural light at all. Just a strange white glow. Not quite a prison cell, more a bleak interview room at a police station. He was sitting at the end of the table. She was two minutes late, like yesterday. He'd brought a pen and note book with him. To make notes. How efficient. He stared at the white wall reflecting the strange white light. Just time for a quick reflection on last night's dream. They were coming thick and fast these days. But no mermaids or sirens last night. They'd moved on to the Old Testament. Right back to the beginning in fact. Adam and Eve. Both naked apart from fig leaves. And the serpent, the tree of knowledge, the apple. There was Polonius in the tree. He didn't say anything. George was Adam. Who was Eve? Maybe Dawn, maybe Linda, or someone far younger. Temptation was in the air. A bit of dreamy meandering, but quickly on to horror story finale. The serpent rose up, expanded and enveloped George's head with its jaws. He could see its giant fangs. He could feel his whole body being squeezed down the creature's gullet. He'd woke up shouting and thrashing. Dawn had rolled away and pulled the duvet over her head.

*

"Morning George. You're looking well. I don't think yesterday's news was a complete shock to you was it? I expect you're making plans for the future already. Or maybe take a bit of time out. A holiday in the sun perhaps."

She seemed to walk in the room, greet him, and sit down in one smooth movement. She sat sideways on the chair facing him across the corner of the table. Maybe a slight pout of the lips, the long neck and elongated legs on full display, with the rose tattoo smiling up at him. It was a different black suit today. A softer material but still smart. Different colour eye-shadow as well. Deep purple. Yesterday it had been dark green. He'd remembered. Maybe Eve was Long Tall Anna. Temptation was definitely in the air.

"I've updated my CV. Put out some feelers. There's some interesting opportunities out there. I'm feeling confident about the future, Anna."

All the time he looked her directly in the eye. Pushed back. No defensive moves here. He wasn't sure where he'd dredged up the self-confidence from. But he had, even if only for a few moments.

"That's good George. I'm glad you're feeling so positive."

She was disarmed, and looked away. But not for long. She opened a file with her long fingers, and smiled that cruel smile again. He could imagine her in an S&M dungeon about to dish out a taste of the whip. Instead, she handed him a letter with the details of his departure. A lot of legal stuff, and a number – £17,397.23. More than he expected, and not bad for two years of steadily increasing failure. They would transfer it into his bank account on the day he left, which as Tommo had predicted was a week on Friday.

"Samantha will see you this afternoon George. To talk about the handover to Angel Wei. You'll like her. She's destined for great things."

Well bully for good old Angel Wei, he thought. Couldn't happen to a nicer person.

"Armando's flying in today or tomorrow. I don't suppose you'll get to meet him before you leave."

Probably not. Unless we manage to squeeze in six pints in the Lamb and Flag, plus a kebab.

"I'm in the office the next week or so George, although I work from home some days, so I'll definitely see you before you go."

"Look forward to it Anna." How about that for a bit of ambiguity. Look forward to going, or look forward to seeing you Anna?

There was embarrassment in her final smile. It was no longer cruel. Then she rose, turned, and exited. He watched her go, with one last glimpse of the rose tattoo. He looked at the letter, signed by Anna Templeton, Senior HR Manager.

There was a black marker pen on the table. It looked new. He took the top off, breathed in the distinctive smell, and walked to the whiteboard in the corner. It was daubed with the hieroglyphics of an obscure IT project plan that he should probably understand.

He wrote 'ARM THE POOR', and popped the marker pen in his pocket, thrilled by a small act of defiance.

*

Back at his desk, he scanned the detritus of the last two years. Yellow stickers with actions, not actioned. Piles of papers to be filed, not filed. Dust between the piles, where the cleaner had given up. Crisp packets to be thrown away, not thrown away. More dust. Coloured paper clips, never to be used. There was even a pencil sharpener. With some pencil shavings in, unemptied. No pencil in sight though. Dawn would say it was a metaphor for the life of George Stephenson. Badly in need of tidying up.

He fired up his desktop. Somehow there was a light and airy feel about the process. Unlike yesterday. Sure enough, there were no threatening e-mails from Bud. George was yesterday's man. No need to intimidate him anymore. There was even a vaguely warm message from Samantha, sent to everybody, about him moving on. Restructuring to improve focus. Thanked him for his contribution. Wished him well for future challenges.

Anna had sent him a soft copy of the letter that she'd just handed to him. The leaving date was confirmed for 17

November, a week on Friday. They obviously didn't want him hanging around, writing strange messages on whiteboards and stealing pens. There was another message from Samantha about the arrival of Angle Wei, the new messiah, and one about Armando jetting in from India. Wasn't he supposed to be jetting in from Singapore yesterday? Perhaps they'd all have to form a guard of honour for the Supreme Commander as he finally entered the premises astride a white stallion. A fanfare of trumpets worthy of Julius Caesar or Napoleon. Mandatory whooping.

A few people came over to say 'sorry you're leaving'. Not many though. Johnny Johnson from IT congratulated him on escaping, and reminded him to hand in his laptop and mobile phone when he left.

There'd be a few other things to sort out, including one big one. Nothing to do with IT. At some point he'd have to say goodbye to Linda. Unless he could avoid her until he left. That would be the better option. The coward's way out. Tommo would know about her movements, but George didn't think he could hide in the bushes for the next week. Or the stationery room. Or that she'd let him get away with no confrontation. Well, he wasn't going to think about Linda now. He'd file her away for as long as he could get away with it. Like Project Argonaut. In the bottom drawer. Out of sight.

Whilst filing Linda away in a plain manila folder, he spotted Samantha walking towards him. She had that busy determined look on her face, and she'd adapted her movement to the new hairstyle. When she got to his desk, she held her head still, and smiled. A friendly smile, which appeared genuine.

"How's it going George? I think you've seen Anna to sort out the details. I hope that's all as you expected. A man with your experience should be able to walk into another job."

A man of your experience. This was almost warm. He didn't detect a hint of irony.

"We've arranged the meeting with Angel Wei tomorrow. I think everybody just calls her Angel. Heavenly eh!"

Not a bad attempt at a joke Samantha. Keep going. You're starting to get the audience on your side.

"Just give her an overall view of the project. No need to get into detail."

She lowered her voice a bit.

"She's supposed to be the whizz-kid that turns everything around. We'll see though."

Sounds like you're deviating from the party line Samantha. Wash your mouth out.

"I'm looking forward to meeting her."

"Yes, I know what you mean George."

He thought she was going to wink to reinforce their conspiracy, but it didn't happen.

"Anyway George, on to more important things. I presume you'll be staying in Last Man Standing. No need to drop out just because you're leaving HG."

He'd always thought of Anna and Samantha as straight down the line corporate citizens. But Anna had the rose tattoo, and something else that he couldn't put his finger on. And Samantha had the joiner, the hairdo, the horses, and football. Rumour had it that her father was a race horse trainer, and her uncle a professional footballer. Usually she got her PA Monika to handle the detail of the various schemes. Collecting cash, handing out winnings, updating spreadsheets, adding witty comments to the results. Monika could spin that out all day by the time she'd finished chatting to everybody. But here was Samantha herself, getting down with the people.

Despite no interest in gambling, George had been persuaded, or coerced, to join Samantha's various syndicates to do the Lottery, the Grand National, and various football challenges. He'd had one win in two years. Twenty pounds on the National. He hadn't even selected it. You just grabbed a screwed-up piece of paper from a box.

He'd usually been knocked out in the first few rounds of Last Man Standing. You put five pounds in, picked a team from the English leagues. If your team won you stayed in, if your team lost or drew, you were out. Samantha loved it. She'd won it three times. It added up to nearly five hundred pounds. Lucky girl.

"OK Samantha, I'll stay in. I'll give my personal e-mail to Monika."

Very delicately she leaned on the corner of his desk, folded her arms, and carefully turned her head towards him. It was bordering on intimacy.

"I had a very big win last week George. A Premier League accumulator. I've got a formula. I know everybody says that, but it works. On average. Have you got a gaming account? If you set up a new one, you can get twenty-five pounds of free bets."

She glanced over her shoulder, leant in a bit closer, lowered her voice still further, and whispered to him.

"Do you want me to set one up for you?"

He struggled to answer. The transformation of Samantha Pena enthralled him. She'd had her knives out for him for the last six months, waiting to carve him up like a Christmas turkey. Without the cranberry sauce. But now the carcass had been thrown in the bin, she was looking more kindly on him. Maybe the joiner was a positive influence.

"That sounds like an offer I can't refuse Samantha."

He'd used that line on Linda when she'd asked him to join her governance and compliance steering group.

A curl of the lips and a flicker of amusement.

"Is that your personal mobile George? Let's get you going on one of the accounts. I prefer Bet-Happy. It's the easiest to use and you definitely get twenty-five pounds of free bets. Some of them have cut it back to ten. You have to put twenty-five pounds of your own money in though."

He picked up his phone, tapped in the code, then delicately handed it to her. There was the tiniest touch of fingers as the manoeuvre was completed.

Now he remembered the adverts and the football shirts. Bet-Perfect, Bet-to-Win, Bet-Cos-You're-a-Tosspot. They advised you to bet responsibly. Beer adverts advised you to drink responsibly. But wasn't that the point of gambling and drinking? You weren't acting responsibly. Would the adverts advise you to commit adultery responsibly? You cheated on your wife because you were irresponsible, and only cared about yourself. That was the whole point. He remembered his Uncle Tim, the one who worked at the brewery when it was still open. He went to the betting shop on a Saturday morning. He'd taken young George there when he was sixteen. To introduce him to the ways of the world. It was full of smoke and men, betting slips and pencils, and strange coloured newspapers. His uncle chewed on his pen, weighed up the odds, had a chat to the other blokes, placed a few bets, watched the races on the telly, lost the money, then went to the pub and got drunk on a Saturday afternoon. Then went home and shouted at Auntie Joyce. Perhaps not such long-lost idyllic days after all.

Samantha had been tapping away on his phone whilst he'd been reminiscing. She handed the it back to him. This time their fingers didn't touch.

"You'll have to input a password and your bank details. I'll just go over and have a chat to Luther about his budget overrun, then I'll come back and we'll set up a bet."

George saw Luther out of the corner of his eye, weighing up whether he could make a run for the gents before Samantha got to him. But he'd hesitated, and she was closing in.

He fumbled with his debit card, input the usual details, ticked the box that he'd read the full terms and conditions, then had to go back and re-input details because the invisible eye informed him he hadn't done it properly. Eventually he finished, transferred the twenty-five pounds, and wrote the password down in his little black book.

"You should use facial recognition George, it's a lot easier," she said, stealing up beside him. He handed the phone back before she asked for it.

"We'll have a small bet tonight on the Europa League. To get you started. A five-pound minimum bet on Legia Warsaw to win. That's Monika's team. She slept with the goalkeeper once. Then the other forty-five pounds for Saturday. We won't bother with the Sunday matches. The same accumulator I've used. There's a twist to it which boosts the odds. One long shot. There's no point in winning the odd twenty pounds. They're all three o'clock kick-off matches. I should be charging you for this advice George. I'll take a share of the winnings – shall we say ten percent? There, that's all set up."

She placed the phone on his desk, rather than handing it back to him, and she spoke whilst turning and striding away.

"I'll get Monika to contact you about the meeting with Angel Wei. It'll be tomorrow sometime."

The corporate mode had reasserted itself.

Chapter 8

She slept with her head resting peacefully on her chest, which was rising and falling with a gentle action. She wore the beige cardigan and beige-and-white check skirt that Dawn had chosen for her last Christmas. And the plumb-coloured slippers chosen by him for her last birthday. Her hair had been carefully crafted into shape by the mobile hairdresser. He'd left work very early at just after three. He knew she'd be asleep. She always was at this time, but he'd come anyway, and he might wake her in ten minutes.

She sat in her usual chair by the window, with some precious light seeping into the room. On the table next to her were photos in various unmatched frames of different sizes and shape. He noticed that they'd been rearranged by the cleaner. He preferred them in chronological order. Holding the baby. First day at school. The trip to London zoo. The graduation. The wedding. All with his mother and him. Except for the wedding. And no pictures of his father of course. He'd been air-brushed out a long time ago. 1973 to be precise. He rearranged the photos. As he placed the last one down, the one of him and Dawn in the ornamental gilt frame, a cup of tea appeared next to it. He hadn't heard Mildred come in.

"There you go George. I was doing the round anyway."

A simple act of human kindness. A cup of tea. Along with all the other acts of human kindness in looking after old people. Being paid the minimum wage to care for somebody else's mother. His mother hadn't paid strangers to look after her own mother. Her and Auntie Joyce had done that between them.

"Thanks Mildred. She's looking peaceful. Has she been OK today?"

"She's been fine George. The dreams seem to have stopped. She hasn't been waking up in the night."

He wished his dreams had stopped. He tried to think what life would've been like for Mildred if she hadn't left Nigeria to look after his mother. Not just his mother obviously. Lots of strangers' mothers. And some fathers. Maybe this life was better. He'd seen a documentary about shanty towns in Lagos. Frantic colourful pictures. But crime, corruption, traffic jams, and hassle. Did Mildred have a boyfriend, a fiancé perhaps? Maybe he shared that tiny flat with her in Harehills, and cooked her tea before she got home. Or maybe he drank whiskey and gambled, treated her badly, and wasn't worthy of her. Just like his father had not been worthy of his mother.

"We'll wake her up in about twenty minutes George. For her tea. Or we could wake her now if you want to."

"No, let her sleep. I've got to go anyway."

He didn't have to go. They went through this routine on most of his visits, except when his mother was actually awake when he arrived, and this was rare. So, although he visited her most weeks in the Sunnybank care home, he probably only spoke to her once a month. Once a month from him. The sacrifice of a lifetime from her. Another woman let down by George Stephenson. Like father, like son.

For most of the time, life just motored along without a single thought about him. His father. It was only during these dutiful interludes in the care home, or sometimes when he was speaking to Paul, that there was any fleeting glimpse. A passing view of someone out of the corner of your eye in a speeding car, half seen, half recognised. The rest of the time he was incarcerated in a medieval tower, under lock and key, guarded by a jailor.

It must have been quite a thing in 1973. It had only been legal for a few years, and where did he meet an exile from Pinochet's Chile, a revolutionary socialist on the run – in a pub over a pint of mild and a bag of pork scratchings?

Unspoken love blossoming over a pickled egg. He worked on the railways for God's sake, or he did do before he ran off with Vincente.

Chapter 9

They'd decided on a Chinese takeaway that night. The place down the road wasn't too bad, and there was the comedy value. It really was called 'Hong Kong Garden'. Same as the Siouxsie and the Banshees song. And the owner really was called Jim Fuk Yu. It said so on the website. When there used to be *Yellow Pages*, he was listed as Fuk Yu, Jim, as in Stephenson, George. The old jokes were the best ones. His wife was called Mary, which sounded English, but she was Chinese as well. If you ordered chicken, she would ask, 'you want breast?', and smile mischievously. It's because you could choose between breast and leg, but it sounded like an invitation. George always ordered breast.

He spooned the takeaway dishes onto their plates. George preferred his own dish for himself. But Dawn wanted them to order a number of dishes, and share them. That was reasonable really, you got more variety, and it was probably better for your relationship – sharing and all that. But deep down, he wanted his own food, on his own plate.

They ate in silence for about a minute, George still hiding his resentment, then Dawn thought of something to say.

"Maybe we should get a dog, George."

"What do you mean a dog?"

"You know, it's got four legs and barks. It would be good company. We could get a puppy. Train it. Take it for walks."

"We haven't got time to take it for walks. We're both at work."

"Well you won't be at the end of next week. That's when you're leaving isn't it?"

He studied her face carefully. She wasn't joking.

You could look at this two ways, he thought:

Option one. The optimistic view. If she was about to leave, she wouldn't suggest getting a dog. It would be one more complication. Who would get custody?

Maybe it was a genuine attempt to give them a common interest.

Option two. The pessimistic view. She was about to leave. But felt guilty about leaving him on his own and out of work. So the dog would keep him company. In addition to Polonius.

"Let's think about it Dawn. It's a big step. Like having a baby."

This was his usual stalling tactic, but she didn't press on.

"What's it like at work now George? Is Samantha sorry to see you go, or glad to see the back of you?"

Dawn had met Samantha at last year's work Christmas party. They seemed to get on very well. They'd stood in a corner together, away from George, and seemed to be laughing a lot in a conspiratorial way. He was sure they were comparing notes on him.

"Glad to get rid of me I think, although she was nicer to me today. They've got some young hot-shot flying in from the Far East to take over the project. I've got to brief her tomorrow. Angel Wei. She's the most well-qualified person ever, apparently. Can't think why they need her to do my job, but there you go."

"Don't put yourself down. It's not a complete disaster, your project, is it?"

"Pretty much so, I'd say. It's only six months' behind and one hundred percent over budget. Par for the course for me really."

He chewed on a prawn. He'd given himself eight prawns, and Dawn seven. That wasn't very gentlemanly. But after chicken breast, the spicy Sichuan prawn dish was his next favourite, and he didn't think Dawn had noticed.

"Dawn, I meant to tell you – Derek called round last night while you were out. He wanted to have a chat with you. Said you were 'advising' him on something."

He hadn't meant to emphasise the word 'advising' or add a sarcastic tone. It had just come out that way. But she couldn't miss it really. He might as well have said 'having sex with'.

She looked back at him. Then she looked at the prawn on the end of her fork, and placed it carefully in her mouth. She didn't speak for a few seconds. Giving herself time to get her story straight, thought George. Then she spoke carefully and deliberately.

"I truly feel pity for you, George. You're like a small child who needs his mother to explain everything, wipe his nose, do up his top button, and walk him to school. You're a child in a man's body."

That was a bit cutting, he thought. He was supposed to be on top here. It was up to Dawn to come up with a good excuse about the Derek issue. Not for him to rationalise why he'd never grown up.

"I was just explaining that Derek came round, that's all. And I did wonder what you were advising him on."

Dawn placed another prawn in her mouth, and so did George. Two could play at that game, he thought, defiantly. He could tell that she was weighing up what to say to him.

"He's got some financial difficulties George. Overstretched himself. He's not the sort of client I usually deal with, but I think I can help. I'm a neutral person to talk to. He hasn't told Cassandra. I want you to keep this to yourself George. I really mean that."

He placed two prawns in his mouth at once, and looked up at the ceiling. Although really, he was looking up to the heavens. There is a God. There really is. And he's sent his only son to a housing development just outside of Leeds to bring joy into the world. Thank you God. Thank you so much.

"Dawn, I won't say a word. I promise. It must be tough for them. He seemed to have everything."

He managed to keep a straight face while saying this. It wasn't easy. He could feel the corners of his lips wanting to curl up. He wanted to get to his feet, pick up a tambourine, shout 'hallelujah', and dance around the kitchen to the sound of an evangelical Baptist choir.

She just about bought it.

"If I find out that you've said something George, I'll deal with you. Do you understand? I mean it. There will be consequences."

She placed another prawn in her mouth. He moved to do the same, but all his prawns were gone.

Saved by the bell. The awkward silence was broken by the phone ringing. The landline again. The phone that never rang. But had now rung two nights running. As he picked the phone up, he somehow knew that there would be silence. And there was. Just like last night. And the same strange feeling that there was somebody on the other end. Somebody who didn't speak. Then his mobile. This hadn't happened last night. It rang twice and then stopped. He didn't have time to pick up. The number was not in his contacts.

"Sounds like somebody's desperate to speak to you George," said Dawn as she opened the kitchen door. "I'm going upstairs to pack for the weekend."

He'd seen it before, she just ran out of patience with him, and sought sanctuary in the bedroom. He heard her footsteps on the stairs, and the bedroom door being closed very firmly, not slammed, but the message was clear. Don't come in until I've gone to bed and switched the light off.

Gathering up the empty takeaway cartons and cramming them into the bin, the elation from the news about Derek ebbed away more quickly than he expected. Stripping away the macho gloss to reveal an undercoat of vulnerability might just make Derek more attractive to Dawn. They could be developing a new closeness, with Derek turning threat into opportunity. So best not to lower your guard George, and make sure you get a few kidney punches in wherever possible.

The bin bag was overflowing, and the smell of congealing takeaway food was already hanging in the air. It would be twice as bad in the morning, and his fault. So he pulled out the bag and carried it outside to the dustbin. It was only about nine thirty, but Sycamore Meadows was closed for the night. Curtains drawn, doors shut, residents safely locked away. The black cat was nowhere to be seen, and it would be ten o'clock before Bernard took Lucy out. There was the faint hum of cars on the main road, but even that seemed fairly quiet. There was no moon showing, and no owl hooting. As he surveyed the estate, he was filled with the profound thought that for some of those houses, with chinks of light flickering past wary curtains, he had no idea who lived there, even after seven years. There could be a de-frocked priest, an opera singer, a future lover. Then he pictured his only son Paul, sitting on the dusty old brown settee in his flat, Danni with her knees curled up against him, both watching something on the laptop. He should have phoned Paul today. He must have subconsciously put it off again. It was too late to ring now, and he reassured himself that their son sitting on that settee fifty miles away, was at ease with the world. He'd definitely ring him tomorrow.

Walking back inside, George looked at the football results on his phone. Legia Warsaw nil, Steua Bucharest one.

She'd tried four times now. But couldn't bring herself to speak to him. She'd written some notes about what she planned to say. A logical sequence. This was the third version, and there were still plenty of corrections and crossings out. And two tear stains in the corner of the page. How could you bring all of this down to five bullet points? You couldn't. Her mouth had been even dryer tonight than last night. She stared at the glass of water that she'd placed beside the piece of paper. She'd drunk half of it before ringing. She drank the rest of it now, and stared out of the hotel window. It had been warm this afternoon when she'd said goodbye to Rupert.

She'd write a letter instead. It was the only way. That's what you used to do. She still had her fountain pen. The one her mother bought her for her eighteenth birthday. Yes, she'd write a letter. She'd do it now. It was more dignified than an e-mail.

Friday 10 November

Chapter 10

Sitting at the breakfast table, piecing together last night's dream – just the usual stuff, a shaman dancing round a blazing fire conjuring up spirits – he'd noticed Dawn watching him eating his toast. He had an awful feeling she was mentally scoring him on some unknown matrix. As he considered how he could put in a good word for himself, there was a knock at the door. That was twice in one week. If it was Derek again, he didn't think he could hold back on the sarcasm. Either way, opening the door seemed a better option than being examined under a microscope by his wife.

Two keen blue eyes looked up at him. Dorothy was the best of the old ladies from the flats round the corner, despite being the owner of the evil cat. She must be well into her nineties, but always immaculately turned out. A smart grey winter coat, a purple wool scarf, and a red beret. Stylish dark brown leather gloves. He'd met most of the ladies while helping out at the Round Table Christmas dinner. It wasn't really his cup of tea. A bunch of solicitors and doctors, all socially superior to him, and they knew it. But there were some good comedy moments. Magda got rolling drunk last year. Hitched her skirt up, started dancing, singing and shouting. Knocked over a full bottle of red wine. Said something terrible to Millie, and hadn't been forgiven yet.

"George, good morning, I've been thinking about Polly."

"Morning Dorothy. You're looking well. He's called Polonius. He's a male."

"I can hear him squawking while you and Dawn are both at work. I think he's lonely. I looked it up on the new laptop that my son Raymond bought me. It says that African greys are highly intelligent birds, but they need enrichment and attention in captivity or they can become distressed."

That's what I need, he thought.

"I think he's alright Dorothy. He's still in good condition. I did him a nice fruit salad last night. With sunflower seeds. I put a pomegranate in as well. That's his favourite."

She held her ground on the doorstep, despite not being invited in, and despite the chilly wind whipping up.

"Yes, but it says they can develop behavioural problems due to their sensitive nature. Social isolation, that's the problem. They can get stressed."

"We're doing our best Dorothy. We do talk to him, and he talks back to us."

"But I thought he only says two things. Maybe that's a sign of stress George. If you like, you could leave me a key, I could call in a few days a week, have a chat to him. I'd be happy to. I wouldn't bring Timothy with me. I don't think cats and parrots mix well."

Oh God, all this kindness is killing me, thought George. It's a nice offer but I can't deal with it right now.

"Dorothy, I'll have a chat to Dawn. It's kind of you. I have to go now. I've got a few things to sort out."

"Oh George. One more thing. Have you seen Derek recently? He looks terrible. Not his usual self. And he's got a strange nervous twitch. He used to be such a fine figure of a man. He's all hunched up now. Mr McManus thinks it's stress. We're all worried about him. Maybe you could have a word with him. See if everything is alright."

He was cherishing Derek's downward spiral, but he smiled sympathetically back at Dorothy.

"Dawn and I are keeping a close eye on him. We've all got his best interests at heart."

The sarcasm didn't register with her. She seemed well set to continue the conversation. But at that point Victor, who ran the management committee, came round the corner to save the day. She spotted him, and marched over for a confrontation.

"Victor, have you organised for the aerial man to come round yet? BBC2 is still awful. I thought you were going to fix things by the end of last month. What do we pay our management fees for? It's a disgrace. You're supposed to be responsible, Victor."

George saw the look of terror on Victor's face, and quietly closed the door.

*

It had been a rather awkward goodbye to Dawn before he'd set off for work. She'd be away for three nights. He knew she was looking forward to a break from him. He'd hung around at home, but got in the way, and only succeeded in irritating her. Even fixing a new coat hook by the back door, a job that had been outstanding for eternity, didn't gain him extra credits. So, in the end, he'd admitted defeat and set off for the office at about nine thirty. He'd tried to kiss her goodbye. This wasn't part of the usual routine. He'd placed one hand on her shoulder, and moved to kiss her on the cheek. She'd turned her head a few degrees and he ended up kissing her on the ear. It was not an unpleasant sensation, but they'd both looked embarrassed and she'd turned her eyes to look at the floor.

"See you on Monday George," she'd said as he'd placed a reluctant step outside the front door. She'd closed it quickly behind him, as if about to start a teenage party with vodka, cigarettes, and snogging.

But right now he was at his desk talking to Anna. Or listening to Anna rather, while he scrutinised her ear studs. He'd noticed one of them as he was imagining kissing her ear – with purpose rather than the accidental joining of lips and earlobe with his wife. He was squinting to see the motif, without appearing to squint. This was not an easy procedure, but it did identify an unmistakable skull and crossbones in the silver stud.

"Have you got something in your eye George?"

"No, it's just the sun."

This was a puzzling response as the window was behind him, without the faintest trace of sunlight peeping in.

"As I was saying, we don't usually provide this outplacement support, but I think I can bend the rules a bit for you."

She emphasised the 'bend the rules' bit with a nod of the head in an arc left and right, and a smile most people would call cheeky.

"You get a morning session with a consultant who does a competency and skills assessment, gives you feedback, and advises on the best routes to find a new job. Shall I set something up for next week if he can fit you in? He's called Dominic. He's quite young, but most people find it a positive experience."

George struggled to think of many worse things in life than young Dominic doing a competency and skills assessment of him. Maybe being burnt alive would just about knock it into second place. But he was still thinking about the skull and crossbones ear studs. When you combined these with the rose tattoo, and the dress-down Friday jeans and red T-shirt emblazoned with clenched fist logo, there was a definite blurring of the lines of corporate mainstream and mild rebellion.

"What do you think George – shall we give it a go?"

There was probably no intention of suggestive ambiguity, but when he smiled back, she returned his smile whilst standing up from the chair she'd pulled up next to his.

"I'll try for Tuesday. I think he might be coming in that day anyway. By the way, I think Samantha has arranged your meeting with Angel Wei this afternoon at two o'clock. Her flight was delayed, but she wanted to meet you before the end of the week. You know, to keep the momentum going."

Thoughts of momentum were far from George's mind. If he'd just arrived from Hong Kong on a Friday, he'd have holed up in the hotel over the weekend, hit the minibar, and strolled in on Monday morning. But that's the point. George got nothing done and was on his way out. Angel Wei got things done and was on her way up.

Enigmatic Anna had walked away now. He watched her open the smoked-glass door into the reception area, half expecting a wave as she disappeared from view. There was no wave, but with the general excitement of Anna out of the way, he was left with a few hours to kill.

He spent the rest of the morning e-mailing various documents to his private e-mail address. Nothing too sensitive, just the sort of things that he might need in a future job. He was never quite sure what the IT department could monitor, so he didn't take any chances, not wanting to put the seventeen thousand pounds at risk. He thought about ringing Paul. He really ought to, but he convinced himself that everything was fine and there was no need. He walked into the town at lunchtime, took an hour and a half, and came back just before two in time for his meeting with Angel Wei. He'd got a few documents together, worked out his story.

Samantha was going to come along as well, but phoned to say that Armando had just arrived from Jakarta and they were both attending a conference call on margin contraction. Should be a barrel of laughs. So it would be just the two of them. Angel and George. Expectations were high. Monika had sent him a biography on Angel. She'd worked all over the world, degrees and masters from the best academic institutions. Her MBA thesis had been published in the *Wall Street Journal*, something about Digital Production Flows. Twenty-seven years old compared to George at forty-nine. Still, he always had his 2:2 from Hull to fall back on.

Bang on time, he walked into the meeting room at two minutes past two. The mystery continued as to why he could never be on time, even with three hours' notice. Angel Wei was sitting at the table in all her glory, her laptop primed for action. She stood up and smiled at him, holding out her petite hand in a genuine act of warm greeting. The brain that he only knew by repute was housed in a head and body of undoubted beauty. George managed to suppress a slight gasp, as he lightly touched her delicate hand taking care not to squeeze too tightly for fear of damage. He couldn't help adding it all up. The perfection of the smooth pale skin, and the gleaming silky hair. The gorgeous brown eyes, and the mathematical symmetry of her features. The delicate slim figure. Smartly dressed but not too formal. Stylishly understated. And all of this after flying half way round the world.

His was more of a buffoon-like grin, but hers was a true smile, and she held it as she looked directly into his eyes.

"Hi George, I'm Angel Wei. Thank you for sparing the time to see me. I really appreciate it. I know how busy you are."

Spoken in perfect English, a slight transatlantic twang. And such sensitivity. To beauty and brains, you had to add overwhelming politeness, and even compassion. He wasn't busy. He had an abundance of free time.

As sure as night follows day, he stumbled over his words.

"No, that's not a problem, hello. I'm George, you know that already. Pleased to meet you. I might be able to help… I'm not sure really…"

She laughed ever so slightly, perhaps a little embarrassed, but it was just enough to ease the tension. Still she held his gaze. For fear of gawping, and as if losing a game of chicken, he looked away, and started to fumble with the disorderly pile of papers that he'd emptied onto the desk.

"Did you have a good trip from Hong Kong? You must be tired. We could move the meeting to Monday if that would be better for you."

"I'm OK George, I've had a good trip thank you. I'm fine to go ahead this afternoon. I'd just like you to take me through the key points on the project. I know there've been some major challenges that you've had to deal with. I think you've done well to get the project to this point."

The humility was overwhelming.

He spent the next hour fumbling through his pile of papers, and trying to find the right files in the right folders. Hard copies and digital copies agreed on the chaos. The project updates were not filed in proper date order, you couldn't trace whether issues had been actioned and closed or were still open. His embarrassment grew, but she maintained the dignified responses.

"OK." "Got that." "Understood." "See your point."

It might have been less humiliating if she'd taken out a revolver, and despatched him with a single shot like an incapacitated racehorse. She didn't take many notes, just tapped the keyboard a few times, smiled, nodded, listened. After about an hour and a half, he sensed she was running out of diplomatic responses.

"I think I've got what I need now George. I just wanted the big picture. I'd like to spend some time on Monday morning with you cleaning up the files on the system. Then I can go through the detail of it myself. I'll meet or call the key people next week. I'm meeting Armando later. He's dealing with some local trouble in Singapore at the moment."

George wondered how you dealt with local trouble in Singapore. Send in a gunboat presumably.

"George, I noticed the café round the corner when I got a taxi from the hotel. Shall we pop out for a quick tea or coffee? We've been in this room long enough. It might be a bit more relaxed there. You could take me through some of the people issues."

He couldn't work out whether it was an act of human kindness, or just another technique that she'd learnt in business school. But what the hell. He did want to get out of the office. He'd had enough for this week. Very briefly an image of a bottle of German Weiss-beer appeared, his tongue drying up in sympathy and sticking to the roof of his mouth. But what was left of the business side of him felt suggesting going to the pub would be inappropriate, and he couldn't imagine Angel sinking a glass of strong German beer at quarter to four in the afternoon. Anyway, he had to drive home. Drive home. To the empty house. Just him and Polonius bickering away all weekend.

*

So the café it was, and he walked out the office with the beautiful Angel, who brought her halo and wings with her. Even better, as they strolled through the reception area, Anna and Samantha were chatting animatedly, and both turned their heads as they watched them leave. Was that a touch of jealousy? George mixing with the stars. Eat your heart out ladies. I haven't got time for all of you at once. Form a line. Pity Tommo wasn't there as well. Must have been doing his rounds.

The café that Angel had spotted was called Luciano's. George had only been there a couple of times because he normally went to Starbucks. You knew where you were with Starbucks. But he didn't want to admit that to Angel. Didn't want to present himself as the sort of guy who prefers mass-produced coffee from an international chain, rather than the artisan mill-ground stuff from an independent. Mr Luciano was pitching at New York Italian American ambience. The stocky former cruise-ship crooner with dyed black hair, open-necked shirt, cream waistcoat, flared trousers and platform shoes, provided the entertainment himself. Short bursts of light opera, or easy-listening swing.

In another life, George imagined himself marching into the establishment with his new gal, Mr L gesturing to the waiters to clear the best table, spread out a clean red-and-white check freshly-laundered tablecloth, pull the chairs out for them to sit down, and bring the order to the table.

Instead, they joined the short queue of customers at the counter.

"I'll get these George. What would you like?"

To counter the feeling of emasculation he ordered an Americano with hot milk, which is what he usually ordered in Starbucks, but added a shot of espresso as well. Just to impress her. Angel ordered a green tea, and paid on her corporate credit card. George didn't have one of those.

They sat at a table in the corner by the window. It was a bit cramped, and he was aware that he was sitting very close to her. For one thrilling moment his knee slightly touched hers, and he felt a definite electrical pulse in his system. He concluded that she'd taken a shower at the hotel after the long flight, and washed her hair. There was a hint of a delicious shampoo smell. He wondered what the handful of customers thought of him and Angel. Perhaps the two construction workers in the corner, anchored down by the biggest muddiest boots in the land, might think they were boyfriend and girlfriend. But that didn't really work with a twenty-two-year age gap. Maybe richer older man and attractive Far Eastern new young wife. Perhaps there was a bit of reflected glory here for you George.

He blinked himself back to reality, and found himself asking her about her background in Hong Kong. She was very open about the family complications, the intricate web of uncles and trading companies and worries about China. It was obvious there was family money there somewhere, but she'd got this far on merit. He'd noticed a lot earlier that she didn't wear a wedding ring or an engagement ring, and she didn't mention a boyfriend or partner. There was a ring with an unusual emblem on her little finger. The emblem wasn't a dragon, but some other mythical creature he didn't recognise. She had the same design on a necklace which hung around her lovely neck. The creature on the necklace rested on her chest just above the top of the black T-shirt. He tried not to stare.

They hadn't spent any time going through the people issues on the project as Angel had originally suggested. He'd run out of steam, and she'd been bombarded by flurries of e-mails and phone calls. That saved him from having to explain his family circumstances, although outwardly everything appeared under control. A wife and one son. Eventually Angel apologised and said that she'd have to get back to the office. The polished armour of self-control began to look slightly tarnished.

He walked her back, like a schoolboy walking his new girlfriend home. She didn't have a satchel for him to carry. They stopped outside the revolving door into the building and turned to face each other. Out of the corner of his eye, he could see Tommo watching. The thought of kissing her floated mischievously through his mind, but she held out her hand to be shaken not kissed.

"Thanks again George. That's been really helpful. I'll see you on Monday. Have a good weekend."

As he was about to reply, she turned her head to look at the man approaching her from one side. He was wearing the sharpest suit George had ever seen. Light grey, but it seemed to glisten. A crisp white shirt and a navy blue tie. This was all expensive stuff. Tight curly grey hair cut short, a slight tan. He was speaking Spanish on his phone, but hung up and greeted Angel in English. He didn't have to introduce himself. This was Armando, and within a few seconds Angel was looking ruffled by the presence further up the food chain.

*

About to turn the key in the ignition to drive back to his deserted residence, and with what he knew was an unwarranted degree of optimism, he checked his phone for any messages. There could be a cheery text from an old school chum, maybe young Alan Goldsborough who lived in a picture book village out towards York, inviting George to a wine tasting evening in the village hall. He could get a taxi and drink his fill. Or old Dodger Jones from university wanting to go out for a few beers to catch up on the good old days. They could cry with laughter as they remembered filling Porky's room with a selection of wet fish when he went home for the weekend. Or sultry Welsh Denise Richardson who he'd met on his first day at work. There'd been a mutual attraction, and he'd kissed her passionately at the end of an away-day in Cleckheaton. She was on the city council now. He'd seen her picture in the local paper. She'd aged well, and still had a naughty glint in her eye. Perhaps there could be one more kiss before the end of time.

There were no messages from Alan, Dodger, or Denise. He hadn't seen any of them for about three decades, and he wondered how he conjured up their memories in the few seconds it takes to ram in a car key. If he'd had a new car with an instant push button ignition, maybe all three would have stayed locked away in the vaults. There were however, two missed calls, both from George's present day. He'd switched his phone to silent when he'd started the meeting with Angel. He fast-forwarded his brain by thirty years.

The first was from Paul. That focused the mind on the here and now. It was the first time Paul had tried to contact him this week. There must be trouble brewing. There was no message. George phoned him back but it went to voice mail. He sent a text: 'Paul, sorry I missed your call. Ring me again. Dad.' He'd ring him again later. He still didn't really want to know what was wrong.

The second missed call was from an unknown number. There was a voice mail.

'George, my name's Bill Parkinson. I run a medium-size transport firm in Hull. I saw your CV on a recruitment website and wanted to have a chat to you about a possible opportunity. I've sent you an e-mail. Get back to me.' George pulled the key back out of the ignition, and fumbled to open the e-mail on his phone. There some background on the company, the role, the project. Could he make it for a meeting next Friday afternoon at their office? He fired off a response. He'd be happy to meet up. That would look good. Still open for business at five fifteen on Friday. He got a reply straightaway. The meeting was arranged for two in the afternoon. There was a map and a post code. Well, things were looking up. An interview already, or a chat at least, something in the pipeline. Somebody was interested in the services of George Stephenson, married man of the parish. In demand, or at least not completely ignored. He conjured up a picture of Bill Parkinson, or Parky as he'd named him. Overweight, with a pink chubby round face topped with greying hair combed over the top of a shining chrome, but with a kindly Father Christmas smile. Bedecked in a beige-and-white check blazer-style jacket, on top of a moss green V-necked jumper, cream shirt and brown tie. Dark brown slacks to match. 1970's Man at C&A.

He threw his phone on to the passenger seat, and began to pull out of the car park. Through the side window he spotted Angel and Armando. She'd stepped back two paces, flailing one arm in the air, with an indignant look on her face, appeared to be shouting. Very strange. But best to look the other way.

He remembered reading somewhere that the worst song for making you drive fast is 'Bat out of Hell' by Meatloaf. He flicked through the iPod list, found it on a drive-time classics compilation, and spent the next few minutes listening to it thundering out. It didn't quite sound the same at 30 mph in rush-hour traffic, but despite that frustration his spirits had been lifted. The afternoon with Angel, and now some form of job prospect.

Chapter 11

The heady days of that optimistic drive home seemed a long way off now. Walking into the empty house brought him crashing back down to earth. The emptiness seemed to expand in front of him, room to room, with a chilling silence settling throughout. A version of the future without Dawn in the house brought on a bilious rotting taste in his mouth. He filled a glass with water in the kitchen and drank it down in one. The taste was still there.

It really was cold. He put his hand on the kitchen radiator. No warmth. No hint of warmth. The central heating wasn't on. He checked the boiler. No pilot light. He couldn't find the manual. Dawn usually sorted these things out. Christ, why did the boiler have to pack in when he was on his own, in November. He pressed a few buttons at random, cursed, and then sat at the kitchen table, a defeated man. Who did you ring to get the boiler repaired? Dawn had all the numbers. She sorted out the servicing.

No warmth, and a creeping hunger. Fleetingly he imagined a note on the table.

'George, I've left you some tea in the oven. Chicken casserole. There's a problem with the boiler, but I've arranged for the heating engineer to come in the morning. I did a big shop today, so there's plenty in the fridge. Have a good weekend. See you on Monday. Love Dawn, XXX.'

There was no note, and there were no frozen chips in the freezer. There were two fish fingers in an old packet. Captain Birdseye smiled up at him. A crumpled packet of frozen peas, and a box for two spicy bean burgers, with nothing in. The long expanse of the weekend without food, warmth, and basic human contact stretched before him. He needed a plan. Angel wouldn't be beaten by this adversity. She'd write a list and storm into action. He could do that as well. He'd ring a plumber in the morning, and go to the Fox and Hounds for tea. That was it. His action plan. It wasn't exactly the Normandy landings to liberate Europe, but it would do for tonight.

*

He'd timed his run carefully, and selected his table carefully. The Fox and Hounds was a ten-minute walk from their house, so he'd delayed his departure until six fifty, to arrive at seven. That meant sitting at the kitchen table for around forty-five minutes, shivering and feeling sorry for himself. He wavered in the final ten minutes without the benefit of a communal sing-song to keep his spirits up, but in the end held out and stuck to his plan. General Eisenhower would have been proud.

He didn't want to get there too early, as he envisaged an evening of sitting alone. But he wanted to get there early enough to claim a favourable position – a view of the big screen to watch the football starting at eight, combined with reasonable access to the bar and toilets, and the ability to defend that position. He was an infrequent visitor, but could just about remember the layout.

Despite some initial jostling as he walked through the doors, he completed an out-flanking manoeuvre by placing his coat on his chosen seat first, remembering to note the table number, and only then going to the bar to buy beer and order food. Armed with a pint of German Weiss-beer, the one that he'd dreamed about earlier, and the receipt for steak-and-ale pie and chips, he then sat down with the quiet satisfaction of a plan well executed, a beachhead established.

At this stage, ten minutes past seven, there was nobody that he recognised. He estimated, with little statistical insight, that the clientele was weighted towards the Grimes Pride estate rather than Sycamore Meadows. At seven twenty, the food arrived. By seven thirty he'd finished the meal, and his first pint. By seven fifty-five he'd finished pint number two, and by eight twenty, pint number three. Three pints at 5.5% in an hour and twenty minutes was starting to take its toll. The match was rumbling on with little incident, and he'd tired of checking his phone. He'd visited the toilet twice, and he'd lined up pint number four. With his head swimming, and his vision clouding, it was time to take stock of the week's developments. He pictured a game show format of green lights and red lights, smiley faces and sad faces, thumbs up and thumbs down, claxon horns and alarm bells. A manic compere in a cheap suit and a glamourous hostess in a revealing dress.

Firstly, the big picture. Dawn hadn't left him. She'd left him for the weekend in Harrogate, but not forever. Yet. He was clinging on by his fingertips to the edge of a rock face, his legs kicking below, fearing to peer down into the crevasse. But he hadn't fallen yet.

He took a sip of beer to fortify himself. OK, he was still nearly fifty, still couldn't communicate, still drove a seven-year-old Toyota Yaris. But all of this was countered by the shifting tectonic plates of Derek's fortunes. Hero to zero in less than a week. The twitch was just an outward sign, pleasing none-the-less, but the inner turmoil would be even better. It was all so uplifting, and would brighten up the long winter nights. Cassandra could be packing her bags as we speak. Gunter from Stuttgart, the tennis coach, waiting outside the house, keeping the engine running. But then the newly vulnerable Derek would be on his own and available. It was a difficult call, but on balance it would be better if Cassandra stayed for the time being.

Having settled that, George took another two sips. He was on a roll, turning threat into opportunity. Redundancy bad. Pay-off good. Interview and job prospect good. Smiley face. Sound the claxon horn.

He peered deep into his glass. The volume of the surround-sound chattering increased as the pub filled up. There might have been a goal scored, but he couldn't see properly now unless he stood up. Swilling a few more mouthfuls down, he carried on with his analysis. Samantha and Anna. They could hardly bear to be in his presence on Wednesday. Was it Wednesday? Yes, Wednesday. But now they seemed… well, interested in him. And what about Angel? My, oh my, sweet Angel. She was positively keen. Only to be expected, poor girl. Green lights, thumbs up, smiley faces.

He sighed to himself. What could go wrong? Oh dear. The house was empty. The central heating boiler had packed in. There was no food. The conservatory was still leaking. He had to fix that. Dorothy might get the RSPCA round to rescue Polonius from the utility room.

He wanted a packet of crisps now. Cheese and onion or prawn cocktail. Despite the pie sitting heavily in his stomach. He'd get a packet of barbecue beef when he next went to the bar. His glass was nearly empty. He emptied it. Churlish not to. What about the strange things? The cat. The dreams. The phone calls. Feeling watched. Paul. He should have phoned Paul. It was too late now. It was all too late.

The haze descended further as Friday night in the Fox and Hounds accelerated to its dazzling crescendo. A smoke machine of early morning mist mixing in with a New Orleans jazz night. An eighties disco firing up in the corner, a glitter ball spinning right round, baby right round. Boy, if only he'd known earlier there was such a wild night out, just around the corner. He could've been down here with Dawn every week. Patching up their relationship, while strutting their funky stuff. Shaking his groove thing right down to the ground. You should be dancing, yeah.

Soon, he abandoned the seat that he'd been guarding so carefully all evening, and started gibbering enthusiastically to strangers at the bar, his tongue loosened by the onslaught of alcohol. Then someone that he really did know. Bernard, and Lucy the dog. He shook Bernard's hand and told him he was the salt of the earth. He stooped to kiss Lucy on the head, telling her that she was the most beautiful girl in the world. And Bernard's two sons. He'd met them before. Alan and Dave. Or Steve and Pete? Clearly, they'd forgiven Bernard for murdering their mother. Truth and reconciliation. They were the sort of boys you'd want on your side in a bar room brawl. Alan, or was it Steve, must have been nearly seven foot tall. A giant. George bought them both a double whiskey, maybe two, and squeezed in a half price cocktail for himself before the nine-thirty deadline. He swapped a few lines with one of the girls behind the bar. She didn't want to swap any lines, gritting her stained teeth adorned with a tooth brace looking like a row of unpolished diamonds. He remembered the teeth, and the hair piled up on top of her head like a specialist bread loaf. She was to feature later in his epic dream saga.

Reality became completely blurred from this point, not that he knew he'd reached any specific point, but somehow, he must have stumbled home. The cold November air cleared a short window of memory for him, and he could see himself fumbling with his key in the lock, turning to see who was looking over his shoulder, with the certain knowledge that he would see no one. And he saw no one.

Inside the house, the cold and darkness drove him to bed. He took time only to remove his coat and shoes, neither without a struggle. His belt dug into his waist as he pulled the duvet over his head like the theatre curtain drawing the evening's performance to a close.

But in that dark space, it got darker still, a gothic horror of dreams. Worse than anything he'd had all week. Dante's Inferno material. Devils and hell-fire. He could live with that. But he recognised the cast. Credits rolled for some of the stars of the week. Angel was there. The evil black cat was there, only double the size. Angel turned into the cat, and the cat turned into Angel. The dragon-like creature from Angel's ring and necklace was dancing around. There was a pile of gold coins cascading around the creature. Danni danced with the creature, turning to smile at the camera as Dracula's bride. Paul and Dawn watched her. There was a short cameo role for the girl behind the bar as she flashed her teeth, showing off extended canines. She joined Anna and Samantha to dance around as the three witches in *Macbeth*.

It was a full-length feature film version of a dream, going on all night while he slipped in and out of half drunkenness, half sleep. At some point the Sahara-like dryness of his mouth, and a bladder about to burst, forced him out of bed and into the bathroom. He splashed cold water on his face, and coughed as if he'd smoked forty a day. The remnants of the dreams clung to life, but eventually began to fade, cold reality overcoming the nightmare world.

Staring hard at his sorry reflection in the mirror, he had the strangest feeling that the events of this week were about to ramp up – one hundred-fold.

PART TWO

Saturday 11 November

Chapter 12

Before she got out of the car, she took a quick look at herself in the rear-view mirror. She'd been putting it off, but the result was not as bad as she'd feared. The short-term damage from last night was visible, but overall she felt satisfied. She turned her head to hide the graze on one side of her forehead. The only war wound from last night. Physical wound that is. The rest was just, well, fatigue. The underlying bone structure, the foundations you might call it, were sound. The eyes, the high cheekbones, the well-formed lips, were all in good shape. She'd only started using the hair colour last year, and it was working efficiently.

She blew herself a kiss, got out of the car and immediately took a deep breath, filling her lungs with the air which was probably as good as it gets in this part of North Leeds. She took her second swig of Harrogate spring water of the morning, drinking from the small plastic bottle which luckily, she'd remembered to put in her bag. Then she slowly turned her head to look up at the concrete block rearing up in front of her.

She inspected it carefully, adjusting her eyes to focus on the window on the far side of the first floor. The one displaying the 'To Let' poster at a slightly odd, even disturbing angle. Taking her final gulp of water, she looked up at the sky. Just a hint of pale winter sun would do it. The merest sliver, just to inject a bit of optimism into the bloodstream. But it was a sludgy monotone. She swivelled her head around in a mini panoramic move left to right, but no, the palette didn't change.

The thumping in her head was starting to build. The nausea from last night, which she thought she had under control, started to bubble up insistently like a hot swamp.

Was this really what she wanted?

Good question.

A few rooms carved out of a dirty grey oblong, just about distinguishable from the dirty grey backdrop of sky. She'd call it a block of flats, but the estate agents had christened them apartments. It looked as though it had been built in the 1970s, but it was only four stories-high. She'd printed off the details before she left yesterday.

'5 Paradise Court. Montague Avenue. Prosser and Butcher are excited to offer this well presented one bedroom first floor apartment, located in central Headingley. Offered furnished, with neutral décor. Ideal for single professional. £535 pcm. Immediately available. £650 deposit.'

It was difficult to see what Prosser and Butcher were getting so excited about. Still, it was about all she could afford. Or more accurately, it would leave minus fifty pounds at the end of each month. But she'd never get George to budge. She had to initiate it. She pictured the board on the wall at work with the coloured stickers, each with a helpful action.

'Improve engagement score by 10%.' 'Develop stakeholder contact.' Somebody had taken down the one that simply said 'bollocks'. Then she imagined her own stickers.

'Take back control.' Where had she heard that before?

'Need some space.' Not bad.

'Some time to think.' OK.

'Accept things, or make a change.' Who said that to her?

Then a stream of them. 'Only get one life.' 'Whole world out there.' 'So much to give.' 'If I really thought I could make things better with him, then I'd stay'. That was too long for a sticker.

But honestly, there was just one massive question mark. Surely, after all this time, nearly twenty-five years, she would know. George was never going to change. Those personality characteristics were set in stone years ago. She'd looked at him long and hard yesterday morning before he left for work. He hadn't noticed her doing it. He was eating a piece of toast in that annoying way of his. Leaving half the crust. Not all the crust. Just half of it. She thought the crust was the best bit. It was an irreconcilable difference. Way down the list of irreconcilable differences, but symptomatic. He'd still be leaving half the crust in five years' time, ten years' time, twenty years' time. When she was nearly seventy. Quite a thought that. Just about your entire adult life with one man. A flawed man. Lots of deep flaws. Profound flaws. Flaws that you couldn't patch up with Polyfilla.

Maybe he wouldn't be there at seventy. But his mother was still going strong. His father as well, as far as they knew, although no one had seen him for decades. What a terrible thought. Of course, she didn't wish for that.

But before she could mentally reverse the darkest thoughts, she was interrupted.

"Hello Miss Stephenson. Pleased to meet you. I'm Angelica. I'll take you round number five. It's very spacious. The landlord fitted a new kitchen nine years ago, and redecorated the whole place at the same time. It's on the corner so you get lots of light. Fully furnished. Neutral décor. Tenants like that. Ideal for the single professional."

Angelica said all of this without looking up from her phone. She pressed the screen triumphantly to send a message of some sort, and only then looked up at Dawn, displaying a weak smile but bearing her small glossy white teeth to the full. She had those strange painted eyebrows that make you look like a clown, and an orange tint pervaded her face.

"It's Mrs Stephenson actually," corrected Dawn with an indignation that she didn't understand. Strange, in the circumstances, that she was so fiercely protecting her marriage title.

"Sorry, of course, yes," replied Angelica with no interest, as she looked back down at her phone to compose the next message. At the same time turning and confidently leading the way, head still bowed, up the path through the small area of grass to Paradise Court. Only coming back up for air when she reached the front door to fumble with the keys in the lock. Dawn followed two paces behind. There was a blackbird pulling a worm out of the ground. The worm was putting up a struggle. Clinging to the earth. The bird didn't look up.

Dawn observed Angelica's slimness, accentuated by the stilt-like high heels, on which she appeared perfectly comfortable, despite the altitude. Her long black hair, well-provided by product, was about the same colour as the classic black jacket and skirt. Dawn estimated her age at twenty-three. Dawn had married George by that age. Her mother had been outraged, told her that she'd expected her to get married at twenty-seven. Quite why her mother had set an exact age for marriage was a mystery, but maybe she'd been right all along. Both her parents had been ambivalent about George. If she'd waited until she was twenty-seven, maybe she wouldn't have married him.

Dawn stood beside the slim Angelica, picking up the faint scent of expensive perfume as Angelica struggled to turn the key in the lock, poking her tongue out of her mouth to one side, and pressing the key harder with both hands. There was the tiniest sign of perspiration on her forehead.

She was an attractive girl. Dawn wondered if Andrew Prosser had eyed her lustfully in the office. Made a few slightly inappropriate comments while leaning over to look at some property particulars, but spending a few seconds examining the back of her neck. Dawn had met him when he'd been round to value their house. The last time her relationship with George had plumbed the depths. A tall man with a red nose and a bad squint which made it difficult to look him in the eye during a conversation. She thought he was looking away in embarrassment when he gave them the bad news on the valuation.

Eventually the slim girl won the battle, the key turned with a sympathetic click, and the door swung open to reveal a small tiled communal entrance hall with a lone empty plastic cup standing in the corner for no good reason. Paradise Court beckoned them in.

*

It had only been a tiny white lie that she'd told George. She was going with Sandra to a spa weekend at a country hotel. But it was only the Saturday and Sunday nights. Arrive at 4.00 pm on Saturday afternoon, and vacate the room by 10.30 am Monday morning. You got to use the spa between 6.00 and 8.00 pm on Saturday evening, followed by a Sicilian-themed gala fish dinner. 5% off the second bottle of Prosecco. The offer applied per person. The mini bar in the room was complimentary, apart from alcohol. In the morning there was a continental breakfast, or porridge option. All in all, it fitted into the budget range of spa weekends. And when she'd found the hotel on Google maps, there was no sign of countryside around it.

Last night she'd spent at Sandra's, and she'd meet her at the country hotel tonight, countryside or not. She had to talk to somebody, try to make sense of it all. Her and George. Should I stay or should I go? God that sounded awful, even if she'd only said it in her head and nobody else could hear it. But last night she'd said it to Sandra, her best friend for years. This was the first time they'd talked about it properly. They'd sat at Sandra's kitchen table, drank far too much wine, and made a list. Dawn felt guilty about it. You couldn't bring nearly twenty-five years of marriage down to a ten-point list. But the bottle of Sauvignon Blanc loosened them up, and Sandra got the pen and paper out. They'd started with a table with three columns – Vote Remain. Vote Leave. Then the different points. But they couldn't split it out like that. So Dawn tore it up, and started a fresh page of random points. There was nothing new, no startling insight that was going to solve the equation. In fact, it read like a rather bland clichéd list. She'd started to feel embarrassed about it. But they'd pressed on.

In his favour. He wasn't a bad man. He wasn't a bad father. They'd been together for nearly twenty-five years – that kept cropping up. They had a son who still needed his mum and dad despite being twenty-two. They'd had some happy times. He could still make her laugh, sometimes. She was still fond of him, sometimes. They had a nice house – they'd have to split the money if they separated. She wanted to discount the final point – the 'nice house'. Did that rank alongside feelings, emotions, fondness, fatherhood, love, tenderness? But it was there somewhere. Sandra hadn't let her cross it out. So that was seven or eight points in his favour, depending on whether you counted the house.

Then there was a final point which Dawn hadn't written down in front of her best friend. Sandra had decided to leave her husband, she was on her own, and she wasn't happy. That sounded so harsh, but honestly it was true, she was just lonely. She hadn't gone travelling, hadn't done that creative writing course, hadn't done the oil painting master class, hadn't met a new loving partner, hadn't moved to India to do yoga at sunrise and sunset. She had the same job, still drank too much, still swapped religions too much. And ultimately, she was on her own and wanted someone to share her life with. So that was the point really. You knew what life was like with George, and you could probably predict what it was going to be like next year, and the year after that. There wasn't a fully developed Plan B. Just a few preliminary sketches, with a lot of doodles around the edges.

Dawn thought the list of negative points would be a lot easier, that the prose would flow smoothly from the pen. She started with 'lying cheating bastard', double underlined it with a flourish. Not very original, but a good opener. Sandra gave the thumbs up, snorted approval, took the biggest gulp of wine in history, and banged her glass down before finishing off her Eccles cake. So that was point number one. Or maybe it was the overall summary.

She was about to write 'Linda' as the second point, but hesitated. That seemed too easy, and she wasn't even sure it was his worst crime. So, she put it in square brackets in a corner and carried on writing – 'weak', 'lost his enthusiasm for life', 'nothing in common anymore', 'refuses to communicate'. Connection and communication. The two Cs. That was the main fault line. On Thursday night she'd even suggested getting a dog, just to see how he reacted. 'Let's think about it,' he'd said. And what about when they went out for a meal, and he had notes in his pocket about what to say. He might as well have rigged up an autocue. 'Say something.' 'What do you want me to say?' Hardly the free-flowing chatter of young lovers.

She'd paused for thought at that point, chewed on the end of the pen, then wrote 'selfish and does nothing around the house'. Maybe that was two points. But she did all the cleaning. And she knew that he'd eaten the last Cornetto on Wednesday night, and given himself more prawns on Thursday night. He still hadn't bought a new teapot, still hadn't fixed the outside light. He'd left a wine stain on the carpet on Tuesday night. He showed no inclination to do anything about the leaking conservatory. OK, he'd fixed a coat hook by the back door yesterday. Oh God, did it come down to this – Cornettos, prawns, teapots, and coat hooks? It was about all these things, but about none of them. What really got to her, like an arrow through the heart, like a steel bar over the head, was that when she looked at George, most of the time she just didn't know him anymore. He was a stranger. Before she knew him, he was a twenty-one-year-old stranger. Now he was a forty-nine-year-old stranger looking back at her across the breakfast table, eating toast in an annoying way. Somewhere in between they had known each other. They really had.

"Sandra, I need a break, I just do. I didn't think it would be this hard. I feel a bit sick if I'm honest. I'll just go outside for some fresh air."

She thought Sandra would be disappointed, keen to carry on the George character assassination, but the response was different.

"It's not easy at all Dawn. And look at me. No sunlit uplands. Go for a walk, and we can carry on if you want to. Or we can stop."

They put their arms around each other for a bear hug, then Dawn pushed the door open, and walked into the car park in front of the flat. It felt like she should light a cigarette, inhale and collect her thoughts. But she hadn't smoked since university, so made do with a wine gum from the pocket of Sandra's Kagool which she'd borrowed. It was a red one, her favourite. There was an incredibly bright beautiful moon; it would disappear in the morning and the sun would rise, whatever happened to her and George. She leaned against the side of her car, and stared at the moon for inspiration. There should've been a wolf howling on a distant prairie, but there was only a scruffy lurcher sniffing around an empty Chinese takeaway carton. It looked up momentarily to check that its supper was not under threat, then tucked in.

There were two more points to consider.

Point one. George thought she was having an affair with Derek Pearson. Derek Pearson, for God's sake! If he was the last man on earth, she wouldn't. Well not without a lot of soul searching. Although he did have muscly legs. And Derek's arrogance had ebbed away over the last few weeks as the extent of his financial predicament became clear. Distinct traces of vulnerability crawling out of the bunker and blinking in the midday sun. That'd made him more interesting, easier to talk to. Poor Derek, saddled with the beautiful, well-connected, but ultimately stomach-churning Cassandra. She didn't need a white horse, a personal trainer, and tennis lessons twice a week with Gunter from Stuttgart, but Derek hadn't felt able to turn the dial down on the spending. Cassandra might stop loving him, and love Gunter instead. Now all Derek had to show for it was a house with two mortgages, a series of credit and store cards beyond their limits, and a dreadful twitch, which of course George had spotted and was delighting in. And things were going to get a lot, lot worse for Derek. Next week probably. She knew that. But if she was being brutally honest, and the moonlight and the alcohol were good bedfellows for brutal honesty, she'd have to admit, if pushed, that she'd let George run away with the idea about Derek. Just a bit. To keep him on his toes. And as a punishment.

Which brought her on to point number two. Lovely Linda, who'd been conveniently parked in square brackets. It hadn't been hard to find out what was going on. As soon as the suspicion arose, she simply waited until George was in the shower, picked up his phone, keyed in his mother's birthday, and read the string of text messages. It was that easy and George was that stupid, that naïve. Dawn had to ask herself why she hadn't confronted him about it. This was the easiest punch to land. But there was a mass of intertwining reasons like a bunch of cables twisted up behind the TV.

Cynically, she could just be keeping it up her sleeve for a later date. The nuclear option to be used when he went beyond unbearable. Or maybe she felt he was just too pathetic to bother with. She wanted to see how many lies he was willing to tell her. Watch him dig himself deeper and deeper into the hole. At some point he'd work out that she knew, and that would punish him more. Perhaps she didn't want Paul to find out that his father was an adulterer. Especially with the scandal of George's father, the stranger in the attic who she and Paul had never met. The thing was, as she'd kept reading the texts, which she did on a regular basis, she realised that George wasn't enjoying it very much. He was trying to get out of it, pretty much as soon as he got into it. Within two weeks he'd stopped calling her Lindy (how sick was that!), and went back to the formalities of Linda. Dawn had almost started to feel sorry for her. Two nights in a Premier Inn was hardly Romeo and Juliet. Then the texts ended. Along with the relationship, presumably.

*

"Shall we go in now Mrs Stephenson. Do you feel alright? You look a bit pale."

In truth, Dawn felt awful, with a major relapse taking hold. Thank God they'd stopped drinking after the interlude in the car park, even though Sandra had suggested getting a taxi to the twenty-four-hour shop to buy more wine. Dawn had summoned up enough self-control to declare the end of proceedings and retirement to bed, or the settee to be precise as Sandra only had one bedroom after the divorce. Dawn had stumbled as she'd stepped into the sleeping bag, but only slightly grazed her forehead as she hit the standard lamp.

Blinking her eyes as wide as possible, and with an unconvincing feigned heartiness, she eventually replied to Angelica

"I'm fine thanks, yes let's see the flat. Let's go for it!"

Puzzled why she added the call to arms bit, Dawn trudged slowly up the stairs, without purpose, a half-heartedness in each step, still clutching the now empty bottle of water. Angelica trotted up the two flights of stairs with a disrespectful breezy air.

The flat was alright. That's about all you could say about it. Alright. Dawn took the opportunity to view the galley-style kitchen first, and fill up the water bottle. There was an unnerving series of banging noises when she turned on the cold-water tap. Angelica explained without knowledge or conviction that it was 'to do with the pipes', as she watched Dawn drain the whole bottle and then refill it.

As promised, there was a large window in the sitting room which really did let a lot of light in. Angelica had been right about that. On a day with just a few of the sun's rays smiling through, perhaps Dawn would have been able to picture herself sitting in that room, with a cup of Costa Rican coffee from the specialist shop in the arcade, re-reading *Middlemarch* – Dawn as Dorothea. But the sun was nowhere to be seen, and it was just the greyness that flooded in.

The bathroom was awful. Even Angelica, already schooled in the estate agent's prose, failed to come up with a positive spin. The avocado suite may have been a collector's item, but it wasn't clean, and there was a faint smell of drains. Maybe that was a metaphor for life with George. One nice room with the potential for sunlight to come flooding in, but just a few paces away the faint smell of drains.

Dawn didn't commit.

"I'll think about it," she told Angelica. Just like she was thinking about everything else.

"Fine," replied Angelica, somehow forcing the corners of her lips in a vaguely upward direction as she locked the door behind them. Eyes down for the next phone call, which was to her boyfriend.

The boyfriend was called Pascal. You knew that because Angelica used his name at the beginning of each sentence, just to emphasise the point that she was young and had a handsome French boyfriend.

"Pascal, you'll never believe what Belinda told me last night."

"Pascal, that's wonderful, I've only been to Val d'Isère once before."

"Pascal, you didn't, did you? What did he say, was he livid?"

Or maybe Pascal wasn't handsome and French. Maybe he was from Dewsbury and worked in a fish and chip shop.

Dawn walked down the path away from the flats, back towards her car parked on the road. She needed more time, and she needed to think about it all without a stinking hangover. Why had they drunk so much wine? When did one more glass of wine turn from being a bad idea into a fantastic idea? She regretted it of course, but you always did. Maybe the time at the Spa would help – detox on the cheap, it would clear her head. She and Sandra could talk some more about things tonight.

*

It didn't work out like that. They checked into the hotel, which was a lot nicer than the mental picture she'd built up. It wasn't really in the historic spa town of Harrogate, more on the outskirts on a business park next to a climbing centre. They used the spa. It didn't provide full rejuvenation from the excess of last night, but it took the edge off it, and allowed them to make a valiant attempt at the gala fish dinner, both of them foregoing the Prosecco offer. They didn't talk about George. Dawn noticed a missed call from him, but she had no intention of ringing him back. She tried ringing Paul, but it went to voicemail.

At about ten o'clock, with both of them nodding off, Dawn admitted to running out of steam, said goodnight to Sandra, and went back to her room. Sandra reluctantly accepted defeat, but said she was going to the bar to read her book.

Dawn was relieved that they'd got separate rooms. It was supposed to be a twin room, but they'd been offered two rooms for the same price, because the hotel wasn't full. Sandra was her friend, her good friend, but Dawn wanted her own space, and Sandra's night time ramblings had stopped being funny. Dawn had heard them the first time when they'd shared a room in Edinburgh for Jackie's hen night. Third hen night that is. Three marriages, two to the same person, and one in the middle. She'd woken up and heard Sandra shouting and thrashing about in bed, rolling from one side to the other, and yelling about various men. Mostly about John, her husband at the time. But also the tall distinguished retired army captain in the cheese shop, not far from Sandra's house. The one she shared with John before she left. Timothy, that was his name, the same as Dorothy's cat. Dark hair, but a grey moustache. Also, Jonathan the mobile hairdresser. Dawn couldn't work out whether they were all the objects of Sandra's desire, or just a collection of random men.

Then it got a bit stranger when they shared a room after Sandra's divorce party at the bar in Manchester. John, Timothy, and Jonathon all got a mention. And also Horatio, God knows who he was. And then the name George. That had made Dawn sit up. It was probably George the pizza delivery chap who worked in the shop near Sandra's new flat. That would be it. It would be a surprise if it was the other George. George Stephenson. Married to Dawn Stephenson. But it was an unusual feeling to think that somebody else, Sandra even, could find George worthy of a dream. Strange that.

Pushing those thoughts aside, Dawn unzipped the pocket in her case, and took out the photo album that she'd brought with her. There was that familiar smell. The old photo, old paper, old plastic smell. A pleasant mustiness. This could go either way, but she'd take the risk. It wasn't really a properly catalogued collection of their lives together, lots of the photos were on her laptop now. It wasn't always in chronological order, there were big gaps mostly in the last five years, and it had a cheap plastic cover with the price still on – £2.99 sale price. But basically, it was all here.

She flicked through the first few pages. Her as a young girl growing up in Streatham. A happy childhood. Her and her sister Sam. The two of them beaming self-confident smiles, with their mum and dad. The modest three-bedroom terraced house five minutes' walk from the railway station. It would be worth one and a half million now. The short walk to the station made a big difference. There was a direct train into Blackfriars. Mum carried on living there even after Dad died. Lots of the neighbours had sold up. Mrs Priestly from next door had moved up to Birmingham to be near her son. The two lawyers had moved in then, extended the kitchen and made a decking area, with an enormous gas-fired barbecue. It was South facing. They'd invited Mum to one of the parties, but she'd only stayed half an hour. Dawn felt a small tear appear in the corner of her eye as she thought about her parents – they'd been happy. It had all been so straight forward. Get married, have two children, stay happy. Dad dies, and Mum carries on stoically, accepts what life has thrown at her. Just like that.

As she wiped away the tear with one finger, she turned the page and came to the first photo with George on. That party in that awful student house in Hull. There were two photos, both in the kitchen. One earlier in the evening, lots of people packed in the kitchen, George at one side, Dawn at the other. There was a guy in the middle dressed as a woman. A six-foot rugby player, with a beard, in drag. She and George didn't know each other at that point. Then the second one with a beer stain on the corner. A lot later in the evening, after they'd talked, after they'd kissed, after they'd talked again. George with his arm around her. She was shouting, had her arm raised in the air. She could have been singing along to something. George had a beer can in his hand. She had a half pint glass with white wine in. She had that red crushed-velvet dress on, shoulder-less. And the Eighties hairstyle. She'd had the perm the week before. The two photos were right next to each other. George's friend had taken both of them, and given them to George when the two of them got together properly. There was a momentary hesitation as she turned the page, but she carried on. Too late to stop now.

The next page was right there in front of her, with the two of them again smiling at the camera. George with the check suit from Next, and her with the wedding dress that she'd chosen with her mum from the shop on Streatham High Street. All the family there. Mum and Dad. George's mum.

She turned the pages quickly. The honeymoon. A couple of holidays, just the two of them.

A few more random ones of relatives that they hadn't seen for years.

Then they were out of order. A few of the dog from her childhood. Two pages just of the dog. Beauty, an Alsatian.

Then a picture of baby Paul. And a picture of Dawn holding baby Paul. And a picture of George in bed holding Paul.

More pictures of the dog.

A picture at Nanna's funeral.

A whole page of pictures from Sorrento. That had been Mum and Dad's first holiday abroad on their own. There was a postcard as well, written to her and Sam. Dad's writing but signed by both of them. Three kisses.

Then a page with no photos. She couldn't remember why.

She turned the page. She knew what was coming. A picture of her and George at cousin Michael's wedding. It was only a month after it had happened. She'd got her figure back though.

She closed the album, sobbing quietly as she put it back in her case. Then she lay on the bed with her clothes on, and the lights still on. She stared at the ceiling. There was a small yellow stain next to the light fitting. You've bought yourself a bit more time George, she thought, but you're not out of the woods. I am going to tackle this.

Chapter 13

As he looked up at the lights shining through the grubby windows of the flat above the corner shop, he imagined his mother watching him – watching him with love, worry, and a tiny bit of disappointment. If his father was also watching, he'd be less concerned, probably trying to steer clear of any trouble. But what did they really think of their only son? They'd brought him into the world – their genes; and they'd brought him up – their nurture. It was strange that this mattered to him. He was making his own way in the world – for better or worse. Mostly worse.

He tried to imagine himself and Danni living in something similar to his parents' house in twenty-five years' time. She'd still be stunningly attractive, the same breathtaking features, just with a few more lines, and the tattoos fading. Two dysfunctional grown-up sons slouched on the settee playing video games, empty pizza cartons and beer bottles strewn across the carpet, a plastic bag of cocaine stuffed in the older one's pocket, a police car parking up outside.

Or the alternative future. Married to Lucy from the 6th form. A safer attractiveness. On her way to being a doctor now, with Matthew the steady boyfriend with glasses in tow. But if he, Paul Stephenson, turned up on her doorstep, declared his love and proposed marriage, he felt she'd say yes, discard Matthew, and fix a date. How arrogant was that? Then in twenty-five years it would be something similar to Derek Pearson's house, but in the country somewhere, with two Labradors, and two sons at university.

The prospect of settling down with either Danni or Lucy, or any normal life free from a ton weight of worry, seemed way over a distant horizon at the moment. There was a dark cloak of misery shrouding his life. He could throw off the white duvet in the morning, only for this second black one to be there in the first seconds of awakening. Sliding down a snake, not climbing up a ladder.

They, his parents, didn't know about any of this yet. They were the people he should have been confiding in, but he hadn't. He couldn't face revealing what his weakness had brought upon him, couldn't face his mother's worried look, his father's realisation that he'd passed on that faulty gene to his only son.

He pulled the collar of his jacket up, buttoned up the front against the cold and wet. It wasn't a jacket designed for winter. It felt like he'd been standing there for ten minutes, but it was a lot less than that. The rain was getting heavier, and the skies were very dark now. It was early evening, and peering up he could see shimmering lights and shapes moving around in the flat. His flat.

He'd been sent to buy beer. They sold beer in the corner shop below his flat, but he'd walked to the larger store on the avenue round the corner. The beer was cheaper, but he wanted the fresh air and the cold, and he wanted to be out of the flat.

Danni was in there. You could almost say they were living together, but there'd be nights when she was somewhere else, and he didn't always know where. Walker was in there as well, her half-brother, and he'd invited a few mates round. It was Paul's flat, but Walker treated it as his own territory when he was there. They wanted plenty of beer before they went out for the night to pubs and clubs. They already had a good stock of pills. Paul was expected to buy the beer for all of them, to offset against the other obligations.

He would spin it out a bit longer before going in. He didn't mind the rain. He huddled up to the wall next to the shop, but water started to gush down from the overflowing gutter, so he moved into the alley which ran at the side. They had a bottle of vodka in the flat, which he'd bought for them earlier. That would keep them going a bit longer. He stared at the row of fast-food outlets on the opposite side of the road. The bright lights and signs looked almost psychedelic through the driving rain. Unpleasant cuisine from around the world – kebabs, pizzas, burgers, curry sauce and chips, fried chicken. The Alabama Authentic Dixy-fried Chicken Shack even had a pink neon happy chicken whose head rocked from one side to the other. An illuminated chicken, and some shady coming and goings. The one bright spot was Norman's traditional café. It displayed a Union Jack as a mark of patriotism and quality. Fried sausages at their best. He and Danni ate out there a couple of times a week, their dining experience of choice.

He looked at his watch. He'd wait one more minute, give it until half five. He could feel water dripping down the back of his neck with a slight tickle. Then a different sensation on his neck, shock and pain, a tight squeezing, a pincer grip. Instinctively he hunched up his shoulders, and tried to turn around.

"Now then Pauly, what are you doing standing out here all on your own. You're wet. We thought we'd lost you. Wondering where the beer had got to."

Walker gripped Paul's neck with his big hands, gave it a final extra painful squeeze, and then let go. Paul spun around and saw Walker grinning at him. One look at Walker and you knew he was bad news. The grin was the default position; but there was a snarling, animal-like look when he lost control. His neck swelled, his face reddened, and he was truly dangerous at that point. Paul had seen him like that. But for now, it was just the grin. The grin and the staring blue eyes.

The alley at the side of the shop led to a yard at the back, and there was a fire escape down from the flat. It wasn't a safe structure, it hung off the wall in the middle, but you could get down it if you were careful. Or drunk enough. Walker must have come out that way, and crept up on him.

"Let's get you in Pauly, out of the rain. Danni's missing you. Jonno and Stag are getting thirsty. Stag's finished off the vodka – he's in a bit of a mess already, God knows what he'll be like later. He can be trouble when he's like that. Thanks for the beer Pauly, we'll knock it off what you owe me."

So, the two of them walked into the flat through the door at the side of the shop, up the narrow stairs, onto the landing, and then opened the door into the sitting room. Walker followed one pace behind, like a prison guard. Paul had been renting the flat for nearly three months, since he'd started the job. There was a sitting room with two windows looking out onto the street, a tiny kitchen and bathroom both frequented by mice, and a bedroom carved out of the roof space up an even narrower staircase.

As they walked into the sitting room, Danni ran up to him with that smile on her face, put her arms around him, pressed her body against his, and kissed him on the lips. It was a lingering affectionate kiss, and he could feel the stud in her tongue. That smile was his weakness, you couldn't resist it, it drew you in. The smile, the mischievous sense of humour, the alternative charm. And the green eyes. The beautiful green eyes. Only two per cent of the world's population had them, and Danni did. A rare creature.

"Where've you been? You left me with these idiots."

She had a slightly gravelly voice, as if she had a permanent cold, but it made her even more attractive. Her lipstick was smudged from the kiss. He liked the maroon lipstick, but he imagined his mother wouldn't. Danni used lots of dark eye shadow, lots of mascara, lots of hairspray. There were remains of faded red streaks in her peroxide blonde hair, a couple of dreadlocks on one side which she'd twisted when she was bored. She bleached her own hair. It was a military operation with the smell of ammonia hanging in the air all day, but it ended up as a work of art. He'd got used to the stud in her tongue, and the small silver ring through her left nostril. She nearly always wore black. She'd worn the short mini skirt and fishnet stockings to his graduation ceremony which had annoyed his parents, although he'd spotted his father glancing at those gorgeous legs. And that was the quandary. It wasn't completely black and white. Good fun, sexy, irreverent, the smile, the green eyes, a little dangerous; all of which he liked. But then a terrible dark side which scared the hell out of him. And indirectly she'd got him involved with Walker and his mates. She hadn't connived in Walker's entrapment. It had all just happened, a terrible comedy of errors.

He looked around the room, his heart sinking even though he knew what he would see. Empty beer cans, an empty vodka bottle, crisp packets, chocolate bar wrappers, the congealed remains of a half-consumed kebab. The TV on full blast but nobody watching it. The radiators and gas fire on high, but both Jonno and Stag in shorts slumped on the settee each with a games console, no attempt to look up as he came in the room. His room, his flat, the flat that he paid the rent for; drinking the beer and eating the crisps and chocolate bars that he'd bought. And the awful stench of it all, it could be rotting corpses on the Somme. He wanted to push open the sash windows and let the cold damp air in. Any air would be better than this. But they were jammed closed, painted over and stuck a long time ago.

Amongst the detritus, there was one other thing that you couldn't avoid looking at. On the small table in the corner that they used for eating on, sat a long survival knife. Walker's knife. A symbol of authority.

*

It was difficult to piece together how it had got to this point. Random events rather than a grand design. But he could remember very clearly how it had started. Happily-drunk at the beginning of his final summer term, he'd started a babbling conversation with the girl with the green eyes and the perfect curves, who just happened to be standing next to him in a dark heaving club. Perfect karma that had led to this perfect storm. He knew straight away that she was trouble, but after splitting up from Lucy for the second time, he thought he was ready for a bit of trouble. Life in the fast lane rather than the thirty miles per hour of Sycamore Meadows.

His friends were jealous to start with. Not now. They'd all extricated themselves from friendship. But it wasn't Danni herself that was the problem. Somehow Walker had appeared on the scene, ingratiated himself, and then he was always there, an ever-present picture of malevolence. Mr Generous at first, buying them drinks, taking them to a gig – no need to pay for the tickets, they were complementary. It was a tried and tested technique. Walker was the alpha wolf, and he'd targeted Paul as the weaker than average deer, to be manoeuvred away from the herd, isolated, ready for the taking. An obligation had started to build. A debt. Slowly at first. But no need to worry, he could tide you over, see you right. And if you needed some pills, just to enjoy the night a bit more, or to relieve the pressure of exams, then he had the contacts and the supply chain. Credit facilities, if the student loan was running out. A small advance when he'd quit his bar job to focus on his finals. A week in Greece for the two of you when the exams were finished – you deserve it. Why not. A line of credit for the deposit on the flat. Pay me back when you start work. It built and built, nothing in writing, a bit here, a bit more there. Until you were in deep, and he had control of you. A fly in the spider's web.

He, Paul, was supposed to know about these things. Three years to get a degree in economics. You should understand finance, balanced budgets, fiscal discipline, tight monetary policy – his grandmother understood all of that. She didn't need a degree in economics. It got worse – now he had a job, a trainee accountant. Income and expenditure. Profit and loss accounts. Balance sheets. Cashflow forecasts. None of this was relevant for dealing with Walker. Psychology and behavioural science might help a bit, with an extended essay on intimidation and terror. Boxing lessons would be better.

There was no documentation. No records were kept. There were no statements. No disclosure of the APR or the terms and conditions. Paul reckoned he'd borrowed about three thousand pounds, if you added in all the things that he thought were for free at the beginning. Walker told him he owed ten thousand all-in, explaining how the arrangement fees, and late payment fees, and penalty interest, and administration fees, had all added up. Complex loan arrangements backed up by the threat of physical violence. It was the perfect business model. With enough real threat to stop you going to the police. The survival knife was never far away.

He had no hope of paying it back now. Interest was added daily. Interest on interest. Compound interest. He was supposed to be paying back two hundred pounds a month from his salary, but the monthly interest was more than that, so the debt kept accumulating. Walker liked it that way. He could get Paul to do little jobs for him. Nothing illegal at this stage, just being his manservant, his butler. But there were hints of bigger jobs in the future, more responsibility, 'promotion' as Walker called it.

Danni knew that Walker had his claws into him, and that he had trouble sleeping at night. It was her idea to go to Spain for a few days two weeks ago. She'd paid for it all. God knows where she got the money. Mysterious Danni. It was best not to ask. Somehow, they'd managed to keep it from Walker. And they'd had some good nights out in Granada. Got talking to a few people. With the help of the tapas and the local wine he'd managed to forget about his troubles for a few hours. But his nemesis was still casting his shadow out there. Walking back to the apartment, you could see him lurking in a shop doorway, or hear him following you a few paces behind. Looking down on you from a balcony. Ever watchful. Protecting his investment.

He'd come close to asking his parents for help. He'd phoned his mother this week. He'd meant to tell her everything, but then bottled out. Then he'd not replied to his father's calls or messages. He couldn't face the shame of it all, the disappointed looks, the whispered comments. Why didn't you stay with Lucy? We thought the world of her.

No, he'd soldier on a bit longer. Something might turn up. Maybe Danni did have a secret plan. She seemed to have been deep in thought since they got back from Granada. Rat poison in his cocoa. Bleach in his vodka. Maybe the boys in blue would catch up with him for one of his other business ventures. Maybe one of his 'associates' would deal with him, or Mr Big would sweep in and despatch him. Or the two of them could head back to the Greek islands, find a really remote one, grow olives, keep a donkey. His grandfather in South America could be the best bet. The ex-communicated one, if he could be tracked down. Or what if Walker simply dropped dead, hereditary heart condition? Unexpected, tragic, a promising life cut short. One in a million chance.

"C'mon Paul, day-dreaming again. They're heading out now. They'll be gone hours. They might not even come back here. With any luck they'll all get arrested and spend the night in the cells. You never know your luck." She squeezed his hand, looked up at him with the startling green eyes, smiled that smile. Everything would be fine.

Chapter 14

Lying in bed at twenty-nine minutes past ten, with most of his clothes still on, he didn't yet know that he was about to share his wife's hangover experience for the rest of the day. A minute later he did. There was no gradual awakening, no relaxing half sleep on a Saturday morning. He just sat up in bed, wide awake but disorientated. His tongue was stuck to the roof of his mouth. The radio was on. It'd probably been on all night. Immediately, a wave of nausea swept over him. He leapt out of bed and ran for the tiny en-suite bathroom. There was an empty wine glass and a piece of cheese on the window sill. He retched but he couldn't be sick. Then the patchwork of memories started to build. He turned the tap on and splashed water on his face, drank as much as he could from his cupped hands. A few more memories came back. The images started to spread like a virus, contorted faces from the pub and the nightmares flickering in an ancient newsreel. He stared at himself in the mirror. He saw a face that was panicky and alone. But at least there was no devil standing behind him. Not yet anyway.

He stumbled back into the bedroom, and then hurried down the stairs, still in the clothes that he'd slept in. He flung open the front door, still unlocked from last night, and took two unsteady steps outside, no shoes on his feet. The cold stung his still wet face. That felt a tiny bit better. Outside it was a chilly wet November morning. That felt good, that felt normal. A car drove past, that felt good as well. He wasn't living in a world of strange creatures and demons. It was the ordinary world of Sycamore Meadows. As if to cement the normality, Bernard and Lucy walked past. They always went out later on a Saturday morning. Routine. Wonderful. Bernard stopped when he saw George.

121

"Good night last night George. Alan and Pete really enjoyed it. Thanks for all the drinks, but I don't think the Pernod and Baileys was a good idea. I bet those glace cherries have been hanging around for a long time. How are you feeling? You don't look too good. Probably a sore throat from all that singing as well."

The beer, the aniseed and sweet sickly tastes and smells, the saltiness of the crisps, the full-throated drunken communal singing, the girl behind the bar, the noise, the shouting, the walk home, the feeling of being watched. Then the dreams. A catalogue of confused images of last night, but at least some normality building this morning.

"I've got the worst hangover ever Bernard. Good job Dawn's away. I feel like death."

"Take care George, a big mug of tea with lots of sugar. That should do the trick."

George watched Bernard start to walk off with Lucy following. Bernard turned and shouted back.

"Alan will be round soon to look at the boiler George. I'm sure he'll get it fixed for you."

God, he'd forgotten about that. Alan knew how to fix boilers. A man of many talents. George hadn't noticed the cold in the house first thing, but he felt it as he walked back in, through the hall into the kitchen.

Maybe that's all it was then. A drunken night, some bad dreams brought on by the alcohol. Nothing to worry about. Just a fleeting return to the excesses of his younger days. He put the kettle on. Put a teabag in a cup. No need for the teapot, there was only him in the house. He found the paracetamol, swallowed a couple down with a large glass of water, made some toast. Drank the tea, ate the toast, made more tea, drank it. Began the long road to recovery. Read the paper. Yes, there'd been a goal in the last minute. He remembered now, vaguely. A few sketchy scenes appeared. The tape replayed more embarrassing things he'd said. He might have told Bernard and his two sons about losing his job; that he was worried Dawn had had enough of him, and that Dawn might be having an affair with Derek Pearson. Oh God, but Bernard knew Derek. He might have told them about Derek's money problems. Even though Dawn had sworn him to secrecy. If that got back to Dawn, there would be hell to pay. He wasn't sure if he'd said all of that. He screwed his eyes up and concentrated hard. Maybe that way, he could drag the memory back. It didn't work. It just made his headache worse. And did you really want the full picture anyway? In technicolour, with surround sound?

He wished Dawn was here, not to see him in a mess like this, but just to have somebody to talk to. To take his confession. To judge him. To condemn him even. He could ring her, but what would he say? 'I got rolling drunk in the pub and made a fool of myself, and had a bad dream about a girl I've just met at work turning into that black cat from next door. I feel terrible. And I might have told Bernard and his sons about Derek's money problems. Despite you giving strict instructions not to. Sorry about that Dawn.'

No, it was probably best that he was on his own. Apart from the bird of course. He walked into the utility room, plonked his cup of tea down onto the top of the washing machine and stared at Polonius.

"What do you think Polonius? What's your angle on things? Have you worked out the secret of life yet? How to make your mate happy? Not that you've got a mate. I know that African greys are supposed to be monogamous. But you haven't got anybody to be monogamous with, have you? But if you did have. Although at your age you might be past it. At least you haven't got the distraction of alcohol. You don't have to hold down a job or worry about bills. The food is just delivered to you, even if it's a bit dull. I know that you've been displaced. You should be flying around the tree tops in Africa and all that, but you haven't got the complications of my life, have you?"

The bird cocked his head to one side, thought hard, and chose his reply.

"Watcha Brian."

It made as much sense as anything. George walked back into the kitchen and sat down at the table. Whatever happened in the pub was embarrassing, but at least it was real. Stupid drunken behaviour. But who knows what those dreams were about. The darkest recesses of his subconscious. Prophesies perhaps. Freud and Nostradamus could both have a field day. Angel, the poor girl, he'd only met her yesterday and there she was cavorting around turning into a giant evil black cat. Bet she wasn't expecting that on the plane over from Hong Kong. And they had their doubts about Danni, but she wasn't the bride of Dracula.

*

He spent the rest of the morning in the company of tea, toast, paracetamol, and water. The crashing waves of nausea and headaches gradually settled into calmer waters. The rest of the day stretched out before him, not as a landscape of opportunity, more like a giant hole in the ground that needed to be filled. Strange how the total freedom to do whatever he wanted weighed so heavily on him. He half-wished that Dawn had left him a list of jobs to do. At the easier end of the DIY spectrum. Fixing the curtain rail that was about to fall off in the dining room. No, that was at the hard-to-impossible end. You could always do some jobs anyway George, even if Dawn hadn't left a list. Make some progress on the huge pile of ironing building up. Iron the Egyptian cotton duvet cover. The expensive one. The one with all the pleats and the ruffled bit around the edges. That would please Dawn. Actually, what he really wanted to do was to go back to bed. Could you do that at nearly midday and at nearly fifty? What if you were in bed and somebody knocked on the door?

There was a knock at the door.

A half familiar face looked back at him as he reluctantly opened it.

"Morning George. Do you still want me to have a look at the boiler? If you've recovered from last night that is. I'm just about back on my feet myself."

There was a conspiratorial grin on Alan's face. An illicit activity shared. A drunken night with incidents best forgotten, or actually forgotten. George would have preferred not to have Alan in the house smiling at him knowingly, but on the other hand Alan was doing him a favour, he was Bernard's son, and the prospect of getting anybody else to fix the boiler over the weekend was pretty remote. He could imagine Dawn returning on Monday to an icy cold house, and being galvanised into leaving him straight away.

So Alan was invited in, shown where the boiler was, given a cup of tea, and provided with a modicum of polite conversation. George made himself a cheese sandwich. There was just enough bread after the toast marathon, and he recovered the lump of rock-hard cheddar cheese from the bathroom.

The news turned out to be good from Alan. George didn't listen to the technical detail properly, but the boiler was fixed, tested and working. The cost was modest. The house was warming up, and there'd be some hot water for a shower. His marriage was saved. Or at least one threat averted. George made yet more tea, there was an introduction to Polonius, then the two of them sat down at the kitchen table. Alan had half an hour to spare before he took his six-year-old daughter to a birthday party.

The thoughts had been gathering in George's mind, but as he listened to Alan talking about his two young daughters with real warmth and obvious love, his mind fixed on a single thought. Your father murdered your mother. You seem like a decent well-adjusted bloke, but that really happened. And here you are sitting at my kitchen table, and last night you were drinking in the pub with your father and your brother. Life has gone on, and it's normal. You look like your father. Your face is the same shape. You've got

125

dark black hair. It'll be greyer when you're the same age as Bernard, just like his is now. Somehow, you've all got over it.

George wanted to know more about what had happened, but you couldn't just come out with it, could you? Thank God, he hadn't asked anything about it last night. His memory was hazy, but he was sure he hadn't been that stupid.

"You live pretty close don't you Alan, just round the corner?"

"You can walk it in twenty minutes George. It's good to be near Dad. I've come in the van this morning though. I've got all my gear in there. I'm self-employed but there's loads of work around. I turned out for you because you're a friend of Dad's. He says he sees you every morning and evening. You always speak to him. Not everybody does."

George had never thought of himself as a kind and caring neighbour. This was a whole new side of himself being revealed. If only Alan could give a sworn statement to Dawn.

"We didn't grow up around here though. A small village in East Yorkshire. Just off the motorway. But we moved to Leeds. Pete and I spent a lot of time with Nanna. Then Pete went in the army, and I went to college to do the plumbing course. We've been here ever since. We're settled."

Well, that was carefully done. A brief summary, but avoiding one huge piece of information. But it was a mutual conspiracy of, what was the word, obfuscation. Alan must know that most people around here know; and he, George, knows that Alan knows that. But they simply ignore it. It all made perfect sense.

*

The shower had been partially successful. He was feeling a bit more human now, but he'd decided that it was too risky to drive. Too much alcohol still in the system. The number seven bus was a better option, and avoided the extortionate car parking charges. Saving the environment as well. What a green champion you are George.

He'd decided to buy a new suit for the interview next week. He'd been alternating between dark navy and charcoal grey for the last year. Even with dress-down Friday, that was still a lot of wear and tear. The trousers had started to glisten under the lights in the office, particularly the navy blue ones. But best not to spend too much. He could be out of work for the next six months, so you didn't want a brand new suit hanging in the wardrobe doing nothing. It was obvious. Like his mother before she moved into the home, refusing to buy ripen-at-home bananas. What if you died the next day? You'd wasted your money. Something mid-range from Discount Menswear would do the trick. Designer suits at discount prices. Right up his street. Probably best to stick with navy blue as well.

You could pay with a contactless debit card these days. The wonders of modern technology. As he slipped the card back into his wallet and looked down the bus, he did a double take. Bernard's son number two, Pete, sitting half way down. He couldn't face another session of dredging up the memories of last night, however much of a good neighbour he was to Bernard, and however curious he was about their past. Fortunately, Pete was penned into the window seat by a large dishevelled gentleman, so George wasn't left with the dilemma of whether to sit next to him or not, settling for a quick nod.

"Hi George. Good night last night. Think you made some new friends!"

What did that mean? He couldn't bear to think about it. He hoped he hadn't said anything too bad to the girl behind the bar. He just remembered looking at her, that's all.

"Give Alan and I a shout if you need any of that other stuff sorting out. We can always help."

"Thanks, I will, see you," replied George as he hurried past, looking away and down.

What did that mean? – 'any of that other stuff sorting out'. Put out a contract on Derek Pearson? Despatch Derek directly – the hands-on approach? Provide cut-price marriage guidance counselling? Or maybe it was just the boiler he was talking about. That could be it. Alan had already been round after all.

With half-hearted reassurance, he sat down on the back seat of the bus and knew straight away that this was a bad idea. The engine was at the back, and despite it being cold outside, it was oppressively hot sitting here, on the engine. He only just made it to the city centre without some form of bodily disaster. Eventually he stumbled off the bus, bought a bottle of water and some Polo mints – a childhood comfort thing, and took advantage of the Marks & Spencer toilet facilities after queuing for an uncomfortable few minutes.

It was an even rockier, higher temperature, road in Discount Menswear. He'd picked up the nearest navy blue suit that was the right size, but it was as hot as a furnace in the cramped changing room with the slightly stained beige curtain pulled across. He bent and turned and twisted. It felt like trying a suit on in a broom-cupboard-sized greenhouse on a hot summer's day. His palms were sweating, his armpits were wet, and there were beads of sweat building on his forehead. Watching his contortions in the mirror, he was struck by the ashen-grey face looking back at him, a ghostly apparition in a business suit. His bowels rumbled like steadily-building thunder. They were not done with him yet. He'd had the last of the paracetamol, and finished off the bottle of water.

The assistant had been waiting to pounce as soon as he left the changing room.

"How does it feel sir?"

Do you mean the suit, or the pit of my stomach, or depths of my bowels?

"Fits across the shoulders well. Maybe the trousers need taking up an inch. Shall I pin them up sir?"

He wanted to get it over with as soon as possible, even with trousers an inch too long. But Brian the sales assistant (he wore a badge) was already kneeling down, pins in hands, the scent of a sale in the air. Maybe this was the Brian that Polonius was referring to.

In the end Brian, parrot reference or not, completed the process efficiently and politely. The suit, with the freshly turned-up trousers, would be available for collection on Tuesday. Brian told him that it was 50% wool, and 50% polyester, which meant that it would wear better. That's a relief. George bought a white shirt and a dark red tie. He'd look like he was running for President.

*

It was nearly five o'clock now. He'd completely run out of steam and just wanted to get home and lie on the settee for five hours and then go to bed. A Chinese takeaway to fill him up. Surely a hangover couldn't last this long. Even his bones had started to ache.

He walked back through the city centre towards the bus station. Early Saturday night revelry was mixing with late Saturday afternoon shopping. Hordes of people with shopping bags from different stores, a job well done having bought five new T-shirts and a pair of unwearable shoes. Mingling with the girls and the boys limbering up for a big night out, some warm-up exercises for their livers before the onslaught. Happy days he thought. Thirty years ago you'd be about to start Saturday night. Second year of university. You hadn't met Dawn yet.

For once the timing at the bus station worked in his favour. He'd only had to wait ten minutes, and now he was sitting on the bus, looking forward to getting home. The bus was full, and struggling through the late afternoon traffic. It had started to rain quite heavily. Christmas lights were glistening and flickering through the rain. Even at forty-nine, Christmas lights lifted the spirits.

He heard a beep on his phone. It could be a text from Paul, or maybe Dawn. He'd settled into his solitude now, and didn't want to deal with anything. He pulled the phone out of the pocket of his jeans, fumbled with the code. No, it wasn't a text, that was a different beep. It was an alert from one of the apps. Bet-Happy. A few more touches and a password took him to his Bet-Happy account, the one that Samantha had set up. It was all unfamiliar. Pictures and messages. A flashing blue smiley face with a pound sign. A flashing red sign which said WIN. He squinted to see it properly. It was dark outside now, away from the city centre, and the lights were not good inside the bus. He pressed a few more screens, picking his way through. There was a table of the matches selected for the accumulator, now with results added. Seven matches, no, eight. There was a number in a box, then there was his account with debits and credits. £50 credit when he opened the account. £25 from Bet-Happy, £25 from him. £5 debit for the bet on Legia Warsaw. £45 debit for the Premier League accumulator. And £83,509 credit for the win on the accumulator.

Sunday 12 November

Chapter 15

It can work both ways. When the dream ends and real-life kicks in. It could be a nightmare. The vampire zombies are closing in. You've done no revision for an exam about to start. Then you wake up to the warmth of your own bed, the familiarity of the curtains and the poster on the wall, the morning smell of the girl next to you. No monster, no exam. But if you're strolling along a beach on an island in the Indian ocean, the heat of the soft white sand warming your feet, your best gal by your side; then you might not be that keen to wake up. Especially to this. This crashing and banging in the street. The shouting. The obscene slurred deep voices – some familiar, some not. The bin being kicked over. Bottles breaking, glass shattering. The twisting of the key in the lock. The front door banging open. Boots on bare floorboards. The noise moving from outside to inside, the volume being turned up. You'd rather be back on the beach.

He looked at his phone. It was 3.56 a.m. He knew it wouldn't last. The dream, or the comforting normality of last night, just the two of them. They'd tidied the flat, swept the debris into rubbish bags and put them in the bin outside. It felt symbolic. Just had one glass of wine each to finish the bottle, and watched a dreadful rom-com. Danni had cried when the lovers and the guinea pig were reunited. They'd gone to bed before midnight. He'd kissed the Sanskrit tattoo on her naked shoulder as she fell asleep in his arms. He could feel her toes touching his, and the rising and falling of her breasts as her breathing slowed. For once she was asleep before he was.

They'd left a bottle of Bacardi on the table. He'd found it under the sink. It might have been left by the previous tenants. And a box of cornflakes. Bacardi and cornflakes for his tormentors. Not quite sherry, mince pies, and carrots for

Santa and Rudolf. There'd be no presents in the morning. More like an offering to the angry gods to keep them at bay. The sacrifice might keep them quiet.

It didn't.

He could hear them moving around in the sitting room below. It wasn't shouting and crashing now. More a deep rumbling, a steadily building threat. For a few minutes he'd held out the hope that they'd eat and drink, and then go off to Stag's appalling bedsit a few streets away. Walker never appeared to have 'a place'. He was a business man continually on the move, a citizen of the world, shifting from one deal to the next. He didn't seem to need any sleep. Perhaps he disappeared to his coffin as the sun rose. Jonno was simply of no fixed abode. If he had a bed it was either the filthy sleeping bag on Stag's floor, or Paul's sofa.

Walker, Stag, and Jonno. The terrible threesome. Walker was the undisputed leader, defending his territory with ruthless efficiency. No challengers in sight. Not a scratch on him. The brains. Even though he boasted of leaving school at fourteen and never returning.

Stag's job was just to be as scary as possible. You felt that at least Walker's violence was controlled. To be used at the appropriate time. Vicious but fair. Stag's violence was random and uncontrolled. He didn't have a neck. His body just tapered to his head at the top. Fists like melons. Bulging muscles pumped up with steroids. They were good for you he said. Like fresh fruit and vegetables. He didn't have a brain. He didn't need one.

Jonno's role was more ill-defined – general heavy lifting and hard manual labour. And the comic stooge. The butt of the jokes. They ordered him around, and he was happy to be ordered around.

Paul had thought that there was a Dickensian air about the three of them. Carefully crafted characters, with some definite comedy in there somewhere. But mostly darkness and threat. Real harm could be done to you.

At four o'clock this morning, it felt like darkness, threat, and harm.

*

He felt the gush of wind from the bedroom door being kicked open – before he heard the bone-crunching sound of it hitting the wall. One day it would come off its hinges, but it clung to the doorframe for now. He'd known it was coming for a few seconds. He'd heard the footsteps on the narrow staircase up to the attic bedroom, amplified because the carpet had worn so thin. It sounded like they were dragging a horse up. They'd have to come up in single file, in order of importance. Walker, Stag, Jonno. At least Walker was a general who led from the front.

It was a dramatic entrance, and now the three of them were standing just inside the doorway. Sometimes you could see the moon through the skylight window. And when it was a full moon, or close to it, the eerie whiteness shone like a spotlight. Tonight was one of those nights, with three ghostly figures picked out in the moonlight.

Paul reached out and switched the bedside light on. The harsh electric brightness was better than the natural graveyard illumination. It stung his eyes open. He squinted up at Walker who was looking over him now. There was an awful smell of stale beer and urine.

"Come on Pauly, let's have a chat. Need to sort out that little job. Get up, there's a good boy. It'll be next week, Friday probably."

Walker's voice was hoarse, from an evening of shouting in loud bars probably, but it was controlled. Paul had seen how much Walker could drink and still remain relatively coherent. You'd think he was out of his head on the dance floor, but then he could seamlessly switch to business mode.

Stag obviously felt the need to back up his commander-in-chief.

"Get out of the fucking bed Paul. Now. Do as you are told."

Stag sounded hopelessly drunk and incoherent, but he could be at his most dangerous like this. Paul's eyes were drawn to those enormous fists. He was wide awake now, and could imagine the damage Stag could do with one punch.

"Shut up Stag," said Walker, "go back downstairs with Jonno. I don't need you up here. In fact, go round to your flat and I'll see you there. Take that bottle of Bacardi with you. I only want a chat with Pauly. Just to arrange things. It's business, that's all."

The foot soldiers trouped out of the room and back down the stairs, without any backchat.

Paul was sitting on the side of the bed now. He'd pulled on a T-shirt and a pair of jeans. It was an old Gestapo tactic to interrogate you whilst you were in the nude. He felt Danni sitting up in bed, and saw that she'd pulled the duvet up to her shoulders. Generally, she knew how to handle Walker. She spoke to her half-brother softly, without confrontation.

"Walker, can't this wait until the morning. Or do what you've got to do, then we can go back to sleep."

"No problem babe. Pauly and I just need to agree a couple of things. Then I'll be gone. We're going back to Stag's place. We've got a few old mates with us. And we're meeting a couple of young ladies. It's Saturday night after all. Well, Sunday morning."

Lucky ladies thought Paul, but said nothing. Out of the corner of his eye he saw Danni roll over and pull the duvet fully over her head. It was probably the best thing to do. It left him simply to listen to what Walker had to say, and be fully compliant. He just had to get through this. Endure.

Walker sat on the bed next to Paul. Right next to him. Their bodies were touching. Walker turned his head to look directly at him. The closeness was both intimidating and embarrassing. Should he look back into those staring blue eyes, or look down with compliance and subjugation? He settled on a respectful glance at Walker and then looked back down. He thought he knew Walker's face pretty well, but noticed a single gold tooth as Walker smiled at him. Walker's smell was more noticeable as well. The accumulated aromas of the night out – beer, spirits, wine, smoke, an expensive aftershave, and a hint of perfume from one of the girls no doubt.

"It's all falling into place Pauly. Door to door distribution. A pyramid system. Click and collect. I want you to be a part of it. You'll need to collect and then deliver. It's all straightforward. Excellent customer service. Friday, probably. Then the next week. I need somebody I can trust. Somebody who won't stand out. That's all you'll need to do. And we'll adjust what you owe me. I promised that."

The steely politeness was chilling. You could almost believe Walker meant what he said. You were just delivering a box of stationery from the wholesaler.

"Thing is Pauly, I need you to do what I say."

Because they were so close, he could feel Walker's movements. He could feel him pulling something out of his jacket, out of the inside pocket. The survival knife.

"I don't want anybody to get hurt Pauly. I really don't."

Walker held up the knife, but didn't point it at Paul. Didn't threaten him with the blade. Instead, he held it in his right hand and ran it across the back of his own left hand. Purposely cut the back of his own hand. Not a deep cut, but it drew blood, and the blood trickled down his hand and onto the white duvet. The terror was complete.

You had to hand it to Walker. He knew a thing or two about dramatic impact. Speak slowly and deliberately. Throw in a couple of extended pauses. A bit of alliteration. Build the tension. Build it some more. Then the drop.

Walker stood up, put his bleeding hand softly on Paul's shoulder as if to comfort him, then walked gently out of the bedroom, almost tip-toeing, and closed the door quietly behind him.

At that point the theatre curtain could have come down, and the audience started to applaud.

Paul lay back down on the bed. It felt like lying on a beach of wet sand with cold water lapping over his body.

Chapter 16

George woke at five in the morning. At about the same time as Paul managed to drift off into a disturbed half sleep. He opened his eyes and was immediately wide awake. He sat bolt upright and stared into the darkness. There was nothing to see. It was pitch black, with just the tiniest sliver of light from the street lamp falling on the other side of the bed. The empty side, without Dawn lying there.

Unlike yesterday, there was no searing hangover, and no images of terrible nightmares to greet him. In fact, after going to bed at just after eight o'clock last night, and with nearly ten hours of uninterrupted sleep in the bag, he was feeling pretty good in the cold and dark of that November Sunday morning. He switched on the bedside lamp, stepped out of bed, and picked up his dressing gown from the hook on the bedroom door. He wrapped it around him for a bit more warmth. The central heating hadn't come on yet, and now you could taste the cold in the air. Dawn had bought him the dressing gown as a Christmas present just after Paul started at university. It had a dark maroon swirling paisley pattern. He hadn't liked it at first, thought it was a bit old-fashioned and middle-aged, but its warming qualities had grown on him. He sniffed at the collar hoping to find the faintest smell of Dawn, but there was no trace.

He walked downstairs, made a cup of tea, and sat down at the kitchen table. It would be a few hours before there were any stirrings of life on Sycamore Meadows. It reminded him of being in their first flat, getting up very early on Sunday morning with baby Paul, the crying alarm clock. Dawn's turn to get up on Saturday, his turn on Sunday. Did he wish he was back in that world now? With the opportunity to do everything differently? Yes, please. Where do I sign?

But it was time to think about this moment. For some reason, he'd parked the big thoughts since he'd woken up, but now he was going to deal with yesterday's events. Not sitting alone at the kitchen table though. He left the tea with only a few sips taken, walked into the hall, and pulled on his old ski jacket. They'd been to Austria about ten years ago to 'give it a go'. The German instructor, the one with the large moustache and the puzzled look, said in his best English that George looked like a new-born giraffe strapped to the skis. That got a few laughs, but on that Thursday afternoon in the Alps, George's humiliation was complete. Skiing was banished to the history books. It was a good jacket though. Nearly new. One careful owner. He zipped it up, and then stepped into his Wellington boots. Another present from Dawn, to encourage gardening duties. They too looked nearly new.

He unlocked the door, and switched on the outside light. It flickered apologetically. There'd been a faulty connection for a long time now, but it was half-working, just enough light to avoid tripping over the step. Good enough for him. Disappointing for Dawn. Now he stood outside in the cold night air, a dampness hanging over him, completely alone. A good job he thought, looking down at himself. Green Wellington boots, blue striped pyjama bottoms, maroon paisley dressing gown peeping out, black and lime-green ski jacket, unshaven chin, uncombed hair. What would his mother say?

His bare feet rubbed against the inside of the boots as he marched across their drive and onto the street. He could feel mud and leaves and dry grass inside the boots as they wobbled around his shins. He walked down the street, then turned onto the main road. One car drove past. He imagined the driver on his way to an early shift at the 24-hour Tesco on the huge roundabout on the ring road. Lucky chap. He walked past the Grimes Pride estate. There were no shadowy figures waiting to pull a knife on him. He approached the Fox and Hounds. The street light picked out a banner advertising the Sunday lunch special. There was a picture of a giant burger and a modest salad. He quickened his pace to hurry past. The memories of Friday night were still raw. Then past the hand car wash, advertising for new recruits, and on to his final destination. He pushed open the unlocked metal gate, walked past the slide and the see-saw, pulled the hood of his jacket over his head, and sat down on the bench in the children's playground, brushing an empty crisp packet on to the ground. This would be where he would do his thinking. Don't ask why.

By any standards, you'd have to think that the bus ride home on Saturday night was an unusual one. The most unusual bus-ride ever. A rocket to the moon. In the blink of an eye, or the few seconds it took to flick through some screens on a smart-phone, his life had changed. Fate. Predetermination. Somebody sneezes in Africa and a sink hole appears in Wakefield. Well, there must have been a lot of sneezing going on in Uganda, because it really was £83,509.

When he'd got home last night, he'd sat at the kitchen table, with yet another cup of tea in front of him. He'd stared at the screen. It was a kaleidoscope of unintelligible opportunities. Super Saturday Price Boost. In Play Enhanced Accumulator. Bet-Happy Vegas. Bet-Happy Double Casino. He'd logged out of the Bet-Happy app, then logged back in again, and the result was the same. Over £83,000 sitting in his account. He'd phoned the helpline number that he'd eventually found somewhere on the website. He'd spoken to Bernadette in a call centre in Dundee. It was true. She congratulated him. She veered off the script. Said it was the first time that she could remember a virgin punter as she called him, having a win as big as that, and she'd worked for Ladbrokes for nineteen years before joining Bet-Happy. Explained that was how an accumulator worked. The odds doubled up and doubled up again. All eight teams had to win, and all eight teams had won. She asked him how he'd decided on the teams. Was he a keen fan or was it just guesswork? He'd said it was guesswork. He didn't mention Samantha. She asked him if he was married, or was he available. He'd said he was happily married, and in his head he thought, only just. She said she was available. Then he'd said goodbye to Bernadette. He'd ordered a takeaway pizza, rather than a Chinese. He'd splashed out £1.99 on extra topping. He'd tried to ring Dawn, but she hadn't answered. He wasn't sure what he would have said to her anyway. He tried to ring Paul, but he hadn't answered either, and George wasn't sure what he would have said to him. And after he'd eaten the pizza, he'd simply gone to bed. He couldn't think of what else to do.

And now here he was sitting on a bench in a children's playground at just after six o'clock on a Sunday morning, with at least an hour and a half to go before it got light. He felt in the outside pockets of the ski jacket. There was one glove. It fitted onto his right hand. That was one hand a bit warmer. He rummaged around in the inside pocket, pulled out a ten-year-old receipt for a lift pass, and a liquorice allsort. The one with pink coconut on. He ate it despite the fluff.

So, what was the big picture view? How was it going to change his life? £17,000 from HG. £83,000 from Bet-Happy. £100,000 in total. A peculiarly nice round number. Pre-ordained almost. More money than he'd ever seen in his life before. Money that had just dropped into his lap. Pennies from heaven. Life changing. But didn't all the lottery winners end up getting divorced, have to move house because the neighbours hated them? His mother told him about a woman from Leeds who'd had a massive win on the football pools in the early sixties. Equivalent to millions today. Said she was going to 'spend, spend, spend'. It all went horribly wrong. Broken marriages, alcoholism. All the money disappeared.

Well, this wasn't that sort of money. Not enough to retire on. Not enough to buy a yacht. Not that he wanted to buy a yacht. Although he'd always fancied a speedboat. But it was enough to make a difference. He could pay off the credit card bills. He could pay off the mortgage. Stick that in your pipe Derek Pearson. It would give him security, that was the main thing, a cushion, some flexibility.

Another car drove by. A small bird hopped past. A nightingale was the only bird that he could think of that came out at night, apart from owls. A nightingale sang in Berkeley Square. This was hardly Mayfair.

What about Dawn? How would this change things? Surely it was a positive. New opportunities would open up. A new lease of life for their marriage. A turning point. Fix the conservatory. Go on an expensive holiday. Buy a new bedroom carpet. Pay an electrician to fix the outside light. Help Paul with a deposit to buy a new flat. But would Dawn see it that way? How many times had she told him about what she'd seen at work – people getting into debt with online gaming. It could bring misery to people's lives. She'd be angry with him. See it as a betrayal.

As the bird hopped back the other way, a darker thought crept into his mind. What if getting her hands on half of the money, gave Dawn the financial clout to leave him? It could be a threat not opportunity. She could get divorced, hook up with Derek, and pay off Derek's credit card bills as a mark of her love. He saw an awful vision of Dawn and Derek lying on a bed in a hotel suite, drinking champagne, running their fingers through a pile of twenty-pound notes, toasting him, laughing at him. No, no. For God's sake stop it. Banish those thoughts George. Dawn isn't like that. She doesn't think that way. You might do. But she doesn't. She's your wife, you still love her. You want a second chance. This could be it.

He stood up, stretched his legs, and looked hopefully up at the sky. There was not the slightest sign of light yet. His friend the bird had disappeared, he was cold and needed the toilet. He took the single glove off, relieved himself in some bushes at the edge of the park, and then put the glove back on the other hand, pushing his little finger in the space for the thumb. To balance out the cold hands.

He started to walk back the way he came, passing the same landmarks. One car, and a cyclist with no lights passed him. He had to think this through very carefully. Especially with the perilous state of his marriage. There were a few problems. Samantha Pena had set this up for him. It was her work. She'd joked that she'd take a cut of the winnings. There weren't supposed to be any winnings. It was just a bit of fun. Except now it had got all serious. What was his opening line going to be to her on Monday morning? His boss for one more week. She'd had him made redundant, but then won him a pile of money. What was she going to say to him? That would wait.

But what should he tell Dawn? This was the tricky thing. It might help if he could just keep it quiet for a bit. Give himself time to think. See how things worked out. That might be the best option. But not leave £83,000 sitting in Bet-Happy pockets. He wanted to close the account, take the money and walk away. No more bets. No handing money back to the thieving gaming company, despite the friendly lady in Dundee.

His feet were cold now, and there was a blister building on his right heel. He should have put some socks on. His legs were even colder. He reached down and felt his pyjama bottoms with his gloveless hand, as he was still walking. There were droplets of moisture building. He carried on walking and carried on thinking.

He wanted to extract the money and park it somewhere. The £25 to open the Bet-Happy account had come from his sole account, not the joint account. So that Dawn wouldn't ask any awkward questions. They had the joint account for paying the mortgage and bills. Both their salaries went into that. Then he had an old account that he sometimes used for other things. Dawn knew about it. She had her own account as well. It was no big deal. Except it would be if you used it to hide £83,000. But it wasn't hiding it. He'd tell her about it, eventually. He'd got another old building society account somewhere that he hadn't used in years. His mother had set it up for him when he was sixteen. In fact, there might be two accounts at two different banks. So, transfer the £83,000 out of Bet-Happy into the sole account, then transfer that out to the two savings accounts – £40,000 to each, leaving £3,000 in the sole account. That would work.

He was turning back into Sycamore Meadows now, on the home stretch despite having lost all feeling in his feet, wondering why he'd embarked on this route march in the dark. His thoughts turned to Dawn and the gas fire. Why was he bothering with this elaborate deception with the money? He'd just tell her face to face when she got back on Monday. That was settled, and it wasn't seven o'clock yet. He'd get home, put the fire on, and find something for breakfast. He might even go to Tesco later this morning to do a massive shop to make sure the fridge was well stocked when Dawn got back tomorrow. George Stephenson, man of substance, and thoughtful husband.

With his head down, deep in thought, talking to himself, he hardly noticed Bernard and Lucy walking towards him.

"Morning George. Seems like we both couldn't sleep."

George looked up, then looked down at his wellies, pyjamas, and dressing gown, but eventually answered.

"Oh, morning Bernard. You're right. I woke up really early. I guess I'm missing Dawn, she's away for the weekend. So I went out for a walk. Bit of a stupid idea really. I should have got dressed properly."

"It's difficult for me to sleep just about every night George. Too many memories, too many ghosts."

Bernard walked past without saying any more.

Monday 13 November

Chapter 17

"She's had it all cut off. It's short now. Darker colour as well. The wife says it'll be more manageable. Less work in the morning. It used to be called a Mary Quant. Iconic apparently. 1960s again."

He was going to miss this. Tommo's commentary as you walked into the reception area. Particularly the reviews of Samantha's hairstyle switches.

Tommo continued, not waiting for a reply.

"Perhaps she wants to give him plenty of variety. Keep him keen. Bob the builder. The new chap."

"Thanks for the update Tommo. I'll look out for it."

Or splashing out some of her winnings from Saturday thought George. What if she'd bet twice as much, or ten times as much? She might be handing in her notice as we speak.

"Didn't see if she had a mini skirt on though. You know, 1960's style. But she had a new coat. Full length. Navy blue. Cashmere I'd say. Not cheap. And shoes to match."

George was wondering whether Tommo had spent any time as a correspondent on a hair and beauty magazine.

"What about her skin tone Tommo. Do you think she's switched moisturiser as well?"

"Because she's worth it you mean?"

George smiled back and started to walk past, but Geoff Thompson hadn't finished yet.

"The other one's not in again today. Old Lindy Lou. London again. Back in tomorrow though. You'd better see her before you go. That's my advice."

It was probably good advice. From an old hand. But George was set on an avoidance strategy for Linda this week. His last week at HG. He'd walk out the building on

Friday afternoon, and never come back. That was quite a thought.

He was about to reply to Tommo when he heard a beep on his phone. He looked down to see a text message from Bill Parkinson about the job opportunity. Could they bring the interview forward to Wednesday afternoon? They were looking for a candidate who could start right away. They seemed keen, very keen. Desperate almost. That was the sort of employer that suited him best. £100,000 and stroll into a new job. Unopposed. It could happen. You just need to hang on to Dawn now.

George didn't reply straight away. Best not to look too eager. He promised Tommo that he'd pop down and have a chat later, then went up to his desk, made a leisurely cup of coffee, then replied to Bill Parkinson. Parky, that's what he'd call him. It was all arranged. Two o'clock on Wednesday afternoon.

Feeling a bit of momentum, like the world was mysteriously turning in his favour, he took another positive step forward. He could meet Paul after the interview. Try to find out if there really was something wrong or not. He'd suggest the old pub on the corner near Paul's work. George could remember it from his student days. If he allowed two hours for the interview and the tests and everything, and a half hour drive from the interview to Paul's work, he could be there by five, easily. He'd buy Paul a meal in the pub, then drive back to Leeds. He quickly fired off a message. He scrolled through the other messages. It was a long time since Paul had replied to anything. But it was difficult to see how he could avoid replying to this one – a specific time and place to meet. He waited for a response, but there was nothing. Give it time, he thought.

So here he was, sitting at his desk, with nothing to do really. It was ten in the morning, he'd got to work a lot later than usual, and he hadn't bothered to switch his computer on yet. He was thinking about Samantha and the bet. Intrigued by Geoff Thompson's description. Would she come and see him, or should he go and see her? Should he just say nothing, completely ignore what had happened?

George Stephenson – man of action. It was a new persona for him, even if not fully formed. He was strolling up to Samantha's work space. She didn't just have a desk. She had a workspace, on the top floor, with a larger desk, a leather swivel chair, a round meeting table, three chairs (one was missing), and a corporate rubber plant in a brown pot – apparently you got that above a certain grade. She looked up as he approached, smiled as she removed the expensive sunglasses, and stood up to greet him. Briefly looking round to make sure nobody was watching or listening in. She spoke in a slightly hushed tone.

"Georgie boy, how are you today?"

She'd never called him Georgie boy before. Nobody had.

"All the better for seeing you Samantha."

"I bet you say that to all the girls George."

This was an unusual exchange of greetings between master and servant. Boss and subordinate. She really did look very smart. The new hair-do and the expensive clothes. It wasn't a mini dress. But it was above the knee. There were some very stylish new earrings as well. She'd look better without the sunglasses though, however expensive they were. She looked sinister, and it was November. For a second he wondered why he hadn't been out on Sunday updating his wardrobe. He could be standing here now in a black Armani suit, hair remodelled and slicked back, Ray-Ban sunglasses, dealing in international espionage. He'd like to see the look on Dawn's face.

"Sit down George."

They sat at the round table. She asked Monika to bring them some coffee. Maybe Monika had been in on the bet as well. She was smiling, but she was always smiling.

"Well, I hope that's helped you out a bit George. You might have lost your job, but that should be a nice little financial boost. You didn't cash out before the end did you? I hope you got the full benefit."

He had only the vaguest idea of what cashing out meant, but he explained that he hadn't, so he'd got the full value. Samantha seemed to know what that added up to. She didn't reveal how much she'd won, and it would have been ungentlemanly to ask.

She carried on as Monika put the coffees on the table. "I was only joking about me taking a commission on the winnings George. It's all yours, enjoy", sounding like a waitress who'd just delivered the main course. At that point there was an unnerving sound of cannons. Tchaikovsky's 1812 overture. One of the few pieces of classical music that he recognised. The Russian defence against Napoleon. Samantha's new ringtone. She looked at the screen, announced "It's Bud, I'd better take this", and walked off. George was left sitting there wondering whether to wait for her to return or simply retreat, like Napoleon.

Then a beep. His own phone. A text message from Paul. At last. And it was good news. He was fine to meet up on Wednesday. Could you tell from a text whether everything was OK? It was a neutral reply, there was no mention of trauma or disaster. Without any real basis in fact, George concluded that Paul was fine. And the meeting up was some good news to give to Dawn when he saw her this evening. He'd tell her about Paul, and he'd tell her about the money. Samantha had disappeared into a meeting room, and he felt that they'd drawn things to a conclusion anyway, so he set off back downstairs to his own desk, grinning back at Monika as he left.

*

He was due to meet Angel at some stage this morning, but when he eventually looked at his e-mails, she'd asked him to move the meeting until three this afternoon. That was fine. It meant he had nothing to do this morning. That was even better. He decided that lunchtime started at eleven thirty, and at eleven twenty he left the office on his mission to track down the old building society accounts. He'd brought all the documents with him that he could think of. Old bank statements, passport, drivers licence, two utility bills with his name on, HMRC letters to their home address, payslip with national insurance number, and a lock of Jesus' hair just in case.

He went into Santander first. The new home of the old Bradford and Bingley building society. There was a greeter waiting to greet him, showed him to a sofa, sat down with him, with an iPad. She was called Adeeba – she had a badge to prove it. Adeeba was very efficient, and he'd brought the right documents along. They found the old bank account. They'd update all the records, but that would take twenty-four hours so he'd need to call back tomorrow. They'd also get the new savings account up and running. No problem said George, hinting that he had some 'significant amounts' to transfer in. He played it cool. George Stephenson was the sort of man dealing with such amounts now, restructuring his portfolio. She asked him if he wanted to speak to their financial adviser. He declined. Said he already had one that he'd been working with for a number of years. Based in Guernsey for tax reasons. The lies flowed off his tongue.

It wasn't quite as straightforward at the Halifax. New home of the old Leeds Permanent building society. There was still the greeter (the badge said Laura), and the sofa. But you needed an appointment. You couldn't just stroll in and speak to somebody. Luckily, there was a free appointment at two this afternoon due to a cancellation. So, they booked him in.

That meant it was going to be a very long lunch hour, but he'd have enough time to get back for his meeting with Angel. He whiled away the extra hour in Smiths looking at some music magazines, and then went to the expensive sandwich shop. With his new-found wealth he decided to splash out – £4.99 for rare beef and horseradish, and £1.75

for a bottle of posh lemonade, made from freshly-squeezed lemons. Spending that much on lunch didn't come easily to him, but maybe he'd get used to it. At two o'clock he went back to the Halifax. Laura took him into a cubicle where they could be more private. It was a similar routine to earlier. It was all there, but he'd need to come back tomorrow. And with his hints of moving significant amounts of money in, they insisted on him seeing a financial adviser. He gave in, ignoring his imaginary chum in Guernsey, and made the appointment for twelve-thirty tomorrow, with Roger, one of their more senior advisors. Boy, he was making lots of new friends, and his horizons were being opened up.

By now it was nearly twenty to three, so over three hours for lunch. That was more like it. He managed to get back to the office and rush into the meeting room at two minutes past three with his pile of papers. He was sweating, flustered, and ill-prepared, after the lunchtime excitement. Angel was sitting there – beautiful, serene, completely in control.

"Hello George. Sorry I asked you to rearrange the meeting. Is it still convenient for you? You look as though you've got a lot on. I hope you haven't had to completely reschedule your day. Are you sure you're feeling well? Can I get you a glass of water?"

"I'm fine thanks," he replied, embarrassed by her concern, "Did you have a good weekend? Did you manage to go out? I hope you weren't stuck in the hotel working all the time. You need some fun."

He felt amused at himself. On reflection, Angel Wei probably didn't need any advice from George Stephenson on how to run her life. She was making a pretty good job of it without his guidance. He wondered if there was a gentleman friend somewhere in the background. Even though she wasn't wearing a ring. Perhaps a rich American investment banker that she'd met at Harvard. Or a Chinese property magnate with a London residence in Belgravia.

"I had a good weekend thank you George. I met up with some relatives on Saturday night. I have a cousin at the university, and another cousin who's visiting. How about you?"

Well, I got totally pissed on Friday night, couldn't remember getting home. Got a new suit on Saturday afternoon, then won eighty-three grand from those sharks at Bet-Happy. Not a bad weekend really.

"A bit quiet, but I've got an interview for a new job on Wednesday."

"That's great George, I'm sure you'll be a strong candidate."

She was just too nice, so supportive, so respectful. They spent an hour and a half going through more detail on the project. She'd said she wanted to discuss people issues. If he'd been more insightful, and learned something over the last twenty-five years, he'd have avoided criticising everybody in sight. But he wasn't, and he hadn't, and he didn't. So the session ended up as a catalogue of grumbles and complaints. Even George felt embarrassed with himself at the end, but still Angel didn't judge him. He couldn't help making comparisons. Samantha judged him. Anna judged him. Dawn judged him. God knows what Linda thought of him.

They walked out of the meeting room at just after four thirty. He found himself brushing against Angel as they stepped into the corridor. He was very close to her, and sensed a very slight fraying at the edges. Hardly noticeable though.

*

Looking at Dawn that evening, he saw the same fraying at the edges, more noticeable in his wife. He was sitting opposite her at the kitchen table. He hadn't seen her since Friday morning, and it felt so good to have her back in the house. When he'd kissed her on the cheek as they said hello, his nose and lips had brushed against her hair. He'd felt the softness and he'd smelt the different shampoo. It must have been from the hotel. His fingertips had touched her waist. She hadn't pulled away. But what were those big brown eyes telling him? He sensed she'd gone away with Sandra to review her options, to make a momentous decision about the future. Was she about to deliver the result?

"It's nice to see you. Did you enjoy the weekend?"

"It was good George. We enjoyed it."

That was it. Not a lot of verbal inter-connection from either side. But from her eyes, he could tell that it was still a 'don't know'. He was still in limbo. Or was it purgatory? It was a bit too soon, but he decided to play his trump card.

"I've been in touch with Paul. He seems OK. I'm meeting him on Wednesday. I've got an interview for a job in Hull. It seems promising. I'll meet him after the interview."

She smiled ever so slightly. There was a bit of a thaw.

"That's great news George. I mean the interview and meeting Paul. Do you think he's alright? I'm still worried about him."

"I only swapped texts with him. But I'll see him on Wednesday."

"I'll get us some tea George. I saw that you went to the supermarket. I've never seen the fridge so full. I didn't realise they sold fresh calamari at Tesco. You got the garlic mayonnaise and lemon juice as well. Thank you."

His inner voice spoke to him. Tell her about the money now George. Do it. This is the moment. There's some positive vibes there. She just smiled at you. Tell her about the money now, or the moment will be lost.

"I'll just go and sort out a few papers, ready for the interview. Get things straight. Then I'll come down and give you a hand."

He did sort out a few papers. He did come down and give her a hand. They ate their tea. He did the washing up. They watched a bit of TV, and they went to bed. Went to sleep.

Things didn't seem so bad after all. But George didn't tell Dawn about the £83,000. Why the hell not, he thought to himself as he lay in bed. It would have been so easy. It was the right thing. But his inner voice was right. The moment had gone now. He could do it tomorrow, but he knew that was unlikely. From now on, if he did tell her, or if she found out, there would always be the question. Why didn't you tell me George? Didn't you trust me? Did you think I'd try to steal it? And he wouldn't be able to give a proper answer.

Chapter 18

About fifty miles away, at nearly midnight, Danni was also listening to her inner voice. As she looked up at the tiny attic window, she knew there was only a fifty/fifty chance that he would be in there. And there was only a fifty/fifty chance that somebody would open the front door and let her in. And if she managed to get in, what were the chances of her having the courage to confront him. And if she confronted him, what were the chances of him changing his mind in any way. All of that added up to pretty long odds. About the same odds as what had happened in Spain, maybe.

This was Stag's awful bedsit. A single room in the attic of a tall three-storey house. There was a huge tree, roots overflowing from the front garden, protruding through the pavement. It must have been planted when this was a stylish tree-lined boulevard. About one hundred years ago. There were still some vestiges of that affluence. Like the ornamental fountain with the strange sea creatures, half-human-half-fish, blowing on shell-shaped trumpets. The water still flowed at certain times of the day. Now it was silent, the empty cans and other rubbish floating in the waters. These days, this was the sort of area where someone like Stag lived. You could only just see the attic window through the branches at the top of the tree, a few leaves left on, waiting to fall for the winter. There was a faint light flickering through the window.

She'd been here twice before, and felt physically sick both times. The second time she'd actually been sick. Out of that same attic window. You could still see some of the mess on the window frame. It churned your stomach when you went in. The rancid smell, the misery, the unwashed clothes and plates, the filthy bed. It reminded her of the dreadful places her mother had dragged them to. Her and

Walker. After Danni's father had left the scene, and after Walker's father had died. Dragged them around so that her mother, Karin, could live with a series of men. Live with them, sleep with them, drink with them, and take drugs with them. How was she supposed to get on at school, when all of that was going on? There wasn't even a table to do your homework on most of the time. Or a pen, or any paper. Let alone a laptop. All there was, was a leering man with his eyes fixed on her. A leering man that smelt bad. It was amazing that she'd managed to get five GCSEs, including an A in Maths and English. It had all fallen apart after that though. Seven years were just a blur. That's a long time for a blur. But things had got a lot better since she'd been with Paul. The tall, good looking, hopelessly drunk university student standing next to her in the club. It had been a hot night, he was wearing shorts showing off his strong sturdy thighs. He'd shouted in her ear and started a conversation. She hadn't heard a word he said, but she let him kiss her anyway. She could tell he had plenty of courage in him, as Auntie Lelia used to call it. Part of him was attracted to the trouble in her. She knew that. But not this much trouble. Not the level of trouble that Walker brought with him. Not the level of trouble that would send Paul running back to pretty, sugary sweet, safe Lucy. That would break Danni's heart.

This was the best place to try to find Walker. In her lost seven years, Walker had transformed himself from a petty criminal to someone far higher up the ranks. Still not top of the pile though. Danni hadn't worked out how he'd done it, but he'd emerged as some sort of business man. But a business man who would happily use violence when necessary. Or when not necessary. Her and her half-brother both had brains. They got that from Karin. Their mother was smart – she could have done a lot more with her life, if she hadn't hooked up with the foul-smelling men. But Walker had the brains and the darkest evil as well. She'd tried to see a good side to him, to see some chance for redemption. They shared blood after all. But it just wasn't there. It was a devil looking back at her.

They hadn't seen this devil since he'd crashed into their bedroom in the early hours of Sunday morning. She'd rolled over and buried her head under the duvet. But that didn't mean she hadn't been listening. She understood what Walker's threats were all about. They weren't threats, they were promises of action. She understood it all too well, and she'd been walking the streets today, trying to work out what to do. She must have tramped around for about ten miles, thinking so hard that her brain hurt. She'd sat on a bench on the old corporation pier, looking out onto the River Humber, searching for inspiration in the expanse of the grey-brown tidal estuary. The river didn't give up any secrets. She'd watched a seagull pick at a discarded chip. There was no moment of revelation from the seabird. All she got was the clarity of what she already knew, like a camera coming into focus. The only way to get Walker off their backs, barring divine intervention, was to give him what he wanted –the practical down-to-earth solution.

Sitting on that bench in the middle of the afternoon, hungry because she'd had no lunch and had no money with her, hands deep in her pockets for warmth, she'd watched the pilot boat guide a large container ship safely through the navigable channel. It would dock at the port further down river. There was a set course, and everybody knew where it was going.

She tried to picture where she was going. Where her and Paul were going. Tonight, next week, next month. She screwed up her eyes, and tried to conjure up a picture. Auntie Lelia had said that she had this awareness, this gift. Auntie Lelia told fortunes, read teacups, read palms, held séances if you were really brave. She came from Irish traveller stock. The sister of Danni's father's father. The father she never really knew. She'd told Danni that she, Danni, had the power as well. Danni was a young girl then. She didn't know what her auntie meant. It seemed like a game. But every now and then, she did sense things. See things. And the night Auntie Lelia died. Danni had been in the room next door. She'd seen the glow of light through the glass partition. A blindingly bright glow. The old lady passing over.

But no vision of the future came to her with her eyes screwed up, sitting on the bench that afternoon. There'd be no magic to make Walker disappear. No puff of smoke, as he turned into a toad. It was the realistic option that she'd take, and she was about to offer it to Walker. If she could manage to get into the house at midnight – you didn't just ring the bell, there wasn't a bell. You didn't book an appointment. Walker asked you to attend. You had an audience with him. By invitation only. He phoned you. You weren't supposed to call him. He had a range of business premises to choose from, including Paul's flat – not through their choice, Stag's flat, and the Alabama Authentic Dixy-fried Chicken Shack (tradesman's entrance).

But tonight, she was in luck. The front door opened. The thinnest man she'd ever seen walked out of the door. He was from one of the other flats. She'd seen him once before. It was an icy cold night, she had her long black coat buttoned up to the top, but he wore only a black T-shirt, black drainpipe jeans, and red plastic sandals, no socks. He saw her, didn't say a word, and looked straight away again as he walked off with his long white arms clasped around his chest for a bit more warmth. But he left the front door open.

She slipped inside, paused in the hall way, and leant her back against the wall, taking a few deep breaths to steady her nerves. Perhaps this wasn't such a great idea after all. You never knew how he was going to react. She took her phone out, and checked for any new messages. Perhaps there'd be some communication from on high with an alternative solution. There were no messages from on high, and strangely, no messages from Rachel. The last one was from a week last Saturday, 4th November, at 23.58.

"I'm planning on coming to the UK the week after next. I'll be back for a few weeks, so let's make sure you and I meet up, just the two of us."

Danni, had replied straight away.

"Great. Let me know when you've booked your flight."

Then a few days later.

"Any news on the flight? Let me know."

But no reply. Nothing.

Well, she had other things to sort out now. The hesitation was over. She'd stick to her plan. She ran quickly up three flights of stairs, and was now standing outside the door into Stag's bedsit. Her heart was pounding, not just because she'd run up the stairs, but because she could hear Walker's voice inside, shouting, angry. This was not a good time, but the odds had narrowed. She'd got in the front door, Walker was in the bed-sit, and she was going in, however frightened she was. She knocked on the door, and within a few seconds, Stag opened the door and let her in.

159

Tuesday 14 November

Chapter 19

There was not a lot to do at work now. Angel had everything she needed from George on the project. He had nothing left to give. Not that he'd given too much in the first place. Anna had told him that the redundancy money would be transferred into his bank account on Friday, his last day. He'd managed to persuade her to cancel the competency and skills assessment with young Dominic. He'd told her that he had a bad knee. She was so impressed with the excuse that she agreed. Things had all been squared up with Samantha. They'd both had an amazing win. He hadn't seen her since she'd disappeared over the horizon into the meeting room yesterday, but judging by the hair, the clothes, and the body language, her win might have been twice as big as his. Good luck to her.

So really, he was just going through the motions at work for a few more days.

But he, and a number of the residents of Sycamore Meadows, had not been going through the motions as he set off for work this morning.

It was nearly ten o'clock when he'd started walking towards the garage. Dawn had left a lot earlier. She still had a proper job. The old lady contingent – Dorothy, Millie, and Magda (it looked as though Millie and Magda had finally made up), and the old gentlemen contingent – Bernard and Victor, and the old dog contingent – Lucy, were gathered in a conspiratorial huddle.

Dorothy elected herself as spokesman, and hurried up to George.

"George, have you heard the news?"

She didn't wait for a reply.

"It's Derek. He's been arrested."

Those words were still swirling around in his mind as he parked his car. He'd phoned Dawn as soon as Dorothy told him. George had moved on from the sheer unadulterated joy of Derek's debt problems, to blinding curiosity about what was happening, why his love rival had been carted off in a police car. He'd been magnanimous in victory when talking to Dawn, and she'd been circumspect in her explanation. But she did know what was going on. She'd expected something to happen this week. Derek really was confiding in her.

Derek hadn't been arrested. There was an investigation going on, into the Chinese bank that he worked for. A fraud investigation. Two officers from the Fraud Squad, the City of London police, were up in Leeds to take statements. Derek had a solicitor. He was going to the police station voluntarily. But there'd been some confusion about the time of the meeting. That's why the police car had turned up earlier this morning at Sycamore Meadows. Not really a dawn raid. More of an unwanted taxi service. That's what got the tongues wagging. And boy, they had been wagging. The Chinese whispers were obviously working overtime. Dorothy had looked as though she was going to wet herself with excitement. Bernard had looked nervous.

It wasn't often that the constabulary turned up at Sycamore Meadows.

Did George feel a tiny twinge of sympathy for Derek? Maybe the minutest, sub-atomic particle of pity. Only a week ago, George had waited outside his own house, in the rain, giving the omnipotent Derek the opportunity to nip out the back. Now, Derek was deep in debt, and helping the police with their enquiries, or whatever they called it. And he, George, was rolling in money, with prospects. Rise and fall. Fall and rise. Watch this space, he thought.

The Derek saga. The building epic tale. It had diverted George off his path this morning. But he'd get things back on-track. Today, was the day, to sort the money out. His plan was

162

to drive to the office mid-morning, park the car in the car park, and then walk straight into the centre of Leeds. Pick up the suit for the interview tomorrow, make sure the savings accounts were up and running, then move the money around. He still couldn't work out why he hadn't told Dawn last night about the gambling win. He'd do it this evening. He really would. He could tell her that he wanted to get the money out, then close the Bet-Happy account, then tell her about it. That would work. He'd almost sound responsible.

He locked the car, set off walking, but then saw Angel. Or rather she saw him and waved. He couldn't ignore her. It looked as though she'd just walked over from the hotel. Probably had a breakfast meeting. He couldn't imagine her having a lie in and then strolling over to the office at eleven o'clock. She trotted up, ran her fingers through her hair, and spoke to him with surprising friendliness.

"Hi George. How are you? I'm pleased I bumped into you. Do you fancy having some lunch together. I've got a meeting at two this afternoon, but I'm free up to then."

He was struggling to work this one out. She was the bright young thing, sweeping in to clear up the mess left by the aging failure – him. She mixed with the high flyers and the go-getters, not the losers. So why would she want to have lunch with him? No need to be tainted. She'd be better off having a working lunch with Armando while he was in town.

She was slightly pale and drawn. Not quite as fresh-faced as when he'd first met her last Friday. She looked as though she needed a good night's sleep. Combing her hair properly would help as well. For a moment he pictured her in the drunken dream from Friday night. The mysterious character changing into the strange creature. But he quickly banished it to a dark recess of his memory.

"I'd really like to Angel, but I need to sort things out for the interview tomorrow. I've got to pick up a new suit, and there's a few other things. I need to go into the town."

She looked genuinely disappointed, hung her head slightly. She couldn't possibly, well, find him attractive could she? No, that was ridiculous. There'd be a queue of investment bankers waiting round the corner.

"How about Thursday Angel? We could go to the Greek restaurant. It's only ten minutes away. I could let you know how the interview went. Go through any last points on the project."

"Oh, that would be fantastic George. There's a few things I'd like to get your advice on. Not work. A few personal things."

It was a business lunch with a work colleague, that's all. Not a date with an attractive twenty-seven-year-old. It was understandable why she'd want to draw on his vast experience. To give his advice on personal matters. A man of his standing. Completely reasonable.

"I'll meet you in reception on Thursday at twelve," he said with assurance. This sort of thing happens all the time.

"Great, George. And good luck for tomorrow. I hope it goes well."

She turned and walked into the office, disappearing through the revolving door. A bit of a mystery that girl, he thought.

*

The business of the day went rather well. He picked up the suit, tried it on, observed himself in the mirror. Not bad. Discount Menswear would do for now. He didn't need Mr Armani just yet. He'd work out his story in the morning – how to handle the interview. He was feeling surprisingly confident.

The savings accounts were both up and running properly. Ready for the influx of funds. The staff seemed to view him in a different light. Not exactly the hot-shot businessman, but a man of substance at least. Someone to be reckoned with. Somebody for the bank to send a Christmas card to. Well, that probably didn't happen anymore. They both wheeled out financial advisers. Both of them under thirty. Adeeba at the Halifax introduced him to Laura. She was perfectly reasonable. She had a dog called Norman, which he thought was a great name for a dog. Dawn had made no more mention of getting a dog. He listened to Laura. But Roger at Santander was a tosspot with annoying bouffant hair which he'd had coloured. A harsh description, but accurate.

George sat on a bench in the shopping centre and completed the transactions. Amazing that you could do it like this on a mobile phone. The full range of humanity walking past – some fat, some thin, some talking, some arguing, some eating a cheese sandwich, and here you are transferring tens of thousands of pounds around. He managed to extract £83,484 from Bet-Happy. He'd spoken to his friend Bernadette in Dundee again. You had to leave £25 on the account to keep it open. He explained that he didn't want to keep it open, but Bernadette said it was a load of hassle to close the account, so best just to get the money out. She was still available for romance. Then he managed to transfer £40,000 to both Santander and the Halifax. He'd phoned First Direct earlier to alert them, and he had to go through some extra security, remember more passwords, pressed more buttons on little tokens, but it had all worked in the end.

Mission accomplished. A general feeling that fate was smiling on him. A mysterious hand guiding him in the right direction. A mysterious foot tripping up Derek. If only the hand could guide him in the right direction with Dawn. But overall, sitting on that bench, George Stephenson was feeling fine with the world.

It's strange how quickly things can change. In a flash. Does the mysterious head of the mysterious hand suddenly decide that you've had enough good luck for one day? Decide that it's time to turn the tables on you. Just enough to disturb you, interrupt your chain of thought, place a few doubts in your mind.

He was walking back to work, and passed Santander bank, the bank that he'd just been in. He remembered the poster in the window. The smiling celebrity faces encouraging him to open a new account. But it was another face that caught his attention. Dawn. Walking into the same bank, strolling through the open doors, looking purposeful. She hadn't seen him. He was walking on the other side of the road. But what was she doing? Their joint account wasn't at Santander. That's why he'd transferred the money here. Anyway, the mystery could be easily solved. Just walk up to your wife and say hello. She'd probably tell you what she was doing, without you asking. You could go for a coffee together. A late lunch. How difficult could that be? There'd be a simple explanation. Something to do with her mother. Or closing an ancient bank account that she'd had as a student. On the other hand, there could be a more sinister explanation. She'd made the decision over the weekend. Now she was sorting out the detail. Renting a flat. On her own. Or with Derek, despite his financial problems. Making the most of their last few months together. Before he ended up in Alcatraz. Cream carpets everywhere, a leather settee, a minimalist kitchen, paintings on the walls, a water bed, mirrors on the bedroom ceiling.

Then, you'd better go up to her now George, stop it happening. This could be your last chance. You'll regret it if you don't do something. But in the end, indecision and procrastination won the day. Put it off. Best not to know. If you don't know the truth, there's still a chance it may never happen. Look the other way. Cross the road. Walk on by. Which he did. And by the time he'd walked on by, it was too late anyway, the moment had passed. His overriding feeling was one of relief. There'd been no awkward encounter. No difficult conversation. Actually, he was feeling relieved that Dawn hadn't spotted him in the bank an hour earlier. That could have been a lot of explaining to do.

Chapter 20

He looked at his watch. It was nearly three o'clock. No point in going back to the office, and he suddenly realised that he hadn't had any lunch. He called in to Starbucks, got himself a small Americano and another expensive sandwich, and sat by the window. He took out his phone and double-checked the transactions that he'd just completed. It was a lot of money after all. Yes, it really was all done and dusted. He sipped his coffee, breathed a deep sigh of satisfaction, and looked out the window.

Linda was looking back at him. What was it Humphrey Bogart said in *Casablanca*? 'Of all the bars in all the world'. She turned and walked in through the door.

Of course, he knew he'd have to deal with the Linda thing at some point. Just not today, this week, this lifetime. He'd deal with it in an unspecified future, at an unseen point over the horizon. The voice on his left shoulder nearly always won out. Right shoulder voice: 'do the right thing, deal with it properly'. Left shoulder voice: 'look after number one, avoid the issue.' Why hadn't he told Dawn about the money? Because he thought there might be an angle in it for him. He knew the strategy would end in tears, but he didn't seem able to change tack. Weakness and indecision would always triumph for George. Never put off until tomorrow what you can put off until the day after.

Except there was no putting this one off. The chance encounter, the cruel twist of fate. Linda was marching towards his table with a purposeful look. He briefly wondered if feigning a heart attack was an option. Clutch your chest, gasp for air, crash to the floor knocking over the coffee. Perhaps a spasm on the floor, a bit of writhing around. That would certainly liven up Starbucks. The ambulance would arrive pretty quickly, and you'd be whisked off to A&E, well away from Linda.

But he didn't, he didn't have time – Linda was only two paces away. He couldn't help noticing her red stiletto shoes. Bright scarlet, warning of danger. There was no fire escape nearby. There was no escape at all. He'd have to deal with it.

Did your life really flash in front of you in the moments before death? Hopefully he wouldn't get to find out just yet. But certainly, the calamitous times with Linda rushed through his brain as she completed the final two paces to the table. He could taste the shame on his lips. He hadn't planned it. It had just happened. But isn't that what every adulterer says – 'I never meant it to happen'. 'I never meant to hurt you'. 'It didn't mean a thing'. But how can you say all of that? Booking the Premier Inn in Rochdale doesn't just happen. You have to press some keys on a computer keyboard. Enter your credit card details. Enter the details again when you put the wrong security code in. At any point you could not complete the booking. There's even a final question, 'complete booking now?' You could not press the enter button. But he had done. He'd completed the booking. And he'd told Dawn that he was working away, that he had a business dinner, and then an early morning meeting with a supplier. He'd lied to his wife of over two decades, the mother of his only son. And he'd driven to Rochdale with Linda in the Toyota Yaris. She'd sat in the passenger seat next to him, where Dawn usually sat. How many times did he have the chance to back out of it? But he hadn't. The momentum had been unstoppable. He'd completed the act. The deed had been done. Only the paralysing shame was left.

It started after Paul went to university. The Spring term, February. He'd spotted Linda in a few meetings at work. She smiled at him. Not many people did. She was out of the 1980s. Power dressing. High heels, padded shoulders, lots of pouting, plenty of hair spray. No wedding ring. What is it the adulterer says? One thing led to another. And as one thing was leading to another, he still had opportunities to switch it off, in fact never switch it on in the first place. But he didn't take them. And the next thing he knew it was late one Tuesday afternoon, and he was driving to the Premier Inn in Rochdale, with Linda at his side, two overnight cases in the boot, and two condoms in his wallet. They weren't heading for a trendy urban boutique-style hotel in a rejuvenated marina development. They weren't even heading for a mid-range international chain with a respectable presence in the UK market. No, they were heading for a budget hotel in the north of England. He'd selected it on the basis of proximity and cost. Not too far away, but far enough. Handy for the M62. It was a Tuesday night and there was a special rate. Thirty-seven pounds, and a discount on the Harvester restaurant next door. Not a fashionable area in a resurgent city, more a beige box on the edge of a slightly faded business park. It didn't seem to bother Linda. She talked incessantly all the way driving over. She'd dressed up for the journey. Full warpaint make-up just for the short trip on the motorway. With another outfit lined up for the evening. She seemed to be looking forward to the proceedings. A night with George Stephenson.

In the reception area, there was an automatic check-in system. You put your credit card in a slot, and a key card came out. But it didn't work and they had to call over an assistant. A smiling lady, who actually said, 'Are you here on business or pleasure sir?' Linda smiled knowingly at him, but he prayed at that point for God to send a thunderbolt and set light to the Premier Inn Rochdale. To burn it to the ground, and then they could have driven home. No act of adultery would have been committed. But God didn't answer his prayer. It was something to do with free will. Taking responsibility for your own actions.

So they'd gone through with it. Getting the keys, taking their bags to the room. He'd waited downstairs while Linda got changed into a little black number. She looked good when she came downstairs, and his spirits lifted for a few minutes. But as they strolled through the light drizzle into the Harvester restaurant at seven fifteen, armed with the discount voucher, his faint hopes became fainter. It must have been running at 150% capacity, with the last throes of a children's party. A bunch of eight- or nine-year-olds visiting the ice-cream station for the free refill, hyped up to breaking point, stinging tears only a matter of time. He should have pre-booked for later in the evening. He should have booked a stylish tapas bar in the Spanish quarter with bleached oak and tarnished leather interiors and a good bottle of Rioja in the offing, but there wasn't a Spanish quarter. Only a TK Maxx one side, and a Carphone Warehouse the other. The stuff of dreams.

They'd waited over an hour for the food. The children eventually cleared off, clutching their party bags, some with tears streaming down their cheeks. Linda was undaunted, chatting merrily as if the evening was going well. She ordered jumbo haddock and chips. He thought she was joking at first, going for a comedy moment, but it was for real. The unfortunate battered fish was hanging over the plate on both sides, and there was a shovel-full of chips. It was of mammoth proportions. Did you get haddocks that big in the North Sea, or were these genetically modified in a fish farm in Romania? Why on earth would you order jumbo haddock and chips when you were on an adulterous night away? He'd watched mesmerized as she'd polished off the whole lot, except for three chips. Why did she bother to leave three chips? After what must have been 1,500 calories of food, you might as well finish the job. It was like doing a marathon and stopping five metres from the finishing line. Perhaps she was trying to demonstrate restraint.

He'd had rack of lamb. The menu was limited and he'd run out of imagination. The lamb was cooked to exhaustion. While they were waiting for the food, he'd had a pint of beer, and she'd had a gin and tonic, a large one. Another imaginative move for both of them. Then they'd finished off a bottle of Cabernet Sauvignon. He declined a pudding, but Linda had ice cream, three balls not two. All three chocolate flavour. She'd gone up to the ice cream station to fill her bowl, the same way as the eight-year-olds had. She'd drizzled some cherry sauce on the ice cream, and wolfed it down. It took four minutes. He'd timed it. Overall, it was an astonishing performance from Linda. If smoking had been allowed, he felt sure she could have slotted in an Embassy king-size as well. But defying the laws of nature, she was slim with a good figure, just turned forty, so she must have top-of-the-range metabolism.

They both declined coffee. He'd half expected her to ask for Belgian chocolates and brandy to round off the evening, but no, she must have had enough. He paid the bill, left a very modest tip, and then they headed back to room 201. He felt like a virgin honeymoon groom from the 1950s. Maybe some stirrings of anticipation but mostly an impending sense of doom. Linda, on the other hand, had a definite spring in her step. Fortified by a Christmas dinner style tuck-in, she was now ready for action. There was still no divine intervention in sight, and he knew he would have to see the process through. The moment had come.

He was about to dredge up the full horror of room 201 – the nervous fumbling, the challenge of the clasp, the untimely sneezing fit, the dampening effect of the beer and red wine, but the ultimate achievement of the task – when Linda finished the final pace to his table in Starbucks. He was still seated. She stood only inches away and placed her hands on her hips, legs slightly apart. A power pose. She peered down at him, further elevated by the stilettos.

"Well hello George, what a coincidence. Not your lucky day. I bet you didn't expect to see me here. Probably just enjoying a quiet cup of coffee."

"Hello Linda, you're looking well, as always. Can I get you a coffee? Large Americano isn't it, and would you like a chocolate muffin?"

"No George, I don't want a cup of coffee or a fucking chocolate muffin. You're so pathetic it's unbelievable, you know that don't you? You weren't going to say anything were you? You were just going to leave, without a word. That's true isn't it George? You're a snivelling little shit. You're a pile of human excrement with flies buzzing around."

He thought maybe that was going a bit too far. Momentarily he considered a cutting sarcastic response. But in that moment, common sense prevailed. He valued his life. But more than that. He knew that searing guilt hung over him. He hadn't been honest with Dawn, and he hadn't been honest with Linda. But in their 'one thing led to another' phase, he'd told Linda who was divorced, that his marriage to Dawn was over as well. That they were separated, only living in the same house for practical reasons, until it was sold. That wasn't true. Well done George, you've let two women down, not just one.

It wouldn't have been so bad if they'd both got drunk at a work Christmas party. Overcome by passion brought on too many free bottles of Prosecco, cheap cocktails, chicken supreme and chocolate mousse, and a discount rate for a room at the Marriot which worked out about the same as a taxi home. They could have both woken up in the morning, looked at each other in horror as they pieced together the events of the night before. Terrible hangover and a terrible sense of guilt, but you could blame it on the boogie, and the booze.

But this was different. It was planned, and executed. At the Premier Inn Rochdale. And what was worse, a lot worse; was that it was planned and executed again. A second time. At the Premier Inn, Sheffield. At least the second time was in a trendy part of town. There was no kids' party in the restaurant. Linda had still packed in the calories –

172

Cumberland sausage and creamy mashed potato, followed by treacle tart – and then the night in room 403. Why a second time, when he felt sick with himself the first turn around? He couldn't explain it. Just the general pathetic weakness. But they'd called it quits after the second time. Not a conscious decision, but he'd managed to avoid Linda, steered clear, avoided eye contact. Always had an excuse not to meet. That was effective, but it meant there was no clean break. No mutual decision to finish it, draw it to a close for the sake of all concerned. And that was why Linda was looming over him now, all powerful and threatening.

"I wish I'd never met you George. You're an excuse for a man. And the time in bed was unpleasant, and uncomfortable. I pity Dawn."

Although he was sitting with his head bowed, he was aware that Linda had raised her voice. Sort of shouting in a hushed tone. A stage whisper. But it was half three in the afternoon. It wasn't packed. There was no general hub-bub to drown out what she was saying. He was sure that the people at the tables around could hear her, easily work out what was going on, view his abject humiliation.

In the next few seconds he remembered the most painful moment he had experienced up to that point. It was at the dentist when he was fourteen. He had to have three teeth out in one go, so they could fit a brace to press the other teeth into the gaps. One tooth had broken as the dentist yanked it out, and the manoeuvres to extract the rest of the tooth were excruciatingly painful, even with the anaesthetic. But at the age of forty-nine, he now experienced worse pain. He'd expected mental anguish, but not physical pain. It was only one kick. But the end of Linda's right shoe connected perfectly with his left shin. It felt that she had steel toe-caps in the stilettos. There can't have been much of a backswing, but boy there was plenty of power in the forward propulsion. He actually screamed, and then clutched his shin in agony. If the people at the tables around had not worked out was going on before, they would now. He half expected some follow-up. A left uppercut to his chin, a right hook to knock him to the floor, followed by a couple of well-placed kicks to the head and groin. But she'd made her point. As he gasped for breath, she turned and walked away, opened the door and made the perfect victorious exit.

Chapter 21

Limping back to the office, he knew it was time to just get in the car and drive home. Lick your wounds and live to fight another day. Retrench and regroup. It was nearly four o'clock, darkness was starting to etch the monochrome sky, and wisps of damp mist floated in the air. The city's lights were on now. The power of electricity balancing out the onset of early evening in November. And on balance, Linda's revenge was proportionate. If this was it, he'd accept it as a fair and reasonable punishment by society. A hundred pound fine, and bound over to keep the peace for twelve months. A low-level public order offence. Urinating in a shopping arcade. Dealt with by the local magistrate, disappointed yet again by the weaknesses of his fellow human beings. Yes, if this was the end of it, he'd take it now. Where do I sign? But it might not be it. This could be the opening salvo. It could go to the Crown Court. Judged by his peers in the presence of the two women that he'd wronged. With a range of other offences taken into account. Oh dear. Just when things were going so well.

Whatever form of justice lay ahead, best to go home now, see Dawn, talk to her, connect. Find out a bit more about Derek. But don't gloat. Definitely don't gloat. Maybe find out what she was doing in the bank this afternoon. Without making it too obvious. And there's the interview tomorrow. Get your story straight. Get your brain into gear. Make a few notes. Do some research. Make sure you know the route. Have a quiet night in, and a good night's sleep.

But as he got closer to the office, the voice on his left shoulder started to whisper, got the map out, suggested a different direction, an alternative route. Like it had steered him along the M62 to Rochdale.

Why was Angel so keen to meet up for lunch? That voice had a point. She'd seemed so in control when he'd first met her. Perfectly turned out, immaculate hair and skin. Like one of those futuristic streamlined trains gliding on a cushion of air into the station, sleek and frictionless. But when he'd bumped into her this morning, things were definitely different. Troubled in some way. Looked like she'd slept in a hedge, not at the Marriot. She hadn't turned into an old diesel train labouring over the Pennines. Not yet. But she definitely looked in need of a good service and a polish. Maybe that was what was intriguing him. The vulnerability drawing him in, playing on his declining masculinity.

It only took a couple of text messages. One from him to Angel, and one back again thirty seconds later. He'd managed to limp over to the same café that they'd gone to last Friday. It closed at six, and it was empty, apart from a weather-beaten old lady holding a bad-tempered terrier on her lap. The dog snarled and displayed a set of sharp yellowing teeth to George, as a warning shot not to sit anywhere near. There was just Mr Luciano himself behind the counter, looking ready to go home. He wouldn't be belting out 'Nessun Dorma' anytime soon. A lone waitress was wiping down the tables. She didn't look up as he walked up to the counter. He'd had enough caffeine for one day, so picked up a small plastic bottle of something pink. Red berries and an exotic mix of things he'd never heard of. It promised a full cleansing de-tox. Just what he needed.

He sat at a table in the window. Hopefully he wasn't tempting fate. A second coming by Linda would overwhelm his defences. He put his coat on a chair to save it for Angel, even though there was no chance of anybody else sitting there. He checked his phone a few times. There was an e-mail from Bill Parkinson, telling him that he'd need to do some psychometric tests after the interview tomorrow. That was fine, he'd worked out the technique. The tests couldn't predict his failings. He looked at his watch. It was nearly five, and he began to think this wasn't such a great idea. Dawn would be at home. It was her half day, although she sometimes took it in the morning. He'd couldn't leave now though. He'd just have a quick drink with Angel, a quick chat, then head off. He could be back before six thirty.

He looked up and saw Angel hurrying towards the door. She spotted him, smiled bashfully, pushed the door open, and walked over to the table. A similar manoeuvre to the one performed by Linda a couple of hours earlier. His shin still hurt now. Perhaps that was why he didn't stand up to greet her. And would he have shaken her hand or kissed her on the cheek? That was always the dilemma for an Englishman. And was this a business meeting or something else?

She stood above him, continued to smile. She'd recovered some of her composure, brushed her hair, a dab of moisturiser maybe.

"Hi George, it's great to see you. I'm really glad we could meet up. Oh, you've got a bottle of something. It's very pink. But do you know what I'd really like to do?"

No, go on, tell me Angel.

"Go for a drink. I mean a proper drink. I could really do with a large glass of wine. I've had a crap afternoon, in a meeting with Armando, linked in Bud via a conference call. It's all a bit stressful at the moment. A lot going on. I'm not comfortable with it. I'll tell you about it later."

It was the word 'crap' that did it. Maybe that marked Angel's transformation from the elite to the masses, even if only a few steps down the ladder. And she wanted him to be her confidant, her trusted partner. This was a role he hadn't tried before. He put on his serious face.

"George, I spotted that bar by the river. It's Colombian. It's a bit lively out front. They had Salsa dancing when I walked past last night. But there's a quiet room at the back. We can talk there. It's less than ten minutes away."

Talk about what? Armando, Bud, and the guys? But his willpower melted in a nanosecond. He could just have a small glass of wine, and still drive home. Not be too late. Dawn wouldn't miss him for just an hour. The problem was, she might not miss him at all. That's what you're supposed to be sorting out George. But he was intrigued. Hooked. He took a hesitant sip of the pink liquid, wincing slightly at the aroma – did you get tomato scented floor cleaner? – then they walked out together.

*

It was, as Angel had predicted, only ten minutes away. The Colombian bar was in fact called Cuban Heels, but Angel explained it was a style of boot. The main bar was remarkably full at half five on a Tuesday afternoon, but at least there was no salsa dancing in sight, and as Angel had said, there was a quiet room at the back. She must have reconnoitred the place. Or perhaps she'd hit the dance floor with Armando last night. He was still in town after all.

George found himself sitting at a small table waiting for Angel to come back from the bar. She'd insisted on getting the drinks, despite his protests, and despite his £83,000 win – he hadn't told her about that, obviously. He'd said he'd have a small glass of whatever she was having. He looked around the room, self-consciously. Aware of himself as the forty-nine-year-old man sitting on his own, waiting for the twenty-seven-year-old young woman to return. The music from the noisy bar filtered in. He'd recognised it when they'd walked in. She'd been impressed and squeezed his arm. He'd swallowed hard, very hard.

There were three other couples in the room, although obviously he and Angel weren't a couple. Three young couples, probably still in their twenties looking at each other and talking, smiling, laughing, listening to what the other one was saying, touching, making eye-contact. There was animation. The body language was unmistakable. Perhaps they weren't all absolutely head-over-heels in love, but there was some electricity. That was his problem. The battery was flat and the jump leads were missing.

He worked out what had happened in his twenties. He'd met Dawn at his twenty-first birthday party. Just a few weeks after the thing he didn't talk about, but the thing he didn't stop thinking about. Dawn was nineteen. They got married four years later. There was a six-month gap in between when they split up, but they got back together and were happy. He remembered, with great clarity, being very happy on his wedding day. Hugging his mother hard, a tear in his eye. He was twenty-five. Paul was born two years later. Earlier than they'd planned, but there you go. He was twenty-seven. And what was he doing as he turned thirty? They were just getting by, that's all. Managing jobs and a three-year-old. They didn't think about body language and electricity, just about getting up and going to bed. And when he was thirty-one, Dawn had the miscarriage. He couldn't remember what he was thinking at forty-one. But here he was at forty-nine, waiting for Angel.

The couple nearest to him were luxuriating on a low-slung leather settee. The girl had looked over at them when they'd walked in. Her perfectly coloured and shaped blonde hair sat on her head like a German helmet. She spotted Angel squeeze his arm, and from that deduced that they couldn't be father and daughter, uncle and niece, it was something more complicated than that. She was looking over at George now, with disdain. Trying to work out what was going on. Wasn't that the joy of sitting in a bar or restaurant? Judging strangers. He was still being judged when Angel walked back from the bar carrying a bottle of white wine, and two large glasses. She looked at him all the way, and smiled. The lady in the German helmet carried on watching and judging. Angel sat down on the stool right next to him, and poured out two large glasses, full to the brim, as if to make a statement. Those glasses were 250 cl, which is a third of a bottle. You won't be driving home if you drink that, he thought. But he didn't say no.

Angel had drunk nearly all of her glass after less than ten minutes, and George thought it would be ungallant not to follow her blistering pace. So, he did. He'd never bothered to learn a lot about wine, but he knew this was a nice bottle of Sauvignon Blanc. And as the sharpness hit the inside of his mouth, and the alcohol started to cloud his brain, he realised very quickly that he'd gone past the point of driving home. But it could be the bus. He'd share this bottle with Angel and get the bus home. He shouldn't be too late. He looked at his watch. It was only six o'clock. He could handle it. He was enjoying himself. He wasn't doing anything wrong. Well, nothing too wrong. You couldn't go to jail for it.

Angel was talking at one hundred miles an hour now, sometimes loud, sometimes soft, waving her hands about, rolling her eyes. Describing the ups and downs of corporate life, of family life.

"Bud thinks he can just parachute me in somewhere, and sort everything out. Just because I've got an MBA from Harvard. I haven't got a magic wand George."

George was nodding a lot.

"I'm on conference calls, and Skype calls. I had a call from Chuck at midnight once."

He carried on nodding, a bit dutifully now.

"And honestly, do I trust Armando?"

Was he supposed to say yes or no?

"No. And he's got me involved in this tax scheme. I'm a director of a company in the Cayman Islands. I think it's dodgy, George."

He wondered if the Cayman Islands were next to the Isle of Man. He'd been there on holiday with his mother when he was seven. It rained a lot. Angel was definitely kicking off her corporate shoes, letting her corporate hair down, and undoing a top button. She did actually undue a top button. He watched her do it.

She picked up the bottle of wine to fill their glasses, stared at it, and then shook it.

"God, it's empty George. How did that happen?"

It's something to do with physics, he thought. By now there was no real question of George leaving and getting the bus home. So he walked to the bar and got another bottle. Twenty-seven pounds. But he was a man of means, he could afford it. For the first time in his life, he could afford twenty-seven pounds for a bottle of wine in a Cuban bar, no, a Columbian bar, without feeling worried or guilty. Well actually he was feeling a bit guilty, but not about the price of the wine. He marched back to their table, concentrating hard on walking normally and not tripping up. He just about succeeded. Then he poured out two more full glasses. Not to be outdone, right to the top. And kept topping them up when they were half full. They were on a roll.

But there was something fuzzy swirling around his head. He had to concentrate very hard to speak properly. It was quarter to seven. The quiet room was not so quiet now. He had to visit the gents. When he returned Angel was sitting at a different table, and had bought another bottle of wine. They hadn't finished the second one yet, and she'd bought number three. So, there was a bottle and a quarter of wine on the table, and two full glasses. He could order his thoughts enough to know that this could end badly.

As they progressed to the third bottle, Angel slipped from high to low. There were no more endearing smiles, no giggles, no more tossing the head. That was replaced by hunched shoulders, deep sighs, and long pauses for reflection. George stared into the distance, fixing his gaze on the picture of the South American gaucho behind the bar, to keep his thoughts just about on track.

"It's my family as well George. They are proud of me. They made sacrifices for me to go to university, to get my Masters in the US…"

She paused, as if to give herself time to remember how to speak. George willed her on, waiting expectantly for the next line.

"Yes, they are proud, but they want their pound of flesh. That's from Shakespeare, isn't it? The pound of flesh. I can't remember which play…"

She paused again, longer this time, then took a small sip of wine, wincing as she swallowed it.

"It's not Mum and Dad. It's my brothers, and those cousins. I had to meet them on Saturday night. I didn't want to, but I knew I had to. I've got to deal with all of that, and Armando as well."

There was a deep sigh.

"You're a good man George. I trust you. I know we haven't known each other long, but I trust you."

He nodded slowly, waiting for some sort of punchline.

"Actually, I feel ill George. I feel a bit sick. Can you walk me back to the hotel? I'm drunk."

That was an understatement, he thought.

*

George didn't get the bus home after the drinking session with Angel. He walked her back to the hotel, and although he was very drunk, he knew that Angel was even drunker. Everything is relative. In the kingdom of the blind the one-eyed man is king – so he used his good eye to guide her through the streets of Leeds, interlocking his arm with hers, steadying her when she stumbled down kerbs, and then gently steering her into the hotel reception. The receptionist was only mildly alarmed. She'd obviously seen it all before, but she did look up from her papers and smiled diplomatically.

Angel asked him if he'd help her to her room. She eventually found the key card in her handbag, in the small paper holder with the room number written on in pen. She dropped it on the floor. It fell near her left foot. He bent to pick it up, and saw the simple flat black shoe, matt not shiny. He saw the beautiful small foot and ankle, in close-up, the ribbed black tights. In that moment, he wanted his fingers to very gently touch her ankle. But through the dizzying haze of alcohol, he managed to muster just enough self-control to avert the disaster that would inevitably have followed. They managed to get in the lift together, and stumble along the corridor to the room. Room 201. The same room number as the one in the Premier Inn Rochdale with Linda. He'd noticed it when he'd picked up the key card, when he'd looked at her ankle. Same room number, but what a contrast in shoes. Linda's glitzy black stilettos, Angel's stylishly understated flat shoes. He managed to guide her into the room, without really setting foot in it. He held the door open, and leaned her against the wall inside.

She smiled and put her hand on his shoulder.

"Thank you George, thank you."

"Goodnight Angel. Take care."

Was this the epiphany? He could have gone into the room, courted disaster, but resisted. Finally showed some self-control and maturity. Not yet. Some more water needed to flow under the bridge.

As he strolled past the receptionist downstairs, she looked up again, perhaps surprised to see him. He said goodnight to her as well.

And now, after jumping in the first taxi outside the station, he was putting the key in the lock of his house. It was still only nine o'clock, but it felt like he'd been away a week. The lights were on inside, and Dawn was at home. He pushed the door open, tripped over the step, and for added comedy value, started to hiccup as he said hello.

Dawn had heard the key turning, and was waiting in the hall. She looked him up and down.

"Hello George, you're drunk aren't you?"

After nearly twenty-five years, Dawn could certainly tell when he was drunk. Anyway, he was very drunk.

"A leaving do I suppose George? Well, you're entitled to that."

He was surprised to find Dawn so accommodating, but that was welcome. She had a strange look on her face.

Something on her mind. Something she wanted to talk about. But she'd looked like that for the last couple of years. He wasn't in any state for a heart-to-heart now, this evening. Best to make a tactical withdrawal.

He concentrated hard to get his words in the right order, and spoke slowly and deliberately.

"Thanks, I did have too much to drink, way too much. Sorry, sorry about that. You're right, a small leaving do. I got a taxi home. I'll get the bus in tomorrow morning. Pick up the car and then drive over to Hull for the interview. I'm meeting Paul, remember. I'll do some preparation in the morning. Hic. Sorry. For the interview, I mean. I think I'd better go to bed now."

He'd got the words in the right order. Just about. He managed to get up the stairs without stumbling, and without Dawn pressing him anymore. He knew she was watching him, something churning around in her mind. Maybe it was about Derek. Whatever it was, it didn't look trivial. It hadn't looked trivial for a long while. He was hungry but didn't want to clatter around in the kitchen trying to get something to eat, dragging pans out of drawers, opening tins, sawing up bread, cutting into blocks of cheese, giving her the opportunity to say what she wanted to say. He closed the bedroom door quietly, managed to get undressed and crawl into bed without any crashing around. The evening hadn't ended in disaster after all.

*

The evening hadn't finished though. Dawn did have something to tell him. Some life-changing news. She'd planned to tell him as soon as he got back from work. Straight away. Sit him down and tell him. George coming in drunk, hours late, had thrown her of course. But she was still going to tell him. Tonight.

Chapter 22

She sat at the bottom of the stairs, pulled her knees up and hugged them, catching sight of the dust on the skirting board. She ran her finger through it, marking a clear path. She heard him get into bed. She knew that he'd tried to do it quietly, but there was a spring at his side of the mattress which always squeaked.

She'd been agonising over her and George for too long. It was wearing her down. The weekend had not thrown up any easy answers because there weren't any easy answers. She'd make her final decision in the next few days and stick to it.

But yesterday morning had thrown up another difficult decision. And on this one she'd made up her mind, and put it into practice, despite the pangs of guilt. Because it opened up more opportunities for her. It didn't mean that she was definitely going to leave George, but it did make it easier if she decided to.

The other thing. The thing that happened a few hours ago. The thing that she was going to tell him about tonight, was a lot, lot bigger.

It had started without any mystery. Simply picking up the post late Monday morning. She'd got back from the weekend in Harrogate at about eleven o'clock. The weekend away that was supposed to sort everything out, and ended up sorting nothing out. The only thing she had to show for it was the graze on one side of her forehead. There was a bit of bruising as well – she could just about hide it by brushing her hair forward, and angling her head slightly. Only one person had noticed it at work today, and Dawn had joked that she'd bashed her head opening a kitchen cupboard. It was just about believable.

There had been three items of post on the mat yesterday, just inside the front door.

The first was a stylish clothes catalogue with her name on it. She flicked through it and then tossed it in the bin. The models just got younger, more attractive, and slimmer. She'd singled out Annabel on the front cover for particular disdain. But it wasn't Annabel's fault that she was perfect. She was a model. It was her job to look like that. She might have troubles of her own. Perhaps Annabel was thinking of despatching her boyfriend, because he'd been sleeping with Paulette on pages seven, fifteen, and eighteen. Perhaps Annabel had fallen over drunk on Friday night, with bruising around her left eye, and cheekbone. Stared in the mirror on Saturday morning, worrying about whether make-up could cover up the purple tinge or whether her modelling career was on hold. Paulette could steam in and be on the cover of the next edition.

The second was a letter for George with the logo of an online gambling company on the front. This one was Bet-Happy, but there were lots of others. Dawn had a particular dislike of these organisations. It was too easy to gamble away your wages on a computer screen or a smart phone. Such a lonely death as well. They spent plenty of time at work trying to sort out the results of online gaming. Strange that Bet-Happy was still sending marketing material by post. At least George didn't have that vice, gambling that is. He had enough of the other vices without having to add that one. Dawn ripped up the envelope and threw it in the bin as well.

Then there was the letter addressed to her from Lloyds bank. Not their bank. She suspected it was more marketing material, and was about to throw that in the bin as well. But then the well-rooted deference to banks kicked in. There might be something important in there. So, almost reluctantly, she opened the letter without paying too much attention. As she extracted the contents, one thing caught her eye straight away – a cheque, made payable to her, just to her, not to both of them. For £7,483. There was a letter as well, addressed to both of them. She walked into the kitchen, sat at the table, and put the letter in front of her, next to the cheque, and read the letter. Compensation for Payment Protection Insurance mis-selling, and endowment mis-selling as well, with interest. She paused at that point, letting it sink in. Then she continued. They'd rejected the original endowment claim, but then when reviewing the PPI documentation, decided that the endowment claim was valid after all, as well as the PPI claim. Please find enclosed a cheque for £7,483 as full settlement. George and Dawn had their mortgage on the previous house with Lloyds, and a personal loan as well. She stared at the cheque again, read the letter again, and again. She remembered them putting in a claim, but that was a long time ago. It had only been the pestering phone calls and e-mails and text messages from claims companies that had prompted them to do it. George had started the process, but as usual, lost interest. She'd found all the old paperwork, filled in the forms, sent them off. Basically, done all of the work. She'd spent a full weekend on it. More than that. She remembered the original rejection of the endowment claim, and basically gave up at that point.

It must be a simple mistake, a clerical error. The mortgage was in joint names, the house was in joint names, the personal loan was in joint names, but the cheque was only payable to her, not to both of them. Mrs Dawn Louise Stephenson.

The dilemma lay on the kitchen table. She walked three times round the kitchen. It didn't take long. After the final lap she turned off into the utility room and saw Polonius. George thought that she didn't have a relationship with the bird. But she did. That was another thing her husband got wrong.

"Well Polonius, this is the choice. Tell George about the cheque, and pay it into the joint account. Full disclosure. It's the right thing to do. The money belongs to both of us. Or there is an alternative. Pay the cheque into that old account at Santander. The one just in my name. I did all the work. I deserve it. I could do that, and still tell him about it later. Depending on the other really big decision. What do you think?"

The African grey was non-committal. It had obligations to both of them. It didn't want to choose. But Dawn had already chosen Alternative B. Logically, it kept more options open. She might be able to afford something better than the flat she'd seen on Saturday morning. Avoid an avocado bathroom suite, and the smell of drains. It was the less honest option, but she'd square that with her conscience later. She picked the expensive clothes catalogue out of the bin and ordered the stylish cream winter coat that Annabel wore on page six.

That was yesterday. When she'd woken up this morning, she hadn't changed her mind. In fact, her resolve had hardened. When George came home last night, when they were re-united after her long weekend away, she felt there was something he wasn't telling her about. There was always a secretive side to him. Perhaps not secretive, more that he never opened up. Bottled it all up, kept it to himself. Thought that he could sort things out, didn't want to ask for help, thought that would be a sign of weakness, not what a man should do. She'd come to accept that. She was never going to change it. She'd have to live with it. Or not. But there was a difference between not opening up, and purposefully not telling her something really important. It wasn't quite outright lying, but it was close to it. That's what it was last night. Nothing to do with his guilt about poor old Linda. Something else. There were three giveaway signs. She could always tell.

He rubbed his neck, at the left-hand side, just below his ear. It went slightly red with the rubbing. That was the first sign. The second was the looking away every time she looked at him. He would only look at her for a second, and then look away. He only did that when he had something to hide. And the third thing was saying that he had to go upstairs or go into another room, to sort something out. He'd done that last night, said that he had to go and sort some papers out ready for his interview. She knew that he hadn't sorted any papers out – he wouldn't prepare for the interview until the last minute.

So that sealed it. There was something he wasn't telling her about, and there'd be something she didn't tell him about. That's why she strolled into Santander this afternoon with the cheque and the paying-in book in her handbag. It had taken her a while to find the paying-in book, but it had turned up. It was a strange feeling, she felt a sense of elation, of opportunities opening up. But at the same time, the feeling of guilt was definitely there. And then the strangest thing of all. A feeling that she was being watched. As though somebody was observing her, and judging her. But she'd managed to banish the thought, walked in, and did the deed. She even used the automated paying-in machine. It worked first time, and she had a receipt with a grainy picture of the cheque and paying-in slip as proof.

*

But all of that, the secretive banking operations, were put into the shade by what happened when she got home this afternoon. It was Tuesday, her half day. She'd used it to go to the bank, and got home about four o'clock. There was a letter waiting on the doormat. Letters were supposed to be dying out in the digital age. She couldn't remember how the timings of the post worked, but there it was. A white envelope, addressed to George, handwritten in very neat handwriting, with a fountain pen. The letter G was written with a flourish.

She wasn't sure what made her open it. It wasn't a mistake. It was clearly addressed to George. There was no reason to think it was anything suspicious. Although, most envelopes were printed. They were from the bank, or

HMRC, or the electricity company. Maybe that was it – because it was handwritten. But it could have been from the window cleaner. George arranged that. Or from the paper shop. Or the chap who came round to give them a quote to fix the conservatory.

But for some reason, she'd decided it was something very personal, and something else that George was keeping from her. Maybe it was the thing he didn't tell her about last night. It wouldn't be from Linda. She'd been spurned, cast aside. Linda would confront him at work if there was anything left to say. Without any obvious reasoning, the curious feeling settled on her that this letter was from someone far deeper in George's past. It didn't take her long to find out. She'd opened it, not even carefully. The envelope was torn, and there was no going back. She'd read the letter. Then she'd sat down. Then she'd cried. And for the next five hours, she'd thought about what on earth she would say to George.

And when he came in drunk, she did think twice about whether this was the right time to tell him. But now, sitting at the bottom of the stairs, with George having just flopped into bed, she knew that this was the moment, even if he had been drinking. You couldn't sit on this. He had to know as soon as possible.

She took a deep breath, walked slowly up the stairs and went into their bedroom.

Chapter 23

"Danni, I can't believe you did something so stupid. You know what he's like. He's dangerous. He'll hurt you. Stay out of this. I've got myself into this mess. I need to get myself out of it."

"And how are you going to do that Paul? You haven't got the money to pay him off. Not the full amount. And even if you did, he'd find some other way to control you. You know how he works. And I'm not sure you did get yourself into this mess. I'm partly responsible. If you hadn't met me, you wouldn't have met Walker. He latched onto you as a nice boy from a nice family. He wants to make you suffer because of that. Because he's never had that. He's jealous. We need to pay him off, then make sure he stays away. You need my help. I know things that can hurt him."

Paul stared at her. She was sitting with her back to the window. It was about six thirty, and dark outside. They had no curtains in the sitting room, so the two windows looked like blocks of black spotted with light. There was one street light directly outside, giving out an eerie translucent glow. Then, the bright lights from the flat opposite. It was like a light shop in there. The young Romanian couple had no curtains either, so you could see right in. Elena would sometimes sit in her bra and jeans watching TV. He kept reminding Danni, that 'if they could see into Elena and Andrei's flat, they could see back into our flat'. Either way, there was no danger of Danni sitting in her bra tonight. It was glacial. The timer for the radiators wasn't working, so he'd only just switched the heating on when he got in from work. The gas fire was as temperamental as ever. It usually took about fifty attempts to light it. He'd given up after twenty-five, and put a jumper and fleece on. Danni had also just got in, and simply kept her coat on. A long black trench coat from a charity shop. It fitted her perfectly, tight at the waist, double breasted, buttoned up to the top. You couldn't see her legs because she had a pair of knee-length leather boots on, but he could imagine them.

They were sitting at the rickety table, on the unsteady chairs. You had to balance carefully on the one Paul was sitting on, to avoid one of the legs breaking. The leg was broken in the middle when he bought it. But it was only five pounds for two chairs, so he'd used some masking tape and a splint of wood to hold the leg together. Every now and then it broke and somebody fell off it. But he'd learnt the balancing technique.

She was staring back at him, with those vivid green eyes drilling into him. Cup of tea in her right hand, and using her left hand to point at him, then up in the air, as if to heaven. A fingerless black glove on her right hand, but not on her left hand. Made her look different. Three rings on her left hand, including the large ruby ring on her wedding finger. Not a real ruby, but a dark red colour, the size of a cherry tomato. She'd always worn that ring, so it wasn't a pledge to him.

"You know I'm right Paul. You've got to do something. You can't just let things run on. You know what he's got planned for you on Friday. Do that, and you'll always be in his grasp. You'll never escape. We've got to take the fight to him."

He pictured his father looking at his mother. With the same look on his face that Paul had now. The knowledge that the woman opposite you, was strong and right. And you weren't.

"So what did you actually say to him when you went to Stag's flat?"

"I said that we would give him the money that you owe. Ten thousand pounds. Five thousand tonight, and five thousand next Tuesday night. And I said I'd keep quiet about the other stuff. I've got that on him Paul, he knows that. He's coming round at eleven o'clock."

"Jesus Christ Danni, and where are we going to get five thousand pounds by eleven o'clock?"

"I've got it Paul. I've had it for a while. Don't ask where it came from. But it's mine. I got it out the bank this afternoon. Don't worry, it's all under control. Relax."

He looked hesitantly back into those gorgeous green eyes, full of mysterious promise.

"Relax! That isn't the word that's springing to mind Danni. You can't do this for me. It's not going to happen. I'll find another way. And even if you did hand over five thousand pounds, where am I going to get the other five thousand pounds by next Tuesday? All I've got is a seven-hundred-pound overdraft, and thirty thousand of student debt."

"You don't have to pay off the student debt now, maybe never. I think you should ask your mum and dad. If they knew what was going on, they'd help. You're meeting your dad tomorrow night. Tell him what's happened. He'll help."

"They haven't got any spare cash Danni. I know they haven't. Honestly, I'm not sure they're going to stay together. I think Mum's had enough. And Dad might have lost his job. He said he was coming over for an interview. I'm not asking him for anything."

She stood up, and walked the few paces over to him. He was still sitting down, but he turned his eyes up to look at her.

"I'm not doing it Danni, and I won't let you give Walker five thousand pounds either. It's your money, you keep it."

"He's coming round at eleven o'clock. He's expecting the money. He's angry with me Paul. Because I mentioned the other stuff. He doesn't like me talking about that. But he'll stick to the deal. I'm his sister, or half-sister. That means something. If we give him the money, and I keep quiet, that will be it. He's coming here for his five thousand pounds. Then we've got a week to get the other five thousand. Your dad's the best bet, but if you won't ask him, then I'll have to borrow the money from somewhere else. I can do that. It'll be less dangerous than owing it to Walker. Or you can go to the bank and get a loan. You've got a steady job. We can get the money somehow. Then we can move on. Get on with our lives."

She was standing over him now, she'd unbuttoned her coat, and the silky black blouse. He breathed in the Chanel No. 5 perfume. She ran her fingers through his hair roughly. He turned his head and put his hands on her hips, pressed his face into her body.

*

Paul looked at his watch. His mum and dad had given it to him for his twenty-first birthday. Traditional, understated, with hands and Roman numerals. Not a digital display in sight. They'd chosen it carefully, and he liked it.

It was nearly half eleven. Of course, Walker hadn't arrived at eleven o'clock. The prince of darkness would arrive at midnight. His favourite slot.

As they'd lain on the settee together, she hadn't said anything, she left him alone with his thoughts, she might even have dozed off. Those thoughts had raced through his head like a runaway train in a western. Hopefully not running off the edge of a canyon. The Walker thing was like the sky full of the blackest, most dangerous storm clouds. The wind whipping up the leaves, the lightning about to flash, the thunder about to crash, the heavens about to open with a torrential downpour. Always, about to happen.

Lying there, holding her warm body beneath the trench coat, feeling her slow breath on his neck, it hadn't taken him long to reach a conclusion. Everything that she said was right. This was the best plan there was. He'd get a bank loan for the other five thousand, or a payday loan, anything. He wouldn't ask his parents for the money. Then, he'd gradually pay back Danni, from his salary. He was determined to do that.

They'd got dressed at ten o'clock. Putting back on the small amount of clothing that they'd taken off. The knee-length boots were back in place. She hadn't taken her coat off. The first time, or the second time. Despite the cold, the passion had been high. He'd certainly felt the adrenaline starting to pump at the thought of confronting Walker. And he couldn't help thinking about what it must have been like in the bank this afternoon when Danni had strolled in, in full regalia, to withdraw five thousand pounds in cash. Perhaps a respectable young man in a polyester suit and a badge had taken her into a booth to complete the transaction, eyeing her longingly. God knows where she'd got it from in the first place. Best not to think about that. It hadn't fallen like pennies from heaven.

The flat had warmed up now. The radiators were hot, and Danni had managed to light the gas fire. Her technique was better than his. She'd kept her big coat on though. They hadn't eaten anything all evening, but she'd bought a bag of seedless grapes for tea. They ate those as they waited the final half hour for Walker to arrive.

Paul thought a lot in those thirty minutes. Tactics to deal with Walker. Look confident. Keep the upper hand. Control the agenda. Make sure he doesn't wipe the floor with you. But he knew that as soon as Walker marched in, all of that would go out the window. Would he have Stag and Jonno with him? He wouldn't really need the extra muscle. Would he have been drinking? Probably not. This was business. That's how Paul wanted it as well. As business-like and formal as possible. Obviously, solicitors hadn't drawn up any contracts, there'd be no independent witnesses. And you couldn't really call it a gentleman's agreement, not with Walker involved. So maybe the ace in the pack was this mysterious information that Danni had on her half-brother. It all started to feel a bit tenuous, but there was no Plan B, and at a quarter to midnight Danni went up to the bedroom, and came back down with a brown envelope. She placed it on the table. They both stared at it, but said nothing.

On schedule, at midnight, they heard the door unlock. When all of this was over, he'd change the lock, or move to a new flat, or move to the Outer Hebrides. They heard Walker march the few paces down the hall, trot up the stairs, then open the door into the sitting room. He was on his own. Paul and Danni were sitting on the settee, which was sideways on to the door. Unprompted, they both stood up when Walker made his grand entrance. So much for trying to keep the upper hand. Walker had kept them waiting, and then they'd stood up when he entered the room, like a teacher, or the Queen, or a Roman emperor. Perhaps they should have bowed and curtsied.

Walker put on his best sneering grin.

"Well, well Pauly. What a turn up for the books. Getting my sister to bail you out. I thought you'd want to work for me. Be part of my business empire. We're going places. I've got five people working for me now. Five people and Jonno. I look after my workers. Career structures, targets, bonuses, paid holidays, pensions. What have you got? A poxy degree, training to be a poxy accountant. But in debt to me. I left school at fourteen and they couldn't get me back. I've only decided to take the money because of Danni. She begged me. She must like you. I can't think why."

Paul took two deep breaths before replying. He was going to count to ten, but gave up after three.

"Thanks for agreeing to this Walker. We appreciate it."

The sneer turned angrier. Conciliation wasn't the right approach. You couldn't win. Defiance was no good. Walker wanted subservience, but not exaggerated subservience. And politeness didn't really fit in either. Perhaps silence was better.

"You're a snivelling shit. I might change my mind. I might walk out now."

Danni felt that she ought to step in.

"Your money's here Walker. Here's the envelope. Five thousand pounds. You'll get the other five thousand next week. Paul and I want to get this sorted out. You get on with your business, and we get on with our lives."

Danni could pitch the tone a lot better than he could. Walker took the envelope, didn't look at it, put it in the inside pocket of his jacket. It was a big envelope, stuffed with fifty-pound notes probably. Perhaps Walker had his jackets specially made to accommodate envelopes full of notes. There was no attempt to count it. Obviously he didn't need to. If you short-changed Walker, he'd come looking for you. Paul hoped the respectable young man in the bank had counted it properly.

Walker kept his eyes fixed on Paul, determined to wring a bit more misery and humiliation out of him. He took two paces nearer the table, nearer the chair that Paul had been sitting on a few hours earlier. Just keep calm and see this through, Paul told himself. Just get through the next few minutes, get Walker out of the flat. But Walker hadn't finished, he was getting into his flow, building up the dramatic impact. He lifted his right leg, placed his foot on the chair. Leant forward. Put his hand on his thigh. He could have been on the stage in a Hollywood musical, about to burst into song. But it was just prose that followed, some advice.

"Do you know where you went wrong Pauly? I'll tell you. Give you a little bit of advice. For free."

Paul kept his head down, avoided eye contact. He bit his lip, determined to stay silent.

"Well I'll tell you. No plan. No forward thinking. Just living for the day. Not like me. I know exactly where I'm going."

"You're an example to us all Walker."

For hours, days, months, and years afterwards, Paul asked himself why he'd said that. He'd managed to just about control himself up to that point. Taken Walker's insults. Soaked them up. And Walker hadn't been

197

particularly insulting with his last comments, not compared to some of the earlier stuff. There must have been something in what he'd said that tipped Paul over the edge. An over-stretched elastic band in his head finally gave way. But sarcasm was the last thing to use on Walker.

There was a brief tumbleweed moment. Maybe two seconds, maybe only one. Walker simply stared at Paul with a disbelieving glare. This sort of defiance didn't happen, and had to be dealt with straight away, punished severely. A Nazi colonel in occupied Poland would round up innocent villagers and shoot them, to set an example to anybody resisting. In a flat in a run-down area of Hull, Walker didn't need to shoot anyone. He would sort this out with his bare hands, and he moved seamlessly into combat mode.

When Paul and Danni talked about this later; many, many times afterwards, even when they were explaining it to the police, they struggled to describe properly what happened next. Walker put his weight on his right leg, the one on the chair. Then in the same movement, began to move towards Paul. Paul heard the cracking noise of the chair leg before anything else. He recognised it, it had happened before. As the chair leg cracked, Walker's right leg stamped down, but his whole body rolled forward with momentum, his head tipped forward, his legs moved backwards. He continued to roll forward head first, with real speed. Then, after the cracking sound of the chair leg, and the chair falling over onto the floor, there came the awful sickening crack of something worse. Walker's head, propelled forward by something stronger than the laws of physics, eventually reached a solid object. Not the wooden floor with the threadbare carpet. That might have been alright. Instead, it hit the hard corner of the iron fire surround.

Paul and Danni had watched this like a slow-motion action replay. A freak own goal. The ball bouncing around in the box before rebounding off the goal post onto the back of somebody's head and back into the net. There was a certain beauty to the way that Walker's body had flown through the air. His head following an invisible arc of symmetry, a poetic curve, ending with heavy metal.

They looked briefly at each other, then took a few paces to peer down at Walker. It was tragi-comedy, but there would be hell to pay for this. All the plans had just gone out the window. Walker was obviously badly hurt. In fact, he wasn't moving, and was probably unconscious even. But when he came round, who knows what would happen. Danni knelt down, and observed him more closely. As if he was a dangerous wild animal, sedated, but could turn on them in a fraction of a second when he woke up.

Danni spoke first, whispered, "Walker, are you OK? That was a bad fall. You hit your head. It was all an accident."

She sounded apologetic. She put her face closer to Walker's. Paul looked on, almost an impartial observer. Walker's body was slumped on the floor in a strange contortion, almost foetal, with the side of his head resting on the fire surround. He was looking straight ahead, along the floor, but his head was slightly crooked in relation to his neck and shoulder. It was difficult to work out. Paul felt a repulsion, but also a magnetic draw to the strange sight below. He nudged his foot into Walker's ribcage, very slightly, but there was still no movement. How often has anybody ever done that to Walker, he thought.

"I think he's out cold, he looks as if he's been knocked unconscious. That was quite a bang to the head. We need to bring him round. Have you got any smelling salts Danni?"

"Smelling salts? What are you on Paul? Victoria's not on the throne anymore. No, I haven't got any smelling salts. Have you?"

"No. I haven't got a clue what smelling salts are either. That was a stupid idea. What about a hypodermic needle with adrenaline, like in *Pulp Fiction*? You have to stick it in his heart though."

"We haven't got a hypodermic needle and we haven't got any adrenaline Paul. Go and get a mug of water."

He walked into the kitchen and picked up a large mug from the draining board. It wasn't clean but that was hardly going to matter. He filled it with cold water, walked back in, spilling some water on the floor, then took aim and emptied the water on Walker's face. Another disrespectful act. Paul thought he would rise up as a raging bull. Punch him to the ground, kick him mercilessly around the floor. Danni would scream for him to stop, but he wouldn't, he'd carry on, sickening thuds sounding out as his boot sank into Paul's ribs, then his face. She'd call an ambulance. Mum and Dad would visit him in hospital. His mum would cry. They'd blame Danni.

But Danni wasn't thinking the same thing. A different certainty was washing over her, as she'd seen the blood seeping out from under Walker's head, thick and deep-red like ruby port.

"He's dead Paul."

He didn't reply for a few seconds.

"He can't be. That wasn't enough to kill him, was it? He's as strong as an ox."

"Something happened when he was little. In a play park. Fell off a climbing frame onto concrete. Mum had left him there on his own. They had to do a big operation. It could be connected to that. I don't know. But I really think he's dead. Look at the blood."

The enormity of it began to sink in.

"Christ, Danni, you mean he's dead, here in my flat. Walker's dead? A dead body laid on the floor in my flat. The police are going to think that we killed him. All I had to do was keep quiet, and he'd be gone by now."

She was staring at Walker, but she wasn't panicking. There was a mass of thoughts turning around in her mind, but she was thinking clearly.

"He's gone now Paul. He's not coming back. You'd better ring 999, the police, and an ambulance, or a hearse for the miserable bastard, a horse-drawn one. We'd better not touch anything. The police will be able to tell that it was an accident. The CSI people. The ones in the white overalls. We just need to keep calm, see it through. We've done nothing wrong. We definitely haven't."

She was running things. He knew that. He pulled his phone out of his pocket, and out of habit, walked out of the sitting room onto the landing, and half way down the stairs. That's where you got the best signal. Danni was left alone with Walker's body, her dead half-brother. She knew that she only had about thirty seconds. The calculation that she'd been doing was this. In Walker's jacket pocket, there was an envelope containing five thousand pounds. That was her money. She'd worked for it, well not exactly, but it was her money. She was happy to help pay off Paul's debt, she loved him. But Walker was dead, and when the police searched the body, they would find the money. But who would get the money? The police knew Walker was a criminal, he had a record. He dealt drugs. They'd think it was dirty money. There were no books or receipts. She might be the only surviving relative. No, there was a baby somewhere by that awful girl. But there wouldn't be a proper legal will, lodged with a firm of solicitors. Of course not. Either way, it was going to be complicated. There was a simple solution. Get the money back now. But not disturb the body.

She bent right down, and very gently reached into the inside jacket pocket. Fortunately, the right side was facing up from the body, the side with the envelope in. She'd remembered that. She fumbled around. She could feel an envelope. That was it. It felt about the right size. But there was something else. A second envelope. She pulled both envelopes out. She recognised the first one. It was the envelope the bank had given her. She opened it, it wasn't sealed, and yes, that was the money, she could see the fifty-pound notes. She'd briefly put the other envelope down on the floor next to the body. Now she picked that up, and opened it. Again, it wasn't sealed. Inside, it was full of euro notes. The envelope was about the same size, it felt about the same thickness. So, at a guess, there might be about five thousand euros in there.

Her heart was pumping like a steam engine now. She couldn't turn back. She made up her mind in half a second. She would keep the envelope that she'd given to Walker. What if he'd smashed his head and died before she'd given him the cash? She'd still have it wouldn't she? So that was OK.

But then the next decision; the choices were coming thick and fast. She could hear Paul talking on the phone on the stairs, so he'd got through to the police and ambulance. Maybe she should talk to him, make the decision together. But she knew what he'd say. Put the envelopes back in Walker's pocket. She wasn't going to do that. And she was going to keep the second envelope as well. What did anybody gain by leaving it in Walker's pocket? She'd already strayed to the edge of the law, so she might as well go the whole way. She'd explain it to Paul later.

Should she try to hide them somewhere? There wasn't time. She still had the big coat on. They would easily fit in the outside pockets, they were deep pockets, she could put one envelope in each pocket. There were flaps on the pockets, nobody would see. But the police would ask them to go to the police station. Would they search her? Maybe she should hide them in the flat, after all. But where? She quickly looked around the sitting room. There was hardly any furniture, no obvious place. She could put them under the pillow in the bedroom, or beneath the pile of clothes in the old wardrobe in the bedroom. But then she would have to walk past Paul in the hall, upstairs to the bedroom. That wouldn't work. And the police might search the flat. They'd be sure to find the envelopes and that would mean lots of awkward questions. All these thoughts were buzzing around in her head as Paul came back into the room, still looking at his phone.

In the fraction of a second that it took for him to look up, she managed to shove one envelope into each pocket.

Wednesday 15 November

Chapter 24

The interview hadn't gone too badly. Not exactly sailed through it, but no disasters. And now he was heading west, not on Route 66, but on the A63, out of Hull. He'd just driven past the Humber bridge. The longest single span suspension bridge in the world, when it had been completed just a few years before he'd started at university. It never seemed a source of local pride when he'd lived there. The people of Hull had no desire to be linked to the people of Lincolnshire, or to anywhere else really. Strong in their insularity, self-reliant; but beaten down by decisions taken hundreds of miles away about their industry, the fishing industry. That's what they'd told him. He remembered the tales from the locals in the back street pubs about the heyday of the North Sea trawlers, the men back on shore with money stuffed in their pockets, ready to drink. But that had all gone when he arrived in September 1986 to start his history degree. The dockers were on their way out as well by then. Replaced by huge metal boxes loaded by giant cranes directly on to the waiting lorries. Containerisation. But this year it was the UK City of Culture, a city coming out of the shadows, so they said. Fishermen and dockworkers replaced by poets, writers, and artists. And maybe George Stephenson would be back in town, after all these years.

Bill Parkinson, Parky, the chap who'd interviewed him, was a local. He'd lived and worked in Hull all of his life. He had the accent to prove it. The unmistakeable flattened vowels. He was similar to the image that George had conjured up of him in two respects – he was fat, and he was kindly. In fact, he was a very big man. He'd struggle to get into any normal size bath. But there was no bald head with hair combed over the top. No check jacket, no V-necked jumper and tie, no brown slacks, as George had imagined when he first spoke to him on the phone. Bill had a full head of hair, mostly black, but with grey settling in like a layer of dust. And a dark-grey suit to match, shiny through daily wear, with a sprinkling of dandruff on the collar.

Bill had greeted him with a limp handshake, strangely out of place for such a big man. But he'd left the impression on George of a kind man, a reasonable man, a decent bloke. He hadn't pressed George too much on why he was leaving HG, or the holes in his CV. There were some embarrassing silences or stumbles from George on a couple of questions. He'd given his stock response, without a hint of irony, when asked what he was most proud of in his career, referring yet again to the sales-order-processing system in Wolverhampton fourteen years ago. But trailed off into quiet reflection when asked to give an example of how he'd turned threat into opportunity. Overall though, in the scheme of things, it had gone reasonably well. He'd formed the view that at Whitehead Transport, there wouldn't be the same pace and plot of HG, but it would be a more settled life. Dull but safe. He could handle that. They wanted to re-schedule their distribution network in the Northern Region. Not a complete re-engineering, just some efficiency initiatives, following the purchase of a smaller company. They needed a project manager. It would still be way beyond George's capabilities, but he guessed that it would take them longer to root out his deficiencies. He could work from home two or three days a week, so the travelling wouldn't be too bad. If they offered him the job, and he was somehow sure they would, he'd take it. He'd have a job, and one hundred thousand pounds in his back pocket. Not bad, eh.

As he drove along the dual carriageway in the early evening darkness, with the river still in sight, that all seemed straightforward. Job and money. For the first time in his life, not a problem. The other problem area was still there though. People. His wife and his son. Preserving his marriage, and reconnecting with his son. The reason that he was driving home now was that Paul had cried off at the last minute. They were supposed to be meeting up in the pub near to Paul's work. George had been sitting there, with a lime and soda in front of him, when he'd got the text at five twenty-one.

"Dad, busy at work, really sorry that I can't make it. I'll ring in the next few days. All fine here."

Could you tell from a text that something was wrong? Maybe. They were due to meet up. It was all arranged. Paul could have said that he'd be a bit late. But still come, later. George would have waited. That text sounded too cheery, too matter of fact. It sounded false. He resolved that once he'd got out of HG on Friday, he'd just drive over to Paul's flat and knock on the door. Find out what was wrong. They could go together. Him and Dawn – the other person he was worrying about.

He was looking forward to getting home. The dual carriageway would turn into the M62 motorway soon. The traffic was getting busier, but he was still less than an hour from home. Looking forward to a bit of normality, a quiet Wednesday night. He felt guilty about his mammoth drinking session with Angel. That was two drunken nights in only a few days. But he hadn't disgraced himself. There was no fumbled kiss. No misplaced hand on the knee. You could almost say that he'd behaved like a gentleman. Listened to her problems. Got her back to the hotel. Back to her room even. Shame about the three bottles of wine and the near-miss ankle incident, but there you go. Just not the sort of behaviour when you're trying to hang on to your wife.

His recollection of getting home last night was very hazy. He remembered Dawn standing in the hall when he got in. She knew he was drunk, but she hadn't shouted at him. Not at first. She seemed quite understanding, quite reflective. He'd gone straight upstairs. Managed to get undressed and crawl into bed. Pulled the duvet over his head. Then a few minutes later Dawn came into the bedroom. She'd left the door open to let some light into the room. Sat on the side of the bed. Gently peeled the duvet back, and said there was something they needed to talk about. Something she had to tell him. He could remember the panic. He didn't want to hear whatever it was she was going to say to him. He was half awake, still drunk. She'd carried on. But she hadn't said she was leaving, she definitely hadn't said that. Surely, he'd remember if she had. No, it was something else. But he still didn't want to know. He'd pulled the duvet back over his head and rolled over. She'd carried on. Something about someone she used to know, and her daughter. Or was it something he had to do? Was it about his mother? Or was it his father trying to get in touch after all these years? It was some family stuff. But he didn't hear properly, didn't want to hear. She'd got mad with him. Shouted in frustration. Then started to cry. He just wanted to go to sleep. Avoid whatever it was. Think about it tomorrow. She'd walked out of the bedroom, slammed the door closed. She'd gone back downstairs. He was relieved. He'd talk to her in the morning.

The traffic had slowed right down, but it was still moving. He'd be on the motorway soon. Maybe one of the lanes was closed up ahead. Road repairs or a broken-down vehicle.

In the morning, this morning, Dawn had gone. He'd woken late. He hadn't set the alarm. It didn't look as though she'd gone, gone. That is, never to come back. She'd just gone to work. She'd had some breakfast. Left her bowl, and spoon, and glass, and cup, on the worktop. Left them for him to put in the dishwasher. As a sign that she was annoyed with him. The cereal was still on the table. The teapot was still warm. There was no 'Dear George' note by the bed. No note on the kitchen table. So, no cause for alarm. No immediate alarm anyway.

He hadn't felt too rough. Maybe the Friday night session had helped to prepare for the Tuesday night session, build up his alcohol tolerance. And he and Angel hadn't actually drunk much of the third bottle. He'd eaten some breakfast, the cereal that Dawn had left on the table. While he was eating it, he'd thought again about what Dawn was trying to tell him last night, but still couldn't make any sense of it. Then he'd prepared for the interview. Prepared in the George Stephenson way that is. Casually, superficially, without care. At least he made sure he had the address and post code to find his way. He hadn't bothered with any lunch, as he'd planned to have an early evening meal with Paul. The early evening meal that had never happened. He'd got the bus to the office, picked up his car from last night, and driven over for the interview.

Now he was feeling hungry. But no need to worry. The fridge was well-stocked from his shopping expedition on Sunday. He was looking forward to seeing Dawn. He might still be back in time for them to have a meal together. He'd tell her about the interview. That he thought they were going to offer him the job. They could plan how they were going to see Paul. She could tell him whatever it was she was trying to tell him last night. That could all be sorted out. Maybe he'd tell her about the money. How about telling her about half of it? Sort of, hedge your bets.

He flicked some music on. There was a CD already in. On came Bruce Springsteen's 'Born to Run' album. First track. Thunder Road.

"With a chance to make it good somehow

Hey what else can we do now

Except roll down the window

And let the wind blow back your hair?

Well the night's busting open

These two lanes will take us anywhere."

Maybe this wasn't quite what The Boss had in mind. The A63 in East Yorkshire. In the dark. In the drizzling rain. You couldn't really imagine rolling down the window and letting the wind blow back your hair. And there was no girl sitting next to him, so it wouldn't work.

The motorway network had other ideas as well. It knows how to lull you into a false sense of security and then dash all your hopes on the rocks of despair. Let you think that you're on your way home. Let you picture the meal on the table, smell it, taste it. The glass of wine. Picture your best gal. A better life. A fairer world. Then let another lorry shed its load. Send in some scheduled road works. Bring down a cloak of fog for good measure. Do all of that when you've had nothing to eat since breakfast and your bladder's full.

He was maybe half a mile away from Junction 38. Where the A63 turns into the M62. He'd noticed the traffic slowing earlier, and now he saw the wisps of mist, and the sea of red brake lights up ahead. He knew it was only a matter of time before the 'advisory' flashing speed limit signs appeared. The ones that said forty when you were only just moving forward at all. He ground to a halt in the middle lane, and began to contemplate his car as a prison cell for the next few hours. Nothing to do other than get more frustrated and irritable. Try to blame somebody, that was usually helpful, but who? Then try thinking about how lucky you were. Only stuck in traffic, nothing worse than that had happened – you'd still get home, just a lot later. You weren't in a mangled heap, or in a ditch, or being carted off in an ambulance.

The traffic started to move a bit, then stopped again. It knew how to tease you. It was a cruel mistress. The first flashing overhead sign started to appear in the distance. He could just about make it out. 'Accident, Slow Down'. Stating the obvious. Then the added torment. The flashing sign that shows you how many lanes are closed. He looked across all three symbols, and yes, all three lanes were closed. Then the next cheery message. 'Diversion. Motorway closed'. It was nearly seven o'clock and the misery lay before him.

He spent the next few hours, along with his fellow travellers, crawling along, edging forward, jostling for position, as they were forced onto the slip road, then onto narrow B roads. Everything that was supposed to be joining the motorway was here. All the lorries with their containers loaded on their backs from the port down river. The ones heading for the M1. All the cars heading home for the evening. Just like him. 'Follow Diversion' it said somewhere. The snake of traffic, the large and the small, the great and the good, they were now squashed into one lane, bound together by circumstance, like a string of beads of different shape and colour. But you never saw your compatriots. Each of you locked away in your own tin can. The procession, the motor cavalcade, made its way along a non-descript road sometimes with houses at the side, sometimes open space.

He'd looked at his phone, and worked out that the diversion was taking them along this minor road, then over the motorway, then onto the motorway at the next junction. But there must be something else slowing them down. Another breakdown on this road. Like everybody else, he searched for an alternative route, but there simply wasn't one. This was the only game in town. He'd already sent a text to Dawn to let her know that he was going to be very late. She even sent back a short response 'Sorry to hear that. It's not the end of the world'. Well no, it's not Armageddon with the four horseman of the apocalypse bearing down, but it's pretty miserable all the same. She didn't mean it, he knew that. What else could she say?

It was nearly ten o'clock now. The traffic had thinned a bit. Maybe the road ahead had cleared. Maybe some people had found alternative routes up at the next junction. They were passing through a village called Ellerdyke. He'd seen the sign on the road. 'Ellerdyke welcomes careful drivers.' It wouldn't have been welcoming this lot for the last three hours. It wasn't really a village, more a line of houses along the road. Curtains drawn. No human beings venturing out. But that wasn't what he was thinking about. It was two of his internal organs playing on his mind – his stomach and his bladder.

He'd finished off the wine gums, and then found a very old packet of Werther's Original Soft Caramels in the glove compartment. Half full. He'd eaten all of them now. Probably the equivalent of a bag of sugar, but at least it was keeping him awake. And a small plastic bottle of water in the pocket of the passenger door. Harrogate spring water. The number one British premium bottled water. That's what it said on the label. That was a real find. He reckoned Dawn had left it there about three weeks ago, so there could be some waterborne disease swimming around. But it staved off the thirst. That was the menu so far. Refined sugar and stagnant water. He'd tried to avoid fantasising about sausages. It wasn't the sight of them. It was the smell that was tormenting him. Sizzling in a pan. God, stop it.

His bladder was the more urgent matter. He was at bursting point. That really would set him back, wetting himself in the driver's seat, with at least another hour to get home, maybe two. He'd have to find a quiet spot to relieve himself. But no petrol stations around, no sign of an all-night McDonalds in Ellerdyke. No toilet facilities, so it would have to be urinating al fresco, like in the good old days.

There was a turning off the road. He indicated left, and pulled round. He was immediately very aware of his surroundings. You spend hours in your car in a traffic jam, looking at the road ahead, looking at the car in front. But all around you, there's another world going on. The people in these houses are leading their lives. The ups and the downs. The marital strife. There could be another George and Dawn in Ellerdyke, trying to salvage their relationship. Or not.

They'd started to come out of the built-up area. There were a few houses at the beginning of the turn off and one street light, but the houses gradually ran out, and it became a country lane, with hedges, trees, and fields. It was a bit misty, but the thick fog had lifted. He could see an opening in the hedge not far away. That would do, it was deserted.

*

211

In the moments before it happened, it seemed strangely still. He'd switched the music off long ago. He was idling along in second gear. You could hardly hear the engine. His senses had been deadened by the hours in the car, but at the same time he was acutely aware of this lane, this grassy verge, the hedge, the dark field beyond. Thought bubbles of what Dawn had started to tell him last night drifted through his mind again. Gently touching each other to try to make sense.

In the moments after it happened, it seemed strangely still as well, except that by then his world had changed forever.

It was the look on her face that stayed with him. She looked directly into his eyes, drilling deep into his soul. It had only been a fraction of a second. The look took hold of him, terrified him, but connected with him at the same time. It was a pleading look, but it had an icy determination as well. And the hands held out in front of her, were held out to him, stretching out to touch him. In that instant, that frozen moment in time, he could see her long beautiful hair faintly shining in the moonlight and flowing over her bare shoulders. He could see her elegant long neck, and the delicate necklace. He could see the light cotton dress, the pale floral print, the lacy edging stopping just above the knee, the slim legs, the open-toe sandals, and her toes. He could see all of her. But he focused on the face, the beautiful face. What were her lips telling him? Was there a smile? What about the eyes? They narrowed as she stared at him, and the look was intense. In that moment he couldn't tell if she was frightened, threatening, lost, or even loving. Or a combination of all of them. But it was the connection, the association, her knowledge of him and his awareness of her, that was the most troubling thing of all. Troubling, puzzling, intriguing.

He'd only taken his eyes off the road for a second. He'd reached to grab the bottle of water to take the last few mouthfuls. As he looked back up at the road, she'd been standing there. A young woman, a beautiful young woman, in her mid to late twenties. He could see her clearly, very clearly, standing in front of the car. He'd braked, but he knew it was too late. He would hit her. But in a strange way he knew he wouldn't.

There was no thud, no sound at all, no body hitting the bonnet. Only silence, deafening silence. And nothing to see apart from the road in front, the blackness of the night, and the touch of the moon.

PART THREE

Thursday 16 November

Chapter 25

He stared at the lukewarm cup of tea in front of him. Nettle tea. It was only lukewarm because he hadn't picked it up for nearly ten minutes. He dipped his finger in and circled it. The liquid reminded him of pond water. The smell was of precipitation and vegetation. Not unpleasant, but he had no desire to ingest it. He'd never made the leap from traditional English Breakfast tea. With milk. From a cow. But she hadn't offered him that. The mug was more appealing than the drink. A red capital 'A' in a red circle, on a black background. 'Anarchy is Sanity'. He was back there. Nearly thirty years ago. He looked around her sitting room. It was like the back room of a charity shop. Every last inch of space covered in stuff. Tables, mantelpiece, window sill, shelves, walls, floor. Swamped by paintings, photos, books, records, CDs, papers, etched glass vases, vintage brass trays, wood-carvings, a half life-size ceramic King Charles spaniel. There was an urgent need for de-cluttering. But don't get rid of the posters. From the far side of the room, just to the right of the door, all the way round, to the other side of the door. A pictorial history. Starting with standard 1980's anti-Thatcher, the miners' strike, CND, Greenham Common, animal rights. Veering to mysticism, mostly over the fireplace. Aliens, conspiracy theories, pentangles, pyramids, ley lines, the paranormal. Then a gap for the bay window, and a gap for quiet reflection in your thirties, repositioning, revisionism. Emerging beyond the curtains, in your forties, as more mainstream environmentalism, climate change, local elections, Green Party councillor. Armed revolution to gentle local democracy in the panorama of the front room of a terraced house in Oakwood, not far from Roundhay Park, just inside the ring road.

Walking back into the room, her black dress rustled with the movement of her legs. It was a long flowing evening gown, silk and lace, swirling embossed floral patterns, a hint of glitter. It stopped at her ankles, but there was no glimpse of flesh, as she wore silver Cuban heel boots. He remembered the style from his night out with Angel. So from the waist down, Bohemian evening wear. But from the waist up, starving artist chic. Crocheted baggy dark grey jumper with sleeves too long, scarlet plastic beads and bangle to match, dangly gem earrings, and a shop window display of rings from the dark side – a skull, a serpent, a wolf. Images from some of his latest dreams. She must have put the make-up on since she placed the cup in front of him twenty minutes ago. A touch of lipstick, a dab of eye-shadow. A quick blast of hairspray. She'd have looked at herself in the bathroom mirror, turned her head, puckered her lips maybe, before she came back downstairs. It was flattering that she'd done it for him. On a Thursday morning.

She was sitting in the leather armchair now, directly opposite him, sitting forward, one leg crossed over the other. Revealing some shin at last. Smoking a herbal cigarette in the erotic way that she always used to. Her special cigarettes, imported from China. She placed the packet down on a tower of books next to the fireplace, without looking. It didn't topple. There was no suggestion of opening a window to dissipate the smoke. It hung in the air, the smell teasing out memories in the same way as a classic pop song.

The essence of her face, the look in her eye, the way she carried herself, all of that hadn't really changed over the decades. The poise, the good looks, relaxed superiority, unhurried self-confidence. Handed down through generations of the landed gentry. Why do the children of the wealthy always look so good? And the generous trust fund made your commitment to the proletariat a lot easier. You could despise authority, support the revolution, 'find yourself', but still live quite comfortably. Shop at Waitrose.

Not that George was bitter. He really wasn't. He'd phoned her at nine o'clock this morning, she'd answered the door at half ten, and here he was at ten to eleven watching her smoke the cigarette, and observing the outline of her thighs beneath the evening dress. He wondered if she'd put that dress on just for him, or whether she always wore it during the week. Either way, he was grateful that she was about to listen to his tale.

Miranda spoke first. Her voice had the same easy authority as it always had. The ability to command the room whether there was one person in it, or whether it was a packed town hall.

"Well George, how nice to see you – after about five years I think. You came to the party when I got elected to the council. We didn't really have much time to speak then. And before that my wedding to Antonio. You know that didn't work out. He's back in Milan now, running a gallery. His girlfriend's nineteen. I've met her. She's got beautiful skin."

She leant down to stub out the cigarette in a large glass ashtray on the floor, even though she'd only smoked half of it.

"It's good to stay in touch. I'm pleased you still had my private number. You're probably a high-powered executive by now. Big detached house. Are you still with Dawn? I'm sure you are. A lovely girl. Steady. Wasn't she head girl at school? You were always so well-suited."

Damned by faint praise there, he thought. She continued without allowing him time to answer.

"But I'm sure you didn't just want to catch up on old times. I sense there's something troubling you. You want to ask for my help."

The last couple of lines sounded like she was a medium at a séance, and in some ways that was apt. Finally, she paused to allow him time to speak.

But where would he start?

*

It felt as though he hadn't slept at all last night, but he must
have managed a few hours of disturbed sleep. There were
no nightmares. You didn't need nightmares when the reality
was even more frightening. It had been about one in the
morning when he'd eventually crawled into bed. He'd tried
to eat some toast when he got in, but his mouth seemed
permanently dried up, even after drinking half a carton of
orange juice. The images darting around in his head
deadened the hunger. Dawn had been asleep, with her back
turned towards his side of the bed. She had the nightie on
with the flimsy thread over each shoulder blade. He could
sense the warmth of her body. He could have put his hand
on her shoulder and gently woken her. She'd have
understood. When he told her what had happened. She
wouldn't have been cross. He could have told her about the
money as well. She could have told him what she was trying
to say on Tuesday night. They could have both put on their
dressing gowns and talked through the night. Resolved
everything. And kissed at five in the morning. But he hadn't
woken her. Perhaps because he didn't know what he'd say,
about what had just happened, and about everything else
that had happened. About their life together. So, he did what
he'd always done. Avoided engagement. Pulled the duvet
over his head, and turned away from her. And when he'd
opened his eyes at half past eight, he'd heard her car pulling
away to go to work. They'd missed each other again.

That's when he'd had his great idea. Don't talk to your
wife of nearly twenty-five years. Don't tell her about the
most momentous thing that's happened in your lifetime. No,
why not scramble through an old address book, find a
telephone number, ring up somebody who you knew for a
couple of years at university and slept with once, and met
up with a couple of times since. Somebody who your wife

had met only a handful of times, and was indifferent about. That was the obvious solution wasn't it? Right up your street George. Then, get in your car, follow the Sat-Nav to the post code from your address book, ignore the fact that this was supposed to be your last but one day at work, drive to a large three-storey terraced house in North Leeds, open the front gate as you remember coming to a party here five years ago, look at the strange ornaments in the front garden, ring the bell, and a few moments later be greeted by Miranda in an evening gown, looking great. You could round off the morning by going to bed together, just for old times' sake. You've got it all covered George.

Except there was a semblance of logic to his actions. He'd known Miranda since the beginning of his final year at university. She was a fresher, two years younger than him, starting a psychology degree. She had an interest in the occult. People started calling her Miranda the witch. A few of them had gathered in her room for a session with a Ouija board. They had their hands on the glass and it moved around, spelt out messages. Somebody's dead auntie was getting in touch. It all seemed real and intense. So intense that he'd ended up in bed with her afterwards. But it wasn't all mystery and imagination. She'd gone on to do a PhD on paranormal activity. Joint research with somebody at an overseas university. Proper scientific analysis. Documented first-hand experiences. A balanced view. It had been published. She'd done a lecture tour. Been on the radio. A minor academic celebrity. Maybe a TV series could have followed. But she'd drifted off into other avenues. The doomed marriage to Antonio. The failed organic soap shop in Hebden Bridge. Then the renaissance later in life. A victorious local election campaign. Winning a seat against the odds.

Now here she was. Sitting opposite him, all ears, waiting to hear his story.

"Yes, it is a bit strange me ringing you out of the blue. And I don't know where to start. I'm not a high-flying executive. I lead a pretty normal life really. I'm a project manager at an IT company. Well, I am until tomorrow that is. Then I'm moving on, as they say. I've had an interview for another job. We still live in Leeds. The house is detached, but it's only got three bedrooms. Something to do with the angle of the plot. The conservatory leaks. Dawn's fine. Paul got an economics degree and works in Hull. He's twenty-two now. We're all just getting on with our lives, like most people."

"So, it's really nice that you've come round here to tell me that George."

He continued, ignoring the sarcasm, "I'm fifty next year. It's a normal existence. Nothing out of the ordinary. Coping with the usual disappointments in life, like everybody has to. Son grown up and left home. I've not really achieved very much at work. I'm trying to keep my marriage afloat. I think Dawn's had enough of me. Most of it's my fault."

He paused for a few seconds. He'd summarised his life in a few sentences to a near stranger. Not a counsellor or psychiatrist. She wasn't on an hourly rate. He took a few sips of the nettle tea. It tasted just as bad, but he was glad of some liquid. He cradled the mug in his hands for comfort. Miranda just sat there observing him, staying silent. So he had to go on and fill the void.

"I've had some strange dreams. Really strange dreams. They got rid of me at work. But I've got a good pay off. I won a lot of money on an online gambling site, predicting football results. Not enough to retire on, but enough to make a difference. And people seem to be paying attention to me. Women. I can't understand it. But that's not the reason I've come to see you."

"So you haven't come to see me to tell me that you're flush with cash and women find you attractive. That's reassuring George."

He ignored that one. He was almost ready to say it now.

"I saw something last night Miranda. The motorway was closed. I had to turn off. Down a country lane. It was a

221

young woman. She stared right at me. It happened. I know it did. I can't explain it, but it did happen, it really did. I didn't imagine it."

"You saw a young woman down a country lane George. That's not earth shattering, is it?"

"Not a real young woman."

"A pretend one?"

"Not a pretend one."

"Give me a clue George. How many syllables?"

He knew she was teasing. He was ready to say it now.

"A ghost. An apparition. Whatever you want to call it. She appeared in front of the car. I should have hit her, but I didn't. Then she wasn't there. It was the way she looked at me. Like she knew me."

He knew that Miranda had been watching him intently as he stumbled through his story. She shook her head slightly, and answered with a mix of mild irritation and gentle amusement.

"So you thought you'd come and see me, after all these years, and I'd explain everything. Just like that. It was the ghost of Anne Grey. A clergyman's daughter. Betrothed to her childhood sweetheart. Abandoned at the altar in 1820. Hanged herself. Took her own life. Now haunts that country lane, looking for her lost lover. Lots of wailing and shrieking, and clanking of chains maybe. Why not throw in a headless horseman as well?"

"There was no headless horseman. It was a normal young woman. She had a summer dress on. Sandals. It's the way she looked at me. I can still see it."

He didn't say any more, and Miranda stayed silent for what seemed like an eternity.

Eventually she spoke.

"George, it's nearly twenty years since I wrote my doctorate. I stopped lecturing fifteen years ago. I spent five years on that stupid soap business with Antonio. Ploughed too much money into it. Then he buggered off. With the girl from Naples with the darkest brown eyes you've ever seen.

I've only got things together in the last few years. After I made the switch. And don't think it's a glamorous life on the council. There's a lot of pot-holes and dog poo."

"I didn't expect you to come up with the answer Miranda. Solve the equation, like maths homework. I just needed to talk to somebody with a bit of knowledge, a bit of experience."

"We did the research. Declan and me. Hundreds of interviews. Documented it all. Looked for common characteristics. We didn't bother trying to identify abnormal electrical activity, or ectoplasm, or unusual radio waves. We just concentrated on the human experience."

He'd been watching Miranda intently as she veered through her condensed life story. But his concentration was broken by a noise above his head. A creaking floorboard. There was somebody else in the house. Upstairs. He'd assumed Miranda was alone. Alone and single. But apparently not.

"And there was plenty of human experience. You can't deny that. But we never actually found any science behind it. Plenty of pseudo science. But no physics or chemistry or biology. And I believe in science George. I always did. You can explain dreams with science. Freud came up with a new science one hundred years ago, and changed everything."

He heard three creaks in a row. And a tap running.

"It wasn't a dream Miranda."

"I'm not saying it was. Obviously something did happen to you last night. You had some form of human experience. Not just a bad dream. But it doesn't mean that it's all voices from the grave. Brains are complicated things. There's a lot of electricity flowing around in those neural networks. Particularly when people are in a heightened emotional state."

He wasn't sure that he liked the considered rational Miranda as much as the teenage wild child. But he was struck by the maturity. She'd known life, developed, learnt. The ebb and flow of fortune. She was a different person.

Whereas he was still basically at school. Giggling on the back row. Two-timing Marie Johnson and Dorothy Gamble.

"It wasn't a random event. She was looking at me. I think she knew me. There was a connection."

"George, give it a bit more thought yourself. Think what was going through your mind at the time. There's a lot more research around thought projection now. I can investigate the area where it happened. Give me the postcode. You can work out where it was roughly. I'll dig out all the old material. I've still got it. But I reckon it's something about you. Think about who the girl could have been. Whether you saw her or not, or whether it was something in your consciousness, something deep down, trying to communicate, trying to make you understand something. The idea of a ghost is very emotive. We think science can't explain it, but maybe we just haven't developed the science yet. Imagine trying to explain the Big Bang to somebody one hundred years ago. They'd think you were mad. But now it's accepted wisdom. Have a think about it, and then let's meet up again. I've got a bit of time this week. We can talk it through."

She smiled at him engagingly, and then spoke again, almost in a whisper. "There might be an adventure out there for us."

An adventure with Miranda was the last thing he needed. What did she have in mind? A day out at Alton Towers with a packed lunch? Or solving mysteries at Smuggler's Top?

He returned a nervous, worried, weak smile.

"I really appreciate you listening to me Miranda. And if there is anything more you can come up with, it might help me work things out."

He looked at his watch, and through the misted-up face, he could just about tell that it was nearly quarter to twelve. He stood up, and heard footsteps at the top of the stairs leading down into the hall. Miranda continued to watch him with an amused expression.

"Thanks for the tea. I'd better be going now. I've got things to sort out."

"Yes, that's probably a good idea George. I think Anna's coming downstairs now. She's working from home today, in the second bedroom. It's got a nice view over the garden at the back. I prefer to work in the kitchen."

Miranda followed George out into the hall, just as a tall woman in her mid-thirties, dressed in a red T-shirt and jeans that he recognised, appeared at the bottom of the stairs.

"Hi Anna," said George.

Anna from HR looked at George, brushing her hair back, disorientated for a few seconds.

"Hi George," said Anna.

*

As he turned the key in the ignition to drive away from Miranda's house, he honestly didn't know where he was going to go. Theoretically he was supposed to be at work, but nobody was too bothered whether he turned up or not. Tomorrow was his last day. He'd told Samantha that he was going to interviews. She didn't seem to expect him to show his face. In any case, the betting win had cut across the boss and subordinate roles. They had an understanding. They shared a guilty secret.

And maybe he shared a guilty secret with Anna as well. Miranda was bound to tell her why he'd appeared at her house this morning. But Miranda didn't think he was crazy, and Anna must know about Miranda's research and her past. Anna wasn't married to Nigel, a partner at a local law firm, driving around in a Range Rover Evoque, living in a barn conversion with generous room proportions. She wore smart corporate dress but she had a rose tattoo on her left ankle. She was a senior HR manager at HG, but lived with Miranda, presumably not as her lodger. Shared her bed, and worked from home in the second bedroom on Thursdays, with the view over the back garden. That must have been what Miranda meant when she said she'd 'made the switch' after Antonio and the failed soap business. Well, good luck to both of them. He didn't think Anna would be referring him to the disciplinary committee for not being at work today.

What about the other woman in his work life? Not counting Linda. Angel. He hadn't seen her since he'd escorted her to her hotel room on Tuesday, after the drunken night out. That seemed a lifetime ago now. After what happened last night. Meeting the new woman in his life. He'd catch up with Angel tomorrow. Say hello, wave goodbye.

Pulling away from outside Miranda's house, he was still not sure where he was going to drive to. He was still in first gear, when the fates took over to set out the next step. Mapping out his destiny. Just as they had been doing over the last week and a bit.

His phone rang on the speaker in the car. He pressed the answer button, and the disembodied voice started to speak, amplified, filling the space. It was no phantom though. He recognised the voice of jovial Bill Parkinson straight away.

"George, it's Bill Parkinson here, from Whitehead Transport. How are you?"

"I'm very well Bill."

I've got an unnerving supernatural experience to deal with. A paranormal mystery to solve. But I've always got time for you Parky, and my career.

"We thought the interview went well yesterday George. We want to move quickly to make an appointment. We'd like you to meet our MD. It's short notice, but—" Bill had obviously carried on speaking, but the line crackled and there was a short silence. The signal must have disappeared. Or a spectral intervention.

"I didn't quite get that Bill," interrupted George, speaking both loudly and slowly.

Communication was restored.

"I said, I know it's short notice, but if you could come to the office this afternoon, that would be great."

George was glad of the direction. At least he'd know which way to turn at the end of the road. Bill spoke again, an encouraging tone in the loud speaker voice, but increasingly distorted by echo and feedback, as if speaking from a submarine.

"I'm hopeful we should be able to make you an offer later today George."

Well Bill, I've got a few irons in the fire, but I'm keeping them close to my chest.

"That's good to know Bill. It sounds a really exciting opportunity."

Bill was disappearing beneath the waves, but they managed to agree on three o'clock, and at the end of Miranda's road he turned left and headed in the general direction of the ring road. He'd grab a sandwich on the way. He had plenty of time. He wasn't exactly dressed for an interview. He'd dressed for meeting Miranda to discuss the supernatural. Jeans, a pink shirt, and suede shoes had seemed appropriate. The new suit was still hanging in the wardrobe back home, but his ski jacket was on the back seat of the car. Judging by Bill's tone, George reckoned he could turn up in a clown outfit, throw a few custard pies around, and still get the job.

The comedy vision was interrupted by a thud on the windscreen. A small bird hit it, but then flew away. George wasn't travelling fast, and the bird looked to have survived, fluttering away dazed and confused, but alive. A real live creature hitting the windscreen, unlike last night. Following the signs to the motorway, he was thinking about Paul now. There was still a mystery about why he hadn't turned up in the pub to meet his father. George decided to do the interview this afternoon, and then go round to Paul's flat. Knock on the door. Paul couldn't avoid him then. If he was out, George would wait until he got back from work. Either way, he'd find out what was wrong. Get it out of him.

As he got onto the slip road for the motorway, the phone went again, and the fates sorted out a few more things. The voice was perfectly clear now, female, and familiar.

"George, where are you? I've been trying to get hold of you. I tried your number at work. They said you weren't there. I didn't see you last night, you got back so late, and I left before you woke up this morning. Your mobile was switched off when I tried to ring earlier."

He hadn't seen Dawn properly since Monday evening, apart from the hazy drunken encounter on Tuesday night. She'd left for work before he got up for the last three days. And he did switch his phone off while he was at Miranda's house. But they were both thinking about the same thing now. Paul.

Dawn carried on, not giving him chance to reply.

"I had a missed call from Paul this morning. He's sent me a text. Apologised for not seeing you last night. Wondered if he could come over, or were we planning to go to Hull. He wants to see us George. I know he does. There is something wrong. He was holding back, but I think he's ready to open up to us now. Has he been in touch with you?"

George was suddenly aware of the mounting list of things he hadn't told Dawn about. The money, and the 'human experience' as Miranda put it. The ghost as George called it.

"Hi, I've been sorting a few things out this morning. That's why I didn't go into work."

That was just about true. He reasoned that he couldn't just throw in the bombshells on a speaker phone, and now wasn't the time to mention Miranda.

"He hasn't been in touch with me since he sent me the text saying he couldn't meet up last night. But Dawn, I'm driving over to Hull now. I've got a second interview for that job. At three this afternoon. I'm going to see Paul after the interview. I'd planned to just turn up. Camp outside the door. Definitely see him no matter what."

"Let's both go. I'll contact him and arrange a time. Let's say six o'clock. I'll take the afternoon off and get the train over. I'll meet you at the station. I'll text you and let you know what time the train's due in."

So that was that. All very efficient. A cross between a business meeting and a date. Or a family reunion.

He had a few hours to plan his communication strategy.

Chapter 26

She knew that the young man opposite was staring at her. He'd been doing that since she got on the train at Leeds. He was ridiculously handsome. It'd been impossible not to notice that when she'd sat opposite him in the window seat. Even though the train was relatively empty. She wondered if he'd knowingly modelled himself on Lord Byron, her favourite romantic poet. Renowned for his personal beauty, dark curled locks, soft skin, dark tortured moodiness. That might even have been a dark wool cape and cream open-neck silk shirt that he was wearing. But if he was a modern-day Byron, why was he heading to Hull? The train stopped there. He should be wandering around classical Italy and Greece, putting the finishing touches to lengthy narrative poems. Maybe he had to start his shift at Aldi first.

When she looked up from the newspaper, he held her gaze for a second before looking out the window and grinning. She looked back down at the paper. It had been lying on the table when she'd got on the train. She hadn't bought it. A tabloid with a scantily-clad lady on the front, and a headline about immigration. She'd thought twice about picking it up and reading it. What if somebody that she knew, saw her? An intelligent liberal-minded woman doing a thing like that. But there was an illicit attraction, and she didn't resist it. Flicking through the pages, she appeased her liberalism by shaking her head, smiling disapprovingly, tutting, and laughing gently. 'It's alright everybody. This intelligent woman in her late forties doesn't really believe any of this. It was just there on the train and I picked it up.'

"I read it as well. I didn't buy it either. It had the same effect on me."

His voice was deeper than she'd expected. Both his hands were resting on the table. Big strong hands. She recognised the enigmatic smile. She'd seen it before.

She didn't look up for a few seconds. Gave herself time to think of an appropriate response. Not too dismissive, not too passive. Stay in control.

"Best to keep an open mind," she replied calmly.

That sounded about right. She folded up the paper, put it down on the table. Took out her phone, and called her husband.

"Hi, I'm about twenty minutes away. I'll see you at the station. How did the interview go?"

She could feel her heartbeat picking up, as she listened distractedly to his reply.

"That's great news George. I'm pleased for you. It should only take ten minutes to drive to Paul's place. I'm genuinely concerned, so let's get it sorted out."

As she ended the call with George, her phone started to ring, and the contact name appeared. "Hi Derek."

She could do without this. She listened to his news without a great deal of sympathy.

"Derek, I'm sorry the police want to interview you again. They're obviously being very thorough. I can't really talk now. I'll try to ring you later."

Lord Byron smiled at her, warmly this time. But his charms wouldn't work on Thursday afternoon. Her personal life was complicated enough anyway. He diverted his gaze to watch the flat East Yorkshire countryside rolling by.

Dawn placed her phone down on the table, shuffled her feet, and sat more upright.

Lightning didn't strike twice.

*

It had been a long time since she'd stood waiting in Hull railway station. She hadn't done it while Paul was at university, or since he'd been working there. So it must have been all those decades ago when she'd been a student. A whole lifetime ago. George and her used to meet there sometimes. 'Under the clocks' as they said in Hull. What a shock to the system that had been. Growing up in Streatham in South London, even before it became properly gentrified, and then coming to the city of Hull at age eighteen to study English Literature. Bristol had been her first choice, but she didn't get the grades. Distracted by her first boyfriend. He did get the grades and did go to Bristol. She didn't see him again, apart from the first Christmas back from university, when he introduced his new girlfriend to her in the Pied Bull.

It had seemed a stark contrast. English Literature and Hull. She'd found it difficult to understand the accent when she first arrived, and they couldn't understand her. Thought she was posh. But Philip Larkin had only died a couple of years before she started her first term. Renowned poet and librarian at the university. What was the quote about Larkin? 'Deprivation for him was what daffodils were for Wordsworth'. So the literary heritage wasn't so bad after all, and she'd grown to like the city and its people. And of course, she'd met her future husband, George Stephenson. She had a lot to thank Kingston Upon Hull for. Perhaps.

She looked at her watch. George was a few minutes late. They were about to spend some time together outside of the house. They'd have to talk, communicate. They'd have to meet Paul, their only son, prise information out of him, find out what was wrong, work together to help him. She smiled to herself as she pictured the challenge ahead. It couldn't be any worse than trying to decorate the spare bedroom together. They'd probably come nearer to divorce at that point, compared to all the other low points. Poor George, he'd found it difficult to accept that she was the better decorator. But after that, they'd used Mr McManus' brother-in-law for decorating. On balance, better to pay than stoke up more trouble.

She took another sip of the coffee that she'd bought from the small kiosk when she'd arrived. The handsome young man had given her a cheeky wave as he'd strode out of the station. He was a lot taller than he'd looked sitting down.

A lot had happened in the last week and a half. Her momentous deliberations about George were drawing to a close. But it was the envelopes that were the problem. The first one, the one with the cheque in, that was just a matter of deceit. An ugly word, but she could deal with that. The second envelope was harder to deal with. She opened her handbag, the fake Mulberry one that George had bought from the market for her last birthday. She'd brought the letter with her, still in the torn envelope, the one addressed to him. If only he hadn't been so drunk the other night, the knowledge would already be sitting in his brain. She'd tried, she'd really tried. But he was curled up under the duvet, half asleep, half drunk. You couldn't just come out and say it, you had to build up to it a bit, lay the groundwork, especially when you'd opened his letter, clearly addressed to him. He was half listening, but he kept nodding off. Had any of it got through to him? In the end she'd given up. Only told him half the story. Less than that. Well, she couldn't change that. She hadn't seen him since, not when they were both awake together. She couldn't have just left the letter on the kitchen table, under the pepper pot, on its own or in the torn envelope, without explanation. So now she was standing in Hull railway station, with the knowledge burning a hole in her conscience.

She'd give him the letter after they'd sorted things out with Paul. She wanted to get that out of the way first.

Chapter 27

Striding into the railway station, trying to appear self-assured and purposeful, George was filled with a sudden fear. He was going to spend the next few hours with Dawn, and with Paul. A family again, early on a Thursday evening in a grubby flat in Hull. It must be two months since they'd last visited him. And now he and Dawn had to work together to get Paul to open up, reveal his worries. Probably with Danni sitting next to him, on guard. It was a bit rich asking Paul to lay bare his problems, when you thought about how many things George himself was keeping secret. He wondered if Dawn had worked out a campaign plan, tactical manoeuvres, to get Paul to pour his heart out. Would there be some secret signalling between the two of them? Nods and winks, scratching of heads, rubbing of ears. Or would Dawn simply take the lead? He'd sit there on the periphery, being supportive, or useless, depending on how you looked at it. And all the while George would be thinking about his own 'issues'. The events of last night. His discussion with Miranda this morning.

He was near the platforms now. Paragon station was all completely different compared to thirty years ago. Hull Paragon Interchange it was called now. A new shopping development. A new bus station. But there was the place where they'd agreed to meet. The bronze statue of Philip Larkin, looking like a librarian. And there was Dawn standing next to Larkin, looking like his wife. In a new stylish cream winter coat. Looking a million dollars. A cup of coffee in one hand. The handbag that he'd bought her, draped over her shoulder. He didn't think she'd worked out that it was fake.

She saw him and took a few paces towards him. For half a second he thought she might have given him a kiss, but the moment passed. There was though, a smile. Not quite warm, but at least thawing.

"Hi George. It's all a bit different here now isn't it."

"It certainly is. Sorry I'm a bit late. I didn't realise the car park was so far away. I didn't recognise anything. I like the new coat. You look like a film star."

"Thanks. It was in the sale. That's good news about the job."

"I was only there about ten minutes and they offered it to me. I think they'd have offered it to a monkey. They were desperate. It's more money as well. They actually wanted me to start on Monday, but I said I wanted next week off to get a few things sorted out. And I said that I wanted to talk to you about it. I can work from home half the week, so the travelling wouldn't be too bad."

She'd been looking him up and down as he talked animatedly about the job. "Did you go to the interview dressed like that, or did you change afterwards?"

A lie would have been an easier response, but for some reason he decided to tell the truth, or half of the truth.

"I did go like this. I thought the casual look might be more impressive. You know, show that I'm relaxed about the whole thing."

"Jeans, pink shirt, suede shoes? And that's your old ski jacket isn't it? So, you left the new suit at home?"

"That's right. I decided against the cravat though."

She shook her head and laughed. They were walking together out of the station. Not arm in arm, but at least in step.

"Things are looking up for you then George."

If only you knew the half of it Dawn.

*

It was a relatively short drive to Paul's flat. They'd been there once before, when he first moved in, and they both knew the general area from student days. But it was a complicated route around a different one-way system to that which George remembered, and he went wrong more than once. For some reason he refused to put the Sat-Nav on because he 'knew the way'. Dawn maintained a diplomatic silence.

Eventually they turned onto the Boulevard, running all the way from Hessle Road to Anlaby Road. So grandly named, it could be Paris, but no, it was Hull. The truth was, maybe one hundred years ago, it would have been grand. A wide tree-lined boulevard, with fountains at intersections. Trawler owners and top skippers would have lived in these beautiful Edwardian terraces. But not now. The settees and the fridges in the front gardens were a sure sign. Not even student land. Just poor land.

They turned left at the ornamental fountain with the strange sea creatures. George remembered wading into that fountain at four in the morning once in his second year. He'd been to a few parties in a house nearby. He couldn't remember which one exactly. It was just called The Squat, and he'd been very, very drunk every time he'd been there. All he could remember was a dog with a Labrador's body and a pug's head. He'd seen the Labrador body from behind, and then it turned its head to reveal the pug's face. He could see the squashed face now, looking at him, with the unhappy eyes and the sad downturned mouth. It knew nature had dealt it a bad hand, an unnatural crossing of breeds.

He drove on for fifty yards, then they were outside a small local police station. A strange place to put a police station, but it looked closed and boarded up. Certainly no bobbies on the beat in sight. Somehow it seemed safer to park the car outside though. Not that George had rolled up in a Bentley, although he could probably afford one now.

He switched the engine off, and turned to look at Dawn.

"Have you had your hair done? It looks a bit different."

"I just had it cut. Same style. But it was a different girl. Serena's gone to Tenerife for a week with her sister." She sighed slightly, and there were a few seconds of silence between them.

George spoke first.

"Dawn, have we got a plan with Paul? I agree with you, there's something wrong. But I'm sure Danni will be there as well. Do you think he's ready to open up now?"

"I think he will. Leave the talking to me George."

He locked the car, and they walked together past the row of fast-food outlets, remembering the illuminated chicken with the rocking head, and Norman's café where they'd had something to eat when Paul first moved in. They crossed the road and stopped outside the corner shop below the flat. The door at the side had a bell and a small plastic box with a hand-written sign, 'Number 86 – middle flat'. George pressed it, and there was a strangled buzzing noise. It was just after six o'clock, and they waited a few moments before hearing footsteps on the stairs.

The door opened, and Paul stood in front of them.

George stared at him, Paul looked back, and in that moment George knew.

Chapter 28

She heard Paul opening the door to his parents. It was reassuring to hear it open smoothly. Walker used to jam his key in, and then kick it open. He wouldn't be doing that again.

She was nervous about meeting George and Dawn, especially Dawn, and was determined to make a better impression than the last time. She hadn't had a drink in days, not even after 'the incident', as they now called it. She'd had a bath, combed her hair as straight as she could get it, and put on a simple grey linen dress. It had short sleeves, but that was enough to cover the tattoo on her shoulder, and the dress was long enough to cover the one on the inside of her thigh. It was a summer dress, but she'd had the central heating on all afternoon, and lit the gas fire half an hour ago. She'd bought some flat shoes from the charity shop at the top of the Boulevard. They pinched her toes, but she only had to wear them for the next few hours. The kettle was about to boil, there were teabags waiting in the pot, and she'd scrubbed the mugs as clean as she could get them. In fact, she'd cleaned the flat right the way through, with Elena's help from over the road. Elena worked as a cleaner for an agency, so had all the equipment, and enough all-purpose cleaning liquid to fill the Pacific. Even Elena was shocked at how quickly the vacuum cleaner had filled up. Danni had given her their last bottle of wine as a thank you, but Elena had outdone her by bringing round a warm homemade apple pie twenty minutes ago. A traditional Romanian recipe. To impress the mother-in-law. There was a wonderful smell of apple, cinnamon, and vanilla, which just about overpowered the lemon-fresh cleaning liquid smell. Danni had decided not to take the credit for the pie, but use it as an example of how friendly the neighbours were.

So she was all-set, standing next to the settee, waiting for the Queen and Prince Phillip to arrive.

But in the hours spent getting ready this afternoon, while Paul was at work, she'd replayed the events of Tuesday night and Wednesday morning, over and over. No matter how many times she thought about it, she didn't change her view on how they should handle the consequences.

*

It had been about half past six yesterday morning when they'd got out of the police station. It was cold and still dark, no sunlight to shake them awake. No sign of a rush hour yet. They'd walked around in a daze at first. Lack of sleep, and overwhelmed by events. In the end they'd caught a bus along Anlaby Road, and then walked up the Boulevard. They were followed by a skinny stray dog part of the way, trying to hunt out some breakfast, before giving up and disappearing down an alley. They walked past the house with Stag's flat at the top. They didn't say anything to each other, but they both wondered whether the news had filtered through to him yet. They turned right at the ornamental fountain, walked past their own flat. There was no sign of any activity. They walked on to Norman's café. They knew it opened at seven thirty. By then there was the faintest trace of grey in the sky from the East. It was busy with construction workers stocking up on calories and coffee for the day ahead, converting an old school to a care home further down the road. But they managed to get their usual small table for two in the corner by the window. Danni was aware how hungry and thirsty she was now, and without asking Paul, ordered a full English breakfast, coffee, and orange juice for both of them. Norman's daughter Julie brought the coffee and juice straight away, and after downing the juice and a few mouthfuls of hot coffee, Danni started to feel a bit more human again. She looked at Paul, but his eyes were staring out of the window with the look of a traumatised soldier. For her though, the cogs in her brain were turning, starting to put things in a logical sequence.

The police and the ambulance had arrived at about the same time, just after quarter to one. In the ten minutes before they arrived, Danni simply explained to Paul what their story was going to be. There was no time for agonising and debate. They'd tell the police exactly what happened, but miss out the money. Walker had come round late at night, as he often did, started to goad Paul, then the accident happened. She told Paul that she'd got the envelope with five thousand pounds in, out of Walker's pocket. He hesitated, but she looked him right in the eye, and told him they weren't going to mention the money. She didn't tell him about the five thousand euros. She'd deal with that after they'd got the police out of their hair.

The paramedics confirmed what they already knew. Walker was dead. There were two police officers, both in uniform. One very tall female, and one short male. The very tall female, PC Johnson, was perfectly reasonable, friendly even. Danni thought for one moment that she might have known her from school. The short male, who never introduced himself, was less reasonable, aggressive almost, and briefly acted as though he was in charge – until the detective in the shabby suit, with the complicated personal life, arrived. He introduced himself as Macleod. She couldn't be sure that he had a complicated personal life, but she'd seen enough TV detectives to know that it was a reasonable bet. Anyway, who was she to talk about complicated personal lives. Macleod's suit really was shabby. Plenty of gravy stains down the front of it, with one aging squashed pea stuck to one elbow. She noticed the pea as they all stood on the landing outside the sitting room, the room with Walker's dead body in. There wasn't a lot of room. Macleod asked the short male if he'd contacted CSI. He said he had, and then he and PC Johnson left. Then there were three, plus the body. Paul and Danni explained to Macleod what had happened (minus the money bit). They stuck to their story. Paul seemed in control, and Macleod seemed to believe them. She'd watched his face as he listened. It was a tired and worn face, grey and stubbly. It matched the suit. He explained that they'd still have to go to the police station to give written statements. They weren't under arrest. They weren't under caution. She watched the detective go into the sitting room to take some photos on his phone. The position of the body, the broken chair, the space between. He told them he wanted a review by the investigation team. They might be able to come during the night, or it might be first thing in the morning. There'd be a post mortem. They'd allow them back into the flat as soon as they could.

They'd been driven to the police station in the city centre. Danni was shown into a small interview room with painted white walls and ceiling and a small security camera in one top corner. One grey door, a radiator, a dark grey carpet, a grey plastic table and three grey plastic chairs. Paul was in a separate room. They left her on her own for about ten minutes and she watched a fly buzzing around the florescent light on the ceiling. This one hadn't died at the end of the summer. It made a few concentric circles before what seemed like a kamikaze upward lunge at the transparent case surrounding the light. The radiator was on full blast and it was stiflingly hot. She kept her thick winter coat on. With one envelope with five thousand pounds in the right hand pocket, and one envelope with five thousand euros in the left hand pocket, that made a lot of sense. But in the baking heat, she needed to avoid sweating, turning red, and looking suspicious.

Macleod eventually came into the room. Despite her lost years living life beyond the edge, her record was clean. But she knew they'd have checked on Walker, and probably knew him well. Macleod asked some questions about Walker, and took her statement, but then his phone went, and he disappeared for a long time. When he came back, he was distracted, rushed to finish the statement, and then said she could go. It looked like he'd believed the story, knew Walker was trouble, and wasn't too upset to see the back of him. Then she had to wait another hour before Paul appeared after giving his statement. He'd nodded to her, and without words she knew that he'd stuck to the story.

*

She was looking at him now, as breakfast arrived. She waited for Julie to put the plates on the table, thanked her, watched her go back into the kitchen, and then spoke softly, reassuringly.

"Paul, things are OK. Think it through, it's worked out fine. Ring work. Tell them that you can't come in today. A death in the family. You can explain properly tomorrow. We don't know what time we'll be allowed back in the flat."

The hit of the full English breakfast smell worked its magic quickly. She watched Paul cutting into a sausage, not half-heartedly, but hungrily. There was some weak November sunlight coming through the window, and some colour had come back into his face. She noticed the flicker of light in his eyes, and despite the uncombed hair and stubbly chin, he began to look like the handsome young man that she'd first met in the club six months ago. One thing was missing though. There was no devil perched on his shoulders.

It was still noisy in the café, deep masculine voices, even some deep-throated laughter. Other people's worlds were going on around them. It felt safe to talk.

"I'm not sorry that he's gone Paul. That might sound cruel. But it's the truth. He was pure evil."

Paul nodded slightly, but carried on eating, not looking at her yet.

"We need to keep our heads Paul. We can get through this. It was an accident. We told the truth. He fell and hit his head. That's exactly what happened."

He was nodding more forcefully now, and she could see the logic and the self-confidence building in him.

"That is what happened Danni. We both know that. We both know that's the truth. And I'm not sorry that he's gone. But what about the money? You mean you actually took the envelope out of his jacket, while he was lying there… dead. Where did you put it?"

"I put it in my coat pocket Paul. It's still here. It's my money. I was going to give it to Walker to get him off your back. But I couldn't see the point of leaving it there. What would have happened to it? I don't know. How are we worse off? I could have left it there in Walker's pocket, or put it in my pocket. I put it in my pocket. That's what I did. It's here Paul."

She took the envelope out of her coat and gently placed it on the table.

"How are we worse off Paul? Think about it. Is it better to have five thousand pounds, or not to have five thousand pounds?"

"You're right. I just can't get my head around what happens next Danni. Is that it? Walker's gone and the debt's gone. It can't be as simple as that."

"Maybe, maybe not. We just don't know."

"What about Stag and Jonno?"

"They haven't got a brain between them. They wouldn't have the full picture. They're nothing without Walker. They've been decapitated."

They both smiled at that, both conjuring up the same image.

They were both eating and talking at the same time now. He pushed the mushrooms to the side of his plate, the only thing he didn't like in Norman's full English.

"You never thought Walker had done all of this on his own though Danni. There could still be somebody else behind it all."

"Do you want those mushrooms?"

He used his knife to push them onto her plate.

"Thanks. Paul, we just don't know yet. And think about it. Walker probably didn't tell anybody that he was going to collect the money. And even if he did, he could have died before I gave it to him. I was hardly going to push five thousand pounds into the pocket of a dead body."

He had to admit that there was a compelling logic to what she was saying. He picked up the envelope and put it back in her hand.

"You're right, but put it away Danni. Put it back in your pocket. Put it back in the bank."

*

That's what she'd done this afternoon, Thursday, about a day after they'd been allowed back in the flat, and before Elena came round to help clean. Put the money back in the bank. She'd seen the same nice young man as on Tuesday afternoon when she drew the money out. He looked at her in the same way. He was definitely in love. She explained that they were going to have some building work done, and then changed their minds. He might possibly have believed her. She enquired about opening a euro account, but there was a mountain of paperwork. Anti-money-laundering procedures. Specially designed to catch an envelope stuffed with five thousand euros taken from the dead body of a criminal.

That envelope was still in her coat pocket. The coat was hanging on a solitary hook in the kitchen. She couldn't think of where else to put it. They didn't have a garden to bury it in. Or a treasure chest. They'd have to disappear to Spain for six months to spend it – or she would. She still hadn't told Paul about it. There was a low-level rumble of guilt in her stomach about that, but it was some form of insurance for her. Best not to overcomplicate things.

She could hear the voices on the landing now. She heard Paul apologising to George for not meeting him yesterday. They'd spun out a couple of hours in the café yesterday morning, and then had a call from the police to say they could go back to the flat. It had been a strange feeling walking back into the room she was standing in now. Walker's body had been taken away, and the broken chair, but it felt like there'd been a burglary. Strangers had been in there, rooting around, moving things, intruding, and then leaving. Things were in different places, there was a discarded carton of apple juice in the bin, and smells of other people hung in the air. Maybe the gang of police intruders had replaced the gang of Walker's intruders. They'd gone to bed at midday and slept all afternoon. Paul got up at twenty past five and texted George to say he was busy at work and couldn't meet him in the pub. They'd explain the reason for the lie now. And Paul had phoned his mother this afternoon. He just had to tell somebody else about what had happened. But they'd agreed. Tell them about Walker, but don't mention the money. There's no need to. The problem's gone away. For the time being anyway.

She could tell there was something strange about George as soon as he walked in the room. Paul walked in first, followed by Dawn. Danni had forgotten how attractive Dawn was. She could be a model in a fashion catalogue aimed at the over-forties. The last time she'd seen her was the disastrous day of his graduation, when she'd barely been able to see properly due to the worst hangover of the century. When George and Dawn had helped Paul move into the flat, Danni had arranged a diplomatic visit to Auntie Lelia's bungalow in Withernsea on the East coast. The next time she'd seen Auntie Lelia, was the night she died. The old lady would be interested in the vibrations that George was giving off now.

Dawn was the first to speak.

"Hi Danni. Wow, the flat looks tidy. Way better than when he first moved in. And what's that wonderful smell – some sort of apple pie?"

Danni was lost for words for a few seconds. Dawn was obviously making a big effort to be friendly, and she appreciated that. Dawn held out her hand, and Danni shook it whilst replying nervously.

"Hello Dawn. Yes, Elena from the flat opposite made it. It's a traditional Romanian recipe. Apple, cinnamon, and vanilla."

Paul looked at her and smiled. So far, so good.

George had been hanging back, and was staring at Paul in the strangest way, but not saying anything.

Dawn prompted him into a greeting. "George, it looks a lot tidier than when we helped Paul move in."

George was looking at Danni now, still deep in thought and distracted.

"It does. You're right. Hi Danni."

"Hello George." She looked away as she replied, side-stepping, but not ignoring the unusual communication that was taking place. She hadn't thought about this for a few days. The Walker incident had blocked it out. "Good to see you again," she continued, "I'll go and get the tea and apple pie."

When she returned Dawn and George were sitting on the settee, and Paul was sitting on one of the three remaining rickety chairs. She handed each of them a mug of tea, and a piece of apple pie on a plate. Cups and saucers would have been better, but they only had one of each, and they didn't match. She hadn't been sure whether to put a teaspoon on the plate as well, to eat the pie with, but Elena's pie was more like a cake, so she decided against it. George watched her as she handed out the plates.

Dawn's eyes were fixed on Paul, who'd already started to tell the story. The toned-down version. He took a sip of tea, and then carried on, with heavy editing.

Walker was trouble. He was always hanging around the flat. Bringing friends round that they didn't want. A bad lot. They couldn't get rid of him. Threatening behaviour. They suspected he was involved in criminal activity. Drugs. He was Danni's half-brother, but she hated him. She was completely different to him. Then the incident happened. It was a freak accident. Chance in a million. They'd explained everything to the police. That's why Paul hadn't met up with George. It was a terrible thing. A tragedy. But everything was resolved now. It had all settled down. That's why he'd seemed so distracted over the last few weeks. He should have told them earlier, but he didn't want to worry them.

Danni watched Dawn's face as Paul told the story. A look of horror had appeared at the mention of the dead body. Dawn had looked over at the fire surround where Walker had hit his head, obviously picturing the corpse that had been lying there only yesterday morning. She'd stopped eating the apple pie at that point. Danni had dreamt about the body last night, and then woke up this morning wondering how they'd carried it downstairs. It must have been a difficult manoeuvre. It would need two strong men. The stairs were so steep and narrow. Walker had bounded up them, then was carried down them, presumably in a body bag. Bet you weren't expecting that, Walker.

Danni took a large bite of the pie. It was probably the best she'd ever tasted. She watched Dawn start to relax a bit as Paul reached the end of the story. It had a happy ending. Not for Walker. But for the rest of them. '…everything was resolved now… it had settled down… he should have told them earlier… he didn't want to worry them.'

Dawn took a deep breath, still with her eyes on her son. "God, that's quite a story Paul. I'm relieved that you've told us. I knew there was something wrong, but I didn't realise it was anything like this. What do you think George?"

They all turned to look at George.

"Sounds like you had a bit of help from above."

"What, do you mean, divine intervention? That's one way of looking at it," replied Paul, slightly puzzled.

George was about to say something else, but Dawn spoke over him, "That's a strange thing to say George. Danni, on the one hand we're sorry about what happened. He's your half-brother. You must feel something."

Danni was almost tempted to tell Dawn the full story. The entrapment, the extortion, the violence. But she paused. She'd rehearsed this answer.

"You're right Dawn. There's part of me that has to feel some sorrow. But if you'd seen the way Walker treated Paul. And I think he was involved in dealing drugs. He really was an evil person. I'm sorry to say that, but it's true. He was making Paul's life a misery. I think the world's a better place without him."

How about that for a carefully considered response, she thought.

Paul reached over, put his hand on Danni's hand, and squeezed it. They hadn't rehearsed that, but it looked good.

*

They'd got the main business of the day out of the way. Danni could tell that Paul had lifted a weight off his shoulders by telling his parents about his 'troubles'. At least part of the story anyway. And she could see that he was relieved that things had gone relatively smoothly between his mother and his girlfriend. The two women in his life. He'd said that he was settling into the new job. Danni had dished up more tea, more pie. She told Dawn that she was bored with the job at the health food shop, but planned to start a university access course next September. She'd got some money saved up. She thought about the envelope in her coat pocket as she was saying that. George didn't say a lot. It was obvious his mind was somewhere else. But Dawn forced him to tell them about the new job in Hull. About how they wanted him so badly, even with a pink shirt and suede shoes.

It was nearly eight o'clock now. They'd all run out of things to say. Run out of pie, and run out of tea bags. She should have got some more, but thankfully nobody wanted another cup. They'd said their goodbyes. She thought Dawn was going to give her a hug, but instead it was something between a wave and an acknowledgement. That was enough though.

Danni was standing on the landing, starting to breathe more easily. She could hear Paul talking to his parents outside the front door. She'd go and buy a bottle of wine from the corner shop when they'd gone. They could start to celebrate. She could kick off these uncomfortable shoes as well. She'd visit her mother tomorrow. She'd phoned her yesterday evening to tell her about Walker. She realised she hadn't spoken to her for at least three years before that. Karin sounded drunk, and started crying. They were crocodile tears. Her mother was probably worried about a source of cash drying up. She'd have to buy her own gin. There'd be the funeral to sort out. That would fall on her. She pictured herself giving the eulogy. 'The world has lost a son, and a brother, and an up-and-coming business man.' She and Paul would stand at the front looking serious whilst the priest did the service. All the cousins would turn up to the wake. Stag and Jonno, and the business associates. There'd be some drunken arguments. The obligatory punch-up. Then the complicated financial arrangements. Good luck with that one. She'd already sorted out her share. The Walker storybook might not be entirely closed. There could be one final twist. But they'd just have to deal with that.

She'd picked up the other storybook now. The one that had started in Spain a few weeks ago. Something had happened with George. She could tell. Somehow, she was going to work it out.

Chapter 29

He was turning the key in the ignition as she spoke to him.

"George, what was wrong with you in there?"

"I'm going to tell you Dawn. I'm going to drive somewhere first. It's less than half an hour away."

"Quite the man of mystery aren't we," she teased.

He avoided answering. "I didn't expect you to be so nice to Danni. You've changed your tune."

"I thought I'd give her a break. Paul obviously wants to be with her. She'd made a real effort. If I'm being honest, I'd say she was the strong one in the relationship."

"Like you, you mean?"

She didn't answer. But the silence answered for her.

"Well at least we know what was troubling him Dawn."

She nodded her head, without agreeing. She knew that he'd inherited that trait from George, so she'd been looking out for it while he'd been recounting the Walker story. Paul had rubbed his neck, at the left-hand side, it went red. Just like George. Like father, like son. It didn't necessarily mean that he was lying. Just that he wasn't telling the whole truth.

She hadn't been telling the whole truth either. But that was different.

*

He followed the same route as last night. No music, and neither of them said anything. He was rehearsing his lines. He turned off at the junction just before the motorway began, not prompted by overhead signs this time. He sped along the roads that he'd crawled along last night, then through the village. Ellerdyke. Then slowed down until he found the turning. He was aware of Dawn looking at him now.

"You're not going to murder me are you George?"

"We're nearly there now. I recognise it."

"Are we going to meet someone?"

"Something like that."

He turned and drove slowly past the remaining houses until it became the country lane, grass verges and hedges on either side. It was as he remembered it, except there were no wisps of mist tonight. It was perfectly clear. He spotted the gap in the hedge, stopped the car, turned the engine off, and swivelled around to look at Dawn. She was looking back at him with a bewildered expression, waiting for an explanation. He parted his dry lips and opened his mouth to speak. He remembered his lines, but the words stuck in his throat, anchored down. He'd managed to say it to Miranda. He could imagine himself saying it to Danni. But somehow, he couldn't say it to his wife, the mother of his son. Come on George. You can do it. He took a deep breath, steeled himself. Now he was ready.

"George, I don't know what we're doing sitting in the car, down this country lane. But there's something I've got to tell you."

He was supposed to speak first. He was thrown off course, trying to compute things in his head, and didn't reply. But from the look in her eyes, he knew this was a seminal moment.

"I can't put it off any longer. You're going to be shocked, and you might be disappointed in me. There's no easy way to say it, I've just got to come out with it."

He thought he saw a flash of movement outside, and turned to look, but it was nothing. He shook his head and looked back at Dawn.

"You got a letter on Tuesday. I opened it. I can't explain why, but I did. I read it. I tried to tell you on Tuesday night but you were drunk. I started, but you weren't listening. You fell asleep. So I gave up. And I didn't see you yesterday."

One final pause, one final deep breath.

"You've got a daughter George. Or you did have. She died. She was called Rachel."

"I know. I saw her last night. Right here."

Friday 17 November

Chapter 30

"I think we'd all like to recognise the contribution George has made over the last couple of years at HG. He's really driven the Argonaut project forward like a Formula 1 racing car. It's well in the lead after three quarters of the race, and now Angel just needs to complete the final laps and take the chequered flag. We'll have to start calling him Ferrari Stephenson."

Turning to face him, she held out her arm as if putting him on display.

"And we understand that he's already got a new job lined up. No lengthy pit stops for George. A new race and another famous victory on the cards I'm sure."

Strangely, he felt only mild embarrassment. He hadn't expected Samantha to wheel out this level of sophisticated irony for his leaving speech. And where did the extended motor racing metaphor come from? It was being delivered as an in-joke that he understood, but did everybody else get it – that he was a cart-horse not a Ferrari? He and Samantha were conjoined in their gambling good fortune, and they could both put his work mishandlings behind them. George had his pay-off and a new job (he'd phoned Bill Parkinson first thing this morning to accept the offer), and Samantha had Angel and her substantial brain to sort out the mess. Now he just had to get through this final day, a drink in the pub this evening, piggy backing onto another leaving do, then he could kiss goodbye to HG.

That should be the easy bit. But as he listened to Samantha praise his achievements, with co-opted colleagues from neighbouring desks looking at their watches and gazing into the distance, he was a lot more focused on the other women in his life. Not counting Angel and Linda who were both standing dangerously near.

The explanation from Paul, and the revelations of last night, from both him and Dawn, in his Toyota Yaris, just outside a distant East Yorkshire village, had briefly brought a new intimacy. She'd even given him a brief hug. Reached over from the passenger seat, twisted her body, and wrapped her arms awkwardly around his shoulders. He'd felt the gentle warmth from her body, and smelt the top-of-the-range re-moisturising conditioner that she used on her hair. No kiss though.

They'd started to piece a few things together. He forgave her for opening the letter. It was a minor thing compared to all of the things she had to forgive him for. And they agreed – she had tried to tell him what was in the letter on Tuesday night. Some of it might even have got through. All of it would have got through if he hadn't been boozing the night away with Angel Wei in a Colombian bar. His wife understood about Elaine. It was before he'd met Dawn. A brief encounter. They were young.

Good job she didn't know the whole truth about Elaine.

He'd started to talk about what he saw on Wednesday night, but they hadn't begun to try to make sense of it. Dawn had looked doubtful. Interested, still close, but doubtful. She'd had that look on her face when his phone had rung. He couldn't really not answer it. And when Miranda's voice had echoed around from the speaker phone, the sceptical look on Dawn's face turned back to the default expression of the last few years – grinding disappointment mixed with anger. Miranda was ringing with her initial thoughts on what she called 'the encounter', but she'd kicked off with some cheeky throw-away lines about Anna, and about George making her think again about the 'traditional route'. She was well into this line of thought before George could alert her that his wife of nearly twenty-five years was listening in. Dawn had remained silent, and Miranda had said that she'd ring back in the morning.

As he'd started the three-point-turn so that he could drive back to the main road, Dawn had asked, with a definitely uncharitable tone: "Was that the witch that you used to know? You saw her today did you?"

He'd started to explain that Miranda had written a PhD on the paranormal. That's why he'd met up with her. But it sounded like 'she's helping me with my enquiries', and Dawn's sceptical look about 'the encounter' turned into a sceptical look about George's motives with Miranda. Back to his old tricks was what he thought Dawn was thinking.

And as he'd turned the car back onto the main road again, and his phone had rung again, and he'd seen Angel's name come up on his contact list, and he'd cut the call off, Dawn had asked: "Was that another one of your lady friends George?"

The new-found intimacy was dead in the water at that point. They drove home in silence. Dawn went straight to bed, and left for work before he got up. Again...

He shook his head, and turned his thoughts back to the here and now. Samantha was drawing her speech to a close.

"I'm not going to say too much more George. We know you don't like the limelight. Prefer just to keep your head down and get on with the job, focus on getting things done. But in the usual tradition, we've had a bit of a collection. We've got you a card, and a gift, to remember us all by..."

Pause for dramatic effect.

"...And we wish you all the best for the future George."

There was a modest ripple of applause from the twenty-five or so people gathered around his desk, some of whom he recognised, but most of whom just happened to sit randomly nearby.

George stepped forward to acknowledge the acclaim, raising his right hand as a gesture of acceptance to the masses. Anna gave him an enigmatic smile. Linda gave him a malevolent smile. Angel seemed to give him an adoring smile. That was the hardest one to work out.

"Thank you for those kind words Samantha. It's rewarding to know that your efforts are appreciated, and your achievements recognised. I'm very proud of how far

256

we moved forward on project Argonaut in the last two years, and I'm pleased that I'm leaving it in good shape for Angel to put the finishing touches to."

Two could play at the biting irony.

"But it's not really the work that you remember. What you remember is the people. The friendships you've made, friendships that will last a lot longer than the job itself."

He looked around at the faces of the people that he didn't know, or didn't know their names, or didn't like, or certainly didn't want to see again. They looked back at him, blankly. There was goal congruity there then.

"I'm sure I'll be keeping in touch with many of you, and I'll certainly be watching the progress of HG International".

Longer pause for dramatic effect. Deep sigh.

"It's so nice of you to get me this card, and present."

He carefully opened the envelope and removed the card. He recognised it from Card Outlet, competitively priced at 99p. He'd bought an identical one himself for somebody about a year ago. It was the biggest card that you could get for under a pound. A sailing ship on the blue ocean with the words 'bon voyage' in silver letters. He opened the card, pretending to read the comments whilst smiling knowingly. Then he opened the present, carefully removing the paper. That was a habit he'd got from his mother at Christmas. You could save the paper for next year. The present was revealed as a bottle of his favourite whiskey. Now that wasn't bad. It had probably cost thirty-five pounds from Tesco. Linda was the only person present who knew what his favourite whiskey was, which was worrying. Unless Monika had phoned Dawn to ask. That would be it.

*

He got the trauma of his leaving presentation out of the way by midday. He'd handed in his security card. IT had come to collect his company laptop and mobile phone. He'd said his goodbyes, shook a few hands, had a hug with Monika, avoided all the right people, and left the building for the last time. Avoided Linda. Promised to have a chat to Tommo in the pub this evening. Promised to speak to Angel in the pub. No tears. No embarrassing moments. He'd got it over with.

And now he found himself driving to Miranda's house. Found himself. A strange expression that. Like he'd found himself in a bed in a budget hotel room with Linda. Twice. Like he'd found himself sitting perilously close to Angel, their knees touching, in a bar, less than three days ago. As if by magic. A puff of smoke, and there you are. Like a puzzled time-traveller mysteriously landing in a baffling new dimension. A twist of fate. No self-determination involved.

This was the plan he found himself executing. Drive to Miranda's house. Solve the ghost mystery. Work it all out. In a matter of hours. Let the ink dry. Then drive back to Leeds. Park the car up for the night, and go to the pub for leaving drinks. Get the bus home or a taxi. What could be easier.

Spending the next few hours alone with Miranda was just another classic George Stephenson idea. Designed to calm the waters in a way that could open the floodgates. Things had been going so well with Dawn last night. It had taken the tragic death of his unknown daughter and subsequent reappearance in spectral form, to bring them together. But it had done. With some help from Paul. Only to be knocked off course by Miranda's broadcast phone call. Perhaps irrevocably so. So, what better way to put things right. Swap a few text messages this morning. Arrange to meet at one o'clock. Then head off to Miranda's house. You've got to hand it to yourself George, you know how to treat a woman.

The sun had been shining as he'd driven out of the HG car park. It was a pale watery sun, ephemeral, and surrounded by sludgy grey clouds, with even darker clouds threatening from further away, but it seemed like a hopeful sign as winter approached. Prophetic even. A new phase of life. And he was sure that Miranda could help him dig out the answers to the strange questions laid before him.

The half-hour drive across the city and out the other side, changed all that. By the time he pulled up outside Miranda's house, the dark clouds had won the battle in the November sky. The pagan hordes were triumphant, with the heavens about to open. There would be a deluge. And George's mood had shifted to the darker side as well. It was a truly dark thing that had happened on Wednesday night. He didn't have to close his eyes to picture the look on her face. There was a message there. A troubling message. That's why he was standing outside Miranda's house now, about to knock on the door. She would help in a way that Dawn couldn't. He felt it in his bones.

The deluge started on the second knock. Hailstones – there was no gradual build up, they just fell from the sky, and bounced off the paving stones outside the front door. It felt primeval, the power of nature, forces beyond our control, the insignificance of the individual. It could have been scripted, but it wasn't, it was real. He hunched up his shoulders, and out of the corner of his eye he saw the black cat running for shelter down the alley at the side of the house. A different black cat, obviously.

On the fourth knock, the door swung open. Miranda wore the same flowing black dress and boots, but now she wore a beautiful close-fitting maroon top, buttoned up with silver studs, a few left open at the top. Her hair was bunched up on her head, tied up with a silver and blue ribbon. The make-up was subtly different from yesterday. The lipstick was a subdued pale pink compared to the bright red of Thursday. There was a serious look on her face.

He hesitated on the doorstep. Not just out of politeness, but because this felt like a step into something very different. Not a 'Famous Five' adventure but a worrying black tunnel with only the slightest glimmer of light at the end. The hailstones accelerated, his heartbeat quickened, he breathed deeply.

"Come in George. I've been thinking…"

And with that he stepped into the tunnel.

Chapter 31

It wasn't hard to turn your mind back twenty-eight years. It was easy. That one night that must have started all of this. It did feel like that was the start. The thing that had triggered the strange events over the last week.

So, it had begun in East London. His final year at university. No real thoughts about what he would do next. A visit to a mate at journalist college. Drinks in a pub and then more drinks at a party back at the flat in Hackney. No sign of a gentrification process at that stage. But for him at nearly twenty-one, whose domain was the north of England, it felt like a different world. More people from more countries. Different colours, different accents, different looks. You needed to watch your back, but he liked it. And he liked her.

They'd started to talk in the pub. Found themselves standing next to each other by accident. Life was that random. Gravity didn't control everything. It was the random sub-atomic particles buzzing around that caused it. You just happened to find yourself in a certain place at a certain time. For no good reason. Except there might have been good reason. And in the first few sentences of the conversation, he'd known that it would lead somewhere. Not just a night in the bed in the room at the top of that cold, cold house, with the musty smell and the sound of the music pounding out two floors below. He'd thought that it would lead to a lot more than that.

They'd walked back from the pub to the party together, and they'd stood in the kitchen together, shouting in each other's ears above the deafening sound system pumping out roots reggae. You could feel the bass hanging in the air. They'd stood outside together in the back yard, where it was quieter. They hadn't felt the cold. He'd kissed her, he'd put his hand on the bottom of her back, his other hand on her neck. Her beautiful neck. He could smell her perfume. They carried on kissing. And when they walked upstairs together to find an empty room in the house, it didn't feel sordid, it felt lovely. It felt as though this would last, be forever beautiful. The talking and the laughing came so easily.

In the morning it wasn't awkward. They weren't sure why they'd woken so early. It was probably down to the sun streaming in through the tiny skylight window in the roof. It had been January but the sun had been strong. Almost like a summer's day. They'd sat at the big kitchen table. Cleared a space. Found some awful coffee and some old bread for toast. There wasn't any embarrassment about the night before, or why they'd been so reckless. They were both calm. They carried on laughing. He could see her face now, and the smile.

He had a train booked from Kings Cross at midday. He'd thought about getting a later train but he didn't have the money for another ticket. And they'd see each other in two weeks. He would come down for the weekend and stay with her at her mum's house. It was all arranged. She was only eighteen, doing A levels in the summer. They walked to the tube station together. Then she got the tube with him to Kings Cross. They kissed and held each other standing near the ticket office. She waved as he went through the barrier and turned onto the platform. George looked around one more time and waved.

That was the last time he saw Elaine's face. He'd thought about her just about every day since. Thought about the last time he saw that face. Until Wednesday night. Her face and his nose.

*

Miranda kept her eyes on him as he explained about the letter, the face, the nose, Elaine, and Rachel.

261

"That's quite a story George. And you've come round here again, expecting me to explain everything."

"You're the expert," he said, almost accusingly.

"We've been through all of this," she replied, defensively. "I don't believe that carbon atoms from dead people get recycled into a form of themselves which then reappear. I don't believe it. Science doesn't believe it, and I believe in science. Honestly, I do. But I believe you had some sort of experience. Something happened in your brain. Electricity and chemicals. Remember."

He was sitting in the same chair as yesterday. With another cup of undrunk lukewarm nettle tea sitting on the side table next to him. The hailstones had stopped. It was just raining now. He had his back to the window but he could hear the rain beating against the glass, and feel the darkness outside. The only light in the room was from a standard lamp behind Miranda which illuminated the back of her head with an eerie glow.

"Science can't explain why I saw my dead daughter on Wednesday night. Why she looked like me. Why she looked like my father and my son."

Miranda fixed her eyes on him with the logical cruelty of a convert.

"But you've said that Dawn started to tell you about the letter. You were drunk, but she started to tell you. She wasn't sure whether you were listening or not. Maybe something did get into your brain. Started the electricity and the chemicals flowing."

He'd thought these thoughts himself. Did Dawn's words get through to him in some way? Did she tell enough of the story to lodge in his consciousness through the drunken haze of Tuesday night? So that he already knew about Rachel when he saw what he saw?

Miranda continued, leading him down the path of logic.

"You'd been driving for hours George. You were tired and hungry and thirsty. You've been under pressure. There are big changes in your life. The idea of the long-lost daughter was buried in your mind. It was dark. It had been misty. Your brain projected something, maybe."

"I liked the old Miranda better. You sound like a computer. There's such a thing as soul, you know."

"But think about this George. Rachel didn't know about you. Elaine said that in the letter – she'd never told Rachel about who her real father was. So even if you accept the premise of an afterlife, how did the disembodied Rachel know to track you down?"

He'd had enough of this.

"I want us to go and see Elaine tomorrow. I want you to come with me. That's the way we can sort this out. The address was on the letter. She must want me to get in touch. She still lives in Hackney. That's where I met her. But it's gentrified now. Part of it anyway. Million pound houses. We'll get the train to London, Miranda. I'll pay."

"What, turn up unannounced after twenty-eight years. The ex-lover of one night, and his glamorous assistant. Should I wear a special outfit? I'm a bit long in the tooth to be the magician's visual ornamentation. Despite what you're thinking."

He wondered how she knew he was thinking that.

"Aren't you going to ring her George? Send her a text, a message, an e-mail? Give her some sort of warning. Maybe she expected you to write to her."

"No. We'll just go. If I turn up on the doorstep, she'll invite me in. If I try to arrange something, she might back off. It makes sense."

"It doesn't make any sense George. And as I said, I've been thinking."

*

There was a mirror above the mantelpiece. He could see the window reflected in it, and watched the rain fall for a few seconds. Which gave him time to go back twenty-eight years. Again.

263

'Maybe she expected you to write to her'. Of course he'd written to her. In 1989. He'd written the letter as soon as he got home that Sunday evening, and posted it that night. And on Friday a letter had come back. He'd torn the envelope open. Noticed how neat the writing was. Neat, but the capital letters at the beginning of the sentences were written with a flourish. Just like she started to speak with a flourish. It wouldn't work – him coming down the Friday that they'd arranged. Her mum's sister was coming that weekend. But he could come the weekend after. Her mum was fine with that. Please write back, but probably best not to ring. Her mum could be a bit funny sometimes. No texts, e-mails, or messaging in those days of course. No mobile phones. You had to have a conversation on the phone in the hall with your mum listening. Or in the corridor of the hall of residence with everybody else listening. Or in a call box, slotting in 50p pieces, avoiding the unspeakable debris in the corner, breathing in the unspeakable fumes.

So he'd written back. Tried to make his handwriting a bit neater.

Then there was radio silence.

For twenty-eight years.

No reply. Nothing.

He wrote four more letters. He phoned the number that she'd given him, despite the threat of the mother. But it just rang and rang with no answer. He made another trip down to London. Got the bus to Hackney. The tube was closed for some reason. Knocked on the door of what looked like an old council flat. No reply. He'd walked to a café. Went back in the afternoon. Knocked again, and there was no reply again. He started hammering on the door, banging his fist hard, more desperately. In the end a neighbour came out. 'Can you shut up knocking. They've moved. A few weeks ago. I don't know where they've gone to. To live with her sister maybe. They didn't leave a forwarding address. There was no husband. Elaine went with her. I presume that's who you're looking for.'

And that was that. Elaine had gone. Gone forever. He'd loved her in that one night. She was the one.

But three weeks later he met Dawn.

Then she was the one.

*

"Anyway George. I said I've been thinking. About two things."

He looked back at her and wound forward. He was forty-nine again.

"Is it good news and bad news? I'll have the bad news first. Get it out the way."

"It's not like that. I did do some research on the place where you had the encounter. That's what I was ringing about last night."

"Where I saw Rachel you mean."

She continued, ignoring his comment, "I've still got access to the academic library. They never cancelled it. I looked for any other documented activity in the area.

"Documented activity. What does that mean Miranda?"

"Different people have done different pieces of research. A lot of it's on a single database. Not all of it. But a lot of it. There's a few things recorded for that village – Ellerdyke."

He was interested now. "What sort of things?"

"I can't open up the detailed accounts. I'm going to try and get Declan to do it, my old co-author. But he's working in the US now."

"It's not about that village. It's about me and my daughter Miranda. But thanks for looking at it. I think I'm more confused than ever. What's the second thing?"

"Well, it's very nice you coming to see me after all these years. Catch up on old times. Flirt a bit. Remember the night after the séance. You're not a bad looking bloke George. In another life, who knows? And I know you want to work out what happened. But I think what you should really work out, is what's going on with you and Dawn. Your wife, George."

"Are you a marriage guidance counsellor now? We've already seen one of them."

"I reckon that's at the heart of all your... issues. You want things to be right between the two of you."

"You're a shrink as well."

"And going on a day out to the capital with me is hardly going to improve things is it? Who'd make the sandwiches George? Would we pop into Madame Tussauds?"

"We could always buy the sandwiches."

"Think about how Dawn would feel. If you want to go and see Elaine, you should ask Dawn to go with you."

Chapter 32

He was planning his escape strategy. The problem was in the positioning. The door out of the room was at the far side. That was about ten paces away. That door led to a narrow corridor. It was about five paces down that corridor to a door into another bar. Then you had to walk about ten paces to the main exit. He was pinned in at the far side of the back room as far from the door as possible. It had been a strategic error. He'd allowed himself to get boxed in. Virtually impossible to make any sort of outflanking manoeuvre. The route was lined by HG comrades enjoying the free drinks. Brian had put his credit card behind the bar. George hadn't. George couldn't remember which department Brian used to work in, or what his second name was. Just that Brian had a large mole on the end of his chin, with hair growing out. Like a wizened old lady. You couldn't miss it.

It had seemed like a good idea at the time. As Napoleon said before he invaded Russia. But like the little corporal in Moscow, George was regretting his decision and looking for a way out. He'd never seen it as a joint leaving do. He viewed it as an excuse to leave the office without saying goodbye, make a cursory appearance at the Red Lion, and then disappear into the ether for ever. One anonymous drink, and then drive home.

He should have taken up a position near the door. To allow a quick getaway. But in his current position, he'd have to pick his way through the masses in the full glare of publicity. More importantly, he'd have to get past Angel, and then, worst of all, Linda.

His thoughts drifted back to sitting in Miranda's house earlier that day. The tidal wave of logic and common sense that she'd released in his direction. Maybe her chaotic life had brought her greater insight. Or maybe her insight was just average. It was his insight that was sadly deficient. The thought of him and Miranda dancing around London together, meeting up with the love of his life from nearly thirty years ago, solving the ghost mystery like Holmes and Watson, was plainly ludicrous. However much of an adventure it might have been. And all of that with Dawn waiting dutifully in the wings, ready to welcome him back with open arms at the end of the weekend. There were still plenty of ludicrous elements to his plan. Turning up unannounced on Elaine's doorstep for one. But either way, turning up with your wife rather than a paranormal consultant, must be a better bet.

Which is why Dawn's response was so puzzling. He'd phoned her as soon as he left Miranda's house. It would be like a weekend minibreak. He'd book the train tickets for Saturday morning, a hotel for Saturday night, train tickets back on Sunday afternoon. They were bound to catch Elaine in at some point over the weekend. They could find out about Rachel. What had happened. Maybe he'd tell Elaine about what he'd seen on Wednesday night. Maybe not. He'd play it by ear.

Dawn had answered. She was having her lunch in the park she told him. It had stopped raining and the sun was out again. Her mood seemed to have improved a bit. He'd pitched his suggestion. There'd been a long silence. She'd asked him where he was. That was a tough one. Sitting in the car outside Miranda's house. He'd opted for honesty. On reflection, that might have been an error of judgement. He should have stuck to his usual tactic of half-truths and obfuscation.

She'd hung up. He'd taken that as a 'no'. He hadn't tried again. So before he arrived in the Red Lion, he'd booked himself a return ticket and a night in the Premier Inn Hackney. If he managed to escape early enough tonight, and Dawn was at home, maybe he'd have another go at persuading her.

Which is why he needed to get out of this place. But at the moment, listening to Patrick from Financial Planning and Analysis was driving him to unmitigated despair. Pinned in the corner, having to listen to sodding Patrick talking in a different language ridden with acronyms and unfathomable technical references. Why do some people only talk about themselves, non-stop, at full volume, close into your face, and expect you to be interested?

"You see, George, we've built a new platform for next year's budget. We bought the RD53 system from HLC, but we've had to customise it. Customise it quite heavily. That doesn't come without risk George. I'm not sure that HLC will support all of the changes. And I don't think Change Management have documented things properly. And as Peter says, not all the subsidiaries have bought into it fully. Spain still used Excel spreadsheets for the half-year budget update, when we had the new platform in the test environment. Can you believe it? Peter specifically instructed them not to, but they did it anyway. Internal Audit found out. Peter should have slapped them down, but he didn't do. Backed off, said he didn't have Tim's support. But Tim was right behind the changes. So God knows what will happen when we go fully live in December. The whole thing could come crashing down."

George had developed the technique of pretending to listen, whilst taking his thoughts elsewhere, to a different universe. He'd been nodding periodically during Patrick's tirade, but was mainly thinking about what tomorrow would bring. So when Patrick looked at him for any sort of response, George just said, "I see your point Patrick." George had also allowed himself a few thoughts of dragging Patrick into the yard behind the pub, punching him to the ground, scattering the empty beer barrels in all directions. Patrick would have plenty of time to think about the RD53 system, whist taking in the smell of stale urine as George ground his face into the dirt.

He looked back at Patrick. There was a slow trickle of blood coming from his right nostril. The deep red liquid touched the top of Patrick's lip and then dripped onto his white shirt, a very distinctive red on white. George stared at Patrick who put his hand up to his nose, blood smeared across his palm and fingers, and threw his head back.

The tall lady on the other side of him said, "Are you OK Patrick?".

"It's just a nose bleed Amanda," said Patrick, pulling some tissues out of his pocket and dabbing at his nose. Not the result of the imaginary beating then, thought George.

This was the window of opportunity, a gap had opened up, he could see a route through the crowd of people. He sipped the last dregs of beer, mumbled something about sorting a few things out, completely ignored the blood-stained Patrick, and made his way towards the door. He waved at Samantha and Anna as he picked his way through the bar area. He waved at Tommo as well. He could tell Tommo wanted to spend a couple of hours in deep conversation, but George just didn't have the stomach for that. He couldn't see Linda. Maybe she'd gone home. But as he was about to reach the door and breathe in the sweet air of freedom, Angel suddenly appeared before him. She smiled, and put her hand on his shoulder.

Perhaps she did know that he planned to leave without saying goodbye. The last time that he'd spoken to her properly, was early on Tuesday evening, before the three bottles of wine had kicked in. It was actually only a week since he'd met her, and in that time she'd seemed to be on a rollercoaster. Veering from the totally in-control stylish young executive; to ragged, troubled young woman beset by work and family problems.

Tonight she was back in control, and on the front foot.

"Hi George. I'm so pleased I saw you before you left."

Before I managed to sneak off, he thought.

"I've made some big decisions George. I think it was that drunken night with you on Tuesday that did it. My life had

270

become so complicated. I'd got myself into such a mess, and I had the worst hangover ever the morning after. I'd reached my lowest point George."

You mean the night out with George Stephenson was plumbing the depths, you couldn't sink any lower.

"I couldn't sink any lower George. I didn't go into work on Wednesday morning. I gave myself lots of time to think. Came up with a plan. It means some pretty big changes."

That's just what I need, he thought.

"I'm going to leave HG. I'll finish this project, serve my notice. Then I'm moving to the not-for-profit sector. I've already told Armando. And I've resigned as a director of all of those companies. I feel better already. And I've sorted things out with my cousins. They won't be pestering me any more."

Just like that. A whole life sorted out in a few strokes.

"It's been nice working with you George. I hope you and Dawn get things sorted out."

She held out her hand, and when he hesitated she took his hand, applied an awkward handshake, then turned and left. That was it.

What did he want? For her to fling her arms around him? Press her lips against his, and beg him not to leave? And what was that about him and Dawn. He couldn't remember discussing that with her. But then there was a lot that was hazy about Tuesday night.

He stood there for a few moments. Then remembered that he was walking away from HG. That was his plan.

He walked through the door, into the corridor. There was nobody there. Apart from Linda.

*

"I've got a nice bruise from Tuesday."

"I bet you have George. If you get away with a bruised leg, I think you'll have done pretty well, don't you?"

271

That sounded like a common sense answer. He didn't think there was another good kicking coming.

"I'm getting married George. He's a good man. His wife died a couple of years ago. He's got two sons. I've met them. Believe it or not, they like me."

He looked down at his shoes. They still needed polishing. A wave of shame washed over him. Still looking at his shoes, he started to speak.

"I'm sorry Linda. I didn't treat you right. I should have been more honest. I've been weak. I'm trying to change all that."

"That sounds like a pretty fair summary of your life George. I didn't plan to meet you again. This was an accident."

He looked up at her, and spoke, almost in a whisper.

"I'm pleased you're getting married Linda. Honestly, you deserve better than me."

"You're talking sense at last," she replied, maybe with the slightest inkling of a smile.

"I shouldn't have kicked you earlier this week. You deserved it though. But, it's a long time since I've resorted to violence like that. My first boyfriend in fact. He was weak like you."

There was an embarrassed pause for a few seconds.

"Well, I'll be going now Linda. All the best for the future. And sorry again."

"Work things out with Dawn, George. That's my advice. I feel guilty about what we did, but I can't change that. Don't worry, I won't tell her anything, although I expect she already knows."

"Thanks. I'm trying, but I'll try harder. Bye."

He smiled, she shook her head slightly, then he walked out of the pub.

Saturday 18 November

Chapter 33

He felt completely safe lying in her arms. She'd brushed her hair out. Untangled the dreadlocks. It felt like she was making a statement. Then had a long bath. Washed her hair with the rosewood shampoo from the hippy shop. Then spent a long time brushing and drying it. With just a touch of that oil. He'd watched her do it. In front of the mirror, with the white towelling dressing gown wrapped around her. It was new, and snow white.

And now he was resting his head on her breasts. Her arms wrapped around him, one hand fastened on his shoulder, the other hand touching the back of his head. She must have bought the new sheets at the same time as the dressing gown, and taken the time to iron them. He didn't realise they had an iron. The feel and smell was exhilarating and soporific at the same time. Danni had fallen asleep almost straight away. Sleep had suddenly come easy to her in the last few days. He could just see the radio alarm clock by the bed, without moving his head. The glowing green numbers showed 1.33 a.m. He was happy to stay in this half-awake state. Saturday tomorrow. They could lie in bed tomorrow morning, doze and talk.

It was only three days since it had all happened. They'd settled back into a new normality. Heard nothing more from the police, or anybody else associated with Walker. One day you owed a bad guy a lot of money, the next you didn't. The torment had ended abruptly. It felt like divine intervention.

And it was good that they'd seen Mum and Dad. It didn't seem to matter that they'd only told them half the story. There was no need for them to know about the money. And Mum had been nice to Danni. Impressed by her plans for the future. And Mum and Dad seemed to be getting along. Always difficult to tell with Dad, because he didn't say very much. There was a bit of a mystery there, but Paul couldn't work it all out. Danni had sensed something as well.

Maybe the cat had sensed the more settled conditions in the flat. That's why it'd returned. He could hear it now, prowling around downstairs in the sitting room. He didn't like it, but he was prepared to tolerate it. It had been away for weeks. Keeping out of the way of Walker and his cronies. They made its life hell. About the same as his life. Danni had fed it, and given it a saucer of full cream milk to welcome it back. It seemed restless though, perhaps it was still settling back in. He'd have to get up and let it out. Otherwise it would be making noises all night. It would drive him mad. The bloody cat.

He slipped out of Danni's arms. She didn't wake up. He fumbled at the bottom of the bed and pulled on his boxer shorts and a T-shirt. He opened the bedroom door, walked down the stairs onto the landing and then pushed the sitting room door open.

He knew there was something wrong as soon as he stepped into the room. He couldn't see anything. But he felt the presence in a fraction of a second. There was someone else or something else in the room, maybe both. You could just feel it. And there was a strangely familiar smell. A dark dread enveloped him. It seemed to get colder. There was the tiniest amount of light from outside, but in other ways it was completely dark. There were two things – one drawing him towards it, and another advancing towards him. Then the searing pain, the crack on the head, the falling over, the tumbling towards the ground, the hitting the floor, the weight on top of him. Something bad. But still the feeling from somewhere else of something good. Something that would help. The weight lifted. He felt a hand on the side of his face. It pushed his head hard against the floor boards. Then some footsteps, a shape rushing to the door. He tried to lift himself up, get up on his knees, but his legs buckled, his head hurt so much. He heard the footsteps crash down the stairs, he heard the front door open. He tried again to get up, managed to stumble down the stairs. The front door was wide open, and he staggered outside. He couldn't see anyone…

"Paul, what happened?" Danni was standing next to him now. "I heard the crashing around. Why are you out in the street? It's nearly two in the morning."

"Somebody was in the flat Danni. They've run round the corner."

He was getting his strength back, thinking straight again. He'd started to run as he was talking to her. He rounded the corner of the street and looked down the Boulevard. He could see a figure running. It was about twenty paces away. Danni had caught up with him.

"Who was it. Is that him?"

Paul was already giving chase, stumbling a bit at first, his head was thumping from being bashed on the floor, but the adrenaline had kicked in. He'd been a good runner at school, still went running two or three times a week. He hadn't realised it at first, but he had no shoes on. He was sprinting down the street in T-shirt and shorts and bare feet. He could see him ahead. He was catching up with him.

But as he hit the ground for the second time that night, the chances of catching the intruder disappeared. The man and the woman had stumbled out on to the street, rocking in each others arms. He'd heard the drunken laughter in that split second. He'd only just caught them a glancing blow, but it was enough. He was sprinting, he was knocked off balance, he stumbled, tried to stay on his feet, but fell forward, tumbled over, felt a pain in his shoulder this time. He rolled over a few times, and then came to rest on his back. He lay on the pavement looking up at the night sky. He could see the stars, there was a strange moment of complete peace, he felt a warm glow, something comforting, a feeling of well being. In that moment he remembered what it had felt like a few minutes earlier when he'd gone into the sitting room in the dark. The feeling of being drawn towards something warm, something good.

"Paul, are you OK? He's gone. You won't catch him now."

She put her arms around him. Held him close. Then looked at him, looked into his eyes. For a moment he saw somebody else, just for a fleeting second, somebody he didn't know, but somebody who seemed familiar. Then he blinked and saw Danni.

"Let's get you back to the flat Paul. We'll work out what's happened."

Chapter 34

Looking up at the departure board, he could have convinced himself that things were going according to plan. The 9.30 a.m. train from Leeds to Kings Cross was on time, and he had twenty minutes to get on the train, and find his seat which he'd booked last night. He'd worked out his route to Hackney Central, and his route to Elaine's house. He'd booked a room at the nearby Premier Inn in case an overnight stop was required. He had his rucksack with minimum gear in. So far so good. But that was just the housekeeping.

There were two things weighing him down.

The first thing. He was going to turn up on the doorstep of his long-lost love, who he hadn't seen for twenty-eight years. The long-lost love who was the mother of the long-lost daughter, who he'd never seen. Except perhaps on Wednesday night. The daughter who had died. He didn't know anything about what had happened to her.

The second thing. His wife of nearly twenty-five years had gone missing. She didn't come home last night. Hadn't answered any calls or texts.

He'd got home at about half past seven, hoping to patch things up after the Miranda misunderstanding. When she hadn't appeared by nine, he'd phoned, then at ten, then at eleven. Then sent three text messages before he went to bed at about half past eleven. His messages had been long, rambling, and defensive. In the final one he'd said he was getting the nine thirty train to London in the morning. And before he left home this morning, having slept alone, he sent another message. This one was short, to-the-point, and worried. He was ready to beg if that would work.

That was it. He wouldn't go to London. He'd go home now. Prepare himself for the begging. He walked towards the main entrance, and turned out onto the street.

"Have you given up already," she said, walking towards him.

*

Staring out the window as the train pulled out of the station, Dawn asked a simple question, without turning to face him.

"Would you like a croissant George?"

On the one hand, it required a simple yes or no answer. But he got the feeling that more was expected. A good explanation for a lifetime of excuses.

He looked at the large brown paper bag sitting on the table between them.

"Is there an almond one, or did you just get plain croissants?"

She turned to look at him, but didn't say anything. This could go either way.

He cracked first.

"I'll take whatever's on offer Dawn. I'm more concerned about what happened to you last night. I was worried."

She pushed her hand deep into the bag, took out a cup, then another cup, then two paper bags, one marked plain, the other marked almond.

"I stayed at Sandra's. I had a lot of thinking to do. A few phone calls to make."

It wasn't like him. To splash out on two first class return tickets, the night before, at full price. But then he did have one hundred thousand pounds in his back pocket. Figuratively speaking. As it turned out, it had been a good move. An act of faith, you might say.

"I phoned Miranda, George. It wasn't hard to get in touch. She's on the local council. I'd say she just about confirmed your story."

279

He took a bite of the almond croissant, some of the flaky pastry sticking to his lips as he started to breathe a bit more easily.

"About you wanting her expertise, shall we say."

Good old Miranda.

"And now here we are George. On our grand day out. Going to meet another one of your old flames. This one's a bit more special though isn't she?"

The sweet almond cream was fortifying him. And the caffeine.

"I haven't seen her for all these years Dawn. I've got to try to make sense of what happened on Wednesday night."

"Have you thought about what you're going to say to Elaine, George? Remember, her daughter died in the last couple of weeks. I know she was your daughter as well, but you never knew her. What's your opening line going to be, standing there, when she opens the door?"

"I thought I'd work that out when we get past Grantham."

*

When they got past Grantham, he delayed the decision until Peterborough. After Peterborough, he delayed it to the orange over-ground line to Hackney. And as they walked down the High Street, he decided to do without a script, and play it by ear on the doorstep.

It was a relief that Dawn was walking beside him, trundling her trolley bag behind her. He'd checked that the hotel room had a double bed. It was a relief, but he also felt on trial. She could have had a clip board, and an assessment form, entering ticks and crosses, or marks out of ten, depending on how he conducted himself during the course of the day. He didn't know that Dawn had already completed her twenty-five-year performance review.

As they got nearer to the road where Elaine's house was, there was a kaleidoscope of pictures circling around in his head. In a less noble moment, Dawn had found that the house was worth £1.8m, and that Elaine was a lawyer specialising in asset finance. Whatever that was. It was clear that the real Elaine was going to deviate from the picture he had in his head. There was the mental old photograph in his wallet. Not a real one, an imaged one. Formed from a memory going back nearly three decades, and a memory going back to last Wednesday night. The clear skin, the slightly angular face, the pale blue eyes, and the long straight blonde hair. In his mind, the old photo was a bit crumpled, and creased in one corner. He'd added a few grey tints to the hair, and a few wrinkles around the eyes. That's all. No filling out of the cheeks. No loose skin around the neck. And no expensive house and a career in asset finance. He'd placed her one rung lower than himself on the financial ladder. Before his recent gains, which would have pushed him up another couple of rungs.

He checked his phone. It was nearly one o'clock, and nearly fifty yards before the turning off the High Street. The sun was directly ahead of them, low in the sky, and dazzling. He could feel his heart beating quickly, even some beads of sweat building on his forehead. He was striding out a few paces ahead of Dawn, but above the noise of the traffic he heard her shout his name.

"George."

He stopped and turned to look at her.

"I've been thinking."

This was never a good sign.

"George, I've decided that you should go and see Elaine on your own. At least to start with. You make the initial contact. Rachel was your daughter. Yours and Elaine's daughter. I'm going to go in this café. Have a coffee and something to eat. I'll be waiting here. You can come back here, or give me a ring, and I'll come to the house. We've got the room booked at the hotel for tonight, so there's plenty of time."

There was part of him that had been hoping for this. And part of him that wanted Dawn by his side. But either way, he could see that she'd decided. She wasn't going any further.

"OK, I understand. I'm just really glad you're with me in some way. I appreciate it."

He gave her a slightly awkward hug, turned, and marched forward, squinting in the sunlight. Within a minute, he turned down the road on his left. Elaine's road. His mouth was dry. He wished he'd brought a bottle of water. There were trees on either side of the road and there were still a few leaves left on the branches. He thought they were plane trees. He looked at each of the houses and the house numbers as he walked on. You could tell why they were worth £1.8m. It was a road with terraced houses but they were all so smartly turned out, well decorated, newly refurbished. He walked past number 22, 24, 26; then stopped outside number 28. This was it. The sun shone through the branches of the trees, and there was a dappled effect on the downstairs window. He walked up the short path to the front door. There might have been a slight pause before he rang the bell, but it was only a momentary hesitation. He rang the bell, and knocked on the navy blue door at the same time. He looked through the bay window to the right. It was a glimpse into somebody else's life. Not just anybody. Somebody that he knew well and at the same time didn't know at all.

Ten seconds of silence, then he rang the bell again, but didn't knock a second time. He thought he heard some noises inside. There was a single pane of frosted glass in the door, and through it you could see some movement. The shape moved to the door and opened it.

"Yes, can I help you?" said the young woman. She was probably in her mid-twenties with an Eastern European accent.

"I'm looking for Elaine Rogers. Sorry, Elaine de Villiers. That's what she's called now."

"She's out. Went out about half an hour ago. I'm not sure what time she'll be back. I'm cleaning. I do it every Saturday."

He could just about cope with the anti-climax. He'd prepared himself for nobody being in, but when the door was opened, he'd expected to see Elaine on the other side. He'd expected her to throw her arms around him. Break down in tears, imagining the life they could have had together.

"You can't wait. You'll need to come back. I need to get on with my work."

"Of course. Thank you. I'll come back this afternoon."

The door closed and George turned back up the path. Should he have left his name? He wasn't sure. He could go back now. No, that wasn't the right thing. He turned and looked back at the house, then walked up the road, back on to the High Street. He wasn't sure that he could face going to the café and meeting up again with Dawn only five minutes after he'd left her. He stood on the pavement for a while, got in everybody's way, couldn't decide what to do, and then as a default option, walked back to the café. He pushed the door open, and spotted Dawn sitting at a small table in the corner. It was crowded. He picked his way through the other tables. He stopped in front of Dawn, but his eyes were drawn to the woman sitting at the next table. She had a scarlet scarf in her hair. It was the contrast to the stylish grey jacket that caught his eye. That and the slightly angular face.

She turned to face him.

"Hi Elaine."

It took her a few seconds longer. Maybe for the first second it was like trying to place someone that you half recognise from a previous job. But for the next two or three seconds it was a deep awakening from a pre-historic age, something dragged back from the mists of time, now out of time and place. This person should not be here now.

"George?"

One word. A proper noun with a question mark at the end, but it opened up the lost years.

His eyes had been fixed on her. He could put his hand on her shoulder. Maybe she would respond. Maybe he could say something about that night. But they weren't alone. His wife of nearly twenty-five years was sitting a few feet away. He glanced over to Dawn. She was staring at him and then at Elaine. That look was printed on his memory. Not jealousy. Not anger. A shared human moment. An understanding, compassion. Something in the general vicinity of love. There was a tear in her eye. There was a tear in his eye as well.

"Elaine. Yes, it is me, George, George Stephenson. You wrote to me, about our daughter. This is my wife Dawn."

Elaine looked over at Dawn and then back to George.

Chapter 35

Peeling the last carrot, he couldn't help reflecting on the supreme weirdness of it all. Standing in the kitchen helping your wife prepare the meal. Waiting for a guest to arrive. Having a glass of chilled Chablis. Some music playing in the background.

Except this wasn't his wife. It was the wife that might have been. This was Elaine, who he'd last seen all those years ago. Lover for one night. The mother of his daughter who had died less than two weeks ago. A daughter who he'd never seen. Not alive anyway. The guest about to arrive was Dawn. His actual wife and lover (intermittently), of all these years. Not counting Linda. Mother of his son, who they had seen a couple of nights ago…

After the initial embarrassed greetings in the café, Dawn had suggested that she go for a walk and then go back to the hotel, to allow George and Elaine time to talk. He couldn't imagine himself being so mature and magnanimous if the roles had been reversed.

So he and Elaine had walked to her house, making small talk about the weather as they strolled in the late autumn sunshine to number twenty-eight Morecombe Terrace. The house that was worth £1.8m. As they entered it, George pondered the mystery of how Elaine had managed to do so well for herself, when she hadn't married him. It didn't occur to him that this was precisely the reason why she'd done so well.

It turned out that Elaine was clever as well as beautiful. She'd got her A levels, all grade A, gone to Bristol university to study law. That was where Dawn wanted to go, but didn't get the grades. Elaine got a first, of course; then a training contract with a big London law firm. She'd done all of this despite being an unmarried mum with a young child. Her own mother had looked after baby Rachel, and Elaine had managed to keep the different plates spinning. Eventually she'd married Rupert, the architect and landowner. Same name as the bear with the check trousers. You'd have thought that would have put her off. Had two children – two boys. They were both at university now. But things hadn't worked out with Rupert. They'd separated two years ago.

She'd remembered the night with George with warmth and affection, but not with the earth-moving love that George had somehow conjured up in his imagination. She was going to get in touch in the weeks after that night, but time moved on. When she'd found out she was pregnant, she'd talked about it with her mother, and on balance they'd decided that she'd have the baby and not get in touch with George. It was for the best. Maintained her independence.

All of this hurt a lot. The post-dated rejection. Not so much rejection as not really needed, surplus to requirements. George had imagined that her mother had forbad her to get in touch, locked her in a tower, had moved them away to a remote farmhouse in Wales to make sure George couldn't track down Elaine. And all this time Elaine had cried herself to sleep every night yearning for the love of her life. Thinking of what might have been, the life she'd lost. Thought about becoming a nun. But instead they just moved away. Then she'd married Rupert. A fictional bear in a red jumper and check trousers.

"Let me get you a top-up George. I got six bottles of this in France last summer. Emma and I rented a house in Provence for three weeks. The kids came for one week, but then flew back for some festival. Just the two of us. Not a man in sight. Well, there was that awful Jean-Paul chap who Emma slept with. He really was called Jean-Paul. It reminded me of French lessons."

Elaine filled George's glass pretty much up to the top. This would be his second glass, and it wasn't seven o'clock yet. It would be his last glass though. There'd be no repeat of the night with Angel.

"Oh God, this one's empty, but I've got one more bottle in the fridge."

Elaine opened another bottle and poured herself the third glass of the evening. You had to make allowances, he thought. Her daughter died less than two weeks ago.

As she talked, George observed her. That was the right word – observed. She was an attractive woman. With the money to pay for stylish clothes. She still had the long blonde hair, but he could tell that it had been touched up, to hide the grey that he'd added in his imaginary photograph. It had probably cost one hundred pounds in the top-of-the-range salon next to the top-of-the-range coffee shop that they'd met in. She had an air of money about her.

She was not the person that George imagined. How could she be? He could cope with her being socially superior; with her being twenty times more wealthy than him, even after his recent winnings; with the fact that she hadn't spent decades regretting discarding him. He could even cope with the thought of Rupert.

What was really hard to cope with, was that she wasn't very nice.

*

When they'd got back to her house after leaving Dawn, they'd sat down at the kitchen table and talked. He'd accepted by then that she wasn't going to throw her arms around him. And perhaps by then, he had an inkling that he didn't want her to. They were just going to talk as the people that they were. Two people who'd slept together all those years ago, and hadn't spoken since.

But not quite that. There was Rachel, their daughter. After Elaine told George about her own life story, she carefully told him about the consequence of that one night.

Rachel had been brought up by Elaine's mother in the early years – when Elaine had been at university, and then when she'd been getting her career on the road. Rachel had lived with Elaine and Rupert when they got married, but she'd started to go off the rails as a teenager. Messed up her A levels. Went to live in a squat in Brixton, dabbled with drugs. Started an art course but didn't finish it. Started a creative writing course but didn't finish it. Did waitressing jobs. Sang backing vocals in a couple of bands that never got anywhere. Lived in Madrid for a year. Elaine had kept giving her money to keep her afloat. Still hadn't thought of contacting George – probably thought it was too late by now. Rachel was never going to make anything of her life.

As Elaine was telling him all of this, George recognised the theme. Rachel hadn't achieved anything in life because she had George's genes, and those genes had triumphed over Elaine's genes, despite the overwhelming superiority of the latter. The other two children had Elaine and Rupert's genes. They were from superior stock. Elaine was sad about the death of her daughter. But Rachel was her 'second division' daughter.

It was when she'd gone back to Spain last May. Living in a commune outside of Granada. Living with a Spanish guy in some converted outbuildings next to a remote farmhouse. He was a musician. She was working in a bar. He had a motorbike, and a taste for Rioja. There was never anything on that country road back from the bar to where they lived. Except there was that night. A truck that had turned off the main road and got lost. Going too fast down the hill. Drifted across the road. They'd been taken to hospital. She and Rupert had flown out there. Rachel died a few days later. Tuesday the 7th. That's when she'd decided to contact George. Twenty-eight years too late. She'd found his number. She'd tried ringing, but couldn't bring herself to speak. She'd found his address, and written the letter. They'd flown the body home. That sounds awful, but it's the practical reality. A week yesterday. Friday the 10th. The funeral would be in two weeks' time.

As Elaine was telling him the story, George had tried to keep his eyes focused on her – on Elaine. But most of the time he looked past her, to the photo on the mantelpiece. It was the same person that he'd seen a few nights ago. The face, the nose, the look.

He hadn't told Elaine yet. He wasn't sure that he would do. He'd wait until Dawn came round. She should be here in a few minutes.

"I'll need to use the toilet Elaine."

"The cloakroom's at the back, just before the garden room."

Elaine pointed past the cream Aga to the extension at the back of the house. As he walked through on the stone pavers, the lights came on automatically and the floodlights outside illuminated the decking area. The picture of their sad conservatory appeared in his mind. He pushed the cloakroom door open, stepped in, switched the light on, and closed it behind him quickly. He needed a break. His inadequacy was weighing heavily on him. He was looking forward to seeing Dawn – his wife from his world. But before that the other world stared him in the face. A collage of family photos from Elaine's land. Rupert was still there. He hadn't been edited out yet. Maybe it was a trial separation. That's what Elaine and Rupert would do. All very civilised. The pictures were what you'd expect. The kids starting school, family holidays, playing rugby, riding a pony. And Rachel was there, a few teenage photos. But she was definitely at the edge, not at the centre, and nothing beyond the age of about sixteen.

Opening the door and switching the light out, he heard Dawn's voice.

*

He was hungry now. He'd only had four cups of coffee and an almond croissant all day. He was sitting opposite Dawn at a dining table in an open-plan kitchen, whilst Elaine moved around, ostensibly preparing food. There was a lot of movement and activity. She looked busy, but only a minimum amount of food had appeared so far. She'd put a small dish of olives on the table, but there was no bread in sight. There might have been twelve olives in total, and he reckoned he'd eaten eight of them. Dawn scowled at him as he took another. A bowl of cashew nuts or lightly-salted hand-cooked potato crisps would have gone down a storm. The starter appeared, which was basically salad. He lifted one of the lettuce leaves with his knife in the hope that there might be some meat or fish underneath. But no, just another tomato. With great restraint, he'd avoided even a sip of the wine in front of him. The evening required a clear head. He noticed that Dawn was not drinking either.

He knew there was chicken to come in the main course. Elaine had made a vague reference to it. But he hadn't seen a chicken in the kitchen. Not a whole one, with legs and wings, roasting in the oven. When the chicken did arrive, it was in small chunks in a watery lemon sauce, with a modest amount of rice, and a few strange vegetables. No sign of the traditional carrots that he'd peeled earlier.

Elaine had kept talking throughout, and had kept drinking throughout. She seemed to be on an unnatural high fuelled by the wine, and it was difficult to tell how Rachel's death was affecting her. Now she disappeared from the kitchen and went upstairs, leaving him and Dawn alone.

They spoke in whispers.

"I don't think I'm going to tell her about the ghost, Dawn."

"If it was a ghost George."

"Let's not go through all of that now."

"I can't work her out George. Whether she's upset by Rachel's death or not. But I think bereavement can affect you like that. And she's been drinking all night."

"I think Rachel was peripheral for her and Rupert. And I think Rachel knew that, and that's why she was reaching out to me. Her real father."

"You don't know all of that George. You're making it up. And why didn't she try to contact you when she was alive?"

"Maybe she would have done."

"Anyway, I agree with you. Don't tell her about whatever it was you thought you saw on Wednesday night. She looks pretty fragile to me. You said she'd told you all about Rachel's life. So you've got what you wanted from the day. And I'd just like to get out of here George. Unless there's something else you were looking for in Elaine."

Trust Dawn to get to the heart of the matter.

But the truth was, there wasn't something else that he was looking for in Elaine. In his mind over the years, he'd seen her as his lost love. A life that might have been. Now he didn't see her like that at all.

"George, honestly, I'd just like to go back to the hotel. We don't belong here."

"But I'm starving. I think there's a pudding coming."

"There's a hundred and one takeaways between here and the hotel George. You could have fried chicken and chips."

He looked at Dawn. She knew him so well. He liked the phrase 'we don't belong here', and he liked the use of the word 'we'.

After nearly twenty minutes, they heard Elaine's footsteps on the stairs and she appeared again in the kitchen, without any explanation of her absence. It was nearly eleven o'clock now, and he could tell that Dawn wanted him to say something so that they could get away. But Elaine was opening the fridge.

"I've got this cheesecake from the deli on the corner. They're ridiculously expensive, but taste great. It's a lemon one I think. Sorry I haven't delivered much of a meal this evening. It's been an awful week."

291

The alcohol had really taken its toll on Elaine, but before he had chance to speak, she'd carved the cheesecake into three, and placed a huge chunk in front of both him and Dawn. She clanked down spoons, then placed a small bottle of dessert wine on the table. As she did this, he saw the reddened eyes and smudged eye make-up.

Dawn looked at him, but they realised that they couldn't extricate themselves from the evening yet. They both took up their spoons and dug into the cheesecake. Elaine was right. It tasted fantastic. But where do you go from here? Eventually, they would leave. He and Dawn would go to the hotel. Elaine would collapse into bed. He'd go to the funeral. Would they promise to stay in touch? Send Christmas cards?

Eventually they finished the cheesecake, and ran out of things to say. It was a natural next step for them to leave.

"We'll need to be getting back to the hotel now Elaine. Thanks for telling me about Rachel. I appreciate it. It's helped me understand things."

"I want you both to come round tomorrow. Before you get the train back. Let's talk again. We need to work it all out. I've had too much to drink tonight. I shouldn't have opened that last bottle of wine."

They were standing in the hall now. Escape was within touching distance. They'd both got their coats on.

"Bye Elaine. What can I say? It's been great seeing you. We'll call in tomorrow before we leave."

He'd been dreading the next bit. Should he put his arms around her? Kiss her on the cheek maybe. Shake hands? Or just sort of wave with an embarrassed look on his face. He decided on the hug, and moved one pace forward to attempt the manoeuvre. He knew that Dawn was watching him, but that was OK. Elaine turned to receive the hug, slightly twisting her body, then losing her footing, and crashing to the floor. There was a moment's silence as he and Dawn looked down at her. She'd managed to clamber up onto her hands and knees. She looked like some form of crab-human-dog hybrid. It was then that he saw the splats of blood dripping onto the expensive cream hall carpet. They were big globules of blood dripping slowly from Elaine's head.

Dawn spoke first. "I think she hit her head on the edge of the radiator. It was quite a bash. Elaine, are you alright?"

There was silence for a few seconds, then a few moaning sounds. "Oh God, my head hurts. I hit it on something. I need to sit down."

Dawn brought a chair through into the hall, and between them they lifted her onto it. George brought her a glass of water, and Elaine took a few gulps. As she did that, he noticed the gash on the side of her forehead. Gently, he brushed her hair to one side, and peered closely at the open cut. The realisation crept over him that they would probably spend the next few hours in A&E at the local hospital. They'd seen it as they'd walked from the railway station. And it was Saturday night. They'd be competing with all the drunks in town to see a nurse or doctor. It would need stitches. They'd have to sit there waiting, whilst the alcohol wore off, and the hangover crept over Elaine. He could picture them getting out at six in the morning, having had no sleep.

He heard his phone ring. He still had his right hand on Elaine's forehead looking at the cut, with his left head on the back of her head providing some support and comfort. He thought about ignoring it, but the curiosity was too much. He diverted his right hand to fumble inside his pocket and eventually bring out his phone.

'Paul', said the screen.

What was Paul doing ringing at nearly midnight on a Saturday night?

"It's Paul," he said to Dawn.

"Hi Paul. Is everything OK?" It was a rhetorical question. George knew that everything wasn't OK. He knew there was something awful around the corner.

"I'm in terrible trouble Dad. I need your help. Could you come now."

293

"Paul, I'm in London, what on earth is it? What's wrong?"

"You need to come now Dad. As soon as you can."

The phone went dead at the other end, and despite dialling back there was no response in reply.

George's throat went completely dry, and he could feel an awful sickness coming on.

Chapter 36

He'd dreamt of Andalusia and the Sierra Nevada mountains last night. Of the Alhambra and the twelve lions spouting water into the four rivers of paradise running across the marble courtyard. The intricate arches in the reflecting pools. The sounds and the movement of water, the sense of space. He'd felt the remains of the dimming autumn sun on his back in the late afternoon. Heard the babbling sounds of the small fountain at the end of the elongated pool. Smelt the calming scent of the myrtle hedge. He'd looked deep into the reflecting pool, and seen not his own face, but the face of a handsome young woman looking back at him.

They'd got into bed at about three in the morning. The feel of the new white sheets was still welcoming. The distinctive fragrance of the rosewood shampoo in Danni's hair still brought thoughts of an unknown, far-off land. But as they'd pulled the duvet over their heads for more warmth, and felt each other's soft slow breath in the darkness, they both knew things had changed.

Surprising then, that they both slept so long and so well. It was nearly one in the afternoon when they'd stirred together. But within a few minutes they'd got out of bed, dressed, and walked across the road to Norman's café. Even managed to secure their favourite table in the corner by the window. Danni was wearing a knitted woollen hat, a tea-cosy hat of blended purple and red stripes, with some of her hair appearing out the top of it at the back, and a fringe covering her forehead at the front. Then the gorgeous pale face. Then the winter coat buttoned up to her neck. Paul marvelled at how she'd managed to do all of this, accurately apply the mascara and lipstick, all within a few minutes. When all he'd managed to do was pull on jeans, T-shirt, and leather jacket.

Julie took their order. Norman had expanded the traditional English café range to try to attract the bohemian student market. It was a delicate balance. Fry-ups for the construction workers. Sourdough bread and forest mushrooms for the poets and musicians. They both ordered beans on toast, and coffee. It was difficult to tell, but there didn't appear to be any poets and musicians around.

They looked at each other, and both sensed an awful inevitability hanging in the air. The problem had not gone away. It had shifted somewhere else. Or more accurately, shifted to somebody else. They hadn't talked it through when they'd got back to the flat last night, after the chase. They'd both started to gather their thoughts internally, but then let sleep calm them, and prepare them. Now it was time to piece it together.

"I don't think Stag or Jonno have the brains Paul. They're both nasty pieces of work, but they wouldn't know about Walker's business. Who owed what, how much, when it was due. There'd be plenty of people who owed Walker money, and there'd be people who Walker owed money to. I can't imagine he had a big ledger with it all written down. Most of it was probably in his head. It wouldn't be easy for either of them to pick things up where Walker left off."

"I'm not sure Danni. They wouldn't know the detail of it, but Stag and Jonno would know that I owed Walker money, and they'd know that Walker was chasing me for it. It's Stag that I'm worried about. I don't think that he's really bothered about getting the exact amount of money out of me. I think he just wants to do me harm. A lot of harm. Because of what happened to Walker. I'd have been better off with Walker. It was just business for him. With Stag, there's something personal. He and Walker grew up together didn't they? Went to school together, there was a bond. They weren't family but they were like family. He'll just want revenge, that's all."

Danni looked back at him. She didn't say anything for a while. She could remember that Stag was always at their house, wherever they were living. She remembered the way Stag looked at Walker. Looked up to him, admired him, always totally loyal. Maybe there was something else in the way he looked at Walker, she could never tell. But she knew Paul was right. Stag would want to do them harm. Both of them. And he was capable of it.

"And you think that was Stag last night don't you?"

"I'm sure it was him. I recognised the smell. I'm not sure if he was looking for money, or whether he wanted to just hurt us there and then."

Without showing any emotion, Danni thought of the euros in her coat pocket.

"And there's another thing Danni. I'm not sure that Walker was the top of the pile. What if Walker was working for somebody. Maybe there was somebody else directing operations, and they knew who owed what."

"I don't remember anybody else being around, or Walker talking about anybody else higher up the food chain."

"He wouldn't talk about it would he? He'd keep it to himself. He'd want to make out that he was top dog. And the other guy, the Mr Big, he wouldn't want his name thrown around. He'd just want to sit in his mountain retreat, stroking his cat, and raking in the money."

"What mountain retreat, what cat?"

"I was thinking about a James Bond villain, you know, stroking the cat, and saying 'come, come Mr Bond we both like killing'."

"I'm pleased that you've still got your sense of humour. But I'm not sure there is a Mr Big. I reckon Walker was a lone wolf. Ran his own show."

"I'm not so sure Danni."

"What I don't like, is just sitting around waiting for something to happen. Living in fear. Honestly Paul, I'd rather just get out of here. I don't mean hide away forever. Just maybe let things quieten down."

"But I've got my job, and the rent, and everything else."

"I know, I know. Let's give it another twenty-four hours."

*

They walked a long way that afternoon. Down the Boulevard. Under the flyover. Past the football ground. It was empty. Hull City were playing away. Into West Park. They sat on a bench. They walked around the park, and sat on a different bench. Bought take-away cups of tea. They talked more. But they didn't come up with a better plan. They walked home in the dark. As the hours had passed, so the feeling of dread increased. It did feel as though they were waiting for something to happen, and that giving it another twenty-four hours wouldn't help. They were right. They only had to wait until midnight.

They'd watched a film. But if you'd asked them, neither of them would have remembered what it was. Paul expected Walker's ghost to appear just after midnight. But the gentle yet determined knock on the door came just before the witching hour.

Paul answered the door, and allowed the tall Chinese gentlemen in the slick dark suit into the hall. Danni waited at the top of the stairs, watching and listening. The stranger explained that Paul owed him eleven thousand pounds. The ten thousand owed to Walker, plus a ten percent disruption fee. If it was paid within forty-eight hours, that would be the end of it. If it remained unpaid, it would be necessary to hurt him badly.

Sunday 19 November

Chapter 37

This was getting to be familiar territory. He was tempted to ask Kalil to take a detour. To the country lane in the village in East Yorkshire. But there was a new priority now, and he wanted to press on. Despite the dull ache in his body from the lack of sleep, and the cramp in his legs from being wedged behind the driver's seat, he was feeling reasonably awake.

He rolled his tongue around in his mouth to try to conjure up some moisture. Then he rubbed his eyes and squinted at the digital clock on the dashboard as it stuttered from 6.59 to 7.00 a.m., seeming to draw breath before it moved to the next hour. It looked badly in need of a recharge, but the weak florescent glow of the numbers on the dusty screen was saying morning not night now. And as if to reinforce the point, watery traces of light were touching the darkness ahead, a grey wash being painted on the blackness.

It was surprising how quickly they'd decided on this course of action. Dawn had listened in on Paul's phone call, pressed close up to him. He'd seen the look of fear on her face, but felt a new closeness as they swapped worried looks and nods and whispers in the hallway of Elaine's house last night, not wanting to speak openly in front of her. He knew that both of their imaginations had been forming different versions of what Paul was referring to. All of them troubling. Without speaking properly, they'd reached the same conclusion: that they should head off to see Paul as soon as possible. But with no trains until the morning, and with weekend engineering works, and no through trains until ten o'clock, it meant that they wouldn't get to Paul's flat until early Sunday afternoon.

Seeing the looks on their faces, and with the thought of Rachel still hanging in the air, Elaine had sobered up quickly, brushed aside the wound on her head, and suggested the minicab. Her regular firm from around the corner, and her regular driver Kalil. Old habits die hard, and despite his worry about Paul's trouble, George couldn't help thinking about the cost of a taxi from London to Hull in the early hours of Sunday morning. Looking at Dawn's face though, he knew that three hundred pounds was probably a fair price to pay, in the circumstances.

That left the issue of Elaine's head. But she had a solution for that one as well. Her neighbours were both doctors – Jemima and Richard, and Elaine didn't seem to have any reservation about banging on their door at half past midnight, demanding some makeshift first aid. "I've got plenty on Richard," she'd said. "Jemima still doesn't know the full story."

Richard had dutifully come round while they were waiting for the minicab, cleaned the wound and patched it up with some sort of tape. "It needs stitches though. You must go to A&E first thing in the morning, otherwise it will leave a bad scar," he'd said as he'd left the house. George had thought that it must come in very handy having a doctor next door that you can blackmail into helping you, and avoiding a five-hour wait in A&E at peak time.

Kalil had arrived at just after one in the morning. Dawn said goodbye to Elaine, then waited outside a few minutes while George said goodbye. It was the strangest parting. The last parting had been decades ago.

Kalil drove them round to the hotel to pick up Dawn's bag. Luckily the night porter still had it with him. George reflected on the wasted hotel room that he'd paid for, and the wasted return tickets, but then they were on their way. The streets of East London had still been busy, but they'd got onto the M11 at about two o'clock. At half three they'd stopped at a service station to fill up with petrol, go to the toilet, and get a cup of coffee.

And now they were within half an hour of Paul's flat. They'd spent the first hour of the journey speculating about what was wrong with Paul. They'd gone round and round in circles, over the same old ground. Dawn told him how she knew Paul wasn't telling them the full story on Thursday evening, due to the rubbing the neck giveaway. George rubbed his neck as she told him this.

He'd phoned Paul back as they were setting off, but all he got was, "I'll explain when you get here. It's best not to discuss on the phone." That had worried both of them even more.

At some point after stopping at the service station, Dawn had fallen asleep. And at some point, he must have grabbed a couple of hours of troubled sleep as well.

*

It was just after half past seven when Kalil switched off the engine. They'd parked in the same space where George had parked on Thursday evening. Kalil went for a walk and to hunt out some food. They'd need him to take them back to Leeds. George knocked on the door, and when he saw Paul's face as he opened it, he knew that things were going to be bad.

They sat in the same places as Thursday evening. That night, Paul had unveiled a story about Walker and a bizarre accident. This morning he unfurled a longer story of human frailty and human malevolence. The gradual accumulation of debt, Walker's manipulation, more debt, threats, more threats. Then what seemed like starlight from heaven – Walker's departure to a better place, or a more appropriate place. A few days of freedom, then the enforcement process.

Paul stood up as he told the story. He'd known it was Stag that got into the flat on Friday night, even though he hadn't actually seen him. But it wasn't Stag that knocked at the door last night. It was a stranger, a polite quietly spoken Chinese gentleman in a smart dark suit. He'd fixed his gaze directly into Paul's eyes, and explained that Walker worked for him. He didn't give a name. He knew what Paul owed

Walker, he knew that Walker's death was an accident, but the debt had to be settled whether Walker was alive or not. And it was better to get things sorted out quickly. To keep things nice and simple. So it had to be paid by midnight on Monday. If not, the Chinese gentleman without the name, would find it necessary to hurt Paul very badly. It was nothing personal, it was about settling obligations, balancing the books, maintaining honour. It had been very, very, clear to Paul that he meant it. It was eleven thousand pounds in total.

"I haven't got eleven thousand pounds," said Paul. Danni and I thought we had a way of working it out. Danni had some money saved up, and I was going to borrow the rest. But now we can't get all of that sorted out by Monday evening. In some ways it was better when Walker was in charge. The devil you know and all that."

Dawn had been quiet up to now. Listening in horror to the story. But now she spoke.

"Why on earth didn't you tell us about this earlier Paul? We could have helped you before it all got out of control."

"I know, I know. I'm sorry. I should have done. I wanted to try to sort it out myself Mum."

"Danni, thanks for trying to help Paul. We appreciate it," said Dawn warmly. "But we'll sort it out from here, won't we George," she said turning to look at her husband.

George had been listening, and doing a few sums in his head. Eleven thousand pounds. He had one hundred thousand pounds. So it was eleven percent of his new-found wealth. Let's round it down to ten percent because there was at least a thousand pounds in the current account anyway. It was manageable. He could sort it all out without too much difficulty. He could get the cash out tomorrow. Meet up with his chums at the banks. Dawn already knew about the seventeen thousand. It was just the eighty-six thousand that needed explaining.

"Do you think there'd be any discount for cash Paul?"

"I don't think so Dad. And I've already cut up my loyalty card."

They smiled at each other.

Then George said more seriously. "Do you think that will be the end of it then?"

"There's no guarantees, but I reckon so yes. Walker was trying to get me more and more trapped. The top guy just wants his money back."

"We'll sort it out Paul. I'll get the money out tomorrow. We'll come over tomorrow evening, and you can pay him. Then you can move on with your life."

Paul gave out a deep sigh, just about managed to hold back the tears.

"Thanks Dad."

Chapter 38

Polonius had greeted both of them when they'd walked in with their overnight bags at about eleven o'clock in the morning. Overnight bags which they hadn't used overnight. He'd seemed particularly excited, something close to a squawking fit, but then he'd had about twenty-four hours stuck on his own in the utility room. Maybe Dorothy was right about the need for more stimulation.

Now they were sitting at the kitchen table, eating breakfast cereal. It felt as though they should be doing something more important. But this was the best they could manage. It was the extra-posh muesli that he'd bought last week. The Jolly Gut range.

He'd been thinking about his tactics as Kalil drove them home. There were two big things to sort out with Dawn, and he was going to sort them out now.

They were both chewing hard on the muesli. It required a high degree of mastication.

"Dawn, there's something I need to tell you," he said, still working his mouth hard.

"There's always something you need to tell me George," she said, managing to swallow a mouthful, "what is it this time? Gambling, money, women?"

He decided to deal with gambling and money first, then circle back to women.

"I've got the seventeen thousand pounds from the pay-off from HG. You know about that."

He was building up to it.

"Yes George. I know about that."

"So we can use that to sort out Paul's problem."

"Yes, and you're going to get the cash out tomorrow."

"I am, yes. But I've got some more money as well."

"Right George, so that's OK then," she said, with a look of puzzlement about what the hell he was telling her.

"Quite a lot of money in fact."

She'd put her spoon down now, but carried on chewing the great source of concentrated fibre, eventually managing to swallow it down with a gulp of freshly-squeezed orange juice.

"How much is quite a lot George?"

"Eighty-three thousand pounds, actually."

With perfect dramatic timing, Polonius let out an extra loud squawk, then a double blast of his battle cry (option 1): "At the other end. At the other end."

"That's funny. He doesn't usually say it twice."

"You don't usually throw eighty-three thousand pounds into the conversation George."

"That's true I suppose."

"Where did you get it from?"

"It was a bit of an accident really."

"A bit of an accident? What sort of an accident? It fell off the back of a lorry?"

He allowed himself a nervous smile before he continued. "Samantha at work."

"Go on George," she said, awaiting the revelation.

"Go on George. Go on George."

"Did you hear that Dawn? Did you hear what he said? Polonius? He said 'Go on George'. That's the first time he's ever said that. It's amazing."

"Yes it's amazing George. But why don't you tell me about the money."

"Go on George. Go on George." Polonius was finding his voice now, having extended his vocabulary by fifty percent.

"Samantha set up one of those gaming accounts for me. A football accumulator. It came up. All the teams won. It grosses up the odds."

"I know how it works George. When did this happen?"

"Go on George. Go on George."

"A week ago. A week yesterday. I was going to tell you, but I knew you'd be cross. About the gambling I mean. With what you see at work."

George spent the next few minutes bumbling through an explanation, knowing that he was being observed.

"It was just a bit of fun… Samantha set it up… she knows about these things… I wasn't really sure what she was doing… it was a shock… I was going to tell you… I really was… I wanted to find the right moment… then the other thing happened… Rachel… Elaine."

"That's pretty big news George. Is that it? Was there something else that you wanted to tell me about?"

Was she really expecting a grand reveal on Linda? Did she really want that?

He was half expecting Polonius to start egging him on again, but bird was silent this time. And he wasn't going to go down the Linda path. There were more important things to sort out.

"Dawn, we haven't really talked about Rachel and Elaine."

"Let's do it now then George. You're on a roll. I feel like a priest in the confessional box. Hit me with the next one. Bless me father for I have sinned."

He'd been rehearsing this one in Kalil's taxi on the way over to Leeds. He was battling on too many fronts. The stuff that was happening to Paul was awful. George was determined to sort it out. To help his only son. But he'd got the gambling money story out of the way now. Full disclosure. It looked like he'd got away with it. He was moving on. Even Polonius was moving on. But he had to get the Rachel thing clear in his head. Elaine was sorted out. He didn't love her. He didn't really like her. She could have contacted him at any point in the last twenty-eight years. Why did she wait until Rachel had died? Because she thought he wasn't worth it. That's why.

"I've got to work out what I saw on Wednesday night. Was it just something in my head. Or was it really Rachel trying to get in touch with me?"

"And how are you going to sort that out George?"

"I want to invite Miranda round this evening. She's been doing some research on the place where I saw... what I saw."

"It's been quite a weekend George. For you and your old flames. Elaine, and now Miranda. I think I'm being pretty accommodating, don't you? Not to mention Samantha and the gambling win. And what about the pretty girl from Hong Kong? The one that phoned you on Thursday night. I'm not sure I ever found out her name. Is there anybody else you wanted to invite round? Or maybe I'll ask Derek to pop in shall I? For some nibbles?"

That would be quite a night he thought. George, Dawn, Miranda, and Derek.

He avoided asking if Derek still had his liberty.

"Let's stick to the three of us. I'll get this clear in my head. Then we can sort out Paul's problems tomorrow."

Chapter 39

"Would you like another hors d'oeuvres Miranda? You haven't tried the vegetarian buffalo meatballs with blue cheese dip and celery yet." It was said half in jest.

"No thanks George. I think I overdid it on the herbed vegan mushroom paté. And we've still got your main course to come."

That was the deal with Dawn. Miranda was welcome. Well, tolerated. But you, George, need to provide the refreshments. Which for George, meant that Marks & Spencer were going to provide the sustenance. He could have done with an afternoon in bed rather than circling hesitantly around the plant-only counter, but he managed to emerge relatively unscathed in under two hours.

In reality, there wasn't much difference between the hors d'oeuvres and main course. There was just a series of vegan and vegetarian dishes to sooth Miranda's palate. It was the least he could do, after ringing her at midday and pleading with her (not in Dawn's earshot) to come round that evening. To try to draw a line under the 'Rachel thing'. He thought she'd accepted just because it was all too intriguing and bizarre to resist. But on top of that she told him on the phone that she had some interesting results from her research.

All three of them had agreed to keep a clear head. So he'd dished up a choice of non-alcoholic drinks – tropical breeze party punch, and immune boosting winter citrus smoothie. Get the party going with a swing, and boost your immune system at the same time. It was a win-win.

George and Dawn sat next to each other at the kitchen table – it was getting a lot of use these days for confessions and discussions. Dawn had repositioned from her usual slot opposite George, perhaps as a show of slowly building unity. Miranda was sitting opposite him. George had served up the next round of bought-in dishes, but most of them sat uneaten on a large oval metal foil plate in the centre of the table. He'd bought that today as well, to save on the washing up.

They were ready to start now. George even had a pen and paper in front of him, to make notes. But he'd allowed himself to get distracted by Miranda's perfume. It was the same one as that night all those years ago. Smell is the most evocative sense of all, like cinder toffee magically spiriting back Christmas at primary school. Focus George, focus, he repeated to himself inaudibly, and shook his head slightly.

"Are you OK George?" said Dawn, observing her husband's movement.

"I'm fine," he replied, clicking the end of the ballpoint pen, ready for action.

Miranda smiled, then started to speak.

"I don't think we need to go over all the old ground again. I'm sure George has explained my position Dawn. You saw something, George, but it's entirely possible that the thought of Rachel was already in your head. Dawn had started to explain it to you, the letter and everything."

"I'm not sure what Dawn told me had got into my head Miranda. I was drunk, I just don't know."

"But Rachel didn't know about you George, did she?"

"Elaine told you that George, on Saturday," said Dawn. "She hadn't told Rachel about you. She didn't know who her real father was. So even if you accepted the idea of, you know, the supernatural, why would she appear to you? And why down that country lane in the middle of nowhere?"

"I agree with Dawn, George. But on the country lane, I have found out something."

They both looked up at Miranda.

"You remember I talked about the database of reported paranormal activity in different places. It's reports of activity, sightings, things that people have seen, or think they've seen. None of it's verified. But it can indicate if a certain place is associated with strange things happening. Well, I got the detailed accounts from my old colleague, and it does show a lot happening in Ellerdyke – where you saw what you saw. There are records from local newspapers, one national newspaper; an amateur researcher went up there a few years ago."

They were both hooked on what Miranda was telling them.

"Apparently a young girl went missing from the village in the 1960s. There was a big missing person investigation, but she was never found. People have reported seeing her. But she doesn't fit the bill of what you saw George. She was in her early teens."

They carried on listening.

"Also, there was a murder there. A man killed his wife with a knife."

George interrupted. "What sort of a knife?"

"I think it was a Gurkha knife."

"A kukri?"

"Yes, I think that's what it was called. It was an argument about what to watch on TV apparently. Be careful with the remote control Dawn."

George and Dawn looked at each other.

"He's one of our neighbours," said George. "Nice chap, Bernard. Funny what turns up when you start digging."

"A nice chap who butchered his wife George. Now he's a pot head."

"He's served his time Dawn. And the dog's nice, Lucy. But anyway, I'm not sure where any of this gets us Miranda."

"It just shows that it's a place with a history George. Maybe, just maybe, it helps your argument. Some researchers think there are portals. Places where connections take place. This life and the next. I don't believe that George. Not any more. You know that. But if you accepted the premise of the paranormal, if you accepted that somehow Rachel knew about you, wanted to contact you, then that would explain why it was in that place. It was a random event for you, getting diverted off the motorway, but to a place where things happen. The idea of a portal, an entrance, a gateway."

He wasn't sure if they'd made a lot of progress. It was a tasty titbit about Bernard. And it was interesting about Ellerdyke, the idea of the portal. But Miranda was right, why would Rachel appear to him when she didn't know who he was? Unless it all became clear in the ether, after death.

But as he opened the front door, he was more concerned with physical beings now. Flesh and blood, hair, perfume. Miranda was about to leave, and perhaps he wouldn't see her again. But it was resolved really. The three of them had spent the evening together. There'd been no ugly incidents. No cross words. It had felt like him and Dawn were a proper couple, spending the evening with an old friend.

He stood with Dawn in the hallway, as Miranda left. They stood close together, thanked Miranda, and waved goodbye.

Saturday 28 October

Before

Chapter 40

He'd been on time last week, and he'd actually earned some money. And when he'd walked into the Sala Aliatar bar to pick her up, he'd looked especially handsome. The dark, gorgeous locks had been trimmed. He still looked like a rock star, but you could see more of his chiselled features and dark piercing eyes. She'd seen Isabella looking at him when she took over from her behind the bar. She couldn't take her eyes off him.

But that was last week, and this was this week. It was a more familiar routine tonight. Sitting on her own, drinking a glass of cheap red wine, smoking a clandestine cigarette, occasionally looking at her expensive watch and comparing the time to the clock behind the bar, and wondering whether Roberto would be a better bet than Rodolfo.

It was busy tonight. The German motor manufacturers were in town. One of them was looking at her right now, looking at her legs. That was an expensive suit he was wearing. She flashed a hard stare at him, he smiled briefly before looking away with not a great deal of embarrassment.

This was her usual slot. The terrace area where she could sit on her own, draw on a cigarette, accustom her taste buds to the smack of the wine, and watch the world go by while she waited and waited for her lift back up to the mountains. It was a bit different tonight though. She normally had plenty of space around her. Most people had moved on to the trendier bars by midnight, but because it was so busy, she was crammed into a corner, with a young British couple pinned next to her. They'd been shunted even closer in the last few minutes by the roaring crowd of Germans whose voices were getting louder by the minute.

The girl in black with the green eyes apologised to her.

"Sorry, were getting pushed further your way. You haven't got much room there."

As the girl spoke, Rachel caught a glimpse of a stud in her tongue, then the ring through the left nostril. Earrings were fine, but she'd never liked studs and rings anywhere else. On this girl though, they looked great. And the red streaks in the peroxide blonde hair, and the two dreadlocks. It was hard to go wrong with a beautiful face like that, and legs more gorgeous than her own.

"You were working behind the bar earlier weren't you? Are you staying for a drink as well? I thought you'd want to get off home, or go somewhere else."

"I'm waiting for a lift. I'm usually waiting for a lift around this time. The Spanish boyfriend never has much idea of time. He should have been busking somewhere near the centre of town. He'll roll up at some point. We live up in the mountains. On a sort of farm. A farm with not much farming, if I'm honest."

"Sounds like an interesting life. I'm Danni by the way. And this is my boyfriend Paul. We're just out here for a few days."

The boyfriend swivelled round, leant forward slightly, and moved his face from side to front profile. This was a handsome young man in his early twenties. Her eyes met his and lingered on them for a few seconds too long. He lifted his hand. She thought he was going to offer a handshake, but instead he waved it and smiled. He looked vaguely familiar but she knew she'd never met him before.

"Hi, I'm Paul, nice to meet you."

"Hi, I'm Rachel."

*

It went from there. Paul bought a round of drinks, managing to outflank the Germans and make eye contact with Isabella. Rachel watched him make his way back from the bar, cradling the three drinks with his big hands, not

315

spilling a drop. Maybe he looked like an American actor. That's where she'd seen him before. When they'd finished those drinks, Rachel bought a bottle of the local red, the second cheapest on offer. She didn't even have to fight to the bar. She just sent Isabella a text, and Juan junior, the son of the owner, brought it over with three clean glasses and some tapas, and a flick of the hand to indicate that it was on the house. BMW, Mercedes, and Audi were paying. And all this time there was no sign of Rodolfo.

They took it in turn for life stories. One o'clock in the morning, warmer, more Mediterranean, versions. Without the disappointment, trauma, and rain. Rachel talked about the commune, the absence of agriculture, the eternal wait for Rodolfo. And while Paul had been at the bar, she'd told Danni about the competing attractions of Roberto, his job at the bank, and his regular salary. Danni gave a highly edited version of her life, missing out huge swathes of family history, certainly not mentioning Walker. But when she talked about plans to go to university next year, Rachel could tell that it wasn't a pipe dream.

Paul was reluctant to talk about himself. Rachel noticed his endearing shyness. But he eventually opened up about his time at Hull university, his job as a trainee accountant. More Roberto than Rodolfo she thought. He'd been to the same university as his father, George, twenty-eight years ago. It was just one sentence. It didn't mean anything.

Somebody dropped a heavy glass on the stone floor. The shattering sound was followed by raucous cheers, and the Teutonic scrum squirmed closer, bumping into Paul. She studied his face as he turned his shoulder against the crowd, but even with that strong hand and the fingers clasped around the glass, he couldn't prevent red wine sloshing out onto his jeans. Danni was sitting between them, but she'd leant back, and Paul was leaning forward looking directly at Rachel. He was very close. As the crowd broke up to avoid standing on the shattered glass, the light from behind the bar fell on his face. Not a powerful light, but it had the *effect of a spotlight on a theatre stage beaming onto the face of an actor. The features of his face were so clear now, so familiar. The nose.*

"Oh God, my jeans are covered in red wine. I'll go to the gents and clean them up a bit."

"What did your dad study at university Paul?"

"History."

"He's called George, from Leeds, right? Still lives there?"

"Yes, look, I'll be back in a minute."

*

It was just something she hadn't done. It hadn't been a conscious choice. She'd never sat down and weighed up the arguments for and against. More of an omission. An action not taken. She'd just got on with her life. Like everybody else. Maybe it was on a 'to do' list somewhere. Like retake A level English Literature. She'd got this far without knowing, and life was trundling along fine. Apart from problematic boyfriends and no proper job.

Maybe it was out of loyalty to her mother and grandmother. 'Don't dig into the past, you never know what you might find'. That's what Gran had said. It seemed sound advice. And Rupert had been there most of the time. An honourable man. An officer and a gentleman. A professional and a landowner. Making an effort to treat her in the same way as his two sons. His two real children. But with something imperceptible missing in her. Something hidden away in the body. Flesh and blood, genes and DNA.

She looked at her watch. The expensive watch that he'd bought her. Ten past one in the morning. Not late for Granada on a Saturday night. It'd be ten past midnight in the UK. Rupert would be tucked up in bed now. In the king-size bed in the barn conversion in the Kent village. It was a mystery why he'd moved out of London after he and Mum split up. More room to swing the Bentley round those country lanes perhaps. As far as she knew, he'd be on his own in that king-size bed, plenty of room to spread out. She'd only seen the barn-conversion once. He'd given her a conducted tour when she'd visited one Sunday afternoon. Seen all five bedrooms, and the wine cellar. And Mum would be on her own as far as she knew. In the standard-size double bed in the house in Hackney.

Now she wondered where he would be on this Saturday night. She'd never had this thought before. Not in such a specific way. This time. This night. This month. In a city in the north of England.

She turned to look at Danni, and found her eyes already looking back at her, seeming to sense something, seeming to expect her to say something profound.

"Danni, I want to tell you something. Something that you probably won't believe, but I'm sure it's true. But if I tell you, I want you to promise me that you won't tell anybody else. Not Paul. Not his father. I'll come back to the UK and tell them myself. When I've had time to think."

Monday 20 November

Chapter 41

He was amazed that he'd managed to drag himself into work, and that it had been a pretty normal day. A trainee accountant going about his business in the usual way. Battling the forces of tedium. Spreadsheets, monthly reporting, variance analysis. Sitting at his desk, staring at his computer screen, completing tasks. That was the day job. But by night, it was drug dealers and loan sharks, a dead body, police officers, a mystery Chinese person, and threats of grievous bodily harm. Tracy on reception had said that he looked a bit pale when he'd gone to get a new access pass. The large friendly lady in the canteen had said that she liked his new haircut, even though he hadn't had his hair cut. Apart from that, he wondered if anybody had registered his presence, let alone suspected any form of alternative life.

But now the alternative life, his excursion into the dark underworld at the age of twenty-two, was about to be drawn to a conclusion. He was facing the final curtain. In about three hours' time, if it all went according to plan. He should be celebrating. Walker had been despatched. It was all in the hands of the professionals now. Adults. His father, and the enigmatic Chinese gentleman. They were going to sort it out between them. The grown ups would tidy up the mess. There would be a financial transaction, a balancing of the books, the debt discharged, a line drawn under the whole sorry episode. He'd got himself into this mess, but now he was going to be rescued.

"It's the guy from the Chinese restaurant under the flyover."

Danni was wearing her 'Dawn outfit'. The one from Thursday evening. Smart, respectable, well turned-out. Dressed for an interview almost.

"I've been walking around all day trying to work out where I've seen him before, but that's it. You don't see him there very often, but we saw him sitting in the window seat with the three big heavy guys a few weeks ago. The huge black car turned up outside. Like the President's armoured limousine. They escorted him out. They were bowing. Mr Zhang Wei, that's what they called him. Don't you remember?"

He did remember. It was him.

"It's strange that he came round himself though. When he's Mr Big. You'd have thought that he'd send one of his foot-soldiers. Walker's gone, and he probably wouldn't trust Stag and Jonno, but he'd have other people."

"Perhaps he likes to keep his hand in. Get down with the people every now and again."

He looked up at Danni as he said this, but his mind was somewhere else.

He should be grateful. He was grateful. But he felt like a child. It had all been taken out of his hands.

"Perhaps we should just clear off Danni. Get the hell out of here. Maybe we could track down Granddad in South America. Or Uncle Aidan in Australia. We could get a coach to London this evening. There's still time. I feel so helpless. Dad's going to bail me out. He shouldn't have to do that. I should be able to stand on my own two feet."

He was saying this without any great conviction.

"We've got to see it through now Paul. You can draw a line under it tonight. Your mum and dad want to help you. You said yourself. You felt closer to your dad. Closer than you've felt in a long time. If you run away now, you'll be throwing that away. He'll give the money to Zhang Wei, then that'll be the end of it. The nightmare will be over. You can always pay your dad back over time. So much a month."

He smiled back at her, and then started laughing.

"What are you laughing at?"

"I'm trying to picture the two of us in the spare bedroom of Uncle Aidan's bungalow in that one-horse town in

Western Australia. Holing up like Bonnie and Clyde. Ready for the shoot-out. Forty degrees in the shade. Huge insects and snakes. Maybe you could get a job behind the bar. You'd have all the locals staring at you. I could do the books for the repair garage. We could make a go of it. For a week."

She looked back at him with the mischievous smile, the green eyes focusing on him. "I'd prefer South America. Up in the mountains with your granddad and Che Guevara. Ready to start the revolution. Hanging out with the Mapuche and hallucinogenic toads."

"Or maybe we'll stay in Hull. We could start going to the general knowledge quiz on Tuesday nights at The Grapes. They do pie and peas at half time. Steal my daddy's cue and make a living out of playin' pool."

"Let's just get tonight out of the way. Then we can get on with our lives Paul."

He nodded. That's what they'd do.

She hadn't finished speaking.

"Paul, there's something that I've got to tell you. I should have told you weeks ago."

*

He was standing up. She stayed sitting down, on the old settee, angling her head upwards to look at him.

"It's not that tall good-looking guy with the long hair is it? That one that delivers to the delicatessen. The one that thinks he's a wizard?"

"Have you smelt his breath, Paul?"

"Have you smelt his breath, Danni?"

"You can smell it from fifty yards away. Old dog's breath. Halitosis. He's not a real wizard. They don't exist. Only in Harry Potter. He's got big ears, and I've only got eyes for you. Sit down, you idiot."

He hung his head in shame.

"It's been a long day. A long week," he said, as he lowered himself back onto the settee, a small cloud of dust puffing up from it as he sat down.

She took a deep breath in. He watched her breasts heave upwards. Then she blew out slowly, preparing herself.

"Right here goes."

She left a few seconds, then started to speak.

"You remember the night in the bar in Granada. It was packed. The German car dealers. We got talking to that girl, Rachel."

"Of course I remember. I liked her. You said she was going to get in touch with you."

"She was. She hasn't. But it's who she was Paul."

"What do you mean, who she was?"

"It sounds unbelievable. An amazing coincidence. One in a million chance. She worked it out. Your dad did History at Hull university. He was there twenty-eight years ago. George Stephenson. Her mother didn't tell her very much. Rachel found a letter from George to her mother. From all those years ago. But she didn't seek him out. Her mother got married. A chap called Rupert. He was her stepfather. She kept looking at you while you were talking. She saw your nose."

Instinctively, he touched his nose with two fingers.

"And…"

"She told me when you were in the gents. But asked me not to say anything. She wanted to come to the UK. Meet both of you. Tell you properly. But now she's disappeared. She doesn't answer any texts or messages."

She still hadn't said it to him.

"And…"

"She's your half-sister Paul. George is her father."

There was a long pause.

"Is there any of that cheap brandy left?"

"Just a touch," she said gently, stroking his hair, twisting a strand of it round her finger, looking directly into his eyes.

"But we've only got one glass, and it's got a big chip in it. I'll pour it out. We can share the glass."

He watched her walk slowly into the kitchen, and knew that she was giving him a couple of minutes alone to get his thoughts together. In his mind, he didn't question what she'd said. Didn't try to dismiss it. There was an overpowering truth in her words. He could see Rachel's face now, with the light from behind the bar touching her features, a picture coming into focus.

He watched Danni walk back in, take a sip from the glass, hand it to him, and then sit next to him, very close.

"I don't know why she hasn't got in touch Paul. I got a text from her a week last Saturday. She said she was booking flights. She should be here now. I've sent her lots of messages, but there's no reply. There's got to be something wrong. I can feel it."

"I don't understand why she didn't just tell me. That night. In the bar. Face to face."

"She was trying to make sense of it all Paul. Can you imagine trying to explain that to you, in the crowded bar, after a few drinks. And we were flying home the next day. She told me because she had to tell somebody. She took my contact details. She was going to come back to the UK. Speak to her mother, then contact your dad and you."

He nodded. It all made sense.

"It's just an amazing coincidence. These sort of things don't happen do they?"

"I think they do."

She left a moment's silence, and then spoke again.

"I know you don't believe in that Auntie Lelia stuff."

"What, you mean, she said you had a sixth sense. Some special insight."

"I'm not sure I believe it. Well, I don't believe it. But I've got a strange feeling about your dad, Paul. When he was here on Thursday night. When he was here early on Sunday morning. That he knows something about Rachel. I can't explain it."

"You said it yourself. There's no such thing as wizards."

"I'm not saying your father's a wizard Paul. I can't imagine him dressed up in one of those long robes, with stars on, a pointy hat and a long beard. And I'm not a witch."

"You'd look great in a witch's outfit."

"Thanks. It's just a feeling I've got. I know you think I'm mad. Look, we've got tonight to deal with. Your mum and dad are coming round. Mr Big's coming round. Let's get that out of the way, then we can think about Rachel. We should tell your dad about her. About meeting her. After the money's been sorted out. Maybe that'll throw some light on things. I'm going to pop out now. Get some tea and coffee from the shop."

"For the tea party."

"It's not a tea party Paul. It's serious business. But at least we can be welcoming to your mum and dad. They're going to bail us out after all. And I need to go for a walk. To clear my head."

Chapter 42

"I wish we'd set off earlier George."

"We've got plenty of time. We're only half an hour away now. We'd only be sitting around waiting."

"You've got the money? In that envelope?"

An envelope full of cash. Like when he paid the dodgy builder for the conservatory.

"It's in my jacket pocket. They're getting to know me at the banks in town."

"I don't suppose we'll get a receipt."

"Or a voucher for the local pizza restaurant. Free extra topping on the deep pan special."

"So we just hand over all that money to a complete stranger, and keep our fingers crossed."

"That's right. What else do we do? He's our son. We want to help him."

George briefly turned to look at Dawn as he was saying this. He caught the hopeful, enigmatic smile before turning back to look at the road.

"I saw Bernard as I came back from the town."

"Was he waiting for the man? Twenty-six dollars in his hand?"

"He's not a junkie shooting up on Sycamore Meadows, Dawn. He's an old guy with a lot to try and forget about. You should give him a break. Forgiveness, redemption and all that."

"Dorothy and the ladies would be interested in Miranda's research."

"Let's deal with the Paul problem tonight. Get that out of the way. Then I'll start to think about Rachel and ectoplasm."

He looked at the digital clock in the car. There'd been a fault with the hour number for about a year now. There was just a dot that flashed on and off. But the second number was fine. As long as you knew what the hour was, you knew what the time was. It was 9.58 p.m. He took a quick look at his watch to check, but the numbers in this range were still obscured by the fog of condensation. Every morning for the last four months he'd promised himself that he'd get it fixed. He'd definitely do it tomorrow. Fix the watch, fix the conservatory, and get a new car. Next year's model. Use his new-found financial might on a bit of conspicuous consumption.

Dawn was probably right. They should have set off earlier. He assured himself that there was still plenty of time. The motorway was clear, there was hardly any traffic. Two hours before the allotted time. But the weather was turning. Somebody up above was dialling up the rainfall. A light drizzle when they'd set off, but constant heavy rain now. He slowed down, leant forward, tensed up, felt sweat build on his forehead, felt his lips drying, and started to squint though the windscreen as the visibility worsened. Not quite panic yet though.

Like a carefully timed dramatic moment in a thriller, his phone ringing made him leap up in his seat, and made Dawn let out a cry like a seabird. He turned to the phone in the hands-free holder to answer, but the pressure told on his finger movements, and he pressed the wrong button, cutting off the call.

"Why did you cut if off George? It could have been Paul. There might be a problem."

"I didn't mean to. They'll ring back. Or I'll return the call. Let's not panic."

When the phone rang the second time, George could feel the burden of responsibility. His pulse quickened, he stared at the screen, took his eyes off the road, swerved ever so slightly, but then managed to press the right button.

"Hello…"

There was a pause.

"George, it's Derek."

Another pause from George and Dawn.

"Hello Derek."

"George, it's your conservatory. I went out for a run down the path at the back of your house. It's been raining heavily. One of the frames seems to have fallen in, it's buckled. I think the rain is getting into the house. I knocked on the door, but obviously you're out. I'm not sure what I can do. You should probably come home. I'll help you patch it up if I can."

The thought of Derek as the good neighbour, the good Samaritan, helping out, offering support, just didn't compute in George's brain. Derek had moved from successful alpha male to potential jailbird in less than a week, but what was he now? Good buddy workmate, emergency DIY, a cup of tea and a slap on the back. Anyway, there wasn't time for any of this. There was the debt to settle. It might have been raining back home, but it was raining here and now, bouncing off the motorway, bouncing off the windscreen. A deluge of biblical proportions. Armageddon black outside, except for the fuzzy red spots of the brake lights in front, and the dazzling white of the headlights coming towards them on the other side of the motorway. Caught in the middle of all of this, things closing in on all sides, pressing down, pressing in.

Then the slowing down, no power, dreamily coasting to a halt. Derek's voice fading, Dawn's voice louder, more panicky.

"What's happened George?"

"There's something wrong with the car. We've lost power. It's dead. It must be the rain."

He'd managed to bring the car to a halt on the hard shoulder. He tried turning the ignition on. Nothing happened. He tried again. Nothing happened. Nothing was going to happen. That was another thing on his list to sort out. The AA membership. The cost had gone up so much. He'd cancelled it, and meant to get another provider. Just like he'd meant to get the Uber app sorted out. The enormity of it all sunk in for him.

"The car's finished Dawn. I really don't know what to do."

It was like turning the dial on an old radio. Derek's voice faded out, then faded in again against a background of interference on the airwaves.

"George, are you still there?"

Then Dawn spoke softly and calmly.

"Derek we need to ask a big favour. We're on the M62 on the way to Hull. It's really important that we get to Paul's flat, our son's flat. The car's knackered. It won't start. We can ring the AA, but we can't be sure when they'll get here. Or we could get an Uber, or try to get a local taxi firm, but I'm not sure they'll be able to pick us up on the motorway. Can you get here Derek, and take us to Hull? It's a massive favour I know. The conservatory can wait."

*

It was quarter to midnight when Derek manoeuvred the midnight blue five series BMW up onto the kerb outside Paul's flat. He'd responded to Dawn's cry for help without equivocation. The damsel in distress rescued by the knight in shining armour. A heavily-tarnished knight though. Rusty armour and a soiled reputation.

George had sat in the back, and Dawn in the passenger seat. It seemed like a reasonable distribution. Derek kept glancing at him through the rear view mirror, but there were no horns in sight. The twitch was still there, but less pronounced and less regular. George patted the envelope in his jacket a hundred times on the journey, double-checking, triple-checking that it was still there. Dawn had told Derek half the story about why they had to be at Paul's flat at midnight, and then quickly asked him how the fraud enquiry was going, deflecting any further questions. Derek told them he was 99% sure there would be no charges. He'd been caught up in the middle of something, an innocent by-stander. That wasn't how George would describe him, but he was surprised at Derek's openness, and genuinely grateful for the taxi service.

With his thoughts still mixed about Derek, he pushed the car door open, and even managed a quick thank you. Dawn stayed in the car for a minute longer, talking to Derek. George saw her put her hand on his shoulder in a rather awkward way, then get out of the car. She was wearing the new cream coat, black tights with a sparkle, and black high heels. She was dressed for the occasion.

"I told him to go home George. I said we'd find our own way back. Whatever that means. I just want to get all of this sorted, then we can stop worrying."

Her voice tailed off as she said this. She'd followed George's eyes looking up at the flat.

There were no lights on. The rendezvous was less than fifteen minutes away, but the flat was in complete darkness.

Chapter 43

He wished he hadn't had that third vodka, especially on top of the shared glass of cheap brandy. He'd found the bottle under the sink next to the lemon-fresh disinfectant. Mixed it with the remnants of a 20p litre bottle of value-range lemonade. Just something to calm his nerves, ease his worries about Danni being out so long, and his father using his life savings to pay for the follies of his son. The vodka had the usual effect on him. Dulled the pain, rather than getting him up on the dance floor.

He'd been sending one more text to Danni. The anaesthetic was kicking in, when he'd heard the door downstairs crash open, the thunderous sound of big boots stomping up the stairs. Then the same big boots kicking open the door into the flat.

This wasn't Mr Zhang Wei. They'd only met once, but there was an air of gentlemanly malevolence about him, sophisticated evil, executive threat. Nor was it the ghost of Walker, middle-ranking evil, non-commissioned officer corps. This was the clatter of the lower orders of crime, the plebeian end. A good kicking down a back alley, slashing with kitchen knives, a blood-stained hammer. Probably knuckle-dusters in the good old days.

Stag had landed a single punch directly in his face. His nose had started bleeding, but he could tell that it wasn't broken. Small mercies. There'd been no follow-up. Just one punch had sent the message…

He'd only been in the back of the van a few minutes. They hadn't gone far. Just down the road. He'd had time to press his fingers up to his nose, and could feel the wetness of the blood. Now they were marching him down a passage at the side of the Alabama Authentic Dixy-fried Chicken Shack. It was just closing. The smell of fried chicken mixed with the sweet smell of his own blood. Stag opened a door at the back into a kitchen, pushed Paul through, and forced him to sit down on a wooden chair sticking out from a small table in the middle of the room. Take-away kitchen and interrogation cell combined. The smell of cooking fat was overpowering, but the kitchen was surprisingly tidy.

Stag did the talking. Jonno's vocabulary was limited. He just watched.

"Now send a message to your dad. We know he's coming here with the cash. It's our money. We worked for Walker. It's not Zhang Wei's money."

*

Surveying the scene, he couldn't help a short chuckle. What did it remind him of? It might have been one of those old black and white films on a wet winter Sunday afternoon that he watched with his dad. Ealing comedies. Made in the 1950s in the Ealing Studios in West London. *The Lavender Hill Mob*. Benign, comedy gangsters. No drugs, nobody got hurt. Wholesome family entertainment. Mum just thought it was ridiculous, but she liked the fact that they were laughing. Where did those days go? But he was only twenty-two. It wasn't time to be yearning for the past. There'd be plenty of time for that.

In a way, Stag and Jonno would have fitted in well in one of those old films. He could picture them as the clueless petty criminals trying to blow a safe, or drive a getaway car. Being chased by an old police car with a flashing blue light. But sixty years had passed since then. Time had moved on. Nowadays you could really get hurt. And prison wasn't like Porridge.

Stag had noticed the short chuckle, and now his face was pressed up against Paul's face. Nose to nose. Paul could smell the awful unwashed stench. The sweat, the beer, the foul breath. It was a smell of an animal and of danger. Mixed with the smell of fried chicken. The thoughts of

1950's comedies had disappeared now. Paul was still planted on the kitchen chair. Stag pulled back a few inches, and spoke, revealing a grey-metal tooth next to his front teeth. Walker'd had a gold-tooth, he remembered.

"If you think this is funny Pauly, you're making a big mistake. We can do things just as bad as Walker, and we will do."

Stag looked around the take-away kitchen, and picked up a cheese-grater from the draining board. It wasn't up to the same standard as Walker's survival knife, and there were a few strands of insipid white cheese hanging off the edges, but it would have to do. He pressed it against Paul's cheek, and snarled, revealing the metal tooth again. Paul wondered how much damage Stag could do with a cheese-grater. You could simply leap out of the chair and avoid the worse effects. But if Stag had you pinned to the ground, straddling you, with both knees pinning down your shoulders, it could get pretty nasty. You'd have to stagger round to A&E at Hull Royal. The stray dog would follow you and sniff around. Not an appealing prospect, and it wasn't the time to answer back to Stag. Not like he'd done to Walker last week. You couldn't rely on providence to despatch him the same way.

Paul tried to work out whether to look back at Stag, or look away. The best self-preservation strategy had always been to avoid eye contact. So he bowed his head and looked at the floor. But he was aware of Stag staring at him, and somehow it seemed disrespectful not to look back. So he lifted his head, and set his eyes on his opponent. He'd never paid much attention to him while Walker was around. Walker was the clear and present danger, and Stag was just there, lurking in the background, playing the supporting role. But here he was, taking his opportunity, stepping up. As Paul looked back at him, he noticed he had one brown eye and one grey eye. That was pretty rare wasn't it? Also, he had a small spider's web tattooed on his neck. Did that signify that you'd been in prison, or that you'd killed somebody, or that you liked spiders? And there was a dreadful spot on the end of Stag's nose, with puss oozing out. It was the worst type of spot. The one right on the end of your nose, glowing like Rudolf the red-nosed reindeer. You knew that you shouldn't squeeze it, but the temptation was always too great, and it made it worse.

"You shouldn't have squeezed that spot Stag."

Why did those words come out? A mysterious force had dragged them out. Maybe it was the brandy and vodka. He'd felt the words flowing out, he was aware it was happening, but he couldn't stop it. The second time in a week. And for the second time in a week a brutal twisted face stared back at him, with a look of incredulity, stunned disbelief in both the brown and the grey eye. The victim was not supposed to answer back like this, because… well, because he was the victim, the one being victimised.

For a split second he thought Stag might not have heard, or might not have heard properly. But as he felt the full force of Stag propelling him back against the kitchen worktop, and his head cracking against the overhead cupboard, he knew that the message had been fully understood and processed. There was a terrible beating coming, maybe a horrible grating. And Danni wasn't around to help him. Where was Danni? Where were his mum and dad? He felt Stag grip his shoulders, and drag him along the worktop. The cheese-grater had tumbled away into the corner. He felt his body crashing against the fridge freezer. But no punches or kicks yet, and no words. The lack of expletives was noticeable. Maybe Stag was saving the best 'til last. Paul felt his body being dragged back again along the worktop. Stag had the power of a bull. Then his body crashed against a larder unit at the other end. Honestly, this was getting a bit monotonous. As his body thudded against the melamine, Paul reflected that somebody had done a pretty good job fitting this kitchen. The joints were all holding. That one hurt a bit more though. His head had connected with the edge of the cabinet. Then a punch grazed the side of his head, but failed to connect properly. A few expletives started to pour from Stag's mouth as he got into the swing of things. 'Fucking tosser. I'll kill you.' That sort of stuff. Nothing too original. Paul's head rocked to one side with the glancing blow, and his body swung round with the momentum, almost as part of a dance routine. His hand instinctively gripped onto something. His fingers tightened around a cold metallic object, and he brought that round in an arc perfectly onto the side of Stag's head. There was a reverberating clang as the pan bounced off the reinforced skull. Stag looked back at him with a bemused smile, before steadying himself to fling a clenched grapefruit-sized fist. But Paul had managed to angle his head before the punch connected, and because Stag was off balance, the punch failed to connect properly. Again. Paul tightened his grip on the pan. It was a good-sized frying pan, but a bit lightweight. Probably used to fry onions. Even so, when he swung it round again onto Stag's head, there was a pleasing crack to go with the second clang. Paul wasn't quite sure what had led him to fight back, but now he was on a roll. He pushed Stag onto the table in the middle of the room, then pushed him off the other side, then fell on top of him. He managed to land a couple of punches full in his face, as Stag was still dazed by the battering of the frying pan. Pent-up aggression briefly allowed free rein in the mild-mannered trainee accountant.

That was about the high point for Paul. It was a bit more mixed after that. Despite thuggery being his chosen profession, his core competency, Stag had failed to beat up the weaker specimen. In fact, to most impartial observers, Paul was on course for a points victory, perhaps even a knock-out. But that wasn't factoring in Jonno. He'd been standing on the side-lines, leaving it up to Stag to give Paul a good pummelling after the ungentlemanly comment about the spot. Now intervention was necessary. He swung has boot into Paul's body, knocking the wind out of him. Simple, but effective. That's all that was needed. You didn't need a high IQ for this sort of work. Paul's comeback had been cruelly cut short. A smile spread over Jonno's face as he swung his boot back to get plenty of purchase for the next kick. But it was cramped in the kitchen, and the heel of his boot banged against the fridge freezer with a dull thud. At the same time Paul rolled off Stag, and grabbed both of Jonno's legs together. Jonno was wearing some strange half-mast trousers which left a good proportion of bare leg showing. It was too tempting. Paul sank his teeth into Jonno's right shin, as deep as possible, getting a good mouthful of flesh, and held on like a determined terrier. Jonno let out something between a high-pitched scream and a simpering wail, and shook his leg ferociously to dislodge his assailant. Scrambling among the feet and legs and bodies, Paul reflected that Walker would be turning in his grave looking at the performance of his old mates. Stag and Jonno must have been thinking the same thoughts. Jonno freed his leg, reached down to grab Paul by his hair, and banged his head against the oven door. Stag rolled onto his side, then up onto his knees, and wound his fist back in preparation for a good punch. Third time lucky.

The malevolent forces were reasserting themselves.

*

Still staring at the dark windows, still trying to work out what was going on, George had heard the beep of a text message. In his haste he struggled to get his phone out of the pocket of his jeans, and then keyed in the wrong passcode. He took a few deep breaths, and then entered the code very slowly and deliberately. As he did that, he heard the beep of a second message, and this one appeared on the screen. 'George, Mr McManus here. Water pouring into your conservatory. Come back quickly'. Irritably he flicked off that message, and opened the first one.

'Dad, they've taken me to the fried chicken place – kitchen at back. Please come.'

"What is it George? Is it Paul?" There was panic in Dawn's voice.

"He says they've taken him to the fried chicken place."

"Who have?"

"I don't know."

"It'll be that awful place with the neon chicken's head. You can see it from here," she said, pointing.

As he squinted at the rocking chicken's head, the neon pink dazzling in the darkness, he saw the tall Chinese gentleman in a smart black suit approaching. There was a fleeting second when George thought he might pull out a shiny revolver and point it at him. But as the stranger took a few more paces, appearing under the streetlamp like an actor coming onto the stage, there was no gun in sight. It was the contrast that impressed George. The litter and mud and dirt, some brick dust floating in the lamplight, but the mysterious stranger, tall and imperious. The sharp, beautifully tailored, black suit. The immaculate, perfectly ironed, white shirt. The black tie, expertly tied, no gap between tie and collar. The sallow skin, the dark eyes, almost black, fixed on his own eyes. The black hair, slightly too long, parted at the side, swept back with just a touch of gel. This must be him.

"Mr Stephenson. Nice to meet you. I'm Mr Zhang Wei. I visited your son on Saturday evening. It seems we have a problem. Some young men have intervened. Taken your son. I assume you have the money that is owed to me. But I want to resolve things properly. I suggest we walk to where they will be. It's not far."

Perfect English. Completely in control. Assured, self confident, professional. George struggled to respond.

"Thank you, yes. We'll come with you."

He regretted the weakness of the answer. Taking the submissive position. Sanctioning his control. Even if he is a top-of-the-range gangster.

*

He'd already heard the crashing and banging, before he pushed the door open. It sounded like fitters taking out an old kitchen. George couldn't work out what was going on at first. There was a general picture of mayhem. Three bodies squirming around on the floor, under a kitchen table. But it was the flash of white, cream actually, on his right hand side that really confused him. It seemed to fly through the air, and then land on the other bodies. He screwed up his eyes, looked again, and worked it out. Paul was near the bottom of the pile. There were two strange men on top of him, one of which was trying to get his arm free to land a punch on Paul's head. Then at the very top of the pile, splayed across, was his wife of nearly twenty-five years, resplendent in her new cream winter coat. She'd confessed to him earlier that it had cost five hundred pounds. The edging was hand-stitched apparently. It had ridden up, revealing the tops of her legs clad in black tights as she grabbed the fist about to hit Paul. He couldn't help thinking how shapely she looked, despite the unusual circumstances.

He swivelled around and saw Mr Zhang Wei standing by the door, arms crossed, shaking his head, obviously not about to intervene at this stage. At the same time, George saw Danni walk in through the kitchen door.

She rushed her explanation to George. "I went out for a walk to clear my head. I saw Stag and Jonno take Paul away. Then I saw you and Dawn arriving, meeting Zhang Wei. I followed you round here."

He took his eyes off Danni, and looked back at the two strange bodies. These two must be Stag and Jonno. Then he saw one of them flip Dawn over onto her back. A button sprung off her coat, and her head hit the floor.

This really was the epiphany. The sight of the thugs wrestling with his son, and hurting his wife. Anger, shame, disappointment, and determination pulsed through his veins. Along with the other strange force that he wasn't supposed to mention. And what a happy coincidence that the kitchen was so well laid-out. Everything carefully placed and accessible. Excluding the set of kitchen knives, which fortunately were stashed away in a drawer. He reached out and picked up an orange cast-iron pan. Who knows why they needed this for fried-chicken, but it was an excellent implement of war.

The challenge was finding the right opportunity. When the heads of the two thugs were exposed. But not too close to the heads of the loved ones. It would be bad news to knock out his beautiful wife, as she grovelled in the dirt in her stylish cream coat, trying to rescue their only son.

He could tell Danni was thinking the same thing. As Jonno tried to pick himself up, she placed her boot firmly on his head to hold it down, and at the same time pointed to Stag's head which now bobbed up as a perfect target. George took aim, and brought the cast-iron pan down on the exposed head. From above, like a pump-action. There was an awful sound of hard metal on dense head. The head veered to one side and the body slumped down. God, was he dead? He hadn't meant to hit him so hard. But how hard are you supposed to hit a head with a cast-iron pan? He'd never done it before. Except at school, of course.

His agonising didn't last too long. He felt himself falling backwards. The other body had raised itself up, and flung itself at him. He hit the floor hard, and he felt his shoulder thud against a corner cupboard. The other body was on top of him, and he could smell the foul breath of the enemy. The pan had fallen out of his hand.

Ivander Holyfield. That was his name. Mike Tyson was on his way down by then, but he knew how to fight dirty. Heavyweight boxing wasn't a gentleman's sport, and neither was this. Jonno's earlobe was handily placed. George manoeuvred his head, gripped his teeth around the soft fleshy lobe, and bit hard. Jonno instinctively pulled away, but George kept his jaw closed and his teeth held fast. Something had to give. And it did. An earlobe. He felt it in his mouth. A bit like a boiled sweet, but softer. Hard to describe. He'd never experienced a detached earlobe in his mouth before. Not even at school. He should compare notes with Iron Mike sometime. He spat it onto the floor. There was a scream. A deep-throated man's scream. George saw Jonno clutching his ear, minus the lobe, with a gloved hand. What an interesting night this was turning out to be. Were they still serving fried-chicken out front? George spat again, and saw some flecks of blood flick onto Dawn's coat. The coat that cost five hundred pounds.

Still screaming, Jonno lunged at George. He was going to inflict real damage now. Serious, serious retribution was about to follow. There'd be no help from Paul. He was still dazed. But Dawn was lifting herself up. Enraged by the blood on the new coat, she grabbed at Jonno's head. It was an awkward, fumbling grab, but her fingers managed to grip his nose from the underside, two fingers slipping into his nostrils, pulling his nose and head back. George wondered if it would be possible for Dawn to pull Jonno's nose clean off. No nose, and half an ear missing. That would teach him to mess with the Stephenson family.

In the end it was Danni that despatched Jonno. She'd picked up the cast-iron pan, and had two hands on the handle. When Jonno eventually managed to shake his head free, with his nose intact, she took aim. It was a bit like a golf swing. It hit him on the side of the head, with force, and with a good follow through. His head and body rocked to one side and then crumpled on top of Stag.

A famous victory for the Stephenson family. Plus Danni. Blooded in combat. Forged together in the white heat of battle.

Saturday 4 November

Before

Chapter 44

She'd had enough time to think now. A full week in fact. A full week of churning things around in her head. She'd made her mind up last Monday, had a mini crisis of confidence on Tuesday, booked the flight on Wednesday (one way), and despite some hesitation on Thursday, she'd told Juan when she'd finished her shift behind the bar. She'd work for another week, so that he could find somebody else. Isabella had said that she'd be happy to do more hours, and the motor convention had finished today anyway. She'd texted her mother on Friday, but kept it short and factual. 'Coming home 15 Nov'. The reply had come back straight away. 'Fantastic. Let me know flight time. Pick you up from the airport.' But she could tell what her mother was really thinking, or hoping was, 'coming home for ever, to get a proper job, and a steady husband.' And maybe there was a tiny part of her that was thinking that as well. But first, some family business to attend to. She'd track them down, father and son, father and half brother, then tell her mother. It would all be fine. Happy families.

That just left the two Rs to deal with in the next week or so. She could leave it open, avoid any confrontation. She didn't have to close the book entirely, make the final diary entry, spend one last night together waiting for the dawn to appear, then bid a tearful farewell. Twice. It could be a short trip home, then back again to Granada to carry on where she'd left off. Except she knew that it wouldn't be.

Her arms were gripped tightly around his body now as he accelerated up the mountain road. He'd turned up at about half twelve, and actually apologised for being late. They leant into the first bend. It was a wide arc. They'd left the city behind, past the last farmhouse, and were heading through the woods, still below the treeline. The headlight was on full beam and it threw a wide band of light on the road ahead. Her face was resting on his strong shoulder. The rich oily smell of his old leather jacket was intense from here, mixing in with human smell and touch of his hair. Her hands could feel the taut strength of his stomach muscles. This was the long straight stretch now before the bends nearer the top, and he opened up the throttle. She was going to tell him when they got back. Afterwards, in a matter-of-fact way, in the dark, while he smoked his final cigarette of the day. He wouldn't work out what was going on. And she'd tell Roberto tomorrow afternoon. Somebody would be heading into town in the truck on Sunday afternoon. She'd walk up to his mother's house, have something to eat with him, then they'd go for a walk, and she'd explain. Roberto was smart and perceptive. He might work out what was going on.

*

She'd found it when she was sixteen, looking for her passport in her mother's bedroom drawer. Her first holiday with her friends, without her mother and Rupert. It was her mother's private drawer, but she needed her passport number because Natasha was booking the flights. She'd carefully found the passport without disturbing anything else; resisted the temptation to read the diary, and been shocked to find that her mother was still on the pill. So why had she taken out the cream-coloured envelope, addressed to Elaine Rogers? And why had she taken the letter out of the envelope, unfolded it, read the date – January 1989, and read the letter? 'Dear Elaine', in blue fountain pen, confident masculine handwriting. Ending 'Love, George xxx'. A true love letter. She didn't know why she'd been drawn to it, but she'd always known from that moment, and had chosen to do nothing about it. She'd put the letter back in the envelope, put the envelope back in the drawer, left it there, and left the thought and the knowledge in there as well.

Until now. It was like an archaeologist discovering the tomb of an ancient warrior. A life long forgotten, a memorial suddenly rediscovered.

*

They were on the tight bends now, a lot higher up, out of the trees. The road was narrow, rock face at one side, and a steep fall away to the other side. But there was a good barrier guarding the drop, and the moon was bright, throwing light all around. She normally shut her eyes on this stretch, and buried her face deeper onto his shoulder and back, but for some reason she'd kept them open tonight. She'd sent a text to Danni while she was waiting in the bar. She'd stay at her mother's house one night, and then go to meet Danni. Just her and Danni. Then get his address. George's address. Her father's address. She was just going to turn up and knock on the door. If he wasn't in, she'd go back, then back again. Either way, she was going to meet him. She shouldn't have left it this long. But she was determined now.

They were on the drop side of the road, but Rodolfo had slowed right down, and she felt safe. There was usually no other traffic on the road at this time, but earlier on they'd seen some lights plotting a steady path down.

It would be a bit of a shock. She'd watch the understanding creep over his face. He'd know as soon as he opened the door and looked at her, but it would take a few seconds for it to sink in. She wouldn't say anything, but he would know.

Then in a fraction of a second, it all went dark, until she did see his face.

Tuesday 21 November

Chapter 45

"Why has he invited us here George?"

"I don't know Dawn. This is probably his corporate HQ. Where he masterminds his global operations."

"What, the Oriental Garden Chinese restaurant on Anlaby Road? This was here when we were students. I don't think they've changed the carpet since then."

"Well you can't go wrong with a red floral swirl. Hides the dirt."

"I can't see any red in it anymore. My feet stuck to it when we came in. I reckon it's been down since the Norman Conquest."

"Probably trying to keep his overheads low. Ruthless cost control. That's the name of the game."

"The food's pretty good actually Dad. We come here before we go out," said Paul, turning to Danni, holding her hand under the table, "but people come here after a night's drinking, so they never taste it properly."

"There's never any trouble," said Danni. "People seem to know that he's in command. Even the drunks can sense it." She lowered her voice, her eyes flicked between George and Dawn. "But I never guessed he was running all of this. That Walker was working for him."

They were sitting at a table for four in the window. Mr Zheng Wei had invited them, but they'd all felt the element of compulsion accompanying the generous invitation. He'd just had a word with the waiter, in Mandarin, pointed at a few things on the menu, and had now disappeared through a door at the back. There was one other group sitting in the far corner. They looked like first-year students. Three boys and one girl. The three boys were all asleep. The girl alternated between staring at her phone, and poking one of the boys to try to wake him.

George looked away from the girl, and quickly glanced at Dawn sitting next to him, Paul sitting opposite him, and Danni sitting opposite Dawn. Then he allowed himself a few moments to reflect on what had just happened.

The two strangers – Jonno and Stag, who Paul explained worked for Walker – did not stay unconscious for long. When the brawl had subsided, Mr Zheng Wei had carefully poured a cup of water onto each of them, and they'd each spluttered back to life like an old car engine firing up. They'd looked dazed and confused, but Mr Zheng Wei had asserted his authority without the need for backup. He gave them some piercing stares, took them in a corner and whispered in their ears. Not too close to Jonno's. Not sweet nothings, George guessed. Probably some very substantial threats, careful guidance that they shouldn't get involved after Walker's untimely demise. Then they both disappeared into the night, tails between their legs. Jonno had picked up his earlobe, and put it in his jacket pocket; it wasn't far to walk to the hospital. It was amazing what the plastic surgeons could do these days.

Then Mr Zheng Wei invited the Stephensons and Danni to his restaurant. That wasn't far either. He'd walked a few paces in front of them, then opened the door for them when they arrived. Dawn had examined Paul's nose under a street light before they went in. She'd been on a first-aid course last year. It definitely wasn't broken. Then she'd taken a small bottle of antiseptic mouthwash out of her handbag and handed it to George. He'd swilled his mouth out in the gents. So had Paul. Washed away the taste of Jonno's flesh and blood. Dawn had dabbed some of the mouthwash on her coat to try to remove the flecks of blood, but it had just smudged it into an untidy daub. She said she'd get it dry-cleaned.

A waiter came over and wiped the table down, told them their food wouldn't be long.

George whispered to Dawn. "When do you think I'm supposed to hand over the money?"

"Why don't you go and knock at that door. That must be his office. Where he directs his global operations, as you say. Let's get it over with, and get out of here."

"Do you think we're going to have to pay for the meal as well, or is it on the house? You know, an offering, to seal a peace treaty. Between warring nations."

"This isn't the fucking Treaty of Versailles George. We're just handing over money to a…" she lowered her voice, "…to a gangster. I know he's got a sharp suit on, and he's all business-like and gentlemanly, but that's what he is. Just go and do it George."

*

The food came pretty quickly. And George came back from his mission pretty quickly, walking back to the table in a self-conscious way, aware that Dawn, Paul, and Danni were watching him. The girl at the other table took time out from her phone to watch him as well. She seemed to have given up poking her boyfriend.

"Well?" said Dawn, expectantly.

"All sorted," replied George, looking for praise. "I went in the room. He was sitting at an old table, looking at his laptop. I handed over the envelope. He didn't count it. Then he just said 'Enjoy your meal Mr Stephenson, we've concluded our business,' that was it. I think the meal is on the house."

"That's not the main issue George. That we're getting a free meal. Did he say anything about the other two, what are they called – Stag and Jonno? They're not going to come after Paul again are they?"

"He said not to worry about them. He told them he'd get his nephews on to them and cut them up if they start anything. And he says he knows their families, so he can always intimidate them. He seems to have all the angles covered," said George cheerily.

"All the angles covered! Oh, well that's OK then. Cut them up and intimidate their mothers. That's alright then. Phew, what a relief! Jesus Christ George, what have we got ourselves into?"

"Relax Dawn. I think he likes us. Respects us. We haven't got ourselves into something. We've got ourselves out of something."

"You bit that guy's ear off George."

"Just his earlobe. Not his whole ear. He can get it stitched back on again. Mike Tyson bit Ivander Holyfield's ear off."

"Who?"

"It was in a boxing match. Tyson was past his best though. Do you think this is chicken or pork?" He was looking at a piece of meat that he'd skewered on the end of his fork.

"It's chicken. That one's pork. And there's the prawns – your favourite."

He spooned some prawns onto his plate, and dug into the rice as well. Dawn was breathing a bit more easily now, and smiling at him.

"You've just handed over…" she mouthed the number rather than speaking it "…eleven thousand pounds. But I suppose that's not the point." She looked reassuringly at Paul. "That's the end of it. That's the point. We can all move on. Paul can move on."

Paul looked directly at his father. "Thanks Dad. I appreciate it. I really do. I don't know how I got into this mess. But it won't happen again. You've given me a new start. I'm incredibly grateful. And I'll pay you back. I'll work it all out. So much a month."

George looked back at his only son, sensing the intensity of feeling that was being directed at him. Honest human emotion.

"It's a gift, not a loan Paul. And for once in my life, I've got some money in my back pocket."

"He got made redundant. Got a pay-off. But he's got a new job. In Hull. More money. Starting next Monday," said Dawn.

"Well done Dad. That's great news. You wanted a change didn't you?"

Before George could answer, there was a noise of chairs being pushed away, and people standing up. Three of the students got up to leave. Two boys who had woken up, and the girl. They left the boyfriend slumped in his chair, with the bill and some cash on the table in front of him. The girl linked arms with one of the other boys as they walked past and left.

"And he won eighty-three thousand pounds on a gambling website," said Dawn.

"It was almost an accident really. A football accumulator. Somebody at work set it up for me. I didn't know what I was doing," said George, apologetically.

"Wow, that's amazing Dad. You're rich. You can buy a speedboat. You always wanted one. Moor it up at Bridlington over the winter, and take it out over the summer. Pretend to be James Bond."

"I didn't know you wanted a speedboat George," said Dawn.

"I used to tell Paul stories about that when he was little. Me as James Bond, standing at the wheel. Young Paul beside me. The baddies chasing us, but they couldn't catch up. We were accelerating away, leaving a big spray behind us."

Paul smiled at him, remembering the stories.

"But I don't think Bridlington and the North Sea will be the same as the French Riviera and the Mediterranean somehow. We'd better get the conservatory fixed first Dawn."

*

Danni had been listening to all of this. The Stephenson family re-bonding. It was nice. She was happy for Paul. Happy for all of them. Maybe she was joining them. Ever so gradually. An associate member. She'd had nothing like that. Just a fractured family. A dead half-brother. An estranged mother. But the ambition and aspiration were back. Her money was back in the bank, and she was also five thousand euros to the good. There'd been no mention of it. Walker had got it from somewhere, but she had it now. Mr Zheng Wei was making no claim on it. Stag and Jonno hadn't mentioned it. She hadn't told Paul about it. The envelope was still in her coat pocket now. Just sitting there. Let sleeping dogs lie, she thought. As far as the money's concerned. But she had to tell George about the other thing.

"George, there's something I've got to tell you."

All eyes turned to her. All six of them. Dawn's two were particularly intense. It might have been the first time she'd called him by his first name.

She took a deep breath, briefly moistened her lips with her tongue. Then she told him. About the amazing coincidence. About meeting Rachel. About Rachel working out that George was her father. About Rachel's plan to meet him and Paul. About the radio silence that had followed.

As she told him this, she saw Dawn and George swapping glances. She saw George slowly shake his head. She saw Dawn put her arm around his shoulders. She saw George put his head in his hands.

There was a silence after that, broken only by the remaining student waking up, looking around in puzzlement, throwing some money on the table, then stumbling out. The four of them were alone now. George spoke first.

"And there's something I need to tell both of you." He took a very deep breath, a giant gulp of water. Then he told them. About the letter from Elaine – telling him that he had a daughter, that she'd died. About what he saw down the country lane. About the family resemblance. About meeting Elaine. About Rachel's death.

"I'm trying to piece it all together," said George. "I've even been in touch with an old friend, Miranda, who's researched the paranormal. I've got lots of random thoughts and questions flying around in my head. Dawn started to tell me about the letter from Elaine. That Rachel had died. But I was drunk. I'm not sure whether that got through or not. Then I saw what I saw. Perhaps it was Rachel's ghost. But I was tired. It was dark and misty. What if I saw what I wanted to see? Apparently other people have seen strange things at that same place. Miranda thinks it could be some sort of portal." He turned to look straight at Danni. Her big green eyes had widened even more and were fixed on him. "Until you told me about you meeting Rachel, about how she worked out that I was her father, I didn't think that she even knew I existed. But she did know about me, and you said she wanted to get in touch with me."

George had started off speaking to all of them, but he'd ended just speaking to Danni.

"I can't explain it all George. Maybe it'll just stay a mystery. I believe it was Rachel trying to get in touch with you. But not everybody thinks like that—"

"We're closing now," interrupted the waiter. "It's nearly one o'clock. Mr Zheng Wei's left for the evening."

"Danni's right," said Dawn. "It stays a mystery. We're not going to get Hercule Poirot turning up to tell us whodunnit, or whether it was a ghost or not, or a trick of the light, or a projection inside your head."

"I got to meet her, Dad. I didn't know who she was at the time. But I liked her. I wish she'd told me there and then."

"I know, I know," said George. "Inconclusive. Unless she appears again of course."

They all looked up, expecting to see Rachel float through the door.

Dawn brought them back to earth.

"Let's not think about that George. I'm just pleased we've got things sorted out for Paul. He can move on. We can all move on now."

She took his hand and squeezed it. A definite public show of affection. "I've just booked us into the Station hotel George. I booked online. The reception's still open. It's just a short walk from here. Fifteen minutes maybe. The car's still stuck on the motorway remember, and Derek's driven back. He said he'd contact the police to tell them about the car. We'll have to organise for it to be picked up tomorrow."

"You could have stayed with us Mum."

"What, and slept on that old settee?"

"You could have had our bed. We seem to have got lots of new sheets."

"How much is it a night at the Station hotel, Dawn?"

"You're a man of means now George. You can afford it"

*

They'd said goodbye to Paul and Danni, and watched them walk off down the Boulevard.

"Do you think they'll be OK?" said George.

"He's cleared his debts. Got those awful people off his back. That's the main thing. He's got a decent job. I think he'll be fine. He and Danni will have to work things out for themselves. They're only young. She's gone up in my estimation George. She was really trying to help him. Using her own money. And she wants to turn her life around."

They were walking into the city centre now. Dawn had stopped speaking. It was as if she knew that he wanted some time to think.

It had been an eventful couple of weeks. And up to that point it had been a relatively uneventful life. Not a life completely devoid of incident, more a life of standardised disappointment and average dissatisfaction. A nearly fifty-year-old man, who'd run out of steam. Marriage problems, family problems, work problems, life-in-general problems.

A leaking conservatory. A parrot that could only say two things.

Then, seemingly without rhyme and reason, there'd been a major change of tack. Lost his job. Got a good pay-off. Got a new job, without really trying. Had lots of weird dreams. Really weird dreams. Won a stack of money. Without really trying. Had a financial cushion for the first time in his life. Seemed to attract the attention of the ladies at work – Samantha, Anna, and Angel. Had a drunken night out with twenty-seven-year-old Angel in fact, brushed her knee and been on the receiving end of her affections. Acted like a gentleman in the hotel room. Caught up with Miranda, who'd changed sexual orientation, and switched to the natural sciences from the old ways. Miranda who coincidentally was living with the HG HR Manager. Resolved things with Linda – sort of. The bruise was starting to disappear. Witnessed the sudden decline and fall of his alpha-male neighbour Derek, now twitching and teetering on the edge of incarceration. Heard the parrot utter a different phrase. Found out that he had a daughter. Found out that she'd died. Elation and tragedy were strange bedfellows. Had maybe seen her ghostly apparition rearing up in front of him, trying to make contact, through a portal – where his elderly neighbour had hacked his wife to death. Or maybe he'd just conjured up the image of his beautiful daughter from his subconscious. Thought projection. Some sort of Freudian analysis. Met the mother of his long-lost daughter. Elaine. The girl, now woman, who he'd spent one night with twenty-eight years ago. Gone to visit her with his wife. Realised Elaine wasn't the love of his life. Wasn't very nice at all really. Vanquished his son's tormentors in a bar-room brawl. Bit off somebody's ear. Handed over eleven thousand pounds to a mysterious Chinese restaurateur and crime overlord. Not got a receipt. Helped his son. Re-connected with his son, or made a good start anyway. Thought better of his son's girlfriend, connected with her in a strange way. His son's girlfriend whose half-brother had cracked his head open and died in a bizarre accident in his son's flat.

Boy, when you went through the list, you couldn't make it up.

But if some invisible hand was orchestrating this, it was a shaky, chaotic, invisible hand. If the disembodied Rachel, floating in an ethereal world, had plotted this as part of a coordinated strategy to help her biological father, it was a strange plan and strange execution. If an omnipotent and loving God was directing operations, you'd have to wonder – didn't he have better things to do with his time than inflict a nervous twitch on a white male in a Leeds suburb? Or intervene in a football accumulator? Or set up a night out with a delicious young girl? How did that compare to eradicating global poverty? Or if you approached it from the dark-side, if he'd accidently done a deal with the devil, it was difficult to see what the deal was, and how everybody fitted into the contract. As far as he knew, his eternal soul was still safe.

So perhaps it was a random series of events. Accidents of history. Not important in the great sweep of humanity. Yet, important to him. Larger than life events, crammed into two momentous weeks. But an aberration. Now his life would settle back to a more even-keel. A normal trajectory.

Except the big one was still hanging in the air. The really big one. His wife of nearly twenty-five years. Dawn. Attractive, kind, loving, long-suffering Dawn. The mother of his son. The lady who was walking beside him now at nearly quarter past one in the morning, in the badlands of a port on the East coast.

"Have you made up your mind Dawn?"

"That's a bit direct for you isn't it George? Discussing emotions so openly. A bit female almost. A bit not-very-British. Does it have to be a 'yes or no' answer? Right here, right now?"

"A hint would be good. You know, direction of travel, and all that."

"Let's just say, you're off the critical list. Out of intensive care. Been through the high-dependency ward, and now recuperating in the general ward. But keep taking the tablets. Finish the course."

"On parole you mean? Out on licence? Bound over to keep the peace?"

"Let's stick with the extended medical metaphor shall we George? It's a bit more forgiving. And you've got a night in the Station hotel to look forward to. They only had the honeymoon suite available."

AUTUMN 2018

ONE YEAR LATER

Chapter 46

"George, you look fine. Your tie's straight. And you can see your face in those shoes. What a smart boy you are!"

"That's what my mother used to say."

"Sad that she didn't live to see this George, but she wouldn't have known what was going on anyway. Maybe she's looking down, watching. She'd be happy for Paul."

"I know. I know."

"And it's amazing, after all these years, you know, that he got in touch. And now he's here as well. The male line. Three generations of the Stephenson family for the big day."

"A daughter found and lost. A father lost and found."

"You're a poet George."

"Diplomatic of Vincente to be visiting his niece in Cordoba though. As part of their grand European tour. I'm not sure that I could have handled the two of them being here. Because of Mum I mean, not anything else. Even if he is a famous playwright, and knows Barbra Streisand."

"I don't know. I think he'd have added a bit of Latin American glamour to the proceedings. Especially on the dance floor tonight. Your dad said they'd won the top Salsa dancing competition when they lived in New York."

"Oh God, there won't be Salsa dancing tonight will there? Please don't put me through that, Dawn."

"Have a few drinks and stick to your dad-dancing, George. That's the safest bet. Although the lead singer in the band is from Puerto Rico, so I can't absolutely promise."

She smiled at him mischievously. "George, can you fasten this clasp at the back of my top. I can't quite reach it."

He put his glasses on, squinted, fumbled, apologised, but eventually managed it. Then he kissed the back of her neck.

She turned, and was about to kiss him on the lips when her phone pinged.

"Oh George, look! Jennifer's just sent me a picture of Lucy, with the dress, and the shoes, and the hair, and the make-up. She's ready now, even though they're not leaving for the church for another hour. Always super-efficient that girl. Look, there it is," said Dawn, handing her phone to him. "She does look absolutely beautiful George. She was the best looking girl in their year at school. And she was always keen on Paul. Head girl, and she'll be qualified as a doctor in a couple of years."

True. They both liked Lucy. She was beautiful. She was clever. Her father did own a construction business, her mother did used to read the weather on 'Look North', and her brother was a professional footballer. But despite everything, George had liked Danni. Edgy, dangerous Danni with the curves, and the startling green eyes. Danni with the insight. Danni who'd met Rachel. Paul must have gone through some conversion on the road to Damascus. They'd never seen Danni again after the meal in the Oriental Garden. After he and Dawn had watched her and Paul walk off down the Boulevard, into the night. The next time they'd seen Paul, he was with Lucy. And the time after that, Lucy was wearing an engagement ring. And today they were getting married. The safe option. Rather than a walk on the wild side.

"The car will be here in ten minutes George. Let's have a small glass of the expensive Cuban rum that your father brought us. In the conservatory. There's a bit of sun in the sky."

Santiago de Cuba, 20-year-old extra Anejo. Special Edition. £158.95 a bottle. They'd looked it up. There was a picture of Ernest Hemingway relaxing on the terrace of his house in Havana in 1940 on the label.

It wasn't their conservatory. Well it was now, actually. At the back of the detached five-bedroom house at the far edge of Sycamore Meadows. Derek had to sell it for a knock-down price to raise cash for the legal bills. He'd stayed out of jail so far, at a price, but it was a struggle. Moving in with Cassandra's widowed mother in Sussex had been the only option. To be fair, Cassandra had stuck with him, remained loyal, resisted Gunter. They'd sold Begonia's horse. Derek had hugged Dawn just a bit too hard when they'd said goodbye, but at least he was finally off the scene. There'd been no word from Linda, Anna, Samantha, Angel, Miranda or Elaine. Or Rachel. Or Danni. But Paul had told them that Danni was good, had started a law degree, and had bought a house. Mysterious Danni.

George didn't think they needed five bedrooms. They only needed one most of the time, which was a very good sign. His probationary period was over. But Dawn had argued that when Paul and Lucy were married, when they had children, they might all come and stay. And his father and Vincente might come and stay, when they were over in Europe the next time. Or Dawn's mother. She was staying tonight in fact. And the large garden gave the dog more room to run around. Tommo the Bernese Mountain Dog was the size of a small horse, but they walked him together, talked and talked, communicated. Dawn had been right. As always.

They could afford all of this. The gambling winnings. The new job. The bonus. George's promotion three months after starting the new job. So they'd had the old conservatory repaired. Sold number two, taken Dorothy up on her offer to adopt Polonius after the cat had died, bought the dog, and purchased number fourteen, otherwise known as Daleside. Andrew Prosser had been at his obsequious best, and taken two commissions.

And here they were, in the new water-tight conservatory, overlooking open fields, sipping overpriced Caribbean rum, about to attend their son's wedding. Feeling good about the world. Dawn looked stunning in her wedding outfit. A tight-fitting peacock blue sleeveless dress, with a bit of a sheen to it. Clinging to all the right places. Tall, slim, immaculate hair, pinned up with a few twists and plaits. A simple pillbox hat. A simple cream jacket to drape over her shoulders. It was November after all.

"It just tastes sweet to me George. It's sugar and water. How's it worth one hundred and fifty pounds?"

"That's like saying champagne is just grapes."

He looked out over the open fields– he would see a sunset next summer, sipping chilled Chablis. And the summer after that. Then he turned to look at his wonderful wife in all her finery. She was staring out at the same view.

If Rachel had meant to do all of this, she'd done a good job.

Lightning Source UK Ltd.
Milton Keynes UK
UKHW012243270123
416084UK00005B/437